**Praise for *Shadow and Bone*, the first book of
The Grisha Trilogy**

'A *New York Times* bestseller, it's like *The Hunger Games* meets *Potter* meets *Twilight* meets *Lord Of The Rings* meets *Game Of Thrones*; basically epic magical fantasy but completely for grown-ups' *Stylist*

'*Shadow and Bone* was a dark, rich, utterly compelling book that did not let me go from the very first word to the very last. I loved it, loved it, loved it, loved it!' *Guardian Teen*

'This engaging YA adventure takes a different and distinctly Russian approach to epic fantasy . . . Giving us a convincingly chilly and well-thought-out world as well as a touchingly played romance, Leigh Bardugo's fantasy is effortlessly readable and sets up what looks like a potentially strong story for the rest of the upcoming Grisha Trilogy' *SFX*

'*Shadow and Bone* is the kind of book that I wish I could wipe from my memory just so that I have the pleasure of reading it again for the first time . . . I honestly can't recommend this book highly enough' *Feeling Fictional*

'I haven't felt this way about a high fantasy book since Trudi Canavan's *The Magician's Guild* . . . I was hooked from the beginning. I know we all make an image in our mind of the world that the author has created but the kingdom in *Shadow and Bone* is so richly imagined, I could picture it all . . .' *My Favourite Books*

'I felt like I fell into this book and was lost from reality until the final page; a sign of a talented story teller who draws the reader in and sucks time away from them'

Serendipity Reviews

'. . . brilliantly written and truly spellbinding' *Mig Mag*

'The world building is slow, subtle and full'

Death, Books and Tea

'There is so much to love about this book . . . Leigh Bardugo knows her stuff. The pacing is superb, the climax is faultless, and the immaculate blend of fantasy, action and romance really did make this book unputdownable'

Realm of Fiction

'It was just amazing; so rich and real and vivid and jump-off-of-the-page and unique . . . As for the writing: totally beautiful, but modern and funny . . . Fantasy addicts will adore it, old-timey Russian lovers will adore it. People who love strong characters and amazing relationships will adore it. Magic lovers will adore it. It has something for everyone – including two gorgeous guys . . . I loved every second and can honestly say this is one of my favourite books from 2012' *The Book Addicted Girl*

'In this richly imagined and beautifully written novel, Leigh Bardugo has created a vivid fantasy world drawing on Russian traditions and folklore. With unexpected twists and turns, and plenty of action and romance, this is a pacy and exciting adventure, but also a multi-layered story of self-discovery, with an intelligent and compelling heroine in Alina' *Booktrust*

**Praise for *Siege and Storm*, the second book of
The Grisha Trilogy**

'Wow, wow, wow – that's all I can say. *Siege and Storm* only
confirms that Leigh Bardugo is a must-read author for all
teenage bookworms and fantasy fans! Set in a beautiful
and magical fictional land, the novel draws you in with its
vivid imagery and unique array of characters . . . If you
haven't entered the world of the Grisha yet, then why on
earth not?!' *Feed Me Books Now*

'Leigh is a writer of the best kind because she loves her
characters and the world they live in and makes a reader
jealous that they can't visit it. There is magic in these
pages' *Sister Spooky*

'In so many series the second book is a huge let-down.
Siege and Storm? An exception . . . I adore the writing – it's
so lyrical, so beautiful, yet so modern and witty and funny.
I love this blend of classic fairytale and modern day. And it
always seems to leave me wanting more! And the plot was
amazing too. It was just nonstop action, nonstop thrills,
nonstop suspense and nonstop excitement. I gobbled it up,
falling harder in love each time'
The Book Addicted Girl, Guardian Teen Books

'*Siege and Storm* carries on the fantastic plot which was so
intricately carved in book one, and the writing continues
to be clever, funny and heartbreaking all at the same time.
This book will have you laughing one minute and an
emotional wreck the next, as Alina's powers are pushed to
the limit and her relationships are tested to breaking point.

I for one cannot wait for the third and final book'

Book Chick City

'I was away on the ships and wandering through Ravka with Alina and Mal, I was on the receiving end of his kisses and his annoyances. I felt the sun warm the pages whenever Alina summoned and I felt the fear when The Darkling was around. There is nothing I don't love about the world in which *The Grisha Trilogy* is set and I cannot wait until next year to see how this series is going to conclude' *Readaraptor*

'*Siege and Storm* is a fantastic sequel to last year's debut *Shadow and Bone* . . . This book is truly epic . . .'

Winged Reviews

'. . . a strong and satisfying sequel solidifying my belief that *The Grisha Trilogy* will go down as one of my favourite series of all time' *Jess Hearts Books*

Leigh Bardugo, you sure know how to involve your readers and make them emotional wrecks. *Siege and Storm* is an enthralling sequel that seriously ups the game and expectations of the reader. It is written so beautifully that it flows flawlessly while keeping the magic alive in the reader's mind. If you want to read a fantasy series that has a truly unique world then read this . . .'

Read, Write and Read Some More

Ruin and Rising

Book III of *The Grisha Trilogy*

LEIGH BARDUGO

Indigo

First published in Great Britain in 2014
by Indigo
a division of the Orion Publishing Group Ltd
Orion House
5 Upper St Martin's Lane
London wc2h 9ea
An Hachette UK company

3 5 7 9 10 8 6 4 2

isbn 978 1 78062 116 6

Printed and bound by CPI Group (UK) Ltd, Croydon, cr0 4yy

www.orionbooks.co.uk

For my father, Harve –
sometimes our heroes don't
make it to the end.

THE GRISHA

SOLDIERS OF THE SECOND ARMY
MASTERS OF THE SMALL SCIENCE

CORPORALKI
(The Order of the Living and the Dead)

Heartrenders
Healers

ETHEREALKI
(The Order of Summoners)

Squallers
Inferni
Tidemakers

MATERIALKI
(The Order of Fabrikators)

Durasts
Alkemi

Before

The monster's name was Izumrud, the great worm, and there were those who claimed he had made the tunnels that ran beneath Ravka. Sick with appetite, he ate up silt and gravel, burrowing deeper and deeper into the earth, searching for something to satisfy his hunger, until he'd gone too far and lost himself in the dark.

It was just a story, but in the White Cathedral, people were careful not to stray too far from the passages that curled around the main caverns. Strange sounds echoed through the dim warren of tunnels, groans and unexplained rumblings; cold pockets of silence were broken by low hisses that might be nothing or might be the sinuous movement of a long body, snaking closer through a nearby passage in search of prey. In those moments, it was easy to believe that Izumrud still lived somewhere, waiting to be woken by the call of heroes, dreaming of the fine meal he would have if only some hapless child would walk into his mouth. A beast like that rests; he does not die.

The boy brought the girl this tale, and others too, all the new stories he could gather, in the early days when he was allowed near her. He would sit beside her bed, trying to get her to eat, listening to the pained whistle of her lungs, and he would tell the story of a river, tamed by a powerful Tidemaker and trained to dive through layers of rock, seeking a magic coin. He'd whisper of poor cursed Pelyekin, labouring for a thousand years with his magic pickaxe, leaving caverns and passages in his wake, a lonely creature in search of nothing but distraction, amassing gold and jewels he never intended to spend.

Then, one morning, the boy arrived to find his way to the girl's room barred by armed men. And when he would not leave, they dragged him from her door in chains. The priest warned the boy that faith would bring him peace and obedience would keep him breathing.

Locked in her cell, alone but for the drip of the water and the slow beat of her heart, the girl knew the stories of Izumrud were true. She had been swallowed whole, devoured, and in the echoing alabaster belly of the White Cathedral, only the Saint remained.

The Saint woke every day to the sound of her name being chanted, and each day her army grew, its ranks swollen with the hungry and the hopeless, with wounded soldiers and children barely large enough to carry rifles. The priest told the faithful that she would be Queen one day, and they believed him. But they wondered at her bruised and mysterious court: the raven-haired Squaller with her sharp tongue, the Ruined One with her black prayer shawl and hideous scars, the pale scholar who huddled away with his books and strange instruments. These were the sorry remnants of the Second Army – unfit company for a Saint.

Few knew that she was broken. Whatever power had blessed her, divine or otherwise, was gone – or at least out of reach. Her followers were kept at a distance so they could not see that her eyes were dark hollows, that her breath came in frightened gasps. She walked slowly, tentatively, her driftwood bones fragile in her body, this sickly girl upon whom all their hopes rested.

On the surface, a new King ruled with his shadow army, and he demanded that his Sun Summoner be returned. He offered threats and rewards, but the answer he received came in the form of a challenge – from an outlaw the people had dubbed the Prince of the Air. He struck along the northern border, bombing supply lines, forcing the Shadow King to renew trade and travel across the Fold with nothing but luck and Inferni fire to keep the monsters at bay. Some said this challenger was a Lantsov prince. Some said he was a Fjerdan rebel who refused to fight alongside witches. All agreed he must have powers of his own.

The Saint rattled the bars of her underground cage. This was her war, and she demanded freedom to fight it. The priest refused.

But he'd forgotten that before she'd become a Grisha and a Saint, she'd been a ghost of Keramzin. She and the boy had hoarded secrets as Pelyekin hoarded treasure. They knew how to be thieves and phantoms, how to hide strength as well as mischief. Like the teachers at the Duke's estate, the priest thought he knew the girl and what she was capable of.

He was wrong.

He did not hear their hidden language, did not understand the boy's resolve. He did not see the moment the girl ceased to bear her weakness as a burden and began to wear it as a guise.

Chapter 1

I stood on a carved stone balcony, arms spread, shivering in my cheap robes, and tried to put on a good show. My *kefta* was a patchwork, sewn together from scraps of the gown I was wearing the night we fled the palace and garish curtains that I'd been told came from a defunct theatre somewhere near Sala. Beads from the lobby chandeliers made up the trim. The embroidery at the cuffs was already coming undone. David and Genya had done their best, but there were limited resources underground.

From a distance, it did the trick, sparkling gold in the light that seemed to emanate from my palms, sending bright glimmers over the ecstatic faces of my followers far below. Up close, it was all loose threads and false shine. Just like me. The threadbare Saint.

The Apparat's voice boomed through the White Cathedral, and the crowd swayed, eyes closed, hands raised, a field of poppies, arms like pale stalks shaken by some wind I couldn't feel. I followed a choreographed series of gestures, moving deliberately so that David and whichever Inferni was helping him this morning could track my movements from their position in the chamber hidden just above the balcony. I dreaded morning prayers, but according to the priest, these false displays were a necessity.

"It is a gift you give your people, Sankta Alina," he said. "It is hope."

Actually, it was an illusion, a pale suggestion of the light I'd once commanded. The golden haze was really Inferni fire, reflected off a beaten mirror dish that David had fashioned from salvaged glass. It was something like the dishes we'd used in our failed attempt to stave off the Darkling's horde during the battle in Os Alta. We'd been taken by surprise; and my power, our planning, all of David's ingenuity, and Nikolai's resourcefulness hadn't been enough to stop the slaughter. Since then, I'd been unable to summon so much as a sunbeam. But most of the Apparat's flock had never seen what their Saint could really do, and for now, this deception was enough.

The Apparat finished his sermon. That was the signal to end. The Inferni let the light flare bright around me. It jumped and wavered erratically, then finally faded as I dropped my arms. Well, now I knew who was on fire duty with David. I cast a scowl up at the cave. *Harshaw*. He was always getting carried away. Three Inferni had made it out of the battle at the Little Palace, but one had died just days later from her wounds. Of the two that remained, Harshaw was the most powerful and the most unpredictable.

I stepped down from the platform, eager to be out of the Apparat's presence, but my foot faltered and I stumbled. The priest grasped my arm, steadying me.

"Have a care, Alina Starkov. You are incautious with your safety."

"Thanks," I said. I wanted to pull away from him, from the turned-soil and incense stench he brought with him everywhere.

"You're feeling poorly today."

"Just clumsy." We both knew that was a lie. I was stronger than when I'd come to the White Cathedral – my bones had mended, I'd managed to keep down meals – but I was still frail, my body plagued by aches and constant fatigue.

"Perhaps a day of rest, then."

I gritted my teeth. Another day confined to my chamber. I swallowed my frustration and smiled weakly. I knew what he wanted to see.

"I'm so cold," I said. "Some time in the Kettle would do me good." Strictly speaking, it was true. The kitchens were the one place in the White Cathedral where the damp could be held at bay. By this time, at least one of the breakfast fires would be lit. The big round cavern would be full of the smells of baking bread and the sweet porridge the cooks made from stores of dried peas and powdered milk provided by allies on the surface and stockpiled by the pilgrims.

I added a shiver for good measure, but the priest's only reply was a noncommittal "hmm".

Movement at the base of the cavern caught my attention: pilgrims, newly arrived. I couldn't help but look at them with a strategic eye. Some wore uniforms that marked them as First Army deserters. All were young and able-bodied.

"No veterans?" I asked. "No widows?"

"It's a hard journey underground," the Apparat replied. "Many are too old or weak to move. They prefer to stay in the comfort of their homes."

Unlikely. It would take more than that to stop it. The pilgrims came on crutches and canes, no matter how old or sick. Even dying, they came to see the Sun Saint in their last days. I cast a wary glance over my shoulder. I could just glimpse the Priestguards, bearded and heavily armed, standing sentinel in the archway. They were monks, scholar priests like the Apparat, and below ground they were the only people allowed to carry weapons. Above, they were the gatekeepers, ferreting out spies and unbelievers, granting sanctuary to those they deemed worthy. Lately, the pilgrims' numbers had been dwindling, and those who did join our ranks seemed more hearty than pious. The Apparat wanted potential soldiers, not just mouths to feed.

"I could go to the sick and elderly," I said. I knew the argument was futile, but I made it anyway. It was almost expected. "A Saint should walk amongst her people, not hide like a rat in a warren."

The Apparat smiled – the benevolent, indulgent smile that the pilgrims adored and that made me want to scream. "In times of trouble, many animals go to ground. That's how they survive," he said. "After fools wage their battles, it is the rats that rule the fields and towns."

And feast on the dead, I thought with a shudder. As if he could read my thoughts, he pressed a hand to my shoulder. His fingers were long and white, splaying over my arm like a waxen spider. If the gesture was meant to comfort me, it failed.

"Patience, Alina Starkov. We rise when the time is right and not before."

Patience. That was always his prescription. I resisted the urge to touch my bare wrist, the empty place where the firebird's bones were meant to reside. I had claimed the sea whip's scales and the stag's antlers, but the final piece in Morozova's puzzle was missing. We might have had the third amplifier by now if the Apparat had lent his support to the hunt or just let us return to the surface. But that permission would only come at a price.

"I'm cold," I repeated, burying my irritation. "I want to go to the Kettle."

He frowned. "I don't like you huddling down there with that girl—"

Behind us, the guards muttered restlessly, and a word floated back to me. *Razrusha'ya*. I batted the Apparat's hand away and marched into the passage. The Priestguards came to attention. Like all their brothers, they were dressed in brown and wore the golden sunburst, the same symbol that marked the Apparat's robes. *My* symbol. And yet they never looked directly at me, never spoke to me or the other Grisha refugees. Instead, they stood silently at the edges of rooms and trailed me everywhere like bearded, rifle-wielding specters.

"That name is forbidden," I said. They stared straight ahead, as if I were invisible. "Her name is Genya Safin, and I'd still be the Darkling's prisoner if it weren't for her." No reaction. But I saw them tense at even the sound of her name. Grown men with guns, afraid of a scarred girl. Superstitious idiots.

"Peace, Sankta Alina," said the Apparat, taking my elbow to shepherd me across the passage and into his audience chamber. The silver-veined stone of the ceiling was carved into a rose, and the walls were painted with Saints in their golden halos. It must have been Fabrikator craft because no ordinary pigment could withstand the cold and damp of the White Cathedral. The priest settled himself in a low wooden chair and gestured for me to take another. I tried to hide my relief as I sank down into it. Even standing for too long left me winded.

He peered at me, taking in my sallow skin, the dark smudges beneath my eyes. "Surely *Genya* can do more for you."

It had been over two months since my battle with the Darkling, and I hadn't fully recovered. My cheekbones cut the hollows of my face like angry exclamations, and the white fall of my hair was so brittle it seemed to float like cobwebs. I'd finally talked the Apparat into letting Genya attend me in the kitchens with the promise that she might work her craft and make me more presentable. It was the only real contact I'd had with the other Grisha in weeks. I'd savoured every moment, every bit of news.

"She's doing her best," I said.

The priest sighed. "I suppose we must all be patient. You will heal in time. Through faith. Through prayer."

A surge of rage took hold of me. He knew damn well that the only thing that would heal me was using my power, but to do that, I needed to return to the surface.

"If you would just let me venture aboveground—"

"You are too precious to us, Sankta Alina, and the risk is far too great." He shrugged apologetically. "You will not have a care for your safety, so I must."

I stayed silent. This was the game we played, that we'd been playing since I'd been brought here. The Apparat had done a lot for me. He was the only reason any of my Grisha had made it out of the battle with the Darkling's monsters. He'd given us safe haven underground. But every day the White Cathedral felt more like a prison than a refuge.

He steepled his fingers. "Months gone by, and still you do not trust me."

"I do," I lied. "Of course I do."

"And yet, you will not let me help you. With the firebird

in our possession, all this might change."

"David is working his way through Morozova's journals. I'm sure the answer is there."

The Apparat's flat black gaze burrowed into me. He suspected I knew the location of the firebird – Morozova's third amplifier and the key to unlocking the only power that might defeat the Darkling and destroy the Fold. And he was right. At least, I hoped he was. The only clue we had to its location was buried in my scant childhood memories and the hope that the dusty ruins of Dva Stolba were more than they seemed. But right or wrong, the firebird's possible location was a secret I intended to keep. I was isolated underground, close to powerless, spied upon by the Priestguards. I wasn't about to give up the one bit of leverage I had.

"I want only the best for you, Alina Starkov. For you and your friends. So few remain. If anything were to happen to them—"

"You leave them be," I snarled, forgetting to be sweet, to be gentle.

The Apparat's look was too keen for my liking. "I simply meant that accidents happen underground. I know you would feel each loss deeply, and you are so very *weak*." On the last word, his lips stretched back over his gums. They were black like a wolf's.

Again, rage coursed through me. From my first day in the White Cathedral, threat had hung heavy in the air, suffocating me with the steady press of fear. The Apparat never missed an opportunity to remind me of my vulnerability. Almost without thinking, I twitched my fingers in my sleeves. Shadows leapt up the walls of the chamber.

The Apparat reared back in his chair. I frowned at him, feigning confusion. "What's wrong?" I asked.

He cleared his throat, eyes darting right and left. "It's . . . nothing," he stammered.

I let the shadows fall. His reaction was well worth the wave of dizziness that came when I used this trick. And that's all it was. I could make the shadows jump and dance but nothing more. It was a sad little echo of the Darkling's power, some remnant left behind in the wake of the confrontation that had nearly killed us both. I'd discovered it when trying to summon light, and I'd struggled to hone it to something greater, something I could fight with. I'd had no success. The shadows felt like a punishment, ghosts of greater power that served only to taunt me, the Saint of shams and mirrors.

The Apparat rose, attempting to regain his composure. "You will go to the archives," he said decisively. "Time in quiet study and contemplation will help to ease your mind."

I stifled a groan. This really was punishment – hours spent fruitlessly perusing old religious texts for information on Morozova. Not to mention that the archives were damp, miserable, and crawling with Priestguards. "I will escort you," he added. Even better.

"And the Kettle?" I asked, trying to hide the desperation in my voice.

"Later. *Razru* – Genya will wait," he said as I followed him into the passage. "You needn't scurry off to the Kettle, you know. You could meet with her here. In privacy."

I glanced at the guards, who had fallen into step behind us. Privacy. That was laughable. But the idea of being kept from the kitchens was not. Maybe today the master flue would open for more than a few seconds. It was a slim hope, but it was all the hope I had.

"I prefer the Kettle," I said. "It's warm there." I gave him my meekest smile, let my lip tremble slightly, and added, "It reminds me of home."

He loved that – the image of a humble girl, huddling by a cookstove, hem trailing in ash. Another illusion, one more chapter in his book of Saints.

"Very well," he said at last.

It took a long while to wend our way down from the balcony. The White Cathedral took its name from the alabaster of its walls and the massive main cavern where we held services every morning and evening. Yet it was much more than that – a sprawling network of tunnels and caves, a city underground. I hated every inch of it. The moisture that seeped through the walls, dripped from the ceilings, clustered in beads on my skin. The chill that couldn't be dispelled. The toadstools and night flowers that bloomed in cracks and crevices. I hated the way we marked time: morning services, afternoon prayer, evening services, Saints' days, days for fasting and half fasting. But mostly I hated the feeling that I really was a little rat, pale and red-eyed, scrabbling at the walls of my maze with feeble pink-tinged claws.

The Apparat led me through the caverns north of the main basin, where the Soldat Sol trained. People backed against the rock or reached out to touch my golden sleeve as we passed. We set a slow pace, dignified – necessary. I couldn't move any faster without becoming winded. The Apparat's flock knew I was sick and said prayers for my health, but he feared there would be a panic if they discovered just how fragile – how very human – I was.

The Soldat Sol had already begun their training by the time we arrived. These were the Apparat's holy warriors, sun soldiers who bore my symbol tattooed on their arms and faces. Most of them were First Army deserters, though others were simply young, fierce, and willing to die. They'd helped to rescue me from the Little Palace, and the casualties had been brutal. Holy or not, they were no match for the Darkling's *nichevo'ya*. Still, the Darkling had human soldiers and Grisha in his service too, so the Soldat Sol trained.

But now they did it without real weapons, with dummy swords and rifles loaded with wax pellets. The Soldat Sol were a different kind of pilgrim, brought to the cult of the Sun Saint by the promise of change, many of them young and ambivalent about the Apparat and the old ways of the church. Since my arrival underground, the Apparat had kept them on a far tighter leash. He needed them, but he didn't wholly trust them. I knew the feeling.

Priestguards lined the walls, maintaining a close eye on the proceedings. Their bullets were real, and so were the blades of their sabres.

As we entered the training area, I saw that a group had gathered to watch Mal spar with Stigg, one of our two surviving Inferni. He was thick-necked, blond, and utterly humourless – Fjerdan to the core.

Mal dodged an arc of fire, but the second spurt of flame caught on his shirt. The onlookers gasped. I thought he might draw back, but instead he charged. He dove into a roll, dousing the flames on the ground and knocking Stigg's feet from beneath him. In a flash, he had the Inferni pinned face down. He secured Stigg's wrists, preventing another attack.

The watching sun soldiers broke into appreciative applause and whistles.

Zoya tossed her glossy black hair over one shoulder. "Well done, Stigg. You're trussed and ready for basting."

Mal silenced her with a look. "Distract, disarm, disable," he said. "The trick is not to panic." He rose and helped Stigg to his feet. "You all right?"

Stigg scowled, annoyed, but nodded and moved to spar with a pretty young soldier.

"Come on, Stigg," the girl said with a wide grin. "I won't go too rough on you."

The girl's face was familiar, but it took me a long moment to place her – Ruby. Mal and I had trained with her at Poliznaya. She'd been in our regiment. I remembered her as giggling, cheerful, the kind of happy, flirtatious girl who made me feel awkward and hopeless in my skin. She still had the same ready smile, the same long blonde braid. But even from a distance, I could see the watchfulness in her, the wariness that came with war. There was a black sun tattooed over the right side of her face. Strange to think that a girl who had once sat across from me in the mess hall now thought I was divine.

It was rare that the Apparat or his guards took me this way to the archives. What was different today? Had he brought me here so I could look over the shreds of my army and remember the price of my mistakes? To show me how few allies I had left?

I watched Mal pair sun soldiers with Grisha. There were the Squallers: Zoya, Nadia, and her brother Adrik. With Stigg and Harshaw, they made up the last of my Etherealki. But Harshaw was nowhere to be seen. He'd probably rolled back into bed after summoning flame for me during morning prayers.

As for the Corporalki, the only Heartrenders on the training floor were Tamar and her massive twin, Tolya. I owed them my life, though the debt didn't rest easy with me. They were close to the Apparat, charged with the instruction of the Soldat Sol, and they'd lied to me for months at the Little Palace. I wasn't quite sure what to make of them. Trust was a luxury I could ill afford.

The remaining soldiers would have to wait for a turn to fight. There were simply too few Grisha. Genya and David kept to themselves, and weren't much for combat, anyway. Maxim was a Healer and preferred to practise his craft in the infirmary, though few of the Apparat's flock trusted Grisha enough to take advantage of his services. Sergei was a powerful Heartrender, but I'd been told he was too unstable to be considered safe around students. He'd been in the thick of the fighting when the Darkling launched his surprise attack, had seen the girl he loved torn open by monsters. We'd lost our only other Heartrender to the *nichevo'ya* somewhere between the Little Palace and the chapel.

Because of you, said a voice in my head. *Because you failed them.*

I was drawn from my bleak thoughts by the Apparat's voice. "The boy oversteps."

I followed his gaze to where Mal was moving between the soldiers, speaking to one or correcting another. "He's helping them train," I said.

"He's giving orders. Oretsev," the priest called, beckoning him over. I tensed, watching Mal approach. I'd barely seen him since he'd been banned from my chamber. Aside from my carefully rationed interactions with Genya, the Apparat kept me isolated from potential allies.

Mal looked different. He wore the peasant roughspun that had served as his uniform at the Little Palace, but he was leaner, paler from time spent below ground. The narrow scar on his jaw stood out in sharp relief.

He stopped before us and bowed. It was the closest we'd been allowed to each other in months.

"You are not the captain here," said the Apparat. "Tolya and Tamar outrank you."

Mal nodded. "They do."

"So why are you leading the exercises?"

"I wasn't leading anything," he said. "I have something to teach. They have something to learn."

True enough, I thought bitterly. Mal had got very good at fighting Grisha. I remembered him bruised and bleeding, standing over a Squaller in the stables of the Little Palace, a look of challenge and contempt in his eyes. Another memory I could do without.

"Why haven't those recruits been marked?" the Apparat asked, gesturing towards a group sparring with wooden swords near the far wall. None of them could have been more than twelve years old.

"Because they're children," Mal replied, ice in his voice.

"It's their choice. Would you deny them the chance to show fealty to our cause?"

"I'd deny them regret."

"No one has that power."

A muscle ticked in Mal's jaw. "If we lose, those tatoos will brand them as sun soldiers. They might as well sign up to face the firing squad now."

"Is that why your own features bear no mark? Because you have so little faith in our victory?"

Mal glanced at me, then back at the Apparat. "I save my faith for Saints," he said evenly. "Not men who send children to die."

The priest's eyes narrowed.

"Mal's right," I interjected. "Let them remain unmarked." The Apparat scrutinised me with that flat black gaze. "Please," I said softly, "as a kindness to me."

I knew how much he liked that voice – gentle, warm, a lullaby voice.

"Such a tender heart," he said, clucking his tongue. But I could tell he was pleased. Though I'd spoken against his wishes, this was the Saint he wanted me to be, a loving mother, a comfort to her people. I dug my fingernails into my palm.

"That's Ruby, isn't it?" I asked, eager to change the subject and divert the Apparat's attention.

"She got here a few weeks ago," Mal said. "She's good – came from the infantry." Despite myself, I felt the tiniest twinge of envy.

"Stigg doesn't look happy," I said, bobbing my head towards where the Inferni seemed to be taking out his loss on Ruby. The girl was doing her best to hold her own, but she was clearly outmatched.

"He doesn't like getting beaten."

"I don't think you even broke a sweat."

"No," he said. "It's a problem."

"Why is that?" asked the Apparat.

Mal's eyes darted to me for the briefest second. "You learn more by losing." He shrugged. "At least Tolya's around to keep kicking my ass."

"Mind your tongue," the Apparat snapped.

Mal ignored him. Abruptly, he put two fingers to his

lips and gave a sharp whistle. "Ruby, you're leaving yourself open!"

Too late. Her braid was on fire. Another young soldier ran at her with a bucket of water and tossed it over her head.

I winced. "Try not to get them too crispy."

Mal bowed. "*Moi sovyerenyi.*" He jogged back to the troops.

That title. He said it without any of the rancour he had seemed to carry at Os Alta, but it still hit me like a punch to the gut.

"He should not address you so," complained the Apparat.

"Why not?"

"It was the Darkling's title and is unfitting for a Saint."

"Then what should he call me?"

"He should not address you directly at all."

I sighed. "Next time he has something to say, I'll tell him to write me a letter."

The Apparat pursed his lips. "You're restless today. I think an extra hour in the solace of the archives will do you good."

His tone was chiding, as if I were a cross child who had stayed up past her bedtime. I made myself think of the promise of the Kettle and forced a smile. "I'm sure you're right." *Distract, disarm, disable.*

As we turned down the passage that would take us to the archives, I looked over my shoulder. Zoya had flipped a soldier on his back and was spinning him like a turtle, her hand making lazy circles in the air. Ruby was talking to Mal, her smile broad, her expression avid. But Mal was watching me. In the ghostly light of the cavern, his eyes were a deep and steady blue, the colour at the centre of a flame.

I turned away and followed the Apparat, hurrying my steps, trying to temper the wheeze of my lungs. I thought of Ruby's smile, her singed braid. A nice girl. A normal girl. That was what Mal needed. If he hadn't taken up with someone new already, eventually he would. And someday I'd be a good enough person to wish him well. Just not today.

We caught David on his way into the archives. As usual, he was a mess – hair going every direction, sleeves blotted with ink. He had a glass of hot tea in one hand and a piece of toast tucked into his pocket.

His eyes flickered from the Apparat to the Priestguards.

"More salve?" he asked.

The Apparat curled his lip slightly at this. The salve was David's concoction for Genya. Along with her own efforts, it had helped to fade some of the worst of her scarring, but wounds from the *nichevo'ya* never healed completely.

"Sankta Alina has come to spend her morning in study," the Apparat declared with great solemnity.

David gave a twitch that vaguely resembled a shrug as he ducked through the doorway. "But you're going to the Kettle later?"

"I will have guards sent to escort you in two hours," said the Apparat. "Genya Safin will be waiting for you." His eyes scanned my haggard face. "See that she gives better attention to her work."

He bowed deeply and vanished down the tunnel. I

looked around the room and blew out a long, dejected breath. The archives should have been the kind of place I loved, full of the smell of ink on paper, the soft crackle of quills. But this was the Priestguards' den – a dimly lit maze of arches and columns carved from white rock. The closest I'd come to seeing David lose his temper had been the first time he'd laid eyes on these little domed niches, some of them caved in, all of them lined with ancient books and manuscripts, their pages black with rot, their spines bloated with moisture. The caves were damp enough that puddles had seeped up through the floors. "You can't . . . you can't have kept Morozova's journals in here," he'd practically shrieked. "It's a *bog*."

Now David spent his days and most of his nights in the archives, poring over Morozova's writings, jotting down theories and sketches in a notebook of his own. Like most other Grisha, he'd believed that Morozova's journals had been destroyed after the creation of the Fold. But the Darkling would never have let knowledge like that go. He'd hidden the journals away, and though I'd never been able to get a straight answer from the Apparat, I suspected the priest had somehow discovered them in the Little Palace and then stolen them when the Darkling had been forced to flee Ravka.

I slumped down on a stool across from David. He had dragged a chair and a table into the driest of the caves, and stocked one of the shelves with extra oil for his lanterns and the herbs and unguents he used to make Genya's salve. Usually, he hunched over some formula or bit of tinkering and didn't look up for hours, but today he couldn't seem to settle, fussing with his inks, fidgeting with the pocket watch he'd propped up on the table.

I thumbed listlessly through one of Morozova's journals. I'd come to loathe the sight of them – useless, confusing, and most importantly, *incomplete*. He described his hypotheses regarding amplifiers, his tracking of the stag, his two-year journey aboard a whaler seeking the sea whip, his theories on the firebird, and then . . . nothing. Either there were journals missing or Morozova had left his work unfinished.

The prospect of finding and using the firebird was daunting enough. But the idea that it might not exist, that I might have to face the Darkling again without it? The thought was too terrifying to contemplate, so I simply shoved it away.

I made myself turn the pages. The only means I had of keeping track of time was David's watch. I didn't know where he'd found it, how he'd got it working, or if the time he'd set it to had any correlation to time on the surface, but I glared at its face and willed the minute hand to move faster.

The Priestguards came and went, always watching or bent to their texts. They were meant to be illuminating manuscripts, studying holy word, but I doubted that was the bulk of their work. The Apparat's network of spies reached throughout Ravka, and these men considered it their calling to maintain it, deciphering messages, gathering intelligence, building the cult of a new Saint. It was hard not to compare them to my Soldat Sol, most of them young and illiterate, locked out of the old mysteries these men guarded.

When I couldn't bear any more of Morozova's ramblings, I twisted in my seat, trying to release a crick from my back. Then I pulled down an old collection of what were mostly debates on prayer, but that turned out to also contain a version of Sankt Ilya's martyrdom.

In this one, Ilya was a mason, and the neighbour boy was crushed beneath a horse – that was new. Usually, the boy was cut down by a plough blade. But the story ended as all the tellings did: Ilya brought the child back from the brink of death, and for his trouble, the villagers threw him into the river, bound by iron chains. Some tales claimed he never sank but floated out to sea. Others vowed his body had emerged days later on a sandbank miles away, perfectly preserved and smelling of roses. I knew them all, and none of them said a word about the firebird or indicated that Dva Stolba was the right place to start looking for it.

All our hope for finding the firebird resided in an old illustration: Sankt Ilya in Chains, surrounded by the stag, the sea whip, and the firebird. Mountains could be glimpsed behind him, along with a road and an arch. That arch had long since fallen, but I thought the ruins could be found at Dva Stolba, not far from the settlements where Mal and I had been born. At least, that's what I believed on my good days. Today, I felt less sure that Ilya Morozova and Sankt Ilya were the same man. I couldn't bring myself to look at the copies of the *Istorii Sankt'ya* anymore. They lay in a mouldy stack in a forgotten corner, seeming less like portents of some grand destiny than children's books that had fallen out of fashion.

David picked up his watch, put it down, reached for it again, knocked over a bottle of ink then righted it with fumbling fingers.

"What's the matter with you today?" I asked.

"Nothing," he said sharply.

I blinked at him. "Your lip is bleeding."

He wiped his palm across it, and the blood beaded up again. He must have bitten it. Hard.

"David—"

He rapped his knuckles against his desk, and I nearly jumped. There were two guards behind me. Punctual and creepy as always.

"Here," David said, handing me a small tin. Before I could take it, a guard had snatched it up.

"What are you doing?" I asked angrily. Though I knew. Nothing passed between me and the other Grisha without being thoroughly inspected. For my safety, of course.

The Priestguard ignored me. He ran his fingers over the top and bottom of the tin, opened it, smelled the contents, investigated the lid, then closed it and handed it back without a word. I plucked it from his hand.

"Thanks," I said sourly. "And thank you, David."

He had already bent back over his notebook, seemingly lost in whatever he was reading. But he gripped his pen so hard I thought it might snap.

Genya was waiting for me in the Kettle, the vast, almost perfectly round cavern that provided food for all those in the White Cathedral. Its curved walls were studded with stone hearths, reminders of Ravka's ancient past that the kitchen staff liked to complain weren't nearly as convenient as the cookstoves and tile ovens above. The giant spits had been made for large game, but the cooks rarely had access to fresh meat. So instead they served salt pork, root vegetable stews, and a strange bread made from coarse grey flour that tasted vaguely of cherries.

The cooks had nearly got used to Genya, or at least they didn't cringe and start praying when they saw her any more. I found her keeping warm at a hearth on the Kettle's far wall. This had become our spot, and the cooks left a small pot of porridge or soup there for us every day. As I approached with my armed escort, Genya let her shawl drop away, and the guards flanking me stopped short. She rolled her remaining eye and gave a catlike hiss. They dropped back, hovering by the entrance.

"Too much?" she asked.

"Just enough," I replied, marvelling at the changes in her. If she could laugh at the way those oafs reacted to her, it was a very good sign. Though the salve David had created for her scars had helped, I was pretty sure most of the credit belonged to Tamar.

For weeks after we'd arrived at the White Cathedral, Genya had refused to leave her chambers. She simply lay there, in the dark, unwilling to move. Under the supervision of the guards, I'd talked to her, cajoled her, tried to make her laugh. Nothing had worked. In the end, it had been Tamar who lured her out into the open, demanding that she at least learn to defend herself.

"Why do you even care?" Genya had muttered to her, pulling the blankets up.

"I don't. But if you can't fight, you're a liability."

"I don't care if I get hurt."

"I do," I'd protested.

"Alina needs to watch her own back," Tamar said. "She can't be looking after you."

"I never asked her to."

"Wouldn't it be nice if we only got what we asked for?" Tamar said. Then she'd pinched and prodded and generally harassed, until finally Genya had thrown off her covers and agreed to a single combat lesson – in private, away from the others, with only the Priestguards as audience.

"I'm going to flatten her," she'd grumbled to me. My skepticism must have been evident, because she'd blown a red curl off her scarred forehead and said, "Fine, then I'll wait for her to fall asleep and give her a pig nose."

But she'd gone to that lesson and the next one, and as far as I knew, Tamar hadn't woken up with a pig nose or with her eyelids sealed shut.

Genya continued to keep her face covered and spent most of her time in her chamber, but she no longer hunched, and she didn't shy away from people in the tunnels. She'd made herself a black silk eye patch from the lining of an old coat, and her hair was looking distinctly redder. If Genya was using her power to alter her hair colour, then maybe some of her vanity had returned, and that could only mean progress.

"Let's get started," she said.

Genya turned her back to the room, facing the fire, then drew her shawl over her head, keeping the fringed sides spread wide to create a screen that would hide us from prying eyes. The first time we'd tried this, the guards had been on us in seconds. But as soon as they'd seen me applying the salve to Genya's scars, they'd given us distance. They considered the wounds she bore from the Darkling's *nichevo'ya* some kind of divine judgement. For what, I wasn't sure. If Genya's crime was siding with the Darkling, then most of us had been guilty of it at one time or another. And what would they say to the bite marks on my shoulder? Or the way I could make shadows curl?

I took the tin from my pocket and began applying salve

to her wounds. It had a sharp green scent that made my eyes water.

"I never realised what a pain it is to sit still this long," she complained.

"You're not sitting still. You're wriggling around."

"It itches."

"How about I jab you with a tack? Will that distract you from the itching?"

"Just tell me when you're done, you dreadful girl." She was watching my hands closely. "No luck today?" she whispered.

"Not so far. There are only two hearths going, and the flames are low." I wiped my hand on a grubby kitchen towel. "There," I said. "Done."

"Your turn," she said. "You look—"

"Terrible. I know."

"It's a relative term." The sadness in her voice was unmistakable. I could have kicked myself.

I touched my hand to her cheek. The skin between the scars was smooth and white as the alabaster walls. "I'm an idiot."

The corner of her lip pulled crookedly. Almost a smile. "On occasion," she said. "But I'm the one who brought it up. Now be quiet and let me work."

"Just enough so that the Apparat lets us keep coming here. I don't want to give him a pretty little Saint to show off."

She sighed theatrically. "This is a violation of my most core beliefs, and you *will* make it up to me later."

"How?"

She cocked her head to one side. "I think you should let me make you a redhead."

I rolled my eyes. "Not in this lifetime, Genya."

As she began the slow work of altering my face, I fiddled with the tin in my fingers. I tried to fit the lid back on, but some part of it had come loose from beneath the salve. I lifted it with the tips of my fingernails – a thin, waxy disc of paper. Genya saw it at the same time I did.

Written on the back, in David's nearly illegible scrawl, was a single word: *today*.

Genya snatched it from my fingers. "Oh, Saints. Alina—"

That was when we heard the stomp of heavy-booted feet and a scuffle outside. A pot hit the ground with a loud *clang*, and a shriek went up from one of the cooks as the room flooded with Priestguards, rifles drawn, eyes seeming to blaze holy fire.

The Apparat swept in behind them in a swirl of brown robes. "Clear the room," he bellowed.

Genya and I shot to our feet as the Priestguards roughly herded the cooks from the kitchen in a confusion of protests and frightened exclamations.

"What is this?" I demanded.

"Alina Starkov," said the Apparat, "you are in danger."

My heart was hammering, but I kept my voice calm. "Danger from what?" I asked, glancing at the pots boiling in the hearths. "Lunch?"

"Conspiracy," he proclaimed, pointing at Genya. "Those who would claim your friendship seek to destroy you."

More of the Apparat's bearded henchmen marched through the door behind him. When they parted ranks, I saw David, his eyes wide and frightened.

Genya gasped and I laid a hand on her arm to keep her from charging forward.

Nadia and Zoya were next, both with wrists bound to prevent them from summoning. A trickle of blood leaked from the corner of Nadia's mouth, and her skin was white beneath her freckles. Mal was with them, his face badly bloodied. He was clutching his side as if cradling a broken rib, his shoulders hunched against the pain. And worse was the sight of the guards who flanked him – Tolya and Tamar. Tamar had her axes back. In fact, they were both armed as thoroughly as the Priestguards. They would not meet my eyes.

"Lock the doors," the Apparat commanded. "We will have this sad business done in private."

Chapter 2

The Kettle's massive doors slammed shut, and I heard the lock turn. I tried to put aside the sick twist in my gut and make sense of what I was seeing. Nadia and Zoya – two Squallers – Mal, and David, a harmless Fabrikator. *Today*, the note had said. What had it meant?

"I'll ask you again, priest. What is this? Why are my friends in custody? Why are they *bleeding*?"

"These are not your friends. A plot has been discovered to bring the White Cathedral down around our very ears."

"What are you talking about?"

"You saw the boy's insolence today—"

"Is that the problem? He doesn't tremble properly in your presence?"

"The issue here is treason!" He drew a small canvas pouch from his robes and held it out, letting it dangle from his fingers. I frowned. I'd seen pouches like that in the Fabrikator workshops. They were used for—

"Blasting powders," the Apparat said. "Made by this Fabrikator filth with materials gathered by your supposed friends."

"So David made blasting powders. There could be a hundred reasons for that."

"Weapons are forbidden within the White Cathedral."

I arched a brow at the rifles currently pointed at Mal

and my Grisha. "And what are those? Ladles? If you're going to make accusations—"

"Their plans were overheard. Stand forward, Tamar Kir-Bataar. Speak the truth you've discovered."

Tamar bowed deeply. "The Grisha and the tracker planned to drug you and take you to the surface."

"I *want* to return to the surface."

"The blasting powders would have been used to ensure that no one followed," she continued, "to bring down the caverns on the Apparat and your flock."

"Hundreds of innocent people? Mal would never do that. None of them would." Not even Zoya, that wretch. "And it doesn't make any sense. Just how were they supposed to drug me?"

Tamar nodded to Genya and the tea that sat beside us.

"I drink that tea myself," Genya snapped. "It isn't laced with anything."

"She is an accomplished poisoner and liar," Tamar replied coldly. "She has betrayed you to the Darkling before."

Genya's fingers clenched around her shawl. We both knew there was truth in the charge. I felt an unwelcome prickle of suspicion.

"You trust her," Tamar said. There was something strange in her voice. She sounded less like she was issuing an accusation than a command.

"They were only waiting to stockpile enough blasting powder," said the Apparat. "Then they intended to strike, to take you aboveground and give you up to the Darkling."

I shook my head. "You really expect me to believe that Mal would hand me over to the Darkling?"

"He was a dupe," said Tolya quietly. "He was so desperate to free you that he became their pawn."

I glanced at Mal. I couldn't read his expression. The first real sliver of doubt entered me. I'd never trusted Zoya, and how well did I really know Nadia? Genya – Genya had suffered so much at the Darkling's hand, but their ties ran deep. Cold sweat broke out on my neck, and I felt panic pull at me, fraying my thoughts.

"Plots within plots," hissed the Apparat. "You have a soft heart, and it has betrayed you."

"No," I said. "None of this makes sense."

"They are spies and deceivers!"

I pressed my fingers to my temples. "Where are my other Grisha?"

"They have been contained until they can be properly questioned."

"Tell me they are unharmed."

"See this concern for those who would wrong her?" he asked of the Priestguards. *He's enjoying this*, I realised. *He's been waiting for it.* "This is what marks her kindness, her generosity." His gaze locked on mine. "There *are* some injuries, but the traitors will have the best of care. You need only say the word."

The warning was clear, and finally I understood. Whether the Grisha plot was real or some subterfuge invented by the priest, this was the moment he had been hoping for, the chance to make my isolation complete. No more visits to the Kettle with Genya, no more stolen conversation with David. The priest would use this chance to separate me from anyone whose loyalties were tied more tightly to me than his cause. And I was too weak to stop him.

Was Tamar telling the truth? Were these allies really enemies? Nadia hung her head. Zoya kept her chin lifted, her blue eyes bright with challenge. It was easy to believe that either or both of them might turn against me, might seek the Darkling out and offer me as a gift with some hope of clemency. And David had helped to place the collar around my neck.

Could Mal have been tricked into helping them betray me? He didn't look frightened or concerned – he looked the way he had at Keramzin when he was about to do something that got us both in trouble. His face was bruised, but I noticed he was standing straighter. And then he glanced up, almost as if he were casting his eyes heavenward, as if he were praying. I knew better. Mal had never been the religious sort. He was looking at the master flue.

Plots within plots. David's nervousness. Tamar's words. *You trust her.*

"Release them," I commanded.

The Apparat shook his head, his expression full of sorrow. "Our Saint is being weakened by those who claim to love her. See how frail she is, how sickly. This is the corruption of their influence." A few of the Priestguards nodded, and I saw that strange fanatical light in their eyes. "She is a Saint, but also a young girl governed by emotion. She does not understand the forces at work here."

"I understand that you have lost your way, priest."

The Apparat gave me that pitying, indulgent smile. "You are ill, Sankta Alina. Not in your right mind. You do not know friend from foe."

Goes with the territory, I thought bleakly. I took a deep breath. This was the moment to choose. I had to believe in someone, and it wasn't the Apparat, a man who had betrayed his King, then betrayed the Darkling, who I knew would gladly orchestrate my martyrdom if it served his purpose.

"You will release them," I repeated. "I will not warn you again."

A smirk flickered over his lips. Behind the pity, there was arrogance. He was perfectly aware of how weak I was. I had to hope the others knew what they were doing.

"You will be escorted to your chambers so that you may spend the day in solitude," he said. "You will think on what has happened, and good sense will return. Tonight we will pray together. For guidance."

Why did I suspect that "guidance" meant the location of the firebird and possibly any information I had on Nikolai Lantsov?

"And if I refuse?" I asked, scanning the Priestguards. "Will your soldiers take up arms against their Saint?"

"You will remain untouched and protected, Sankta Alina," said the Apparat. "I cannot extend the same courtesy to those you would call friends."

More threats. I looked into the guards' faces, their fervent eyes. They would murder Mal, kill Genya, lock me in my chambers, and feel righteous in the act.

I took a small step back. I knew the Apparat would read it as a sign of weakness. "Do you know why I come here, priest?"

He gave a dismissive wave, his impatience showing through. "It reminds you of home."

My eyes met Mal's briefly. "You should know by now," I said, "an orphan has no home."

I twitched my fingers in my sleeves. Shadows surged

up the Kettle walls. It wasn't much of a distraction, but it was enough. The Priestguards startled, rifles swinging wildly, as their Grisha captives recoiled in shock. Mal didn't hesitate.

"Now!" he shouted. He shot forward, snatching the blasting powder from the Apparat's hand.

Tolya threw out his fists. Two of the Priestguards crumpled, clutching their chests. Nadia and Zoya held up their hands, and Tamar spun, her axes slicing through their bonds. Both Squallers raised their arms, and wind rushed through the room, lifting the sawdust on the floor.

"Seize them!" yelled the Apparat. The guards sprang into action.

Mal hurled the pouch of powder into the air. Nadia and Zoya lobbed it higher, up into the master flue.

Mal slammed into one of the guards. The broken ribs must have been an act, because there was nothing tentative in his movements now. A fist, a thrown elbow. The Priestguard went down. Mal grabbed his pistol and aimed high, up into the flue, into darkness.

This was the plan? No one could make that shot.

Another guard threw himself at Mal. Mal pivoted from his grasp and fired.

For a moment, there was a hush, suspended silence, and then high above us, I heard it: a dampened *boom*.

A roaring sound rushed towards us. A cloud of soot and rubble billowed from the flue above.

"Nadia!" cried Zoya, who was grappling with a guard.

Nadia arced her arms and the cloud hovered, twisted, siphoned into the shape of a whirling column. It spun away and collapsed to the floor in a harmless clatter of pebbles and dirt.

I took all of this in dimly – the fighting, the Apparat's shouts of rage, the grease fire that had broken out against the far wall.

Genya and I had come to the kitchens for one reason alone: the hearths. Not for the heat or for any sense of comfort, but because each of those ancient hearths led to the master flue. And that flue was the only place in the White Cathedral with direct access to the surface. Direct access to the sun.

"Strike them down!" the Apparat shouted at his Priestguards. "They're trying to kill our Saint! They're trying to kill us all!"

I'd come here every day, hoping the cooks might use more than a few fires so that the flue would open all the way. I'd tried to summon, hidden from the Priestguards by Genya's thick shawl and their superstitious fear of her. I'd tried and failed. Now Mal had blown the flue wide open. I could only call and pray that the light would answer.

I felt it, miles above me – so tentative, barely a whisper. Panic gripped me. The distance was too great. I'd been foolish to hope.

Then it was as if something within me rose and stretched, like a creature that had lain idle for too long. Its muscles had gone soft from disuse, but it was still there, waiting. I called and the light answered with the strength of the antlers at my throat, the scales at my wrist. It came to me in a rush, triumphant and eager.

I grinned at the Apparat, letting exultation fill me. "A man so obsessed with holy fire should pay more attention to the smoke."

The light slammed through me and burst over the room in a blinding cascade that illuminated the almost comical expression of shock on the Apparat's face. The Priestguards threw up their hands, eyes squeezed shut against the glare.

Relief came with the light, a sense of being right and whole for the first time in months. Some part of me had truly feared I might never be restored completely, that by using *merzost* in my fight with the Darkling, by daring to create shadow soldiers and trespass in the making at the heart of the world, I had somehow forfeited this gift. But now it was as if I could feel my body coming to life, my cells reviving. Power rippled through my blood, reverberated in my bones.

The Apparat recovered quickly. "Save her!" he bellowed. "Save her from the traitors!"

Some of the guards looked confused, some frightened, but two jumped forward to do his bidding, sabres raised to attack Nadia and Zoya.

I honed my power to a gleaming scythe, felt the strength of the Cut in my hands.

Then Mal lunged in front of me. I barely had time to draw back. The jolt of unused power recoiled through me, making my heart stutter.

Mal had got hold of a sword, and his blade flashed as he cut through one guard, then the other. They toppled like trees.

Two more advanced, but Tolya and Tamar were there to stop them. David ran to Genya's side. Nadia and Zoya flipped another guard in the air. I saw Priestguards on the periphery raising their rifles to open fire.

Rage coursed through me, and I fought to rein it in. *No more*, I told myself. *No more deaths today.* I hurled the Cut in a fiery arc. It crashed through a long table and tore into the earth before the Priestguards, opening a dark, yawning trench in the kitchen floor. There was no way of knowing how deep it went.

Terror was written on the Apparat's face – terror and what might well have been awe. The guards fell to their knees, and a moment later, the priest followed. Some wept, chanting prayers. Beyond the kitchen doors, I heard fists pounding, voices wailing, "Sankta! Sankta!"

I was glad they were crying out for me and not the Apparat. I dropped my hands, letting the light recede. I didn't want to let it go. I looked at the bodies of the fallen guards. One of them had sawdust in his beard. I had almost been the person to end his life.

I drew a little light and kept it burning in a warm halo around me. I had to be cautious. The power was feeding me, but I'd been too long without it. My weakened body was having trouble keeping up, and I wasn't sure of my limits. Still, I'd been under the Apparat's control for months, and I wouldn't have an opportunity like this again.

Men lay dead and bleeding, and a crowd was waiting outside the Kettle doors. I could hear Nikolai's voice in my head: *The people like spectacle.* The show wasn't over yet.

I walked forward, stepping carefully around the trench I'd opened, and stood before one of the kneeling guards.

He was younger than the others; his beard just coming in, his gaze fastened on the ground as he mumbled prayers. I caught not just my name, but the names of real Saints, strung together as if in a single word. I touched my hand to his shoulder, and his eyes slid shut, tears rolling down his cheeks.

"Forgive me," he said. "Forgive me."

"Look at me," I said gently.

He forced himself to look up. I cupped his face in my hand, gentle, like a mother, though he was barely older than I was. "What's your name?"

"Vladim . . . Vladim Ozwal."

"It's good to doubt Saints, Vladim. And men."

He gave a shaky nod as another tear spilled over.

"My soldiers bear my mark," I said, referring to the tattoos borne by the Soldat Sol. "Until this day you have put yourself apart from them, buried yourself in books and prayer instead of hearing the people. Will you wear my mark now?"

"Yes," he said, fervently.

"Will you swear loyalty to me and only me?"

"Gladly!" he cried. "Sol Koroleva!" Sun Queen.

My stomach turned. Part of me hated what I was about to do. *Can't I just make him sign something? Give a blood oath? Make me a really firm promise?* But I had to be stronger than that. This boy and his comrades had taken up arms against me. I couldn't let that happen again, and this was the language of Saints and suffering, the language they understood.

"Open your shirt," I commanded. Not a loving mother now, but a different kind of Saint, a warrior wielding holy fire.

His fingers fumbled with his buttons, but he didn't hesitate. He pulled the fabric apart, baring the skin of his chest. I was tired, still weak. I had to concentrate. I wanted to make a point, not kill him.

I felt the light in my hand. I pressed my palm to the smooth skin over his heart and let the power pulse. Vladim flinched when it connected, scorching his flesh, but he did not cry out. His eyes were wide and unblinking, his expression rapt. When I pulled my hand back, my palm print remained, the brand throbbing red and angry on his chest.

Not bad, I thought grimly, *for your first time mutilating a man.*

I let the power go, grateful to be finished.

"It is done."

Vladim looked down at his chest, and his face broke into a beatific grin. *He has dimples*, I realised with a lurch. *Dimples and a hideous scar he'll bear for the rest of his life.*

"Thank you, Sol Koroleva."

"Rise," I commanded.

He stood, beaming down at me, tears still running from his eyes.

The Apparat moved as if to stand. "Stay where you are," I snapped, my rage returning. He was the reason I'd just had to brand a young man. He was the reason two men lay dead, their blood pooling over discarded onion skins and carrot shavings.

I looked down at him. I could feel the temptation to take his life, to be rid of him forever. It would be deeply stupid. I'd awed a few soldiers, but if I murdered the Apparat, who knew what chaos I might unleash? *You want to, though*, said a voice in my head. For the months underground, for the fear and intimidation, for every day sacrificed below the surface when I could have been hunting the firebird and seeking revenge on the Darkling.

He must have read the intent in my eyes.

"Sankta Alina, I only wanted for you to be safe, for you to be whole and well again," he said shakily.

"Then consider your prayers answered." That was a lie if I'd ever told one. The last words I would have chosen to describe myself were *whole* or *well*. "Priest," I said. "You will offer sanctuary to all those who seek it, not just those who worship the Sun Saint."

He shook his head. "The security of the White Cathedral—"

"If not here, then elsewhere. Figure it out."

He took a breath. "Of course."

"And there will be no more child soldiers."

"If the faithful wish to fight—"

"You are on your knees," I said. "We are not negotiating."

His lips thinned, but after a moment, he dipped his chin in assent.

I looked around. "You are all witness to these decrees." Then I turned to one of the guards. "Give me your gun."

He handed it over without a second's pause. With some satisfaction, I saw the Apparat's eyes widen in dismay, but I simply passed the weapon to Genya, then demanded a sabre for David, though I knew he wouldn't be much good with it. Zoya and Nadia stood ready to summon, and Mal and the twins were already well armed.

"Up," I said to the Apparat. "Let us have peace. We have seen miracles this day."

He rose, and as I embraced him, I whispered in his ear. "You will lend your blessing to our mission, and you will follow the orders I've laid out for you. Or I will carve you in half and throw the pieces into the Fold. Understood?"

He swallowed and nodded.

I needed time to think, but I didn't have it. We had to open those doors, to offer the people an explanation for the fallen guards and for the explosion.

"See to your dead," I said to one of the Priestguards.

"We'll bear them with us. Do they . . . do they have family?"

"We are their family," said Vladim.

I addressed the others. "Gather the faithful from all over the White Cathedral and bring them to the main cavern. I will speak to them in one hour's time. Vladim, once we're out of the Kettle, free the other Grisha and get them to my quarters."

He touched the brand at his chest in a kind of salute. "Sankta Alina."

I glanced at Mal's bruised face. "Genya, clean him up. Nadia—"

"I've got it," Tamar said, already dabbing the blood on Nadia's lip with a towel she'd dunked into a cookpot full of hot water. "Sorry about that," I heard her say.

Nadia smiled. "Had to make it look good. Besides, I'll get you back."

"We'll see," Tamar replied.

I looked over the other Grisha in their bedraggled *kefta*. We didn't make for a very impressive parade. "Tolya, Tamar, Mal, you'll walk beside me with the Apparat." I lowered my voice. "Try to look confident and . . . regal."

"I have a question—" Zoya began.

"I have about a hundred, but they'll have to wait. I don't want the crowd out there turning into a mob." I looked at the Apparat. I felt the dark urge to humble him, to make him crawl in front of me for these long weeks of subjugation underground. Ugly, foolish thoughts. It might gain me petty satisfaction, but what would it cost? I took a deep breath and said, "I want everyone else interspersed with the Priestguards. This is a show of alliance."

We arranged ourselves in front of the doors. The Apparat and I took the lead, the Priestguards and Grisha arrayed behind us, the corpses of the fallen borne aloft by their brothers.

"Vladim," I said, "open the doors."

As Vladim moved to turn the locks, Mal took his place beside me.

"How did you know I'd be able to summon?" I asked under my breath.

He glanced at me, and a faint grin touched his lips. "Faith."

Chapter 3

The doors flew open. I threw out my hands and let light blast into the passageway. A cry went up from the people lining the tunnel. Those who weren't already kneeling fell to their knees, and a chorus of prayer washed over me.

"Speak," I muttered to the Apparat as I bathed the supplicants in glowing sunlight. "And make it good."

"We have faced a great trial this day," he declared hurriedly. "Our Saint has emerged from it stronger than before. Darkness came to this hallowed place—"

"I saw it!" cried one of the Priestguards. "Shadows climbed the walls—"

"About that . . . " murmured Mal.

"Later."

"But they were vanquished," continued the Apparat, "as they will always be vanquished. By faith!"

I stepped forward. "And by power."

Again, I let light sweep through the passage, a blinding cascade. Most of these people had never seen what my power could truly do. Someone was weeping, and I heard my name, buried in the cries of "Sankta! Sankta!"

As I led the Apparat and the Priestguards through the White Cathedral, my mind was working, turning over options. Vladim went ahead of us, to see my orders done.

We finally had a chance to get free of this place. But what would it mean to leave the White Cathedral behind? I'd be abandoning an army and leaving them in the Apparat's care. And yet, there weren't many options open to us. I needed to get aboveground. I needed the firebird.

Mal dispatched Tamar to rally the rest of the Soldat Sol and search out more working firearms. My control of the Priestguards was tenuous at best. In case of trouble, we wanted guns at the ready, and I hoped I could rely on the sun soldiers to stay loyal to me.

I escorted the Apparat to his quarters myself, Mal and Tolya trailing us.

At his door, I said, "In one hour, we'll lead services together. Tonight, I leave with my Grisha and you'll sanction our departure."

"Sol Koroleva," the Apparat whispered, "I urge you not to return to the surface so soon. The Darkling's position is not a strong one. The Lantsov boy has few allies—"

"I'm his ally."

"He abandoned you at the Little Palace."

"He *survived*, priest. That's something you should understand." Nikolai had intended to get his family and Baghra to safety, then return to the fight. I could only hope he'd succeeded and that the rumours of him wreaking havoc on the northern border were true.

"Let them weaken each other, see which way the wind blows—"

"I owe Nikolai Lantsov more than that."

"Is it loyalty that drives you? Or greed?" pressed the Apparat. "The amplifiers have waited countless years to be brought together, and you cannot wait a few more months?"

My jaw clenched at the thought. I wasn't sure what was

driving me, if it was my need for vengeance or something higher, if it was hunger for the firebird or friendship with Nikolai. It didn't much matter though. "This is my war too," I said. "I won't hide like a lizard under a rock."

"I beg you to heed my words. I have done nothing except serve you faithfully."

"The way you served the King? The way you served the Darkling?"

"I am the voice of the people. They did not choose the Lantsov Kings or the Darkling. They chose you as their Saint, and they will love you as their Queen."

Even the sound of those words made me weary.

I glanced over my shoulder to where Mal and Tolya waited a respectful distance away. "Do you believe it?" I asked the priest. The question had plagued me since I'd first heard word of him gathering this cult. "Do you really think I'm a Saint?"

"What I believe doesn't matter," he replied. "That's what you've never understood. Do you know they've started building altars to you in Fjerda? In *Fjerda*, where they burn Grisha at the stake. There is a fine line between fear and veneration, Alina Starkov. I can move that line. That is the prize I offer you."

"I don't want it."

"But you will have it. Men fight for Ravka because the King commands it, because their pay keeps their families from starving, because they have no choice. They will fight for you because to them you are salvation. They will starve for you, lay down their lives and their children's lives for you. They will make war without fear and die rejoicing. There is no greater power than faith, and there will be no greater army than one driven by it."

"Faith didn't protect your soldiers from the *nichevo'ya*. No amount of fanaticism will."

"You see only war, but I see the peace that will come. Faith knows no border and no nationality. Love for you has taken root in Fjerda. The Shu will follow, then the Kerch. Our people will go forward and spread the word, not just through Ravka but through the world. This is the way to peace, Sankta Alina. Through you."

"The cost is too high."

"War is the price of change."

"And it's ordinary people who pay it, peasants like me. Never men like you."

"We—"

I silenced him with a hand. I thought of the Darkling laying waste to an entire town, of Nikolai's brother Vasily commanding that the draft age be lowered. The Apparat claimed to speak for the people, but he was no different from the rest.

"Keep them safe, priest – this flock, this army. Keep them fed. Keep marks off the children's faces and rifles out of their hands. You leave the rest to me."

"Sankta Alina—"

I held open the door to his chamber. "We'll pray together soon," I said. "But I think you could use a head start."

Mal and I left the Apparat secured in his chambers and guarded by Tolya – with strict orders to make sure that the door stayed closed and that no one disturbed the priest's prayers.

I suspected that the Apparat would soon have the Priestguards, maybe even Vladim, back under his control. But all we needed were a few hours' start. He was lucky I hadn't crammed him into a damp corner of the archives.

When we finally arrived at my chamber, I found the narrow white room packed with Grisha, and Vladim waiting at the door. My sleeping quarters were among the largest in the White Cathedral, but it was still a challenge to accommodate a group of twelve. No one looked too badly off. Nadia's lip was swollen, and Maxim was tending to a cut over Stigg's eye. It was the first time we'd been allowed to gather underground, and there was something comforting about seeing Grisha crowded together and sprawled over the meagre furniture.

Mal didn't seem to agree. "We might as well travel with a marching band," he grumbled under his breath.

"What the hell is going on?" Sergei asked as soon as I'd dismissed Vladim. "One minute I'm in the infirmary with Maxim, the next I'm in a cell." He paced back and forth. There was a clammy sheen to his skin, and he had dark circles beneath his eyes.

"Calm down," said Tamar. "You're not behind bars now."

"I might as well be. We're all trapped down here. And that bastard is just looking for a chance to get rid of us."

"If you want to get out of the caves, then this is your opportunity," I said. "We're leaving. Tonight."

"How?" Stigg asked.

By way of answer, I let sunlight flare for a brief, brilliant moment in my palm—proof that my power had ignited in me once more, even if that small gesture took more effort than it should.

The room erupted into whistles and cheers.

"Yes, yes," said Zoya. "The Sun Summoner can summon. And all it took was a few deaths and a minor explosion."

"You blew something up?" said Harshaw plaintively. "Without me?"

He was wedged against the wall next to Stigg. Our two Inferni couldn't have looked more different. Stigg was short and stocky with nearly white blond hair. He had the solid, stubby appearance of a prayer candle. Harshaw was tall and lean, his hair redder than Genya's, nearly the colour of blood. A scrawny ginger tabby had somehow made her way down to the bowels of the White Cathedral and taken a liking to him. She followed him everywhere, slinking between his legs or clinging to his shoulder.

"Where *did* those blasting powders come from?" I asked, perching next to Nadia and her brother on the edge of my bed.

"I made them when I was supposed to be making salve," said David. "Just like the Apparat said."

"Right under the noses of the Priestguards?"

"It's not as if they know anything about the Small Science."

"Well, somebody must. You got caught."

"Not exactly," said Mal. He'd stationed himself by the doorway with Tamar, each of them keeping an eye on the passage beyond.

"David knew we were meeting in the Kettle," said Genya, "and he guessed about the master flue."

David frowned. "I don't guess."

"But there was no way to get the powders out of the archives, not with the guards searching everything."

Tamar grinned. "So we had the Apparat deliver it."

I stared at them in disbelief. "You meant to get caught?"

"Turns out the easiest way to schedule a meeting is to get arrested," said Zoya.

"Do you know how risky that was?"

"Blame Oretsev," Zoya replied with a sniff. "It was his idea of a brilliant plan."

"It did *work*," Genya observed.

Mal lifted a shoulder. "Like Sergei said, the Apparat was waiting for an opportunity to take us out of action. I thought we'd give him one."

"We were just never sure when you'd be in the Kettle," Nadia said. "When you left the archives today, David claimed he'd forgotten something in his quarters and came by the training rooms to give us the signal. We knew the Apparat would be more likely to trust Tolya and Tamar, so they roughed us up a little—"

"A lot," put in Mal.

"Then they claimed to have discovered a devious plot involving a few wicked Grisha and one very gullible tracker."

Mal gave a mock salute.

"I was afraid he'd insist on putting everyone in the cells," said Tamar. "So we claimed you were in immediate danger and that we had to get to the Kettle right away."

Nadia smiled. "And then we just hoped the whole kitchen wouldn't fall in on us."

David's frown deepened. "It was a controlled blast. The odds that the cave's structure would hold were well above average."

"Ah. Above average," said Genya. "Why didn't you say so?"

"I just did."

"What about those shadows on the wall?" asked Zoya. "Who pulled that off?"

I tensed, unsure of what to say.

"I did it," said Mal. "We rigged it as a distraction."

Sergei paced back and forth, cracking his knuckles. "You should have told us about the plan. We deserved a warning."

"You could have at least let me blow something up," added Harshaw.

Zoya gave an elaborate shrug. "I'm *so* sorry you felt excluded. Never mind how closely we've been watched and that it was a miracle we weren't found out. We definitely should have jeopardised the whole operation to spare your feelings."

I cleared my throat. "In less than an hour, I'll be leading services with the Apparat. We'll leave directly after that, and I need to know who's going with me."

"Any chance you're going to tell us where the third amplifier is?" asked Zoya. Thus far, only the twins, Mal, and I knew where we hoped to find the firebird. *And Nikolai*, I reminded myself. Nikolai knew too – if he was still alive.

Mal shook his head. "The less you know, the safer we'll be."

"So you're not even telling us where we're going?" Sergei said sulkily.

"Not quite. We're going to attempt to make contact with Nikolai Lantsov."

"I think we should try Ryevost," said Tamar.

"Go to the river cities?" I asked. "Why?"

"Sturmhond had smuggling lines throughout Ravka.

It's possible Nikolai is using them to get arms into the country." Tamar would know. She and Tolya had been trusted members of Sturmhond's crew. "If the rumours are true and he's based somewhere in the north, then there's a good chance the drop point near Ryevost is active."

"That's a lot of maybe and not much more," Harshaw observed.

Mal nodded. "True. But it's our best lead."

"And if it's a dead end?" asked Sergei.

"We split up," said Mal. "We find a safe house where you can lie low, and I take a team to find the firebird."

"You're welcome to remain here," I said to the others. "I know the pilgrims aren't friendly to Grisha, and after tonight, I'm not sure how sentiment will change. But if we're captured aboveground—"

"The Darkling doesn't deal kindly with traitors," finished Genya quietly.

Everyone shifted uncomfortably, but I made myself meet her gaze. "No. He doesn't."

"He's had his shot at me," she said. "I'm going."

Zoya smoothed the cuff of her coat. "We'd move faster without you."

"I'll keep up," Genya countered.

"See that you do," said Mal. "We'll be entering an area crawling with militias, not to mention the Darkling's *oprichniki*. You're recognisable," he said to Genya. "So is Tolya, for that matter."

Tamar's lips twitched. "Would you like to be the one to tell him he can't come?"

Mal considered this. "Maybe we can disguise him as a really big tree."

Adrik shot to his feet so fast he nearly bounced me

from the bed. "See you in an hour," he declared, as if daring anyone to argue. Nadia gave me a shrug as he marched out of the room. Adrik wasn't much younger than the rest of us, but maybe because he was Nadia's little brother, he always seemed to be looking to prove himself.

"Well, I'm going," said Zoya. "The humidity down here is murder on my hair."

Harshaw rose and pushed off from the wall. "I'd prefer to stay," he said with a yawn. "But Oncat says we go." He hefted the tabby onto his shoulder with one hand.

"Are you ever going to name that thing?" Zoya asked.

"She has a name."

"*Oncat* is not a name. It's just Kaelish for cat."

"Suits her, doesn't it?"

Zoya rolled her eyes and flounced through the door, followed by Harshaw and then Stigg, who gave a polite bow and said, "I'll be ready."

The others trickled out after them. I suspected David would have preferred to remain at the White Cathedral, cloistered with Morozova's journals. But he was our only Fabrikator, and assuming we found the firebird, we would need him to forge the second fetter. Nadia seemed happy to go with her brother, though it was Tamar she grinned at on the way out. I'd guessed that Maxim would choose to remain here at the infirmary, and I'd been right. Maybe I could get Vladim and the other Priestguards to set an example for the pilgrims and take advantage of Maxim's skills as a Healer.

The only surprise was Sergei. Though the White Cathedral was miserable, damp, and dull, it was also relatively secure. As eager as Sergei had seemed to escape the Apparat's grasp, I hadn't been sure he'd want to take his chances with us aboveground. But he'd nodded tersely and simply stated, "I'll be there." Maybe we were all desperate for blue sky and a chance to feel free again, no matter the risk.

When they were gone, Mal sighed and said, "Well, it was worth a try."

"All that talk of militias," I said, realisation dawning. "You were trying to scare them off."

"Twelve is too many. A group that big will slow us through the tunnels, and once we're aboveground, they'll put us at greater risk. As soon as we have a chance, we'll need to split up. There's no way I'm taking a dozen Grisha into the southern mountains."

"All right," I said. "Assuming we can find a safe place for them."

"No easy task, but we'll manage it." He moved towards the door. "I'll be back in a half hour to take you to the main cavern."

"Mal," I said, "why did you step between me and the Priestguards?"

He shrugged. "Those aren't the first men I've killed. They won't be the last."

"You kept me from using the Cut on them."

He didn't look at me when he said, "You're going to be a queen someday, Alina. The less blood on your hands, the better."

The word *queen* came so easily to his lips. "You seem certain we'll find Nikolai."

"I'm certain we'll find the firebird."

"I need an army. The firebird may not be enough." I rubbed a hand over my eyes. "Nikolai may not even be in Ravka."

"The reports coming out of the north—"

"Could be lies spread by the Darkling. The Prince of the Air might be a myth created to draw us out of hiding. Nikolai might never have made it out of the Grand Palace." It hurt me to say it, but I forced myself to speak the words. "He could be dead."

"Do you believe that?"

"I don't know."

"If anyone could make that escape, it's Nikolai."

The too-clever fox. Even once he'd abandoned his disguise as Sturmhond, that's who Nikolai had been to me, always thinking, always scheming. Though he hadn't predicted his brother's betrayal. He hadn't seen the Darkling coming.

"All right," I said, embarrassed by the quaver in my voice. "You haven't asked about the shadows."

"Should I?"

I couldn't resist. Maybe I wanted to see how he would react. I curled my fingers, and shadows unspooled from the corners.

Mal's eyes followed their progress. What did I expect to see in him? Fear? Anger?

"Can you do more with it?" he asked.

"No. It's just some kind of remnant of what I did in the chapel."

"You mean saving all our lives?"

I let the shadows fall and pinched the bridge of my nose with my fingers, trying to stave off a rush of dizziness. "I mean using *merzost*. This isn't real power. It's just a carnival trick."

"It's something you took from him," he said. I didn't think I imagined the satisfaction in his voice. "I won't say a word, but you shouldn't hide it from the others."

I could worry about that later. "What if Nikolai's men aren't in Ryevost?"

"You think I can track a giant mythic bird, but I can't locate one loudmouthed prince?"

"A prince who's managed to evade the Darkling for months."

Mal studied me.

"Alina, do you know how I made that shot? Back in the Kettle?"

"If you say it's because you're just that good, I'm going to take off my boot and beat you with it."

"Well, I *am* that good," he said with a faint grin. "But I also had David put a beetle in the pouch."

"Why?"

"To make aiming easier. All I had to do was track it."

My brows rose. "Now, *that's* an impressive trick."

He shrugged. "It's the only one I know. If Nikolai's alive, we'll find him." He paused, then added, "I won't fail you again." He turned to go, but before he shut the door, he said, "Try to rest. I'll be outside if you need me."

I stood there for a long moment. I wanted to tell him that he hadn't failed me, but that wasn't quite true. I'd lied to him about the visions that plagued me. He'd pushed me away when I'd needed him most. Maybe we'd both asked each other to give up too much. Fair or not, I felt as if Mal had turned his back on me, and some part of me resented him for it.

I glanced around the empty room. It had been disconcerting to see so many people in here. How well did I know any of them? Harshaw and Stigg were a few years older than the others, Grisha who had made their way to the Little Palace after they'd heard the Sun Summoner had returned. They were practically strangers to me. The twins believed I was blessed by divine power. Zoya followed me only grudgingly. Sergei was falling apart, and I knew he probably blamed me for Marie's death. Nadia might too. Although she'd grieved more quietly, they'd been best friends.

And Mal. I supposed we'd made a kind of peace, but it wasn't an easy one. Or maybe we had just accepted what I would become, that our paths would inevitably diverge. *You're going to be a queen someday, Alina.*

I knew I should at least try to sleep for a few minutes, but my mind wouldn't slow down. My body was thrumming with the power I'd used and eager for more.

I glanced at the door, wishing it had a lock. There was something I wanted to try. I'd attempted it a few times and never managed anything more than a headache. It was dangerous, probably stupid, but now that my power had returned, I wanted to try again.

I kicked off my boots and lay back on the narrow bed. I closed my eyes, felt the collar at my throat, the scales at my wrist, the presence of my power inside me like the beat of my heart. I felt the wound at my shoulder, the dark knot of scars made by the Darkling's *nichevo'ya*. It had strengthened the bond between us, giving him access to my mind as the collar had given him access to my power. In the chapel, I had used that connection against him and almost destroyed both of us in the process. I was foolish to test it now. Still, I was tempted. If the Darkling had access to that power, why shouldn't I? It was a chance to glean information, to understand the way the bond between us functioned.

It won't work, I reassured myself. *You'll try, you'll fail, you'll have a little nap.*

I slowed my breathing, letting power course through me. I thought of the Darkling, of the shadows I could bend to my fingers, of the collar around my neck that he had placed there, the fetter at my wrist that had separated me irrevocably from any other Grisha and truly set me on this path.

Nothing happened. I was lying on my back in a bed in the White Cathedral. I hadn't gone anywhere. I was alone in a vacant room. I blinked up at the damp ceiling. It was better that way. At the Little Palace, my isolation had nearly destroyed me, but that was because I had hungered for something else, for the sense of belonging I'd been chasing my whole life. I'd buried that need in the ruins of a chapel. Now I would think in terms of alliance instead of affection, of who and what would make me strong enough for this fight.

I'd contemplated killing the Apparat today; I'd burned my mark into Vladim's flesh. I'd told myself I had to, but the girl I'd been would never have considered such things. I hated the Darkling for what he'd done to Baghra and Genya, but was I so different? And when the third amplifier was around my wrist, would I be different at all?

Maybe not, I conceded, and with that admission came the barest tremor – a vibration moving over the connection between us, an answering echo at the other end of an invisible tether.

It called to me through the collar at my neck and the bite at my shoulder, amplified by the fetter at my wrist, a bond forged by *merzost* and the dark poison in my blood. *You called to me, and I answered.* I felt myself drawn upward, out of myself, speeding towards him. Maybe this was what Mal felt when he tracked – the distant pull of the other, a presence that demanded attention even if it couldn't be seen or touched.

One moment I was floating in the darkness of my closed eyes, and the next I was standing in a brightly lit room. Everything around me was blurry, but I recognised this place just the same: I was in the throne room at the Grand Palace. People were talking. It was as if they were underwater. I heard noise but not words.

I knew the moment the Darkling saw me. He came into sharp focus, though the room around him remained a murky blur.

His self-control was so great that no one near him would have noticed the fleeting look of shock that passed over his perfect features. But I saw his grey eyes widen, his chest lock as his breath caught. His fingers clenched the arms of his chair – no, his throne. Then he relaxed, nodding along to whatever the person before him was saying.

I waited, watching. He'd fought for that throne, endured hundreds of years of battle and servitude to claim it. I had to admit it suited him well. Some petty part of me had hoped I'd find him weakened, his black hair turned to white like mine. But whatever damage I'd done to him that night in the chapel, he'd recovered better than I had.

When the murmur of the supplicant's voice cut off, the Darkling rose. The throne faded into the background, and I realised that the things closest to him looked the clearest, as if he were the lens through which I was seeing the world.

"I will take it under advisement," he said, voice cool as

cut glass, so familiar. "Now leave me." He gave a brusque wave. "All of you."

Did his lackeys exchange baffled glances or simply bow and depart? I couldn't tell. He was already moving down the stairs, his gaze fastened on me. My heart clenched, and a single clear word reverberated in my mind: *run*. I'd been mad to attempt this, to seek him out. But I didn't move. I didn't release the tether.

Someone approached him, and when he was just inches from the Darkling, he came into clearer focus – red Grisha robes, a face I didn't recognise. I could even make out his words: ". . . the matter of signatures for . . ." Then the Darkling cut him off.

"Later," he said sharply, and the Corporalnik skittered away.

The room emptied of sound and movement, and all the while, the Darkling kept his eyes on me. He crossed the parquet floor. With each step, the polished wood came into focus beneath his boot, then faded away again.

I had the strange sensation of lying on my bed in the White Cathedral and being here, in the throne room, standing in a warm square of sunlight.

He stopped before me, his eyes studying my face. What did he see there? He had come to me unscarred in my visions. Did he see me healthy and whole, my hair brown, my eyes bright? Or did he see the little mushroom girl, pale and grey, battered by our fight in the chapel, weakened by life underground?

"If only I'd known you'd prove such an apt pupil." His voice was genuinely admiring, almost surprised. To my horror, I found that pathetic orphaned part of me taking pleasure in his praise. "Why come to me now?" he asked.

"Has it taken you this long to recover from our skirmish?"

If that had been a mere skirmish, then we really were lost. *No*, I told myself. He'd chosen that word deliberately, to intimidate me.

I ignored his question and said, "I didn't expect compliments."

"No?"

"I left you buried beneath a pile of rubble."

"And if I told you I respect your ruthlessness?"

"I don't think I'd believe you."

The barest smile touched his lips. "An apt pupil," he repeated. "Why waste my anger on you when the fault is mine? I should have anticipated another betrayal from you, one more mad grasp at some kind of childish ideal. But I seem to be a victim of my own wishes where you are concerned." His expression hardened. "What have you come here for, Alina?"

I answered him honestly. "I wanted to see you."

I caught the briefest glimpse of surprise before his face shuttered again. "There are two thrones on that dais. You could see me anytime you liked."

"You're offering me a crown? After I tried to kill you?"

He shrugged again. "I might have done the same."

"I doubt it."

"Not to save that motley of traitors and fanatics, no. But I understand the desire to remain free."

"And still you tried to make me a slave."

"I sought Morozova's amplifiers *for you*, Alina, that we might rule as equals."

"You tried to take my power for your own."

"After you ran from me. After you chose—" He stopped, shrugged. "We would have ruled as equals in time."

I felt that pull, the longing of a frightened girl. Even now, after everything he'd done, I wanted to believe the Darkling, to find some way to forgive him. I wanted Nikolai to be alive. I wanted to trust the other Grisha. I wanted to believe anything so that I wouldn't have to face the future alone. *The problem with wanting is that it makes us weak.* A laugh escaped me before I thought better of it.

"We would be equals until the day I dared to disagree with you, until the moment I questioned your judgement or didn't do as I was bid. Then you would deal with me the way you dealt with Genya and your mother, the way you tried to deal with Mal."

He leaned against the window, and the gilded frame came into sharp focus. "Do you think it would be any different with your tracker beside you? With that Lantsov pup?"

"Yes," I said simply.

"Because you would be the strong one?"

"Because they're better men than you."

"You might make me a better man."

"And you might make me a monster."

"I've never understood this taste for *otkazat'sya*. Is it because you thought you were one of them for so long?"

"I had a taste for you, once." His head snapped up. He hadn't expected that. Saints, it was satisfying. "Why haven't you visited me?" I asked. "In all these long months?"

He stayed silent.

"There was barely a day at the Little Palace when you didn't come to me," I continued. "When I didn't see you in some shadowed corner. I thought I was going mad."

"Good."

"I think you're afraid."

"How comforting that must be for you."

"I think you fear this thing that binds us." It didn't frighten me. Not any more. I took a slow step forward. He tensed but did not move away.

"I am ancient, Alina. I know things about power that you can barely guess at."

"It's not just power, though, is it?" I said quietly, remembering the way he had toyed with me when I'd first arrived at the palace – even before, from the first moment we'd met. I'd been a lonely girl, desperate for attention. I must have given him so little sport.

I took another step. He stilled. Our bodies were almost touching now. I reached up and cupped his cheek with my hand. This time the flash of confusion on his face was impossible to miss. He held himself frozen, his only movement the steady rise and fall of his chest. Then, as if in concession, he let his eyes close. A line appeared between his brows.

"It's true," I said softly. "You are stronger, wiser, infinite in experience." I leaned forward and whispered, my lips brushing the shell of his ear. "But I am an apt pupil."

His eyes flew open. I caught the briefest glimpse of rage in his grey gaze before I severed the connection.

I scattered, hurtling back to the White Cathedral, leaving him with nothing but the memory of light.

Chapter 4

I sat up with a gasp, sucking in the damp air of the alabaster chamber. I looked around guiltily. I shouldn't have done it. What had I learned? That he was at the Grand Palace and in disgustingly good health? Paltry information.

But I wasn't sorry. Now I knew what he saw when he visited me, what information he could or couldn't cull from the contact. Now I had practice in one more power that had only belonged to him. And I'd enjoyed it. At the Little Palace, I'd dreaded those visions, thought I might be losing my mind, and worse, I'd wondered what they said about me. No longer. I'd had enough of shame. Let him feel what it was to be haunted.

A headache was starting in my right temple. *I sought Morozova's amplifiers* for you, *Alina.* Lies disguised as truth. He'd sought to make me more powerful because he believed he could control me. He still believed it, and that scared me. The Darkling had no way of knowing that Mal and I knew where to start looking for the third amplifier, but he hadn't seemed concerned. He hadn't even mentioned the firebird. He'd seemed confident, strong, as if he belonged in that palace and on that throne. *I know things about power that you can barely guess at.* I gave myself a shake. I might not be a threat, but I could become one. I wouldn't let him beat me before I'd had a chance to give him the fight he deserved.

A quick knock came at the door. It was time. I shoved my feet back into my boots and adjusted my scratchy golden *kefta*. After this, maybe I'd give myself a treat and stuff the thing in a stewpot.

The services were quite a spectacle. It was still a challenge to summon so far underground, but I threw blazing light over the walls of the White Cathedral, drawing on every reserve to awe the crowd that moaned and swayed below. Vladim stood to my left, his shirt open to display the brand of my palm on his chest. To my right, the Apparat held forth, and whether out of fear or real belief, he did a very convincing job of it. His voice rang through the main cavern, claiming that our mission was guided by divine providence and that I would emerge from my trials more powerful than ever before.

I studied him as he spoke. He looked paler than usual, a bit sweaty, though not particularly chastened. I wondered if it was a mistake to leave him alive, but without the rush of fury and power guiding my actions, execution wasn't a step I was prepared to consider seriously.

A hush had fallen. I looked down into the eager faces of the people below. There was something new in their exultation, maybe because they'd finally had a glimpse of my real power. Or maybe because the Apparat had done his work so well. They were waiting for me to say something. I'd had dreams like this. I was an actor in a play and I'd never learned my lines.

"I will—" My voice cracked. I cleared my throat and tried again. "I will return more powerful than before," I said in my best Saint's voice. "You are my eyes." I needed them to be, to watch the Apparat, to keep each other safe. "You are my fists. You are my swords."

The crowd cheered. As one, they chorused back to me, *Sankta Alina! Sankta Alina! Sankta Alina!*

"Not bad," Mal said as I stepped away from the balcony.

"I've been listening to the Apparat go on for nearly three months. Something had to rub off."

On my orders, the Apparat announced that he would spend three days in isolation, fasting and praying for the success of our mission. The Priestguards would do the same, confined to the archives and guarded by the Soldat Sol.

"Keep them strong in their faith," I told Ruby and the other soldiers. I hoped that three days would give us plenty of time to get well away from the White Cathedral. Although knowing the Apparat, he'd probably talk his way out before dinner.

"I knew you," Ruby said, clutching my fingers as I turned to go. "I was in your regiment. Do you remember?"

Her eyes were wet, and the tattoo on her cheek was so black it seemed to float on top of her skin.

"Of course I do," I said kindly. We hadn't been friends. Back then, Ruby had been more interested in Mal than religion. I'd been nearly invisible to her.

Now she released a sob and pressed a kiss to my knuckles. "Sankta," she whispered fervently. Whenever I thought my life couldn't get any stranger, it did.

Once I'd disentangled myself from Ruby, I took a final moment to speak to the Apparat in private.

"You know what I'm going after, priest, and you know the power I'll wield when I return. Nothing happens to the Soldat Sol or to Maxim." I didn't like leaving the Healer on his own here, but I wouldn't command him to join us, not knowing the dangers we might face on the surface.

"We are not enemies, Sankta Alina," the Apparat said gently. "You must know that all I've ever wanted was to see you on Ravka's throne."

I almost smiled at that. "I know, priest. On the throne and under your thumb."

He tilted his head to one side, contemplating me. The fanatical glint was gone from his eyes. He simply looked shrewd.

"You are not what I expected," he admitted.

"Not quite the Saint you bargained for?"

"A lesser Saint," he said. "Perhaps a better queen. I will pray for you, Alina Starkov."

The strange thing was I believed him.

Mal and I met the others at Chetya's Well, a natural fountain at the crossroads of four of the major tunnels. If the Apparat did decide to send a party after us, we'd be harder to track from there. At least that was the idea. We hadn't bargained on so many of the pilgrims turning out to see us off. They'd followed the Grisha from their quarters and crowded around the fountain.

We were all in ordinary travel clothes, our *kefta* stowed in our packs. I'd exchanged my gold robes for a heavy coat, a fur hat, and the comforting weight of a gun belt at my hip. If it hadn't been for my white hair, I doubted any of the pilgrims would have recognised me.

Now they reached out to touch my sleeve or my hand. Some pressed little gifts on us, the only offerings they had: hoarded bread rolls gone tooth-breakingly hard, polished stones, bits of lace, a clutch of salt lilies. They murmured prayers for our health with tears in their eyes.

I saw Genya's surprise when a woman placed a dark green prayer shawl around her shoulders. "Not black," she said. "For you, not black."

An ache began in my throat. It wasn't just the Apparat who had kept me isolated from these people. I'd distanced myself from them as well. I distrusted their faith, but mostly I feared their hope. The love and care in these tiny gestures was a burden I didn't want.

I kissed cheeks, shook hands, made promises I wasn't sure I could keep, and then we were on our way. I'd been carried into the White Cathedral on a stretcher. At least I was leaving on my feet.

Mal took the lead. Tolya and Tamar brought up the rear, scouting behind us to make sure that no one followed.

Through David's access to the archives and Mal's innate sense of direction, they'd managed to construct a rough map of the tunnel network. They had started plotting a course to Ryevost, but there were gaps in their information. No matter how accurate they'd been, we couldn't be sure of what we might be walking into.

After my escape from Os Alta, the Darkling's men had tried to penetrate the network of tunnels beneath Ravka's churches and holy sites. When their searches turned up empty, they'd begun bombing: closing off exit routes, trying to drive anyone seeking shelter to the surface. The Darkling's Alkemi had created new explosives that collapsed buildings and forced combustible gases below ground. All it took was a single Inferni spark, and whole sections of the ancient network of tunnels collapsed. It was one of the reasons the Apparat had insisted I remain at the White Cathedral.

There were rumours of cave-ins to the west of us, so Mal led us north. It wasn't the most direct route, but we hoped it would be stable.

It was a relief to be moving through the tunnels, to finally be doing something after so many weeks of confinement. My body was still weak, but I felt stronger than I had in months, and I pushed onward without complaint.

I tried not to think too hard about what it would mean if the smuggling station at Ryevost wasn't active. How were we supposed to find a prince who didn't want to be found, and do it while remaining hidden ourselves? If Nikolai was alive, he might be looking for me, or he might have sought alliance elsewhere. For all he knew, I had died in the battle at the Little Palace.

The tunnels grew darker as we moved further from the White Cathedral and its strange alabaster glow. Soon our way was lit by nothing except the swaying light of our lanterns. In some places, the caverns were so narrow that we had to remove our packs and wriggle along between the press of walls. Then, without warning, we'd find ourselves in a giant cave wide enough to pasture horses.

Mal had been right: so many people travelling together were noisy and unwieldy. We made frustratingly slow progress, marching in a long column with Zoya, Nadia, and Adrik spread out along the line; in case of a cave-in, the air our Squallers could summon might provide valuable breathing time for anyone trapped.

David and Genya kept falling behind, but he seemed to be the one responsible for the lag. Finally, Tolya hefted the huge pack from David's narrow shoulders.

He groaned. "What do you have in this thing?"

"Three pairs of socks, one pair of trousers, an extra

shirt. One canteen. A tin cup and plate. A cylindrical slide rule, a chrondometer, a jar of spruce sap, my collection of anticorrosives—"

"You were only supposed to pack what you need."

David gave an emphatic nod. "Exactly."

"Please tell me you didn't bring all of Morozova's journals," I said.

"Of course I did."

I rolled my eyes. There had to be at least fifteen leather-bound books. "Maybe they'll make good kindling."

"Is she joking?" David asked, looking concerned. "I can never tell if she's joking."

I was. Mostly. I'd hoped the journals would give me insight into the firebird and maybe even into how the amplifiers could help me destroy the Fold. But they'd been a dead end, and if I was honest, they'd frightened me a little too. Baghra had warned me of Morozova's madness, and yet somehow I'd expected to find wisdom in his work. Instead, his journals had provided me with a study in obsession, all of it documented in nearly indecipherable scrawl. Apparently genius didn't require good penmanship.

His early journals chronicled his experiments: the blacked-out formula for liquid fire, a means of preventing organic decay, the trials that had led to the creation of Grisha steel, a method for restoring oxygen to the blood, the endless year he'd spent finding a way to create unbreakable glass. His skills extended beyond those of an ordinary Fabrikator, and he was well aware of it. One of the essential tenets of Grisha theory was "like calls to like", but Morozova seemed to believe that if the world could be broken down to the same small parts, each Grisha should be able to manipulate them. *Are we not all things?*

he demanded, underlining the words for emphasis. He was arrogant, audacious – but still sane.

Then his work on the amplifiers had begun, and even I could see the change. The text got denser, messier. The margins were full of diagrams and crazed arrows that referred back to earlier passages. Worse were the descriptions of experiments he'd performed on animals, the illustrations of his dissections. They turned my stomach and made me think Morozova had deserved whatever early martyrdom he'd received. He'd killed animals and then brought them back to life, sometimes repeatedly, delving deeper into *merzost*, creation, the power of life over death, trying to find a way to create amplifiers that might be used together. It was forbidden power. I knew its temptation, and I shuddered to think that pursuing it might have driven him mad.

If he was led by some noble purpose, I didn't see it in his pages. I sensed something more in his fevered writings, in his insistence that power was everywhere for the taking. He had lived long before the creation of the Second Army. He was the most powerful Grisha the world had ever known – and that power had isolated him. I remembered the Darkling's words to me: *There are no others like us, Alina. And there never will be.* Maybe Morozova wanted to believe that if there were no others like him, there could be, that he might create Grisha of greater power. Or maybe I was just imagining things, seeing my own loneliness and greed in Morozova's pages. The mess of what I knew and what I wanted, my desire for the firebird, my own sense of difference had all become too hard to untangle.

I was pulled from my thoughts by the sound of rushing water. We were approaching an underground river. Mal slowed our pace and had me walk directly behind him, casting light over the path. It was a good thing too, because the drop came fast, so steep and sudden that I slammed into his back, nearly knocking him over the edge and into the water below. Here, the roar was deafening, the river rushing past at uncertain depth, plumes of mist rising from the rapids.

We tied a rope around Tolya's waist, and he waded across, then secured it on the other side so we could follow one by one, attached to the line. The water was ice cold and came all the way up to my chest, the force of it pulling me nearly off my feet as I held on to the rope. Harshaw was the last to cross. I had a moment of terror when he lost his footing and the tether nearly snapped free. Then he was up, gasping for breath, Oncat soaked to the skin and spitting mad. By the time Harshaw reached us, his face and neck were a patchwork of tiny scratches.

After that, we were all eager to stop. Mal insisted we keep going.

"I'm drenched," Zoya groused. "Why can't we stop in *this* dank cave instead of the next dank cave?"

Mal didn't break stride, but hooked a thumb back at the river. "Because of that," he shouted over the din of rushing water. "If we've been followed, it will be too easy for someone to sneak up on us with that noise as cover."

Zoya scowled, and we pushed on, until finally we'd outdistanced the river's clamour. We spent the night in a hollow of damp limestone where there was nothing to hear but our teeth chattering as we shivered in our wet clothes.

For two days, we carried on like that, moving through the tunnels, occasionally backtracking when a route proved impassable. I'd lost all sense of what direction we were heading, but when Mal announced that we were turning west, I noticed that the passages were sloping upward, leading us towards the surface.

Mal set an unforgiving pace. To keep contact, he and the twins would whistle to each other from opposite ends of the column, making sure no one had drifted too far behind. Occasionally, he'd fall back to check on everyone.

"I can tell what you're up to," I said once when he returned to the head of the line.

"What's that?"

"You pop back there when someone's lagging, start up a conversation. You ask David about the properties of phosphor or Nadia about her freckles—"

"I have never asked Nadia about her freckles."

"Or *something*. Then gradually you start to pick up the pace so that they're walking faster."

"It seems to work better than jabbing them with a stick," he said.

"Less fun."

"My jabbing arm is tired."

Then he was gone, pressing ahead. It was the most we'd spoken since we'd left the White Cathedral.

No one else seemed to have trouble talking. Tamar had started trying to teach Nadia some Shu ballads. Unfortunately, her memory was terrible, but her brother's was nearly perfect and he'd eagerly taken over. The normally taciturn Tolya could recite entire cycles of epic poetry in Ravkan and Shu – even if no one wanted to hear them.

Though Mal had ordered that we remain in strict formation, Genya frequently escaped to the front of the column to complain to me.

"Every poem is about a brave hero named Kregi," she said. "Every single one. He always has a steed, and we have to hear about the steed and the three different kinds of swords he carried and the colour of the scarf he wore tied to his wrist and all the poor monsters he slew and then how he was a gentle man and true. For a mercenary, Tolya is disturbingly maudlin."

I laughed and glanced back, though I couldn't see much. "How is David liking it?"

"David is oblivious. He's been babbling about mineral compounds for the last hour."

"Maybe he and Tolya will just put each other to sleep," Zoya grumbled.

She had no business griping. Though they were all Etherealki, the only thing the Squallers and Inferni seemed to have in common was how much they loved to argue. Stigg didn't want Harshaw near him because he couldn't stand cats. Harshaw was constantly taking offense on Oncat's behalf. Adrik was supposed to stay near the middle of the group, but he wanted to be close to Zoya. Zoya kept slipping away from the head of the column to try to get away from Adrik. I was starting to wish I'd cut the rope and left them all to drown in the river.

And Harshaw didn't just annoy me; he made me nervous. He liked to drag his flint along the cave walls, sending off little sparks, and he was constantly slipping bits of hard cheese out of his pocket to feed Oncat, then chuckling as if the tabby had said something particularly funny. One morning, we woke to find that he'd shaved the sides of his scalp so that his crimson hair ran in a single thick stripe down the centre of his head.

"What did you do?" shrieked Zoya. "You look like a deranged rooster!"

Harshaw just shrugged. "Oncat insisted."

Still, the tunnels occasionally surprised us with wonders that rendered even the Etherealki speechless. We'd spend hours with nothing to look at except grey rock and mud-covered lime, then emerge into a pale blue cave so perfectly round and smooth that it was like standing inside a giant enamel egg. We stumbled into a series of little caves glittering with what might well have been real rubies. Genya dubbed it the Jewelbox, and after that, we took to naming all of them to pass the time. There was the Orchard – a cavern full of stalactites and stalagmites that had fused together into slender columns. And less than a day later, we came across the Dancehall, a long cave of pink quartz with a floor so slippery we had to crawl over it, occasionally sliding to our bellies. Then there was the eerie, partially submerged iron portcullis we called the Angelgate. It was flanked by two winged stone figures, their heads bent, their hands resting on marble broadswords. The winch worked and we passed through it without incident, but why had it been put there? And by whom?

On the fourth day, we came upon a cavern with a perfectly still pool that gave the illusion of a night sky, its depths sparkling with tiny luminescent fish.

Mal and I were slightly ahead of the others. He dipped his hand in, then yelped and drew back. "They bite."

"Serves you right," I said. "'Oh, look, a dark lake full of something shiny. Let me put my hand in it.'"

"I can't help being delicious," he said, that familiar

cocky grin flashing across his face like light over water. Then he seemed to catch himself. He shouldered his pack, and I knew he was about to move away from me.

I wasn't sure where the words came from: "You didn't fail me, Mal."

He wiped his damp hand on his thigh. "We both know better."

"We're going to be travelling together for who knows how long. Eventually, you're going to have to talk to me."

"I'm talking to you right now."

"See? Is this so terrible?"

"It wouldn't be," he said, gazing at me steadily, "if all I wanted to do was talk."

My cheeks heated. *You don't want this*, I told myself. But I felt my edges curl like a piece of paper held too close to fire. "Mal—"

"I need to keep you safe, Alina, to stay focused on what matters. I can't do that if . . ." He let out a long breath. "You were meant for more than me, and I'll die fighting to give it to you. But please don't ask me to pretend it's easy."

He plunged ahead into the next cave.

I looked down at the glittering pond, the whorls of light in the water still settling after Mal's brief touch. I could hear the others making their noisy way through the cavern.

"Oncat scratches me all the time," said Harshaw as he ambled up beside me.

"Oh?" I asked hollowly.

"Funny thing is, she likes to stay close."

"Are you being profound, Harshaw?"

"Actually, I was wondering, if I ate enough of those fish, would I start to glow?"

I shook my head. Of course one of the last living Inferni would have to be insane. I fell in step with the others and headed into the next tunnel.

"Come on, Harshaw," I called over my shoulder.

Then the first explosion hit.

Chapter 5

The whole cavern shook. Little rivulets of pebbles clattered down on us.

Mal was beside me in an instant. He yanked me away from the falling rock as Zoya bracketed my other side.

"Lights out!" Mal shouted. "Packs off."

We shoved our packs against the walls as a kind of buttress, then doused the lanterns in case the sparks set off another explosion.

Boom. Above us? North of us? It was hard to tell.

Long seconds passed. *Boom.* This one was closer, louder. Rocks and soil rained down on our bent heads.

"He found us," moaned Sergei, his voice ragged with fear.

"He can't have," Zoya protested. "Even the Apparat didn't know where we were headed."

Mal shifted slightly. I heard the smatter of pebbles. "It's a random attack," he said.

Genya's voice trembled when she whispered, "That cat is bad luck."

Boom. Loud enough to rattle my jaw.

"*Metan yez,*" said David. Marsh gas.

I smelled it a second later, peaty and foul. If there were Inferni above us, a spark would follow and blow us all to bits. Someone started crying.

"Squallers," commanded Mal, "send it east." How could he sound so calm?

I felt Zoya move, then the rush of air as she and the others drove the gas away from us.

Boom. It was hard to breathe. The space seemed too small.

"Oh, Saints," Sergei quavered.

"I see flame!" Tolya shouted.

"Send it east," repeated Mal, voice steady. The *whoosh* of Squaller wind followed. Mal's body was braced next to mine. My hand snaked out, seeking his. Our fingers twined together. I heard a small sob from my other side, and I reached for Zoya's free hand, taking it in mine.

BOOM. This time the whole tunnel roared with the sound of falling rock. I heard people shouting in the dark. Dust filled my lungs.

When the noise stopped, Mal said, "No lanterns. Alina, we need light." It was a struggle, but I found a thread of sunlight and let it blossom through the tunnel. We were all covered in dust, eyes wide and frightened. I did a quick tally: Mal, Genya, David, Zoya, Nadia, and Harshaw – Oncat tucked into his shirt.

"Tolya?" shouted Mal.

Nothing. Then, "We're all right."

Tolya's voice came from behind the wall of fallen rock blocking the tunnel, but it was strong and clear. I pressed my head to my knees in relief.

"Where's my brother?" yelled Nadia.

"He's here with me and Tamar," Tolya replied.

"Sergei and Stigg?" I asked.

"I don't know."

Saints.

We waited for another *boom*, for the rest of the tunnel to come down on top of us. When nothing happened, we started scrabbling towards Tolya's voice as he and Tamar dug from the other side. In a matter of moments, we saw their hands, then their dirty faces staring back at us. They scooted into our section of the tunnel. As soon as Adrik dropped his hands, the ceiling above where he and the twins had been standing collapsed in a billow of dust and rock. He was shaking badly.

"You held the cave?" Zoya asked.

Tolya nodded. "He made a bubble as soon as we heard that last boom."

"Huh," Zoya said to Adrik. "I'm impressed."

At the elation that burst over his face, she groaned. "Never mind. I'm downgrading that to grudging approval."

"Sergei?" I called. "Stigg?"

Silence, the shift of gravel.

"Let me try something," said Zoya. She raised her hands. I heard a crackling in my ears, and the air seemed to grow damp. "Sergei?" she said. Her voice sounded weirdly distant.

Then I heard Sergei's voice, weak and trembling, but clear, as if he were speaking right beside me. "Here," he panted.

Zoya flexed her fingers, making adjustments, and called to Sergei again.

This time, when he replied, David said, "It sounds as if it's coming from below us."

"Maybe not," Zoya replied. "The acoustics can be misleading."

Mal moved further down the passage. "No, he's right.

The floor in their segment of the tunnel must have collapsed."

It took us nearly two hours to find them and dig them out – Tolya hefting soil, Mal calling directions, the Squallers stabilising the sides of the tunnel with air as I maintained a dim illumination, the others forming a line to move rocks and sand.

When we found Stigg and Sergei, they were covered in mud and nearly comatose.

"Lowered our pulses," Sergei mumbled groggily. "Slow respiration. Use less air."

Tolya and Tamar brought them back, raising their heart rates and flushing their lungs with oxygen.

"Didn't think you'd come," slurred a still-bleary Stigg.

"Why?" cried Genya, gently brushing the dirt from around his eyes.

"He wasn't sure that you'd care," said Harshaw from behind me.

There were mumbled protests and some guilty looks. I did think of Stigg and Harshaw as outsiders. And Sergei . . . well . . . Sergei had been lost for a while now. None of us had done a very good job of reaching out to them.

When Sergei and Stigg could walk, we headed back to the more intact part of the tunnel. One by one, the Squallers released their power, as we waited to see if the ceiling would hold so they could rest. We brushed the dust and grime off one another's faces and clothes as best we could, then passed a flask of *kvas* around. Stigg clung to it like a baby with a bottle.

"Everyone okay?" Mal asked.

"Never better," said Genya shakily.

David raised his hand. "I've been better."

We all started laughing.

"What?" he said.

"How did you even do that?" Nadia asked Zoya. "That trick with the sound?"

"It's just a way of creating an acoustical anomaly. We used to play with it back in school so we could eavesdrop on people in other rooms."

Genya snorted. "Of course you did."

"Could you show us how to do it?" asked Adrik.

"If I'm ever bored enough."

"Squallers," Mal said, "are you ready to move again?"

They all nodded. Their faces had the gleam that came with using Grisha power, but I knew they must already be approaching their limits. They'd been keeping tons of rock off us for half a mile, and they'd need more than a few minutes of rest to restore themselves.

"Then let's get the hell out of here," Mal said.

I lit the way, still wary of what surprises might be waiting for us. We moved cautiously, Squallers on alert, twisting through tunnels and passages until I had no sense of which way we'd gone. We were well off the map that David and Mal had created.

Every sound seemed magnified. Every fall of pebbles made us pause, frozen, waiting for the worst. I tried to think of anything but the weight of the soil above us. If the earth came down and the Squallers' power failed, we would be crushed and no one would ever know, wildflowers pressed between the pages of a book and forgotten.

Eventually, I became aware that my legs were working harder and realised the grade of the floor had turned steep. I heard relieved sighs, a few quiet cheers, and less than an hour later, we found ourselves crowded into some kind of basement room, looking up at the bottom of a trapdoor.

The ground was wet here, pocked by little puddles – signs that we must be close to the river cities. By the light from my palms, I could see that the stone walls were cracked – whether the damage was old or the result of the recent explosions, I couldn't tell.

"How did you do it?" I asked Mal.

He shrugged. "Same as always. There's game on the surface. I just treated it like a hunt."

Tolya pulled David's old watch from the pocket of his coat. I wasn't sure when he'd acquired it. "If this thing is keeping time right, we're well past sunset."

"You have to wind it every day," said David.

"I know that."

"Well, did you?"

"Yes."

"Then it's keeping time right."

I wondered if I should remind David that Tolya's fist was roughly the circumference of his head.

Zoya sniffed. "With our luck, someone will be setting up for midnight mass."

Many of the entrances and exits to the tunnels were found in holy places – but not all of them. We might emerge in the apse of a church or the courtyard of a monastery or we might poke our heads out of the floor of a brothel. *And good day to you, sir.* I pushed down a crazed giggle. Exhaustion and fear were making me giddy.

What if someone was waiting for us up there? What if the Apparat had switched sides yet again and set the Darkling on our trail? I wasn't thinking straight. Mal believed the explosions had been a random attack on the tunnels, and that was the only thing that made sense. The

Apparat couldn't know where we'd be or when. And even if the Darkling had somehow found out that we were headed for Ryevost, why bother using bombs to drive us to the surface? He could just wait for us to turn up there.

"Let's go," I said. "I feel like I'm suffocating."

Mal signalled for Tolya and Tamar to flank me.

"Be ready," he said to them. "Any sign of trouble, you get her out of here. Take the tunnels due west as far as you can."

It was only after he'd started climbing the ladder that I realised we'd all hung back, waiting for him to go first. Tolya and Tamar were both more experienced fighters, and Mal was the only *otkazat'sya* among us. So why was he the one taking the brunt of the risk? I wanted to call him back, tell him to be careful, but it would just sound absurd. "Careful" wasn't something we did any more.

At the top of the ladder, he gestured down at me, and I released the light, pitching us into darkness. I heard a thump, the sound of hinges straining, then a soft grunt and a creak as the trapdoor opened. No light flooded down, no shouts, no gunfire.

My heart was pounding in my chest. I followed the sounds of Mal levering himself up, his footfalls above us. Finally, I heard the scrape of a match, and light bloomed through the trapdoor. Mal whistled twice – the all clear.

One by one, we ascended the ladder. When I stuck my head through the trapdoor, a chill slid over my spine. The room was hexagonal, its walls carved from what looked like blue lapis, each studded with wooden panels painted with a different Saint, their golden halos glinting in the lamplight. The corners were thick with milky cobwebs. Mal's lantern rested on a stone sarcophagus. We were in a crypt.

"Perfect," said Zoya. "From a tunnel to a tomb. What's next, an outing to a slaughterhouse?"

"Mezle," David said, pointing to one of the names carved into the wall. "They were an old Grisha family. There was even one of them at the Little Palace before—"

"Before everyone died?" put in Genya helpfully.

"Ziva Mezle," Nadia said quietly. "She was a Squaller."

"Can we host this salon somewhere else?" Zoya asked. "I want to get out of here."

I rubbed my arms. She had a point.

The door looked like heavy iron. Tolya and Mal braced their shoulders against it as we arrayed ourselves behind them, hands raised, Inferni with their flints ready. I took my position in back, prepared to wield the Cut, if necessary.

"On three," Mal said.

A burble of laughter escaped me. Everyone turned.

I flushed. "Well, we're probably in a graveyard, and we're about to come charging out of a tomb."

Genya giggled. "If anyone's out there, we're going to scare the sneeze out of him."

With the barest hint of a grin, Mal said, "Good point. Let's lead with *ooooooo*." Then the grin disappeared. He nodded at Tolya. "Stay low."

He counted down, and they shoved. The bolts shrieked, and the tomb doors flew open. We waited, but there were no sounds of alarm to greet us.

Slowly, we filed out into the deserted cemetery. This close to the river, people buried their dead aboveground in case of flooding. The tombs, arrayed in tidy rows like stone houses, gave the whole place the feel of an abandoned city. A wind blew through, shaking leaves free from the trees and stirring the grasses that grew up around the smaller grave sites. It was eerie, but I didn't care. The air was almost warm after the chill of the caves. We were outside at last.

I tilted my head back, breathing deeply. It was a clear, moonless night, and after those long months underground, the sight of all that sky was dizzying. And so many stars – a glittering, tangled mass that seemed close enough to touch. I let their light fall over me like a balm, grateful for the air in my lungs, the night all around me.

"Alina," Mal said softly.

I opened my eyes. The Grisha were staring. "What?"

He took my hands and held them out in front of me, as if we were about to start a dance. "You're glowing."

"Oh," I breathed. My skin was silver, cocooned in starlight. I hadn't even realised I was summoning. "Oops."

He ran a finger down my forearm where the sleeve had ridden up, watching the play of light over my skin, a smile curling his lips. Abruptly, he stepped back. He dropped my hands as if they were hot.

"Be more careful," he said tightly. He gestured to Adrik to help Tolya reseal the crypt, then spoke to the group. "Stay close and keep quiet. We need to find cover before dawn."

The others fell into step behind him, letting him lead yet again. I hung back, actively brushing the light from my skin. It clung to me, as if my body was thirsty for it.

When Zoya drew level with me, she said, "You know, Starkov, I'm beginning to think you turned your hair white on purpose."

I flicked a speck of starlight from my wrist, watching it fade. "Yes, Zoya, courting death is an integral part of my beauty regimen."

She shrugged and cast a glance at Mal. "Well, it's a little obvious for my taste, but I'd say the whole moon maiden look is working."

The last person I wanted to talk to about Mal was Zoya, but that had sounded suspiciously like a compliment. I remembered her gripping my hand during the cave-in and how strong she'd stayed throughout it all.

"Thanks," I said. "For keeping us safe down there. For helping save Sergei and Stigg."

Even if I hadn't meant a word of it, the look of shock on her face would have been worth it.

"You're welcome," she managed. Then she stuck her perfect nose in the air and added, "But I won't always be around to save your ass, Sun Summoner."

I grinned and followed her down the aisle of graves. At least she was predictable.

It took us far too long to get out of the cemetery. The rows of crypts stretched on and on, cold testimony to the generations Ravka had been at war. The paths were raked clean, the graves marked with flowers, painted icons, gifts of candy, little piles of precious ammunition – small kindnesses, even for the dead. I thought of the men and women bidding us goodbye at the White Cathedral, pressing their offerings into our hands. I was grateful when we finally cleared the gates.

The terror of the cave-in and long hours on our feet had taken their toll, but Mal was determined to get us as close to Ryevost as he could before dawn. We trudged onward, marching parallel to the main road, keeping to the starlit fields. Occasionally we glimpsed a lone house, a lantern glowing in the window. It was a relief, somehow, to see these signs of life, to think of a farmer rising in the night to fill his cup with water, his head turning briefly to the window and the darkness beyond.

The sky had just started to lighten when we heard the sounds of someone approaching on the road. We barely had time to scurry into the woods and take shelter in the brush before we glimpsed the first wagon.

There were about fifteen people in the convoy, mostly men, a few women, all bristling with weapons. I glimpsed bits and pieces of First Army uniforms – standard-issue trousers shoved into decidedly non-regulation cowhide boots, an infantry coat shorn of its brass buttons.

It was impossible to tell what they were transporting. Their cargo had been covered by horse blankets and tightly secured to the wagon beds with rope.

"Militia?" Tamar whispered.

"Could be," said Mal. "Not sure where a militia would get repeating rifles."

"If they're smugglers, I don't know any of them."

"I could follow," said Tolya.

"Why don't I just go do a waltz in the middle of the road?" Tamar taunted. Tolya was hardly quiet on his feet.

"I'm getting better," Tolya said defensively. "Besides—"

Mal silenced them with a look. "Do not pursue, do not engage."

As Mal led us deeper into the trees, Tolya grumbled, "You don't even know how to waltz."

We made camp in a clearing close to a slender tributary of the Sokol, the river fed by the glaciers in the Petrazoi and the heart of commerce in the port cities. We hoped we were far enough from town and the main roads that we wouldn't have to worry about anyone stumbling upon us.

According to the twins, the smugglers' meeting place was in a busy square that overlooked the river in Ryevost. Tamar already had a compass and map in hand. Though she must have been as tired as the rest of us, she would have to leave immediately to make it to town before noon.

I hated letting her walk into what might be a trap, but we'd agreed that she would have to be the one to go. Tolya's size made him far too conspicuous and none of the rest of us knew the way the smugglers worked or how to recognise them. Still, my nerves were jangling. I had never understood the twins' faith and what they were willing to risk for it. But when the time had come to choose between me and the Apparat, they'd shown their loyalty in no uncertain terms.

I gave Tamar's hand a quick squeeze. "Don't do anything reckless."

Nadia had been hovering nearby. Now she cleared her throat and kissed Tamar once on each cheek. "Be safe," she said.

Tamar flashed her Heartrender's grin. "If anyone wants trouble," she said, flicking back her coat to reveal the handles of her axes, "I've a fresh supply."

I glanced at Nadia. I had the distinct impression Tamar was showing off.

She pulled up her hood and set out at a jog through the trees.

"*Yuyeh sesh*," Tolya called after her in Shu.

"*Ni weh sesh*," she shouted over her shoulder. And then she was gone.

"What does that mean?"

"It's something our father taught us," Tolya replied. "*Yuyeh sesh*: 'despise your heart.' That's the direct translation. The real meaning is more like 'do what needs to be done – be cruel if you have to.'"

"What's the other part?"

"*Ni weh sesh*? 'I have no heart.'"

Mal raised a brow. "Your dad sounds like fun."

Tolya smiled the slightly mad grin that made him look just like his sister. "He was."

I looked back the way Tamar had gone. Somewhere beyond the trees and the fields beyond that lay Ryevost. I sent my own prayers with her: *Bring back news of a prince, Tamar. I don't think I can do this alone.*

We laid out bedrolls and divvied up food. Adrik and Nadia started raising a tent while Tolya and Mal scouted the perimeter, setting up stands where guards would be posted. I saw Stigg trying to get Sergei to eat. I'd hoped that being aboveground might bring him around, but though Sergei seemed less panicked, I could still feel tension coming off him in waves.

In truth, we were all jumpy. As lovely as it was to lie beneath the trees and see the sky again, it was also overwhelming. Life in the White Cathedral had been miserable, but manageable. Up here, things felt wilder, beyond my control. Militias and the Darkling's men roamed these lands. Whether we found Nikolai or not, we were back in this war, and that meant more battles, more lives lost. The world seemed suddenly large again. I wasn't sure I liked it.

I looked at our camp: Harshaw already curled up and snoozing with Oncat on his chest; Sergei, pale and watchful; David, back propped against a tree, a book in his hands as Genya fell asleep with her head in his lap; Nadia and Adrik struggling with poles and canvas while Zoya looked on and didn't bother to help.

Despise your heart. I wanted to. I didn't want to grieve any more, to feel loss or guilt, or worry. I wanted to be hard, calculating. I wanted to be fearless. Underground, that had seemed possible. Here, in this wood, with these people, I was less sure.

Eventually, I must have dozed, because when I woke, it was late afternoon and the sun was slanting through the trees. Tolya was beside me.

"Tamar's back," he said.

I sat upright, fully awake. The look on Tolya's face was grim.

"No one approached her?"

He shook his head. I straightened my shoulders. I didn't want anyone to see my disappointment. I should be grateful Tamar had made it in and out of the city safely.

"Does Mal know?"

"No," said Tolya. "He's filling canteens at the creek. Harshaw and Stigg are on watch. Should I get them?"

"It can wait."

Tamar was leaning against a tree, gulping down water from a tin cup as the others gathered around to hear her report.

"Any trouble?" I asked.

She shook her head.

"And you're sure you were in the right place?" Tolya said.

"West side of the market square. I got there early, stayed late, checked in with the shopkeeper, watched the same damn puppet show four times. If the post is active, someone should have spoken to me."

"We could try again tomorrow," suggested Adrik.

"I should go," said Tolya. "You were there a long time. If you show up again, people may notice."

Tamar wiped her mouth with the back of her hand. "If I stab the puppeteer, will that draw too much attention?"

"Not if you're quiet about it," replied Nadia.

Her cheeks pinked as we all turned to look at her. I'd never heard Nadia crack a joke. She'd mostly been an audience to Marie.

Tamar slipped a dagger from her wrist and twirled it, balancing its point on one fingertip. "I can be quiet," she said, "and merciful. I may let the puppets live." She took another gulp of water. "I heard some news too. Big news. West Ravka has declared for Nikolai."

That got our attention.

"They're blocking off the western shore of the Fold," she continued. "So if the Darkling wants weapons or ammunition—"

"He'll have to go through Fjerda," finished Zoya.

But it was bigger than that. This meant the Darkling had lost West Ravka's coastline, its navy, the already tenuous access Ravka had to trade.

"West Ravka now," Tolya said. "Maybe the Shu Han next."

"Or Kerch," put in Zoya.

"Or both!" crowed Adrik.

I could almost see the tendril of hope twisting its way through our ranks.

"So now what?" Sergei asked, tugging anxiously at his sleeve.

"Let's wait one more day," Nadia said.

"I don't know," said Tamar. "I don't mind going back. Though there were *oprichniki* in the square today."

Not a good sign. The *oprichniki* were the Darkling's personal soldiers. If they were prowling the area, we had good reason to move on as soon as possible.

"I'm going to go talk to Mal," I said. "Don't get too comfortable. We may need to be ready to leave in the morning."

The others dispersed while Tamar and Nadia walked away to dig through the rations. Tamar kept bouncing and spinning her knife – definitely showing off, but Nadia didn't seem to mind.

I picked my way towards the sound of the water, trying to sort through my thoughts. If West Ravka had declared for Nikolai, that was a very good sign that he was alive and well and making more trouble for the Darkling than anyone in the White Cathedral had realised. I was relieved, but I wasn't certain what our next move should be.

When I reached the creek, Mal was crouching in the shallows, barefoot and bare-chested, his trousers rolled up to his knees. He was watching the water, his expression focused. At the sound of my approach, he shot to his feet, already lunging for his rifle.

"Just me," I said, stepping out of the woods.

He relaxed and dropped back down, eyes returning to the creek. "What are you doing out here?"

For a moment I just watched him. He stayed perfectly still, then suddenly, his hands plunged into the stream and emerged with a wriggling fish. He tossed it back. No point holding on to it when we couldn't risk making a fire to cook it.

I'd seen him catch fish this way at Keramzin, even in winter, when Trivka's pond froze over. He knew just where to break the ice, just where to drop his line or the moment to make his grab. I'd waited on the banks, keeping him company, trying to spot places in the trees where the birds made their nests.

It was different now, the water reflecting spangles of light over the planes of his face, the smooth play of muscle beneath his skin. I realised I was staring and gave myself a little shake. I'd seen him without a shirt before. There was no reason to be an idiot about it.

"Tamar's back," I said.

He stood, his interest in the fish lost. "And?"

"No sign of Nikolai's men."

Mal sighed and scrubbed a hand through his hair. "Damn it."

"We could wait another day," I offered, though I already knew what he would say.

"We've wasted enough time. I don't know how long it will take us to get south or to find the firebird. All we need is to get stuck in the mountains when the snow comes. And we have to find a safe house for the others."

"Tamar says West Ravka has declared for Nikolai. What if we took them there?"

He considered. "That's a long journey, Alina. We'd lose a lot of time."

"I know, but it's safer than anywhere this side of the

Fold. And it's another chance to find Nikolai."

"Might be less dangerous trekking south on that side too." He nodded. "All right. We need to get the others ready. I want to leave tonight."

"Tonight?"

"No point waiting around." He waded out of the water, bare toes curling on the rocks.

He didn't actually say "dismissed", but he might as well have. What else was there to talk about?

I started towards camp, then remembered I hadn't told him about the *oprichniki*. I stomped back to the creek. "Mal . . . ," I began, but the words died on my lips.

He had bent to pick up the canteens. His back was to me.

"What is that?" I said angrily.

He whirled, twisting himself around, but it was too late. He opened his mouth.

Before he could get a word out, I snapped, "If you say 'nothing', I will knock you senseless."

His mouth clamped shut.

"Turn around," I ordered.

For a moment, he just stood there. Then he sighed and turned.

A tattoo stretched across his broad back – something like a compass rose, but much more like a sun, the points reaching from shoulder to shoulder and down his spine.

"Why?" I asked. "Why would you do this?"

He shrugged and his muscles flexed beneath the intricate design.

"Mal, why would you mark yourself this way?"

"I have a lot of scars," he said finally. "This is one I chose."

I looked closer. There were letters worked into the design. *E'ya sta rezku*. I frowned. It looked like ancient Ravkan.

"What does this mean?"

He said nothing.

"Mal—"

"It's embarrassing."

And sure enough, I could see a flush spreading over his neck.

"Tell me."

He hesitated, then cleared his throat and muttered, "I am become a blade."

I am become a blade. Was that what he was? This boy whom the Grisha had followed without argument, whose voice stayed steady when the earth caved in around us, who'd told me I would be a queen? I wasn't sure I recognised him any more.

I brushed my fingertips over the letters. He tensed. His skin was still damp from the river.

"Could be worse," I said. "I mean, if it said 'Let's cuddle' or 'I am become ginger pudding', *that* would be embarrassing."

He released a surprised bark of laughter, then hissed in a breath as I let my fingertips trail the length of his spine. His fists clenched at his sides. I knew I should step away, but I didn't want to.

"Who did it?"

"Tolya," he rasped.

"Did it hurt?"

"Less than it should have."

I reached the furthest point of the sunburst, right at the base of his spine. I paused, then dragged my fingers back up. He snapped around, capturing my hand in a hard grip.

"Don't," he said fiercely.

"I—"

"I can't do this. Not if you make me laugh, not if you touch me like that."

"Mal—"

Suddenly his head jerked up and he put a finger to his lips.

"Hands above your heads." The voice came from the shadows of the trees. Mal dove for his rifle and had it at his shoulder in seconds, but three people were already emerging from the woods – two men and a woman with her hair in a topknot – the muzzles of their weapons trained on us. I thought I recognised them from the convoy we'd seen on the road.

"Put that down," said a man with a short goatee. "Unless you want to see your girl plugged full of bullets."

Mal set his rifle back on the rock.

"Come on over," said the man. "Nice and slow." He wore a First Army coat, though he looked like no soldier I had ever seen. His hair was long and tangled, kept from his eyes by two messy plaits. He wore belts of bullets across his chest and a stained waistcoat that might have once been red but was now fading to a colour somewhere between plum and brown.

"I need my boots," said Mal.

"Less chance of you running without them."

"What do you want?"

"You can start with answers," the man said. "Town nearby, plenty more comfortable places to hole up. So what are a dozen people doing hiding out in the forest?" He must have seen my reaction, because he said, "That's right. I found your camp. You deserters?"

"Yes," said Mal smoothly. "Out of Kerskii."

The man scratched his cheek. "Kerskii? Maybe," he said. "But—" He took a step forward. "Oretsev?"

Mal stiffened, then said, "Luchenko?"

"All Saints, I haven't seen you since your unit trained with me in Poliznaya." He turned to the other men. "This little pissant was the best tracker in ten regiments. Never seen anything like it." He was grinning, but he didn't lower his rifle. "And now you're the most famous deserter in all of Ravka."

"Just trying to survive."

"You and me both, brother." He gestured to me. "This isn't your usual."

If I hadn't had a rifle in my face, the comment might have stung.

"One more First Army grunt like us."

"Like us, huh?" Luchenko jabbed at me with his gun. "Take off the scarf."

"Bit of a chill in the air," I said.

Luchenko gave me another poke. "Go on, girl."

I glanced at Mal. I could see him weighing the options. We were at close range. I could do some serious damage with the Cut, though not before the militiamen got off a few rounds. I could blind them, but if we started a firefight, what might happen to the people back at camp?

I shrugged and pulled the scarf from my neck with a rough tug. Luchenko gave a low whistle.

"Heard you were keeping hallowed company, Oretsev. Looks like we caught ourselves a Saint." He cocked his head to one side. "Thought she'd be taller. Bind them both."

Again, I locked gazes with Mal. He wanted me to act, I could feel it. As long as my hands weren't bound together, I could summon and control the light. But what about the other Grisha?

I held out my hands and let the woman secure my wrists with rope.

Mal sighed and did the same. "Can I at least put my shirt on?" he asked.

"No," she said with a leer. "I like the view."

Luchenko laughed. "Life's a funny thing, isn't it?" he said philosophically as they marched us into the woods at gunpoint. "All I ever wanted was a drop of luck to flavour my tea. Now I'm drowning in it. The Darkling will empty his coffers to have the two of you delivered to his door."

"You're going to hand me over that easily?" I said. "Foolish."

"Big talk from a girl with a rifle at her back."

"It's just good business," I said. "You think Fjerda or the Shu Han won't pay a small fortune – maybe even a large fortune – to get their hands on the Sun Summoner? How many men do you have?"

Luchenko glanced over his shoulder and wagged his finger at me like a schoolteacher. Well, it had been worth a try.

"All I meant," I continued innocently, "was that you could auction me off to the highest bidder and keep your men fat and happy for the rest of their days."

"I like the way she thinks," said the woman with the topknot.

"Don't get greedy, Ekaterina," Luchenko said. "We aren't ambassadors or diplomats. The bounty on that girl's head will buy us passage through the border. Maybe

I'll catch a ship out of Djerholm. Or maybe I'll just bury myself in blondes for the rest of my days."

The unsavoury image of Luchenko cavorting with a bunch of curvy Fjerdans was driven from my mind as we entered the clearing. The Grisha had been rounded up at its centre and were surrounded by a circle of nearly thirty armed militiamen. Tolya was bleeding heavily from what looked like a bad blow to the head. Harshaw had been on watch, and one glance at him told me he'd been shot. He was pale, swaying on his feet, clutching the wound at his side and panting as Oncat yowled.

"See?" said Luchenko. "With this windfall, I don't need to worry about the highest bidder."

I stepped in front of him, keeping my voice as low as I could. "Let them go," I said. "If you turn them over to the Darkling, they'll be tortured."

"And?"

I swallowed the bolt of rage that coursed through me. Threats would get me nowhere. "A living prisoner is more valuable than a corpse," I said meekly. "At least untie me so I can see to my friend's injury." *And so I can mow down your militia with a flick of my wrist.*

Ekaterina narrowed her eyes. "Don't do it," she said. "Have one of her bloodletters take care of him." She gave me a jab in the back and steered us into the group with the others.

"Spy that collar?" Luchenko asked of the crowd. "We have the Sun Summoner!"

There were exclamations and a few whoops from the rest of the militia. "So start thinking about how you're going to spend all of the Darkling's money."

They cheered.

"Why not ransom her to Nikolai Lantsov?" said a soldier from somewhere near the back of the circle. Now that I was in the middle of the clearing, there seemed to be even more of them.

"Lantsov?" Luchenko said. "If he has a brain in his head, he's rusticating somewhere warm with a pretty girl on his knee. If he's even alive."

"He's alive," said someone.

Luchenko spat. "Makes no matter to me."

"And your country?" I asked.

"What has my country ever done for me, little girl? No land, no life, just a uniform and a gun. Doesn't matter if it's the Darkling on the throne or some useless Lantsov."

"I saw the prince when I was in Os Alta," said Ekaterina. "He's not bad looking."

"Not bad looking?" said another voice. "He's damnably handsome."

Luchenko scowled. "Since when—"

"Brave in battle, smart as a whip." Now the voice seemed to be coming from above us. Luchenko craned his neck, peering into the trees. "An excellent dancer," said the voice. "Oh, and an even better shot."

"Who—" Luchenko never got to finish. A blast rang out, and a tiny black hole appeared between his eyes.

I gasped. "Imposs—"

"Don't say it," muttered Mal.

Then chaos erupted.

Chapter 6

Gunfire shattered the air around us, and Mal knocked me from my feet. I landed with my face in the mulch of the forest floor and felt his body shielding mine.

"Stay down!" he yelled.

I twisted my head to the side and saw the Grisha forming a ring around us. Harshaw was on the ground. Stigg had his flint in hand, and flames shot through the air. Tamar and Tolya had charged into the fray. Zoya, Nadia, and Adrik had their hands up, and leaves lifted in gusts from the forest floor, but it was hard to tell friend from foe in the tangle of armed men.

There was a sudden thump beside us as someone swung down from the treetops. "What are you two doing barefoot and half naked in the mud?" asked a familiar voice. "Looking for truffles, I hope?"

Nikolai slashed through the bonds on our wrists and yanked me to my feet. "Next time *I'll* try getting captured. Just to keep things interesting." He tossed Mal a rifle. "Shall we?"

"I can't tell who's who!" I protested.

"We're the side that's hopelessly outnumbered."

Unfortunately, I didn't think he was joking. As the ranks shifted and I got my wits about me, it was easier to distinguish Nikolai's men by their pale blue armbands.

They'd cut a swathe through Luchenko's militia, but even without their leader, the enemy was rallying.

I heard a shout. Nikolai's men moved forward, driving the Grisha ahead of them. We were being herded.

"What's happening?" I asked.

"This is the part where we run," Nikolai said pleasantly, though I could see the strain on his dirt-smudged face.

We took off through the trees, trying to keep pace as Nikolai darted through the woods. I couldn't tell where we were headed. Towards the creek? The road? I'd lost all sense of direction.

I looked behind me, counting the others, making sure we were together. The Squallers were summoning in tandem, knocking trees into the militia's path. Stigg trailed them, sending up spurts of flame. David had somehow managed to retrieve his pack and staggered beneath its bulk as he ran beside Genya.

"Leave it!" I yelled. If he heard, he ignored me.

Tolya had Harshaw thrown over his shoulder, and the weight of the big Inferni was slowing his stride. A soldier was gaining on him, sabre drawn. Tamar vaulted onto a fallen trunk, took aim with her pistol, and fired. A second later, the militiaman clutched his chest and crumpled midstride. Oncat darted past the body, fast on Tolya's heels.

"Where's Sergei?" I shouted, just as I glimpsed him lagging behind, his expression dazed. Tamar backtracked, dodging falling trees and fire, and forcibly pulled him along. I couldn't hear what she was yelling, but I didn't think it was gentle encouragement.

I stumbled. Mal caught my elbow and shoved me forward, turning to squeeze off two shots from his rifle. Then we were pouring into a barley field.

Despite the heat of the late afternoon sun, the field was shrouded in mist. We pelted over the marshy soil until Nikolai shouted, "Here!"

We skidded to a halt, sending up sprays of dirt. *Here?* We were in the middle of an empty field with nothing except fog for cover and a throng of militiamen hungry for revenge and fortune on our heels.

I heard two shrill whistle blasts. The ground rocked beneath me.

"Hold on tight!" Nikolai said.

"To what?" I yelped.

And then we were rising. Cables snapped into place beside us as the field itself seemed to lift. I looked up – the mist was parting, and a massive craft hovered directly over our heads, its cargo hold open. It was some kind of shallow barge, equipped with sails at one end and suspended beneath a huge, oblong bladder.

"What the hell is that?" Mal said.

"The *Pelican*," said Nikolai. "Well, a prototype of the *Pelican*. Trick seems to be getting the balloon not to collapse."

"And did you solve that little problem?"

"For the most part."

The soil beneath us fell away, and I saw we were standing on a swaying platform made of some kind of metal mesh. We rose higher – ten, then fifteen feet above the ground. A bullet pinged against the metal.

We took up spots at the edge of the platform, clutching the cables while trying to take aim at the mob firing up at us.

"Let's go!" I shouted. "Why aren't we getting out of range?"

Nikolai and Mal exchanged a glance.

"They know we have the Sun Saint," Nikolai said. Mal nodded, snatched up a pistol, and gave Tolya and Tamar a swift nudge.

"What are you doing?" I asked, suddenly panicked.

"We can't leave survivors," Mal said. Then he dove from the edge. I screamed, but he tucked into a roll and came up firing.

Tolya and Tamar followed, cutting through the remaining ranks of militia while Nikolai and his crew tried to lend cover from above. I saw one of the militiamen break free and run for the woods. Tolya put a bullet through his victim's back, and before the body had even hit the ground, the giant was turning, his hand forming a fist as he crushed the heart of another knife-wielding soldier looming up behind him.

Tamar charged directly into Ekaterina. Her axes flashed twice, and the militiawoman fell, her topknot drifting down beside her lifeless form, attached to a piece of scalp. Another man lifted his pistol, taking aim at Tamar, but Mal was on him, knife slicing mercilessly across his throat. *I am become a blade.* And then there was no one left, only bodies in a field.

"Come on!" Nikolai called as the platform drifted higher. He tossed down a cable. Mal braced his feet against the ground, holding the rope taut so Tamar and Tolya could shin up. As soon as the twins were on the platform, Mal hooked his ankle and wrist in the cable and they bent to haul him in.

That was when I saw movement behind him. A man had risen from the dirt, covered in mud and blood, sabre held out before him.

"Mal!" I cried. But it was too late, his limbs were tangled in the rope.

The soldier released a roar and slashed out. Mal raised a useless hand to defend himself.

Light flashed off the soldier's blade. His arm stopped midswing, and the sabre dropped from his fingertips. Then his body came apart, splitting down the middle as if someone had drawn a near perfect line from the top of his head all the way to his groin, a line that gleamed bright as he fell in pieces.

Mal looked up. I stood at the edge of the platform, my hands still glowing with the power of the Cut. I swayed. Nikolai yanked me back before I could tip over the edge. I broke free of him, scooting to the far end of the platform and vomiting off the other side.

I clung to the cool metal, feeling like a coward. Mal and the twins had leapt into that battle to make sure the Darkling wouldn't learn our location. They hadn't hesitated. They'd killed with ruthless efficiency. I'd taken one life, and I was curled up like a child, wiping sick from my lip.

Stigg sent fire licking over the bodies in the field. I hadn't stopped to think that a body sliced in half would give away my presence just as surely as an informant.

Moments later, the platform was hauled up into the *Pelican*'s cargo hold, and we were underway. When we emerged above deck, the sun was shining off the port side as we climbed into the clouds. Nikolai shouted commands. One team of Squallers manned the giant lozenge of a balloon, while another filled the sails with wind. Tidemakers shrouded the base of the craft in mist to keep us from being spotted by anyone on the ground. I recognised some of the rogue Grisha from the days when

Nikolai had masqueraded as Sturmhond and Mal and I had been prisoners aboard his ship.

This craft was larger and less graceful than the *Hummingbird* or the *Kingfisher*. I soon learned that it had been built to transport cargo shipments of Zemeni weapons that Nikolai was smuggling over the northern and southern borders and occasionally through the Fold. It wasn't constructed of wood but some lightweight Fabrikator-made substance that sent David into a tizzy. He actually lay down on the deck to get a better view, tapping here and there. "It's some kind of cured resin, but it's been reinforced with . . . carbon fibres?"

"Glass," said Nikolai, looking thoroughly pleased by David's enthusiasm.

"More flexible!" David said in near ecstasy.

"What can I say?" asked Genya drily. "He's a passionate man."

Genya's presence worried me a little, but Nikolai had never seen her scarred, and he didn't seem to recognise her. I circulated with Nadia, whispering a few reminders to our Grisha about not using her real name.

A crewman offered me a cup of fresh water so that I could rinse out my mouth and wash my face and hands. I accepted it with cheeks burning, embarrassed over my display back on the platform.

When I'd finished, I leaned my elbows on the railing and peered through the mist at the landscape below – fields painted in the red and gold of autumn, the blue-grey glitter of the river cities and their bustling ports. Such was the mad power of Nikolai that I barely thought twice about the fact that we were flying. I'd been aboard his smaller crafts, and I definitely preferred the feel of the *Pelican*.

There was something stately about it. It might not get you anywhere quickly, but it wouldn't capsize on a whim either.

From miles beneath the earth to miles above. I could scarcely believe any of it, that Nikolai had found us, that he was safe, that we were all here. A tide of relief washed over me, making my eyes fill.

"First vomit, then tears," Nikolai said, coming up beside me. "Don't tell me I've lost my touch."

"I'm just happy you're alive," I said, hastily blinking my eyes clear. "Though I'm sure you can talk me out of it."

"Glad to see you too. Word was you'd gone underground, but it was more like you'd vanished completely."

"It did feel like being buried alive."

"Is the rest of your party there?"

"This is it."

"You can't mean—"

"This is all that remains of the Second Army. The Darkling has his Grisha, and you have yours, but . . ." I trailed off.

Nikolai surveyed the deck. Mal and Tolya were deep in conversation with a member of Nikolai's crew, helping to tie down ropes and manoeuvre a sail. Someone had found Mal a jacket, but he was still short a pair of boots. David was running his hands over the deck as if he were trying to disappear into it. The others were clustered into little groups: Genya was huddled with Nadia and the other Etherealki. Stigg had got stuck with Sergei, who slumped on the deck, his head buried in his hands. Tamar was seeing to Harshaw's wounds as Oncat dug her claws into his leg, her fur standing on end. The tabby obviously didn't enjoy flying.

"All that remains," Nikolai repeated.

"One Healer chose to stay underground." After a long minute, I asked, "How did you find us?"

"I didn't, really. Militias have been preying on our smuggling routes. We couldn't afford to lose another shipment, so I came after Luchenko. Then Tamar was spotted in the square, and when we realised the camp they were moving on was yours, I thought why not get the girl—"

"And the guns?"

He grinned. "Exactly."

"Thank goodness we had the foresight to be captured."

"Very quick thinking on your part. I commend you."

"How are the King and Queen?"

He snorted and said, "Fine. Bored. There's little for them to do." He adjusted the cuff of his coat. "They took Vasily's loss hard."

"I'm sorry," I said. In truth, I'd spared little thought for Nikolai's older brother.

"He brought it on himself, but I'm surprised to say I'm sorry too."

"I need to know – did you get Baghra out?"

"At great trouble and with little thanks. You might have warned me about her."

"She's a treat, isn't she?"

"Like a fine plague." He reached out and tugged on a lock of my white hair. "Bold choice."

I pushed the loose strands behind my ear self-consciously. "It's all the fashion underground."

"Is it?"

"It happened during the battle. I hoped it might turn back, but it seems to be permanent."

"My cousin Ludovic woke up with a white streak in his

hair after he almost died in a house fire. Claimed the ladies found it very dashing. Of course, he also claimed the house fire was set by ghosts, so who can say."

"Poor cousin Ludovic."

Nikolai leaned back on the railing and studied the balloon tethered above us. At first, I'd assumed it was canvas, but now I thought it might be silk coated with rubber. "Alina . . . ," he began. I was so unused to seeing Nikolai ill at ease that it took me a moment to realise he was struggling for words. "Alina, the night the palace was attacked, I did come back."

Was that what was worrying him? That I thought he'd abandoned me? "I never doubted it. What did you see?"

"The grounds were dark when I flew over. Fires had broken out in a few places. I saw David's dishes shattered on the roof and the lawn of the Little Palace. The chapel had collapsed. There were *nichevo'ya* crawling all over it. I thought we might be in trouble, but they didn't spare the *Kingfisher* a second look."

They wouldn't, not with their master trapped and dying beneath a heap of rubble.

"I'd hoped there might be some way to retrieve Vasily's body," he said. "It was no good. The whole place was overrun. What happened?"

"The *nichevo'ya* attacked the Little Palace. By the time I arrived, one of the dishes was already down." I dug my nail into the rail of the ship, scratching a little half-moon. "We never had a chance." I didn't want to think about the main hall streaked with blood, the bodies strewn over the roof, the floor, the stairs – broken heaps of blue, red, and purple.

"And the Darkling?"

"I tried to kill him."

"As one does."

"By killing myself."

"I see."

"I brought the chapel down," I said.

"You—"

"Well, the *nichevo'ya* did, at my command."

"You can command them?"

Already, I could see him calculating a possible advantage. Always the strategist.

"Don't get excited," I said. "I had to create my own *nichevo'ya* to do it. And I had to be in direct contact with the Darkling."

"Oh," he said glumly. "Will that change once you've found the firebird?"

"I'm not sure," I admitted, "but . . ." I hesitated. I'd never spoken this thought aloud. Among Grisha it would be considered heresy. Still, I wanted to say the words, wanted Nikolai to hear them. I hoped he might understand the edge it would give us, even if he couldn't grasp the hunger that drove me. "I think I may be able to build my own army."

"Soldiers of light?"

"That's the idea."

Nikolai was watching me. I could tell he was choosing his words carefully. "You once told me that *merzost* isn't like the Small Science, that it carries a high price." I nodded. "How high, Alina?"

I thought of a girl's body crushed beneath a mirrored dish, her goggles askew, of Marie torn open in Sergei's arms, of Genya huddling in her shawl. I thought of church walls, like pieces of bloody parchment, crowded with the names of the dead. It wasn't just righteous fury that guided me, though. It was my need for the firebird – banked, but always burning.

"It doesn't matter," I said firmly. "I'll pay it."

Nikolai considered this, then said, "Very well."

"That's it? No sage words? No dire warnings?"

"Saints, Alina. I hope you weren't looking to me to be the voice of reason. I keep to a strict diet of ill-advised enthusiasm and heartfelt regret." He paused, his grin fading. "But I'm truly sorry for the soldiers you lost and that I didn't do more that night."

Below us, I could see the beginnings of the white reaches of the permafrost and, far beyond, the shape of mountains in the distance. "What could you have done, Nikolai? You would have just got yourself killed. You still might." It was harsh, but it was also the truth. Against the Darkling's shadow soldiers, everyone – no matter how brilliant or resourceful – was close to helpless.

"You never know," said Nikolai. "I've been busy. I might have some surprises in store for the Darkling yet."

"Please tell me you plan to dress up as a volcra and jump out of a cake."

"Well, now you've ruined the surprise." He pushed off the railing. "I need to pilot us over the border."

"The border?"

"We're heading into Fjerda."

"Oh, good. Enemy territory. And here I was starting to relax."

"These are my skies," Nikolai said with a wink. Then he strolled across the deck, whistling a familiar, off-key tune.

I'd missed him. The way he talked. The way he attacked a problem. The way he brought hope with him wherever he went. For the first time in months, I felt the knot in my chest ease.

Once we crossed the border, I'd thought we might head for the coast or even West Ravka, but soon we were tacking towards the mountain range I'd glimpsed. From my days as a mapmaker, I knew they were the northernmost peaks of the Sikurzoi, the range that stretched across most of Ravka's eastern and southern border. The Fjerdans called them the Elbjen, the Elbows, though as we drew closer, it was hard to tell why. They were massive, snowcapped things, all white ice and grey rock. They would have dwarfed the Petrazoi. If those were elbows, I didn't want to know what they were attached to.

We climbed higher. The air grew frigid as we drifted into the thick cloud cover that hid the steepest peaks. When we emerged above it, I released an awed gasp. Here, the few mountaintops tall enough to pierce the clouds seemed to float like islands in a white sea. The tallest looked as if it was clutched by huge fingers of frost, and as we arced around it, I thought I saw shapes in the ice. A narrow stone staircase zigzagged up the cliff face. What lunatic would make that climb? And for what possible purpose?

We rounded the mountain, drawing closer and closer to the rock. Just as I was about to call out in panic, we rolled hard to the right. Suddenly, we were between two frozen walls. The *Pelican* swerved and we entered an echoing stone hangar.

Nikolai really had been busy. We crowded at the railing, gaping at the hectic bustle around us. Three other crafts were docked in the hangar: a second cargo barge like the *Pelican*, the sleek *Kingfisher*, and a similar vessel that bore the name *Bittern*.

"It's a kind of heron," said Mal, pulling on a pair of borrowed boots. "They're smaller. Sneaky." Like the *Kingfisher*, the *Bittern* had double hulls, though they were flatter and wider at the base, and equipped with what looked like sled runners.

Nikolai's crew threw lines over the *Pelican*'s rail, and workers ran forward to catch them, stretching them taut and tying them to steel hooks secured in the hangar's walls and floor. We touched down with a thud and a deafening screech as hull scraped against stone.

David frowned disapprovingly. "Too much weight."

"Don't look at me," said Tolya.

As soon as we came to a halt, Tolya and Tamar leapt from the railings, already calling out greetings to crewmen and workers they must have recognised from their time aboard the *Volkvolny*. The rest of us waited for the gangway to be lowered, then shuffled off the barge.

"Impressive," Mal said.

I shook my head in wonder. "How does he do it?"

"Want to know my secret?" Nikolai asked from behind us. We both jumped. He leaned in, looked from left to right, and whispered loudly, "I have a lot of money."

I rolled my eyes.

"No, really," he protested. "A *lot* of money."

Nikolai gave orders to the waiting dockworkers for repairs and then led our ragged, wide-eyed band to a doorway in the rock.

"Everybody in," he said. Confused, we crowded into the little rectangular room. The walls looked as if they were made of iron. Nikolai pulled a gate closed across the entry.

"You're on my foot," Zoya complained grumpily, but

we were all wedged in so tightly it was hard to tell who she was angry at.

"What is this?" I asked.

Nikolai dropped a lever, and we let loose a collective scream as the room shot upwards, taking my stomach with it.

We jolted to a halt. My gut slammed back down to my shoes, and the gate slid open. Nikolai stepped out, doubled over with laughter. "I never tire of that."

We piled out of the box as fast as we could – all except for David, who lingered to fiddle with the lever mechanism.

"Careful there," Nikolai called. "The trip down is bumpier than the trip up."

Genya took David's arm and yanked him clear.

"Saints," I swore. "I forgot how often I want to stab you."

"So I *haven't* lost my touch." He glanced at Genya and said quietly, "What happened to that girl?"

"Long story," I hedged. "Please tell me there are stairs. I'd rather set up permanent house here than ever get back in that thing."

"Of course there are stairs, but they're less entertaining. And once you've dragged yourself up and down four flights of them enough, you'll find you're far more open-minded."

I was about to argue, but as I took a good look around, the words died on my tongue. If the hangar had been impressive, then this was simply miraculous.

It was the biggest room I'd ever been in – twice, maybe three times as wide and as tall as the domed hall in the Little Palace. It wasn't even a room, I realised. We were standing at the top of a hollowed-out mountain.

Now I understood what I had seen as we approached

aboard the *Pelican*. The frost fingers were actually enormous bronze columns cast in the shapes of people and creatures. They towered above us, bracketing huge panels of glass that looked out on the ocean of cloud below. The glass was so clear that it gave the space an eerie sense of openness, as if a wind might blow through and send me tumbling into the nothingness beyond. My heart started to hammer.

"Deep breaths," Nikolai said. "It can be overwhelming at first."

The room was teeming with people. Some bunched in groups where drafting tables and bits of machinery had been set up. Others were marking crates of supplies in a kind of makeshift warehouse. Another area had been set aside for training; soldiers sparred with dulled swords, while others summoned Squaller winds or cast Inferni flame. Through the glass, I saw terraces protruding in four directions, giant spikes like compass points – north, south, east, west. Two had been set aside for target practice. It was hard not to compare it to the damp, cloistered caverns of the White Cathedral. Everything here was bursting with life and hope. It all bore Nikolai's stamp.

"What is this place?" I asked as we slowly made our way through.

"It was originally a pilgrimage site, back when Ravka's borders extended further north," Nikolai replied. "The Monastery of Sankt Demyan."

Sankt Demyan of the Rime. At least that explained the winding staircase we'd glimpsed. Only faith or fear could get anyone to make that climb. I remembered Demyan's page from the *Istorii Sankt'ya*. He'd performed some kind of miracle near the northern border. I was pretty sure he'd been stoned to death.

"A few hundred years ago, it was turned into an observatory," Nikolai continued. He pointed to a hulking brass telescope tucked into one of the glass niches. "It's been abandoned for over a century. I heard about it during the Halmhend campaign, but it took some finding. Now we just call it the Spinning Wheel."

Then it struck me: the bronze columns were constellations – the Hunter with his drawn bow, the Scholar bent in study, the Three Foolish Sons, huddled together, trying to share a single coat. The Bursar, the Bear, the Beggar. The Shorn Maiden wielding her bone needle. Twelve in all: the spokes of the Spinning Wheel.

I had to crane my neck all the way back to get a view of the glass dome high above us. The sun was setting and through it, I could see the sky turning a lush, deep blue. If I squinted, I could just make out a twelve-pointed star at the dome's centre.

"So much glass," I whispered, my head reeling.

"But no frost," Mal noted.

"Heated pipes," David said. "They're in the floor. Probably embedded in the columns too."

It *was* hotter in this room. Still cold enough that I wouldn't want to part with my coat or my hat, but my feet were warm through my boots.

"There are boilers beneath us," Nikolai said. "The whole place runs on melted snow and steam heat. The problem is fuel, though I've been stockpiling coal."

"For how long?"

"Two years. We started repairs when I had the lower caverns turned into hangars. It's not an ideal holiday spot, but sometimes you just want to get away."

I was impressed, and also unnerved. Being around

Nikolai was always like this, watching him shift and change, revealing secrets as he went. He reminded me of the wooden nesting dolls I'd played with as a child. Except instead of getting smaller, he just kept getting grander and more mysterious. Tomorrow, he'd probably tell me he'd built a pleasure palace on the moon. *Tough to get to, but quite a view.*

"Have a look around," Nikolai said to us. "Get a feel for the place. Nevsky's unloading cargo in the hangar, and I need to take care of repairs to the hull." I remembered Nevsky. He'd been a soldier in Nikolai's old regiment, the Twenty-Second, and not particularly fond of Grisha.

"I'd like to see Baghra," I said.

"You're sure about that?"

"Not remotely."

"I'll take you to her. Good practice should I ever need to walk someone to the gallows. And after you've had your fill of punishment, you and Oretsev can join me for dinner."

"Thank you," Mal said, "but I should look into outfitting our expedition to retrieve the firebird."

There'd been a time, not so long ago, that Mal would have bristled at the thought of leaving me alone with Prince Perfect, though Nikolai had the grace not to register surprise. "Of course. I'll send Nevsky to you when he's done. He can arrange your accommodations as well." He clapped a hand on Mal's shoulder. "It's good to see you, Oretsev."

The smile Mal returned was genuine. "You too. Thanks for the rescue."

"Everyone needs a hobby."

"I thought yours was preening."

"Two hobbies."

They clasped hands briefly, then Mal bowed and moved off with the group.

"Should I be offended that he doesn't want to dine with us?" Nikolai asked. "I set an excellent table, and I rarely drool."

I didn't want to discuss it. "Baghra," I prodded.

"He was impressive in that barley field," Nikolai continued, taking my elbow to steer me back the way we'd come. "Better with a sword and gun than I've ever seen him."

I remembered what the Apparat had said: *Men fight for Ravka because the King commands it.* Mal had always been a gifted tracker, but he'd been a soldier because we were all soldiers, because we had no choice. What was he fighting for now? I thought of him diving from the mesh platform, his knife moving across the militiaman's throat. *I am become a blade.*

I shrugged, eager to change the subject. "There's not much to do underground besides train."

"I can think of a few more interesting ways to spend one's time."

"Is that supposed to be innuendo?"

"What a filthy mind you have. I was referring to puzzles and the perusal of edifying texts."

"I'm not getting back in that iron box," I said as we approached the door in the rock. "So you'd better be taking me to the stairs."

"Why does everyone always say that?"

I heaved a sigh of relief as we descended a broad, delightfully stationary set of stone steps. Nikolai led me through a curving passage, and I shrugged off my coat, beginning to sweat. The floor directly below the observatory was considerably warmer, and as we passed a wide doorway, I spotted a maze of steaming boilers that glowed and hissed in the dark. Even the ever-polished Nikolai had a fine mist of perspiration on his elegant features.

We were most definitely headed to Baghra's lair. The woman never seemed to be able to keep warm. I wondered if it was because she so rarely used her power. I'd certainly never been able to shake the chill of the White Cathedral.

Nikolai stopped at an iron door. "Last chance to run."

"Go on," I said. "Save yourself."

He sighed. "Remember me as a hero." He knocked lightly on the door, and we entered.

I had the disconcerting sense that we'd stepped right back into Baghra's hut at the Little Palace. There she sat, huddled by a tile oven, dressed in the same faded *kefta*, her hand resting on the cane she'd taken such pleasure in whacking me with. The same servant boy was reading to her, and I felt a burst of shame when I realised I hadn't even thought to ask if he'd made it out of Os Alta. The boy stopped as Nikolai cleared his throat.

"Baghra," Nikolai said, "how are you this evening?"

"Still old and blind," she snarled.

"And charming," Nikolai drawled. "Never forget charming."

"Whelp."

"Hag."

"What do you want, pest?"

"I've brought someone to visit," Nikolai said, giving me a push.

Why was I so nervous?

"Hello, Baghra," I managed.

She paused, motionless. "The little Saint," she murmured, "returned to save us all."

"Well, she did almost *die* trying to rid us of your cursed spawn," Nikolai said lightly. I blinked. So Nikolai knew Baghra was the Darkling's mother.

"Couldn't even manage martyrdom right, could you?" Baghra waved me in. "Come in and shut the door, girl. You're letting the heat out." I grinned at this familiar refrain. "And you," she spat in Nikolai's direction. "Go somewhere you're wanted."

"That's hardly limiting," he said. "Alina, I'll be back to fetch you for dinner, but should you grow restless, do feel free to run screaming from the room or take a dagger to her. Whatever seems most fitting at the time."

"Are you still here?" snapped Baghra.

"I go but hope to remain in your heart," he said solemnly. Then he winked and disappeared.

"Wretched boy."

"You like him," I said in disbelief.

Baghra scowled. "Greedy. Arrogant. Takes too many risks."

"You almost sound concerned."

"You like him too, little Saint," she said with a leer in her voice.

"I do," I admitted. "He's been kind when he might have been cruel. It's refreshing."

"He laughs too much."

"There are worse traits."

"Like arguing with your elders?" she growled. Then she thumped her stick on the floor. "Boy, go and fetch me something sweet."

The servant hopped to his feet and set down his book.

I caught him as he raced past me for the door. "Just a moment," I said. "What's your name?"

"Misha," he replied. He was in desperate need of a haircut, but otherwise looked well enough.

"How old are you?"

"Eight."

"Seven," snapped Baghra.

"Almost eight," he conceded.

He was small for his age. "Do you remember me?"

With a tentative hand he reached out and touched the antlers at my neck, then nodded solemnly. "Sankta Alina," he breathed. His mother had taught him that I was a Saint, and apparently Baghra's contempt hadn't convinced him otherwise. "Do you know where my mother is?" he asked.

"I don't. I'm sorry." He didn't even look surprised. Maybe that was the answer he'd come to expect. "How are you finding it here?"

His eyes slid to Baghra, then back to me.

"It's all right," I said. "Be honest."

"There's no one to play with."

I felt a little pang, remembering the lonely days at Keramzin before Mal had arrived, the older orphans who'd had little interest in another scrawny refugee. "That may change soon. Until then, would you like to learn to fight?"

"Servants aren't allowed to fight," he said, though I could see he liked the idea.

"I'm the Sun Summoner, and you have my permission." I ignored Baghra's snort. "If you go find Malyen Oretsev, he'll see about getting you a practice sword."

Before I could blink, the boy was tearing out of the room, practically tripping over his own feet in his excitement.

When he was gone, I said, "His mother?"

"A servant at the Little Palace." Baghra gathered her shawl closer around her. "It's possible she survived. There's no way of knowing."

"How is he taking it?"

"How do you think? Nikolai had to drag him screaming onto that accursed craft. Though that may just have been good sense. At least he cries less now."

As I moved the book to sit beside her, I glanced at the title. Religious parables. Poor kid. Then I turned my attention to Baghra. She'd put on a bit of weight, sat straighter in her chair. Getting out of the Little Palace had done her good, even if she'd just found another hot cave to hide in.

"You look well."

"I wouldn't know," she said sourly. "Did you mean what you said to Misha? Are you thinking of bringing the students here?" The children from the Grisha school at Os Alta had been evacuated to Keramzin, along with their teachers and Botkin, my old combat instructor. Their safety had been nagging at me for months, and now I was in a position to do something about it.

"If Nikolai agrees to house them at the Spinning Wheel, would you consider teaching them?"

"Hmph," she said with a scowl. "Someone has to. Who knows what garbage they've been learning with that bunch."

I smiled. Progress, indeed. My smile vanished when Baghra rapped me on the knee with her stick. "Ow!" I yelped. The woman's aim was uncanny.

"Give me your wrists."

"I don't have the firebird."

She lifted her stick again, but I flinched out of the way.

"All right, all right." I took her hand and laid it on my bare wrist. As she groped nearly up to my elbow, I asked, "How does Nikolai know you're the Darkling's mother?"

"He asked. He's more observant than the rest of you fools." She must have been satisfied that I wasn't somehow hiding the third amplifier, because she dropped my wrist with a grunt.

"And you just told him?"

Baghra sighed. "These are my son's secrets," she said wearily. "It's not my job to keep them any longer." Then she leaned back. "So you failed to kill him once more."

"Yes."

"I cannot say I'm sorry. In the end, I'm even weaker than you, little Saint."

I hesitated, then blurted, "I used *merzost*."

Her shadow eyes flew open. "You *what*?"

"I . . . I didn't do it myself. I used the connection between us, the one created by the collar, to control the Darkling's power. I created *nichevo'ya*."

Baghra's hands scrambled for mine. She seized my wrists in a painful grip. "You must not do this, girl. You must not trifle with this kind of power. This is what created the Fold. Only misery can come of it."

"I may not have a choice, Baghra. We know the location of the firebird, or at least we think we do. Once we find it—"

"You'll sacrifice another ancient life for the sake of your own power."

"Maybe not," I protested weakly. "I showed the stag mercy. Maybe the firebird doesn't have to die."

"Listen to you. This is not some children's story. The stag had to die for you to claim its power. The firebird is no

different, and this time the blood will be on your hands."
Then she laughed her low, mirthless chuckle. "The thought
doesn't bother you as much as it should, does it, girl?"

"No," I admitted.

"Have you no care for what there is to lose? For the
damage you may cause?"

"I do," I said miserably. "*I do.* But I'm out of options,
and even if I weren't—"

She dropped my hands. "You would seek it just the
same."

"I won't deny it. I want the firebird. I want the
amplifiers' combined power. It doesn't change the fact that
no human army can stand against the Darkling's shadow
soldiers."

"Abomination against abomination."

If that was what it took. Too much had been lost for
me to turn away from any weapon that might make me
strong enough to win this fight. With or without Baghra's
help, I would have to find a way to wield *merzost*.

I hesitated. "Baghra, I've read Morozova's journals."

"Have you, now? Did you find them stimulating
reading?"

"No, I found them infuriating."

To my surprise, she laughed. "My son pored over those
pages as if they were holy writ. He must have read through
them a thousand times, questioning every word. He began
to think there were codes hidden in the text. He held the
pages over flame searching for invisible ink. In the end, he
cursed Morozova's name."

As had I. Only David's obsession persisted. It had nearly
got him killed today when he'd insisted on dragging that
pack with him.

I hated to ask it, hated to even put the possibility into words, but I forced myself to. "Is there . . . is there any chance Morozova left the cycle unfinished? Is there a chance he never created the third amplifier?"

For a while, she was silent, her expression distant, her blind gaze locked on something I couldn't see. "Morozova never could have left that undone," she said softly. "It wasn't his way."

Something in her words lifted the hairs on my arms. A memory came to me: Baghra putting her hands to the collar on my neck at the Little Palace. *I would have liked to see his stag.*

"Baghra—"

A voice came from the doorway: "*Moi soverenyi.*" I looked up at Mal, annoyed at being interrupted.

"What is it?" I asked, recognising the edge that came into my voice whenever the firebird was concerned.

"There's a problem with Genya," he said. "And the King."

Chapter 7

I shot to my feet. "What happened?"

"Sergei let her real name slip. He seems to be taking to heights about as well as he took to caves."

I released a growl of frustration. Genya had played a key role in the Darkling's plot to depose the King. I'd tried to be patient with Sergei, but now he'd put her in danger and jeopardised our position with Nikolai.

Baghra reached out and snagged the fabric of my trousers, gesturing to Mal. "Who is that?"

"The captain of my guard."

"Grisha?"

I frowned. "No, *otkazat'sya*."

"He sounds—"

"Alina," Mal said. "They're coming to take her right now."

I pried Baghra's fingers away. "I have to go. I'll send Misha back to you."

I hurried from the room, closing the door behind me, and Mal and I raced for the stairs, taking them two at a time.

The sun had long since set, and the lanterns of the Spinning Wheel had been lit. Outside, I glimpsed stars emerging above the cloud bank. A group of soldiers with blue armbands had gathered by the training area and looked about two seconds from drawing their guns on Tolya and Tamar. I felt a surge of pride to see my Etherealki arrayed behind the twins, shielding Genya and David. Sergei was nowhere to be found. Probably a good thing, since I didn't have time to give him the pummelling he deserved.

"She's here!" called Nadia when she caught sight of us. I went straight to Genya.

"The King is waiting," said one of the guards. I was surprised to hear Zoya snap back, "Let him wait."

I put my arm around Genya's shoulders, leading her a little way off. She was shaking.

"Listen to me," I said, smoothing her hair back. "No one will hurt you. Do you understand?"

"He's the *King*, Alina." I heard the terror in her voice.

"He's not the king of anything any more," I reminded her. I spoke with a confidence I didn't feel. This could get very bad, very fast, but there was no way around it. "You must face him."

"For him to see me . . . brought low like this—"

I made her meet my gaze. "You are not *low*. You defied the Darkling to give me freedom. I won't let yours be taken."

Mal approached us. "The guards are getting antsy."

"I can't do this," said Genya.

"You can."

Gently, Mal laid a hand on her shoulder. "We've got you."

A tear rolled down her cheek. "Why? Back at the Little Palace, I reported on Alina. I burned her letters to you. I let her believe—"

"You stood between us and the Darkling on Sturmhond's ship," Mal said in that same steady voice he'd used during the cave-in. "I don't reserve my friendship for perfect people. And, thank the Saints, neither does Alina."

"Can you trust us?" I asked.

Genya swallowed, then took a breath, mustering the poise that had once come so easily to her. She pulled up her shawl. "All right," she said.

We returned to the group. David looked questioningly at her, and she reached out to take his hand.

"We're ready," I said to the soldiers.

Mal and the twins fell into step beside us, but I held up a warning hand to the other Grisha. "Stay here," I said, then added quietly, "and keep alert." On the Darkling's orders, Genya had come close to committing regicide, and Nikolai knew it. If it came to a fight, I had no idea how we would get off this mountaintop.

We followed the guards across the observatory and through a corridor that led down a short set of stairs. As we rounded a bend, I heard the King's voice. I couldn't make out everything he was saying, but I didn't miss the word *treason*.

We paused in a doorway formed by the spear arms of two bronze statues – Alyosha and Arkady, the Horsemen of Ivets, their armour studded with iron stars. Whatever the chamber had once been, it was now Nikolai's war room. The walls were covered in maps and blueprints, and a huge drafting table was littered with clutter. Nikolai leaned against his desk, arms and ankles crossed, his expression troubled.

I almost didn't recognise the King and Queen of Ravka. The last time I'd seen the Queen, she'd been swathed in rose silk and dripping with diamonds. Now she wore a wool *sarafan* over a simple peasant blouse. Her blonde hair, dull and strawlike without the polish of Genya's skill, had been twisted into a messy bun. The King was apparently still partial to military attire. The gold braid and satin sash of his dress uniform were gone, replaced by First-Army drab that seemed incongruous with his weak build and greying moustache. He looked frail leaning on his wife's chair, the damning evidence of whatever Genya had done to him clear in his stooped shoulders and loose skin.

As I entered, the King's eyes bugged out almost comically. "I didn't ask to see this witch."

I forced myself to bow, hoping some of the diplomacy I'd learned from Nikolai might serve me. "*Moi tsar.*"

"Where is the traitor?" he bayed, spittle flying from his lower lip.

So much for diplomacy.

Genya took a small step forward. Her hands shook as she lowered her shawl. The King gasped. The Queen covered her mouth.

The silence in the room was the quiet after a cannon blast. I saw realisation strike Nikolai. He glanced at me, his jaw set. I hadn't exactly lied to him, but I might as well have.

"What is this?" muttered the King.

"This is the price she paid for saving me," I said, "for defying the Darkling."

The King scowled. "She is a traitor to the crown. I want her head."

To my surprise, Genya said to Nikolai, "I will take my punishment if he takes his."

The King's face flushed purple. Maybe he'd have a heart attack and save us all a lot of bother. "You will stay silent among your betters!"

Genya lifted her chin. "I have no betters here." She wasn't making this any easier, but I still wanted to cheer.

The Queen sputtered. "If you think that—"

Genya was trembling, but her voice stayed strong as she said, "If he cannot be tried for his failures as a King, let him be tried for his failures as a man."

"You ungrateful whore," sneered the King.

"That's enough," Nikolai said. "Both of you."

"I am Ravka's King. I will not—"

"You are a King without a throne," said Nikolai quietly. "And I respectfully ask that you hold your tongue."

The King shut his mouth, a vein pulsing at his temple.

Nikolai tucked his hands behind his back. "Genya Safin, you are accused of treason and attempted murder."

"If I'd wanted him dead, he'd be dead."

Nikolai gave her a warning look.

"I didn't try to kill him," she said.

"But you did something to the King, something from which the court doctors said he'd never recover. What was it?"

"Poison."

"Surely it could have been traced."

"Not this. I designed it myself. If given in small enough doses over a long enough time, the symptoms are mild."

"A vegetable alkaloid?" asked David.

She nodded. "Once it builds up in the victim's system, a threshold is reached, the organs begin to fail, and the degeneration is irreversible. It's not a killer. It's a thief. It steals years. And he will never get them back."

I felt a little chill at the satisfaction in her voice. What she described was no mundane poison, but the craft of a girl somewhere between Corporalnik and Fabrikator.

A girl who had spent plenty of time in the Materialki workshops.

The Queen was shaking her head. "Small amounts over time? She didn't have that kind of access to our meals—"

"I poisoned my *skin*," Genya said harshly, "my lips. So that every time he touched me—" She shuddered slightly and glanced at David. "Every time he kissed me, he took sickness into his body." She clenched her fists. "He brought this on himself."

"But the poison would have affected you too," Nikolai said.

"I had to purge it from my skin, then heal the burns the lye would leave. Every single time." Her fists clenched. "It was well worth it."

Nikolai rubbed a hand over his mouth. "Did he force you?"

Genya nodded once. A muscle in Nikolai's jaw ticked.

"Father?" he asked. "Did you?"

"She is a servant, Nikolai. I didn't have to force her."

After a long moment, Nikolai said, "Genya Safin, when this war is over, you will stand trial for high treason against this kingdom and for colluding with the Darkling against the crown."

The King broke into a smug grin. But Nikolai hadn't finished.

"Father, you are ill. You have served the crown and the people of Ravka, and now it is time for you to take the rest you deserve. Tonight, you will write out a letter of abdication."

The King blinked in confusion, eyelids stuttering as if he couldn't quite comprehend what he was hearing. "I will do no such—"

"You will write the letter, and tomorrow you will leave on the *Kingfisher*. It will take you to Os Kervo, where you'll be seen safely aboard the *Volkvolny* and across the True Sea. You can go somewhere warm, maybe the Southern Colonies."

"The *Colonies*?" the Queen gasped.

"You will have every luxury. You will be far from the fighting and the reach of the Darkling. You will be safe."

"I am the King of Ravka! This . . . this traitor, this—"

"If you remain, I will see you tried for rape."

The Queen clutched a hand to her heart. "Nikolai, you cannot mean to do this."

"She was under your protection, Mother."

"She is a servant!"

"And you are a Queen. Your subjects are your children. All of them."

The King advanced on Nikolai. "You would send me from my own country on so slight a charge—"

At this Tamar broke her silence. "Slight? Would it be slight if she had been born noble?"

Mal crossed his arms. "If she'd been born noble, he never would have dared."

"This is the best solution," said Nikolai.

"It is not a solution at all!" barked the King. "It is cowardice!"

"I cannot put this crime aside."

"You have no right, no authority. Who are you to sit in judgement on your King?"

Nikolai stood up straighter. "These are Ravka's laws, not mine. They should not bow to rank or status." He tempered his tone. "You know this is for the best. Your health is failing. You need rest, and you're too weak to lead our forces against the Darkling."

"Watch me!" the King roared.

"Father," Nikolai said gently, "the men will not follow you."

The King's eyes narrowed. "Vasily was twice the man you are. You are a weakling and a fool, full of common sentiment and common blood."

Nikolai flinched. "Maybe so," he said. "But you will write that letter, and you will board the *Kingfisher* without protest. You will leave this place, or you will face trial, and if you are found guilty, then I will see you hang."

The Queen let out a small sob.

"It is my word against hers," the King said, waving his finger at Genya. "I am a King—"

I stepped between them. "And I am a Saint. Shall we see whose word carries more weight?"

"You shut your mouth, you grotesque little witch. I should have had you killed when I had the chance."

"That is *enough*," Nikolai snapped, his patience fraying. He gestured to the guards at the door. "Escort my father and mother to their rooms. Keep them under watch and ensure that they speak to no one. I will have your abdication by morning, Father, or I will have you in irons."

The King looked from Nikolai to the guards who now flanked him. The Queen clutched at his arm, her blue eyes panicked.

"You are no Lantsov," snarled the King.

Nikolai merely bowed. "I find I can live with that fact."

He signalled the guards. They took hold of the King, but he pulled free of their grip. He walked to the door, bristling with rage, trying to summon the scraps of his dignity.

He paused before Genya, his eyes roving over her face. "At least now you look like what you truly are," he said. "Ruined."

I could see the word hit her like a slap. *Razrusha'ya.* The Ruined. The name the pilgrims had whispered when she'd first come among them. Mal moved forward. Tamar's hands went to her axes, and I heard Tolya growl. Genya halted them with a hand. Her spine stiffened, and her remaining eye blazed with conviction.

"Remember me when you board that ship, *moi tsar.* Remember me when you take your last look at Ravka as it slips beneath the horizon." She leaned in and whispered something to him. The King paled, and I saw real fear in his eyes. Genya drew back and said, "I hope the taste of me was worth it."

The King and Queen were hustled from the room by the guards. Genya held her chin high until they were gone. Then her shoulders sagged.

David put his arm around her, but she shook him off. "Don't," she snarled, brushing away the tears that threatened.

Tamar started forward at the same moment that I said, "Genya—"

She held up her hands, warding us off. "I don't want your pity," she said ferociously. Her voice was raw, wild. We stood there helplessly. "You don't understand." She covered her face with her hands. "None of you do."

"Genya—" David tried.

"Don't you dare," she said roughly, tears welling up again. "You never looked at me twice before I was like this, before I was broken. Now I'm just something for you to fix."

I was desperate for words to soothe her, but before I could find any, David bunched up his shoulders and said, "I know metal."

"What does that have to do with *anything*?" Genya cried.

David furrowed his brow. "I . . . I don't understand half of what goes on around me. I don't get jokes or sunsets or poetry, but I know metal." His fingers flexed unconsciously as if he were physically grasping for words. "Beauty was your armour. Fragile stuff, all show. But what's inside you? That's steel. It's brave and unbreakable. And it doesn't need fixing." He drew in a deep breath then awkwardly stepped forward. He took her face in his hands and kissed her.

Genya went rigid. I thought she'd push him away. But then she threw her arms around him and kissed him back. Emphatically.

Mal cleared his throat, and Tamar gave a low whistle. I had to bite my lip to stifle a nervous laugh.

They broke apart. David was blushing furiously. Genya's grin was so dazzling it made my heart twist in my chest. "We should get you out of the workshop more often," she said.

This time I did laugh. I stopped short when Nikolai said, "Do not think to rest easy, Genya Safin." His voice was cold and deeply weary. "When this war is over, you will face charges, and I will decide whether or not you are to be pardoned."

Genya bowed gracefully. "I don't fear your justice, *moi tsar*."

"I'm not the King yet."

"*Moi tsarevich*," she amended.

"Go," he said, waving us away. When I hesitated, he simply said, "All of you."

As the doors closed, I saw him slump at his drafting table, his head in his hands.

I trailed the others back down the hall. David was murmuring to Genya about the properties of vegetable alkaloids and beryllium dust. I wasn't sure how wise it was for them to be colluding over poisons, but I supposed this was their version of a romantic moment.

My feet dragged at the prospect of returning to the Spinning Wheel. It had been one of the longest days of my life, and though I'd held exhaustion at bay, now it settled over my shoulders like a sodden coat. I decided that Genya or Tamar could update the rest of the Grisha on what had happened, and I would deal with Sergei tomorrow. But before I could find my bed and sink into it, there was something I needed to know.

At the stairs, I grabbed Genya's hand. "What did you whisper?" I asked quietly. "To the King."

She watched the others move up the steps, then said, "*Na razrusha'ya. E'ya razrushost.*" I am not ruined. I am ruination.

My brows rose. "Remind me to stay on your good side."

"Darling," she said, turning one scarred cheek to me, then the other, "I don't *have* a good side any more." Her tone was merry, but I heard sadness there too. She winked at me with her remaining eye and disappeared up the stairs.

Mal had worked with Nevsky to see to our sleeping arrangements, so he was left to show me to my quarters, a set of rooms on the eastern side of the mountain. The door frame was formed by the clasped hands of two bronze maidens I thought might be meant to embody the Morning and Evening Stars. Inside, the far wall was entirely taken up by a round window, ringed in riveted brass like a sidescuttle on a ship. The lanterns were lit, and though the view would most likely be spectacular in the daytime, right now, there was nothing to see except darkness and my own tired face looking back at me.

"The twins and I will be right next door," Mal said. "And one of us will be posted while you sleep."

A pitcher of hot water was waiting for me by the basin, and I rinsed my face as Mal reported on the accommodations he'd secured for the rest of the Grisha, how long it would take to outfit our expedition into the Sikurzoi, and how he wanted to divide the group. I tried to listen, but at some point, my mind shut down.

I sat on the stone bench of the window seat. "I'm sorry," I said. "I just can't."

He stood there, and I could almost see him wrestling with whether or not to sit down beside me. In the end, he stayed where he was.

"You saved my life today," he said.

I shrugged. "And you saved mine. It's kind of what we do."

"I know it isn't easy, making your first kill."

"I've been responsible for a lot of deaths. This shouldn't be any different."

"But it is."

"He was a soldier like us. He probably has a family somewhere, a girl he loves, maybe even a child. He was there and then he was just . . . gone." I knew I should leave it at that, but I needed to let the words out. "And you know the really scary part? It *was* easy."

Mal was quiet for a long moment. Then he said, "I'm not sure who my first kill was. We were hunting the stag when we ran into a Fjerdan patrol on the northern border. I don't think the fight lasted more than a few minutes, but I killed three men. They were doing a job, same as I was, trying to get through one day to the next, then they were bleeding in the snow. No way to tell who was the first to fall, and I'm not sure it matters. You keep them at a distance. The faces start to blur."

"Really?"

"No."

I hesitated. I couldn't look at him when I whispered, "It felt good." He didn't say anything, so I plunged on. "It doesn't matter why I'm using the Cut, what I'm doing with the power. It *always* feels good."

I was afraid to look at him, afraid of the disgust I'd see on his face or, worse, the fear. But when I forced myself to glance up, Mal's expression was thoughtful.

"You could have struck down the Apparat and all his Priestguards, but you didn't."

"I wanted to."

"But you didn't. You've had plenty of opportunities to be brutal, to be cruel. You've never taken them."

"Not yet. The firebird—"

He shook his head. "The firebird won't change who you are. You'll still be the girl who took a beating for me when I was the one who broke Ana Kuya's ormolu clock."

I groaned, pointing an accusatory finger at him. "And you let me."

He laughed. "Of course I did. That woman is terrifying."

Then his expression sobered. "You'll still be the girl who was willing to sacrifice her life to save us at the Little Palace, the same girl I just saw back a servant over a king."

"She's not a servant. She's—"

"A friend. I know." He hesitated. "The thing is, Alina, Luchenko was right."

It took me a moment to place the militia leader's name. "About what?"

"There's something wrong with this country. No land. No life. Just a uniform and a gun. That's how I used to think too."

He had. He'd been willing to walk away from Ravka without a second glance. "What changed?"

"You. I saw it that night in the chapel. If I hadn't been so scared, I could have seen it before."

I thought of the militiaman's body falling in pieces. "Maybe you were right to be scared of me."

"I wasn't afraid of you, Alina. I was afraid of losing you. The girl you were becoming didn't need me any more, but she's who you were always meant to be."

"Power hungry? Ruthless?"

"Strong." He looked away. "Luminous. And maybe a little ruthless too. That's what it takes to rule. Ravka is broken, Alina. I think it always has been. The girl I saw in the chapel could change that."

"Nikolai—"

"Nikolai's a born leader. He knows how to fight. Knows how to politic. But he doesn't know what it is to live without hope. He's never been nothing. Not like you or Genya. Not like me."

"He's a good man," I protested.

"And he'll be a good king. But he needs you to be a great one."

I didn't know what to say to that. I pressed a finger to the window glass, then wiped the smudge away with my sleeve. "I'm going to ask him if I can bring the students here from Keramzin. The orphans too."

"Take him with you when you go," Mal said. "He should see where you come from." He laughed. "You can introduce him to Ana Kuya."

"I already unleashed Baghra on Nikolai. He's going to think I stockpile vicious old women." I made another fingerprint on the glass. Without looking at him, I said, "Mal, tell me about the tattoo."

He was silent for a time. Finally, he scrubbed a hand over the back of his neck and said, "It's an oath in old Ravkan."

"But why take on that mark?"

This time he didn't blush or turn away. "It's a promise to be better than I was," he said. "It's a vow that if I can't be anything else to you, at least I can be a weapon in your hand." He shrugged. "And I guess it's a reminder that wanting and deserving aren't the same thing."

"What *do* you want, Mal?" The room seemed very quiet.

"Don't ask me that."

"Why not?"

"Because it can't be."

"I want to hear it anyway."

He blew out a long breath. "Say goodnight. Tell me to leave, Alina."

"No."

"You need an army. You need a crown."

"I do."

He laughed then. "I know I'm supposed to say something noble – I want a united Ravka free from the Fold. I want the Darkling in the ground, where he can never hurt you or anyone else again." He gave a rueful shake of his head. "But I guess I'm the same selfish ass I've always been. For all my talk of vows and honour, what I really want is to put you up against that wall and kiss you until you forget you ever knew another man's name. So tell me to go, Alina. Because I can't give you a title or an army or any of the things you need."

He was right. I knew that. Whatever fragile, lovely thing had existed between us belonged to two other people – people who weren't bound by duty and responsibility – and I wasn't sure what remained. And still I wanted him to put his arms around me, I wanted to hear him whisper my name in the dark, I wanted to ask him to stay.

"Goodnight, Mal."

He touched the space over his heart where he wore the golden sunburst I'd given him long ago in a darkened garden.

"*Moi soverenyi*," he said softly. He bowed and was gone.

The door closed behind him. I doused the lanterns and lay down on the bed, pulling the blankets around me. The window wall was like a great round eye, and now that the room was dark, I could see the stars.

I brushed my thumb over the scar on my palm, made years ago by the edge of a broken blue cup, a reminder of the moment when my whole world had shifted, when I'd given up a part of my heart that I would never get back.

We'd made the wise choice, done the right thing. I had to believe that logic would bring comfort in time. Tonight, there was just this too-quiet room, the ache of loss, knowledge deep and final as the tolling of a bell: *Something good has gone.*

The next morning, I woke to Tolya at my bedside.

"I found Sergei," he said.

"Was he missing?"

"All last night."

I dressed in the clean clothes that had been left for me: tunic, trousers, new boots, and a thick wool *kefta* in Summoner blue, lined with red fox, its cuffs embroidered with gold. Nikolai always came prepared.

I let Tolya lead me down the stairs to the boiler level and to one of the darkened water rooms. Instantly, I regretted my choice of clothing; it was miserably hot. I cast a glow of light inside. Sergei was seated against the wall near one of the big metal tanks, his knees pressed to his chest.

"Sergei?"

He squinted and turned his head away. Tolya and I exchanged a glance.

I patted his big arm. "Go and find your breakfast," I said, my own stomach growling. When Tolya had gone, I dimmed the light and went to sit beside Sergei. "What are you doing down here?"

"Too big up there," he mumbled. "Too high."

There was more to it than that, more to him letting Genya's name slip, and I couldn't ignore it any more. We'd never had a chance to talk about the disaster at the Little Palace. Or maybe there'd been opportunities and I'd avoided them. I wanted to apologise for Marie's death, for putting her in danger, for not being there to save her. But what words were there for that kind of failure? What words could fill the hole where a living girl with chestnut curls and a lilting giggle had been?

"I miss Marie too," I said finally. "And the others."

He buried his face in his arms. "I was never afraid before, not really. Now I'm scared all the time. I can't make it stop."

I put my arm around him. "We're all scared. It's not something to be ashamed of."

"I just want to feel safe again."

His shoulders were shaking. I wished I had Nikolai's gift for finding the right words. "Sergei," I said, not sure if I was about to make matters better or worse. "Nikolai has camps on the ground, some in Tsibeya and a little further south. There are way stations for the smugglers, away from most of the fighting. If he agrees to it, would you prefer to be assigned there? You could work as a Healer. Or maybe just rest for a while?"

He didn't even hesitate. "Yes," he gasped.

I felt guilty for the rush of relief that came over me. Sergei had slowed us during our fight with the militia. He was unstable. I could apologise, offer useless words, but I didn't know how to help him, and it didn't change the fact that we were at war. Sergei had become a liability.

"I'll see to the arrangements. If there's anything else you need . . ." I trailed off, unsure how to finish. Awkwardly, I patted his shoulder, then rose and turned to go.

"Alina?"

I paused in the doorway. I could just make him out in the dark, the light from the hallway glinting off his damp cheeks. "I'm sorry about Genya. About everything."

I remembered the way Marie and Sergei used to jab at each other, thought of them sitting arm in arm, laughing over a shared cup of tea. "Me too," I whispered.

When I emerged into the hall, I was startled to see Baghra waiting with Misha.

"What are you doing out here?"

"We came to find you. What's the matter with that boy?"

"He's had a hard time of it," I said, leading them away from the tank room.

"Who hasn't?"

"He saw the girl he loved gutted by your son and held her while she died."

"Suffering is cheap as clay and twice as common. What matters is what each man makes of it. Now," she said with a rap of her stick, "lessons."

I was so stunned that it took me a moment to understand her meaning. Lessons? Baghra had refused to teach me since I'd returned to the Little Palace with the second amplifier. I gathered my wits and followed her down the hall. I was probably a fool for asking, but I couldn't stop myself. "What changed your mind?"

"I had a chat with our new King."

"Nikolai?"

She grunted.

My steps slowed when I saw where Misha was leading her. "You ride in the iron box?"

"Of course," she snapped. "I should drag my body up all those stairs?"

I glanced at Misha, who looked placidly back at me, hand resting on the wooden practice sword at his hip. I edged into the horrible contraption.

Misha slammed the grate closed and pulled the lever. I shut my eyes as we hurtled upward, then jolted to a stop.

"What did Nikolai say?" I asked shakily as we stepped into the Spinning Wheel.

Baghra gave a wave of her hand. "I warned him that once you had the power of the amplifiers, you might be as dangerous as my son."

"Thanks," I said drily. She was right and I knew it, though that didn't mean I wanted Nikolai worrying about it.

"I made him swear that if that happened, he'd put a bullet in you."

"And?" I asked, even as I dreaded hearing it.

"He gave me his word. Whatever that's worth."

I happened to know Nikolai's word was good. He might mourn me. He might never forgive himself. But Nikolai's first love was Ravka. He would never tolerate a threat to his country.

"Why don't you do it now and save him the trouble?" I muttered.

"I think about it daily," she snapped back. "Especially when you run your mouth."

Baghra murmured instructions to Misha, and he led us to the southern terrace. The door was hidden in the hem of the Shorn Maiden's brass skirts, and there were coats and hats hung on hooks along her boot. Baghra was already so bundled up I could barely see her face, but I grabbed a fur hat for myself and buttoned Misha into a thick wool coat before we stepped into the biting cold.

The long terrace ended in a point, almost like the prow of a ship, and the cloud bank lay like a frozen sea before us. Occasionally the mist parted, offering glimpses of the snow-covered peaks and gray rock far below. I shuddered. *Too big. Too high.* Sergei wasn't wrong. Only the tallest peaks of the Elbjen were visible above the clouds, and again I was reminded of an island chain stretching south.

"Tell me what you see," said Baghra.

"Mostly clouds," I said, "sky, a few mountain peaks."

"How far to the closest one?"

I tried to gauge the distance. "At least a mile, maybe two?"

"Good," she said. "Take its head off."

"What?"

"You've used the Cut before."

"It's a *mountain*," I said. "A really big mountain."

"And you're the first Grisha to wear two amplifiers. Do it."

"It's miles away!"

"Are you hoping I'll grow old and die while you complain?"

"What if someone sees—"

"The range is uninhabited this far north. Stop making excuses."

I heaved a frustrated sigh. I'd worn the amplifiers for months. I had a good sense of the limits of my power.

I held up my gloved hands, and the light came to me in a welcome rush, shimmering over the cloud bank. I focused it, narrowing it to a blade. Then, feeling like an idiot, I struck out in the direction of the nearest peak.

Not even close. The light burned through the clouds at least a few hundred yards short of the mountain, briefly revealing the peaks below and leaving shreds of mist in its wake.

"How did she do?" Baghra asked Misha.

"Badly."

I scowled at him. Little traitor. Someone snickered behind me.

I turned. We'd drawn a crowd of soldiers and Grisha. It was easy to pick out the red crest of Harshaw's hair. He had Oncat curled round his neck like an orange scarf, and Zoya was smirking beside him. *Perfect.* Nothing like a little humiliation on an empty stomach.

"Again," said Baghra.

"It's too far," I grumbled. "And it's huge." Couldn't we have started smaller? Say, with a house?

"It is not *too far*," she sneered. "You are as much there as you are here. The same things that make the mountain make you. It has no lungs, so let it breathe with you. It has no pulse, so give it your heartbeat. That is the essence of the Small Science." She thumped me with her stick. "Stop huffing like a wild boar. Breathe the way I taught you – contained, even."

I felt my cheeks redden, and I slowed my breathing.

Snippets of Grisha theory filled my head. *Odinakovost.* Thisness. *Etovost.* Thatness. It was all a muddle. But the words that came back to me most strongly were Morozova's fevered scrawl: *Are we not all things?*

I closed my eyes. This time, instead of drawing the light to me, I went to it. I felt myself scatter, reflecting off the terrace, the snow, the glass behind me.

I lashed out with the Cut. It struck the side of the mountain, sending a sheet of ice and rock tumbling with a dull roar.

A cheer went up from the crowd at my back.

"Hmph," said Baghra. "They'd clap for a dancing monkey."

"All depends on the monkey," said Nikolai from the edge of the terrace. "And the dance."

Great. More company.

"Better?" Baghra asked Misha.

"A little," he said grudgingly.

"A lot!" I protested. "I hit it, didn't I?"

"I didn't ask you to hit it," said Baghra. "I told you to take its head off. Again."

"Ten coins says she doesn't make it," called one of Nikolai's rogue Grisha.

"Twenty says she does," shouted Adrik loyally.

I could have hugged him, though I knew for a fact he didn't have the money.

"Thirty says she can hit the one behind it."

I whirled. Mal was leaning against the archway, his arms crossed.

"That peak is over five miles away," I protested.

"More like six," he said breezily, a challenge in his eyes. It was as if we were back at Keramzin, and he was daring me to steal a bag of sweet almonds or luring me out onto Trivka's pond before the ice had set. *I can't*, I'd say. *Of course you can*, he'd reply, gliding away from me on too-big borrowed skates, the toes stuffed with paper, never turning his back, making sure I would follow.

As the crowd hooted and placed wagers, Baghra spoke to me in a low voice. "We say like calls to like, girl. But if the science is small enough, then we are like all things. The light lives in the spaces between. It is there in the soil of that mountain, in the rock and in the snow. The Cut is already made."

I stared at her. She'd as good as quoted Morozova's journals that time. She'd said the Darkling had been obsessed with them. Was she telling me something more now?

I pushed up my sleeves and raised my hands. The crowd went silent. I focused on the peak in the distance, so far away I couldn't make out its details.

I called the light to me and then released it, letting myself go with it. I was in the clouds, above them, and for a brief moment, I was in the dark of the mountain, feeling myself compressed and breathless. I was the spaces between, where light lived even if it could not be seen. When I brought my arm down, the arc I made was infinite, a shining sword that existed in a moment and in every moment beyond it.

There was an echoing *crack*, like thunder from a distance. The sky seemed to vibrate.

Silently, slowly, the top of the far mountain began to move. It didn't tip, just slid inexorably to the side, snow and rock cascading down its face, leaving a perfect diagonal line where a peak had once been, a ledge of exposed grey rock, jutting just above the cloud bank.

Behind me, I heard shrieking and whooping. Misha was jumping up and down, crowing, "She did it! She did it!"

I glanced over my shoulder. Mal gave me the barest nod, then started rounding everyone up and back into the Spinning Wheel. I saw him point to one of the rogues and mouth, "Pay up."

I turned back to the broken mountain, my blood fizzing with power, my mind reeling from the reality, the permanence of what I'd just done. *Again*, clamoured a voice inside me, hungry for more. First a man, then a mountain. There and gone. Easy. I shivered in my *kefta*, comforted by the soft brush of the fox fur.

"Took your time," grumbled Baghra. "At this rate, I'll lose both my feet to frostbite before you make any progress at all."

Chapter 8

Sergei left that night on the *Ibis*, the cargo barge that had been pressed into service while the *Pelican* was being repaired. Nikolai had offered him a place at a quiet way station near Duva where he could recuperate and be of some help to the smugglers passing through. He'd even offered to let Sergei wait and take shelter in West Ravka, but Sergei had simply been too anxious to leave.

The next morning, Nikolai and I met with Mal and the twins to work out the logistics of pursuing the firebird in the southern Sikurzoi. The rest of the Grisha didn't know the location of the third amplifier, and we intended to keep it that way as long as we could.

Nikolai had spent the better part of two nights studying Morozova's journals, and he was just as concerned as I was, convinced that there must be books missing or in the Darkling's possession. He wanted me to pressure Baghra, but I had to be careful how I approached the subject. If I provoked her, we'd have no new information and she'd stop my lessons.

"It's not just that the books are unfinished," Nikolai said. "Does Morozova strike anyone as a little . . . eccentric?"

"If by eccentric you mean insane, then yes," I admitted. "I'm hoping he can be crazy *and* right."

Nikolai contemplated the map tacked to the wall. "And

this is still our only clue?" He tapped a nondescript valley on the southern border. "That's a lot riding on two skinny pieces of rock."

The unmarked valley was Dva Stolba, home to the settlements where Mal and I had been born, and named for the ruins that stood at its southern entrance – slender, wind-eroded spires that someone had decided were the remnants of two mills. We believed they were actually the ruins of an ancient arch, a signpost to the firebird, the last of Ilya Morozova's amplifiers.

"There's an abandoned copper mine located at Murin," said Nikolai. "You can land the *Bittern* there and enter the valley on foot."

"Why not fly right into the Sikurzoi?" Mal asked.

Tamar shook her head. "Could be tricky manoeuvering. There are fewer landing sites, and the terrain is a lot more dangerous."

"All right," agreed Mal. "Then we set down in Murin and come over the Jidkova Pass."

"We should have good cover," Tolya said. "Nevsky claims a lot of people are travelling through the border cities, trying to get out of Ravka before winter arrives and the mountains become impossible to cross."

"How long will it take you to find the firebird?" Nikolai asked.

Everyone turned to Mal.

"No way of knowing," he said. "It took me months to find the stag. Hunting the sea whip took less than a week." He kept his eyes on the map, but I could feel the memory of those days rising up between us. We'd spent them in the icy waters of the Bone Road with the threat of torture hanging over us. "The Sikurzoi cover a lot of territory. We need to get moving as quickly as possible."

"Have you chosen your crew?" Nikolai asked Tamar.

She had practically broken into a dance when he'd suggested that she captain the *Bittern* and had immediately set about getting familiar with the ship and its requirements.

"Zoya isn't great at working in a team," Tamar replied, "but we need Squallers, and she and Nadia are our best options. Stigg's not bad with the lines, and it can't hurt to have at least one Inferni on board. We should be able to do a test run tomorrow."

"You'd move faster with an experienced crew."

"I added one of your Tidemakers and a Fabrikator to the list," she said. "I'd feel better using our people for the rest."

"The rogues are loyal."

"Maybe so," Tamar replied. "But we work well together."

With a start, I realised she was right. *Our people.* When had that happened? In the journey from the White Cathedral? The cave-in? The moment when we'd faced down Nikolai's guards and then a king?

Our little group was splitting up, and I didn't like it. Adrik was furious at being left behind, and I was going to miss him. I'd even miss Harshaw and Oncat. But the hardest part would be saying goodbye to Genya. Between crew and supplies, the *Bittern* was already weighted down, and there was no reason for her to come with us into the Sikurzoi. And though we needed a Materialnik with us to form the second fetter, Nikolai felt David's best use was here, putting his mind to the war effort. Instead, we'd take Irina, the rogue Fabrikator who had forged the cuff of scales around my wrist back on the *Volkvolny*. David was happy with the decision, and Genya had taken the news better than I had.

"You mean I don't get to go tramping through a dusty mountain range with Zoya complaining all the way and Tolya regaling me with the Second Tale of Kregi?" She'd laughed. "I'm crushed."

"Will you be all right here?" I'd asked.

"I think so. I can't believe I'm saying this, but Nikolai is growing on me. He's nothing like his father. And the man can dress."

She was certainly right about that. Even on a mountaintop, Nikolai's boots were always polished, his uniform immaculate.

"If everything goes well," said Tamar, "we should be ready to leave by week's end."

I felt a surge of satisfaction and had to resist the urge to rub the bare spot on my wrist. Then Nikolai cleared his throat. "About that . . . Alina, I wonder if you might consider a slight detour."

I frowned. "What kind of a detour?"

"The alliance with West Ravka is still new. They're going to be feeling pressure from Fjerda to open the Fold to the Darkling. It would mean a great deal for them to see what a Sun Summoner can do. While the others start scouting the Sikurzoi, I thought we might attend a few state dinners, shear off the top of a mountain range, put their minds at ease. I can take you to join the others in the mountains on the way back from Os Kervo. Like Mal said, they have a lot of territory to cover, and the delay would be negligible."

For a moment, I thought Mal might speak up about the need to get in and out of the Sikurzoi before the first snowfalls came, about the danger of any delay at all. Instead, he rolled up the map on the desk and said, "Seems wise.

Tolya can go as Alina's guard. I need practice on the lines."

I ignored the twist my heart gave. This was what I wanted. "Of course," I said.

If Nikolai had been anticipating an argument, he hid it well. "Excellent," he replied, slapping his hands together. "Let's talk about your wardrobe."

As it turned out, we had more than a few other issues to handle before Nikolai could bury me in silks. He had agreed to send the *Pelican* to Keramzin once it returned, but that was just the first item on the agenda. By the time we'd finished talking about munitions and storm patterns and wet weather gear, it was well past noon and everyone was ready for a break.

Most of the troops ate together in a makeshift mess hall that had been set up on the western side of the Spinning Wheel, beneath the looming watch of the Three Foolish Sons and the Bear. I didn't feel much like company, so I grabbed a roll doused in caraway seeds and some hot tea brimming with sugar and walked out to the southern terrace.

It was bitterly cold. The sky was bright blue, and the afternoon sun made deep shadows in the cloud bank. I sipped my tea, listening to the sound of the wind rushing in my ears as it ruffled the fur around my face. To my right and left, I could see the spikes of the eastern and western terraces. In the distance, the stump of the mountaintop I'd severed was already covered in snow.

Given time, I was sure Baghra could teach me to push my power further, but she would never help me master *merzost*, and on my own, I had no idea where to begin. I remembered the feeling I'd had in the chapel, the sense of connection and disintegration, the horror of feeling my life torn from me, the thrill of seeing my creatures come into being. Without the Darkling, I couldn't find my way into that power, and I couldn't be sure the firebird would change that. Maybe it was simply easier for him. He'd once told me he'd had far more practice with eternity. How many lives had the Darkling taken? How many lives had he lived? Maybe after all this time, life and death looked different to him – small and unmysterious, something to be used.

With one hand, I called the light, letting it slide over my fingers in lazy rays. It burned through the clouds, revealing more of the jagged, ruthless cliffs of the mountain range below. I set my glass down and leaned over the wall to look at the stone steps carved into the side of the mountain beneath us. Tamar claimed that in ancient times, pilgrims had made the climb on their knees.

"If you're going to jump, at least give me time to compose a ballad in your honour," said Nikolai. I turned to see him striding onto the terrace, blond hair shining. He'd thrown on an elegant greatcoat of army drab, marked with the golden double eagle. "Something with lots of sad fiddle and a verse devoted to your love of herring."

"If I wait, I may have to hear you sing it."

"I happen to have a more than passable baritone. And what's the rush? Is it my cologne?"

"You don't wear cologne."

"I have such a naturally delightful scent that it seems like overkill. But if you have a penchant for it, I'll start."

I wrinkled my nose. "No, thank you."

"I shall obey you in all things. Especially after that demonstration," he said with a nod to the lopped-off mountain. "Any time you want me to take off my hat, please just ask."

"Looks impressive, doesn't it?" I said with a sigh. "But the Darkling learned at Baghra's knee. He's had hundreds of years to master his power. I've had less than one."

"I have a gift for you."

"Is it the firebird?"

"Was that what you wanted? Should have told me sooner." He reached into his pocket and placed something atop the wall.

Light glinted off an emerald ring. The lush green stone at its centre was bigger than my thumbnail and surrounded by stars of tiny diamonds.

"Understatement is overrated," I said on a shaky breath.

"I love it when you quote me." Nikolai tapped the ring. "Console yourself knowing that, should you ever punch me while wearing it, you'll probably take my eye out. And I'd very much like you to. Wear it, that is. Not punch me."

"Where did you get this thing?"

"My mother gave it to me before she left. It's the Lantsov emerald. She was wearing it at my birthday dinner the night we were attacked. Curiously enough, that was not the worst birthday I've had."

"No?"

"When I was ten, my parents hired a *clown*."

Tentatively, I reached out and picked up the ring. "Heavy," I said.

"A mere boulder, really."

"Did you tell your mother you planned to give it to a common orphan?"

"She did most of the talking," he said. "She wanted to tell me about Magnus Opjer."

"Who?"

"A Fjerdan ambassador, quite a sailor, made his money in shipping." Nikolai looked out at the cloud bank. "Also my father, apparently."

I wasn't sure whether to offer congratulations or condolences. Nikolai talked about the conditions of his birth easily enough, but I knew he felt the sting of it more deeply than he admitted.

"It's strange to actually know," he continued. "I think some part of me always hoped the rumours were just that."

"You'll still make a great king."

"Of course I will," he scoffed. "I'm melancholy, not daft." He brushed an invisible piece of lint from his sleeve. "I don't know if she'll ever forgive me for sending her into exile, especially to the Colonies."

Was it harder to lose a mother or to simply never know one? Either way, I felt for him. He'd lost his family piece by piece – first his brother, now his parents. "I'm sorry, Nikolai."

"What is there to be sorry about? I've finally got what I wanted. The King has stepped down, the path to the throne is clear. If there weren't an all-powerful dictator and his monstrous horde to attend to, I'd be opening a bottle of champagne."

Nikolai could be as glib as he wanted. I knew this wasn't how he'd imagined assuming leadership of Ravka – his brother murdered, his father brought low by the sordid accusations of a servant.

"When will you take the crown?" I asked.

"Not until we've won. I'll be crowned in Os Alta or not at all. And the first step is consolidating our alliance with West Ravka."

"Hence the ring?"

"Hence the ring." He smoothed the edge of his lapel and said, "You know, you could have told me about Genya."

I felt a wash of guilt. "I was trying to protect her. Not enough people have done that."

"I don't want lies between us, Alina." Was he thinking of his father's crimes? His mother's dalliance? Still, he wasn't quite being fair.

"How many lies have you told me, *Sturmhond*?" I gestured to the Spinning Wheel. "How many secrets have you kept until you were ready to share them?"

He tucked his hands behind his back, looking distinctly uncomfortable. "Prince's prerogative?"

"If a mere prince gets a pass, so does a living Saint."

"Are you going to make a habit of winning arguments? It's very unbecoming."

"Was this an argument?"

"Obviously not. I don't lose arguments." Then he peered over the side. "Saints, is he running the ice stairs?"

I squinted through the mist. Sure enough, someone was making his way up the narrow, zigzagging steps along the cliff side, his breath pluming in the icy air. It took me only a moment to realise it was Mal, head bent, pack on his shoulders.

"Looks . . . bracing. If he keeps this up, I may actually have to start exerting myself." Nikolai's tone was light, but I could feel his clever hazel eyes on me. "Assuming we best the Darkling, as I'm sure we will, does Mal plan to stay on as the captain of your guard?"

I caught myself before I could rub my thumb over the scar on my palm.

"I don't know." Despite everything that had happened, I wanted to keep Mal near. I knew that wouldn't be fair to either of us. I made myself say, "I think it might be best if he was reassigned. He's good in combat, but he's a better tracker."

"You know he won't take a commission away from the fighting."

"Do what you think is best." The pain was like a slender knife gliding right between my ribs. I was cutting Mal out of my life, but my voice was steady. Nikolai had taught me well. I tried to hand the ring back. "I can't accept this. Not now." Maybe not ever.

"Keep it," he said, curling my fingers over the emerald. "A privateer learns to press any advantage."

"And a prince?"

"Princes get used to the word *yes*."

When I got back to my room that evening, Nikolai had more surprises waiting. I hesitated, then turned on my heel and marched down the corridor to where the other girls were lodged. For a long second, I just stood there, feeling shy and foolish, then I forced myself to knock.

Nadia answered. Behind her, I saw Tamar had come to visit and was sharpening her axes by the window. Genya sat at the table, sewing gold thread around another eye patch, and Zoya was lounging on one of the beds, keeping a feather aloft with a gust from her fingertips.

"I need to show you something," I said.

"What is it?" asked Zoya, keeping her eyes on the feather.

"Just come and see."

She rolled herself off the bed with an exasperated sigh. I led them down the hallway to my room, and threw open the door.

Genya dove into the pile of gowns laid out on my bed. "Silk!" she moaned. "Velvet!"

Zoya picked up a *kefta* hanging over the back of my chair. It was gold brocade, the sleeves and hem embroidered lavishly in blue, the cuffs marked with jeweled sunbursts. "Sable," she said to me, stroking the lining. "I have never loathed you more."

"That one's mine," I said. "But the rest are up for grabs. I can't wear all of them in West Ravka."

"Did Nikolai have these made for you?" Nadia asked.

"He's not a big believer in half measures."

"Are you sure he wants you giving them away?"

"Lending," I corrected. "And if he doesn't like it, he can learn to leave more careful instructions."

"It's smart," Tamar said, tossing a teal cape over her shoulders and looking at herself in the mirror. "He needs to look like a King, and you need to look like a Queen."

"There's something else," I said. Again, I felt that shyness creep over me. I still didn't quite know how to behave around the other Grisha. Were they friends? Subjects? This was new territory. But I didn't want to be alone in my room with nothing but my thoughts and a pile of dresses for company.

I took out Nikolai's ring and set it on the table.

"Saints," breathed Genya. "That's the Lantsov emerald."

It seemed to glow in the lamplight, the tiny diamonds twinkling around it.

"Did he just give it to you? To keep?" asked Nadia.

Genya seized my arm. "Did he propose?"

"Not exactly."

"He might as well have," Genya said. "That ring is an heirloom. The Queen wore it everywhere, even to sleep."

"Toss him over," Zoya said. "Break his heart cruelly. I will gladly give our poor prince comfort, and I would make a magnificent queen."

I laughed. "You actually might, Zoya. If you could stop being horrible for a minute."

"With that kind of incentive, I can manage a minute. Possibly two."

I rolled my eyes. "It's just a ring."

Zoya sighed and held the emerald up so it flashed. "I *am* horrible," she said abruptly. "All these people dead, and I miss pretty things."

Genya bit her lip, then blurted, "I miss almond *kulich*. And butter, and the cherry jam the cooks used to bring back from the market in Balakirev."

"I miss the sea," said Tamar, "and my hammock aboard the *Volkvolny*."

"I miss sitting by the lake at the Little Palace," Nadia put in. "Drinking my tea, everything feeling peaceful."

Zoya looked at her boots and said, "I miss knowing what happens next."

"Me too," I confessed.

Zoya set the ring down. "Will you say yes?"

"He didn't actually propose."

"But he will."

"Maybe. I don't know."

She gave a disgusted snort. "I lied. *Now* I have never loathed you more."

"It would be something special," said Tamar, "to have a Grisha on the throne."

"She's right," added Genya. "To be the ones to rule, instead of just to serve."

They wanted a Grisha queen. Mal wanted a commoner queen. And what did I want? Peace for Ravka. A chance to sleep easy in my bed without fear. An end to the guilt and dread that I woke to every morning. There were old wants too, to be loved for who I was, not what I could do, to lie in a meadow with a boy's arms around me and watch the wind move the clouds. Those dreams belonged to a girl, not to the Sun Summoner, not to a Saint.

Zoya sniffed, settling a seed pearl *kokochnik* atop her hair. "I still say it should be me."

Genya tossed a velvet slipper at her. "The day I curtsey to you is the day David performs an opera naked in the middle of the Shadow Fold."

"Like I'd have you in my court."

"You should be so lucky. Come here. That headpiece is completely crooked."

I picked up the ring again, turning it over in my hand. I couldn't quite bring myself to put it on.

Nadia bumped my shoulder with her own. "There are worse things than a prince."

"True."

"Better things too," Tamar said. She shoved a cobalt lace gown at Nadia. "Try this one on."

Nadia held it up. "Are you out of your head? The bodice might as well be cut to the navel."

Tamar grinned. "Exactly."

"Well, Alina can't wear it," said Zoya. "Even she'll fall right out of it onto her dessert plate."

"Diplomacy!" shouted Tamar.

Nadia collapsed into giggles. "West Ravka declares for the Sun Summoner's bosom!"

I tried to scowl, but I was laughing too hard. "I hope you're all enjoying yourselves."

Tamar hooked a scarf over Nadia's neck and drew her in for a kiss.

"Oh, for Saints' sake," complained Zoya. "Is everyone pairing up now?"

Genya snickered. "Take heart. I've seen Stigg casting mournful glances your way."

"He's Fjerdan," Zoya said. "That's the only kind of glance he has. And I can arrange my own assignations, thank you very much."

We sorted through the trunks of clothes, choosing the gowns, coats, and jewels best suited to the trip. Nikolai had been strategic, as always. Each dress was wrought in shades of blue and gold. I wouldn't have minded some variety, but this trip was about performance, not pleasure.

The girls stayed until the lamps burned low, and I was grateful for their company. But when they'd claimed the dresses they liked, and the rest of the finery had been wrapped and returned to the trunks, they said their goodnights.

I picked up the ring from the table, feeling the absurd weight of it in my palm.

Soon the *Kingfisher* would return and Nikolai and I would leave for West Ravka. By then, Mal and his team would be on their way to the Sikurzoi. That was the way it should be. I'd hated life at court, but Mal had despised it. He'd be just as miserable standing guard at banquets in Os Kervo.

If I was honest with myself, I could see that he'd flourished since we'd left the Little Palace, even underground. He had become a leader in his own right, found a new sense of purpose. I couldn't say he seemed happy, but maybe that would come in time, with peace, with a chance for a future.

We would find the firebird. We would face the Darkling. Maybe we'd even win. I would put on Nikolai's ring, and Mal would be reassigned. He would have the life he should have had, that he might have had without me. So why did that knife between my ribs keep twisting?

I lay down on my bed, starlight pouring through the window, the emerald clutched in my hand.

Later, I could never be sure if I'd done it deliberately, or if it was an accident, my bruised heart plucking at that invisible tether. Maybe I was just too tired to resist his pull. I found myself in a blurry room, staring at the Darkling.

Chapter 9

He was sitting on the edge of a table, his shirt crumpled into a ball at his knee, his arms raised above his head as the vague shape of a Corporalnik Healer came in and out of focus, tending to a bloody gash in the Darkling's side. I thought at first we might be in the infirmary at the Little Palace, but the space was too dark and blurry for me to tell.

I tried not to notice the way he looked – his mussed hair, the shadowed ridges of his bare chest. He seemed so human, just a boy wounded in battle, or maybe sparring. *Not a boy*, I reminded myself, *a monster who has lived hundreds of years and taken hundreds of lives.*

His jaw tensed as the Corporalnik finished her work. When the skin had knitted together, the Darkling dismissed her with a wave. She hovered briefly, then slipped away, fading into nothing.

"There's something I've been wondering," he said. No greeting, no preamble.

I waited.

"The night that Baghra told you what I intended, the night you fled the Little Palace, did you hesitate?"

"Yes."

"In the days after you left, did you ever think of coming back?"

"I did," I admitted.

"But you chose not to."

I knew I should go. I should at least have stayed silent, but I was so weary, and it felt so easy to be here with him. "It wasn't just what Baghra said that night. You lied to me. You deceived me. You . . . drew me in." Seduced me, made me want you, made me question my own heart.

"I needed your loyalty, Alina. I needed you bound to me by more than duty or fear." His fingers tested the flesh where his wound had been. Only a mild redness remained. "There are rumours that your Lantsov prince has been sighted."

I drifted nearer, trying to keep my voice casual. "Where?"

He glanced up, his lips curling in a slight smile. "Do you like him?"

"Does it matter?"

"It's harder when you like them. You mourn them more." How many had he mourned? Had there been friends? A wife? Had he ever let anyone get that close?

"Tell me, Alina," said the Darkling. "Has he claimed you yet?"

"*Claimed me?* Like a peninsula?"

"No blushes. No averted eyes. How you've changed. What about your faithful tracker? Will he sleep curled at the foot of your throne?"

He was pressing, trying to provoke me. Instead of shying away, I moved closer. "You came to me wearing Mal's face that night in your chambers. Was it because you knew I would turn you away?"

His fingers tightened on the table's edge, but then he shrugged. "He was the one you longed for. Do you still?"

"No."

"An apt pupil, but a terrible liar."

"Why do you have such disdain for *otkazat'sya*?"

"Not disdain. Understanding."

"They're not all fools and weaklings."

"What they are is predictable," he said. "The people would love you for a time. But what would they think when their good king aged and died, while his witch of a wife remained young? When all those who remember your sacrifices are dust in the ground, how long do you think it will take for their children or their grandchildren to turn on you?"

His words sent a chill through me. I still couldn't get my head around the idea of the long life that lay ahead of me, that yawning abyss of eternity.

"You never considered it, did you?" said the Darkling. "You live in a single moment. I live in a thousand." *Are we not all things?*

In a flash, his hand snaked out and seized my wrist. The room came into sudden focus. He yanked me close, wedging me between his knees. His other hand pressed to the small of my back, his strong fingers splayed over the curve of my spine.

"You were meant to be my balance, Alina. You are the only person in the world who might rule with me, who might keep my power in check."

"And who will balance me?" The words emerged before I thought better of them, giving raw voice to a thought that haunted me even more than the possibility that the firebird didn't exist. "What if I'm no better than you? What if instead of stopping you, I'm just another avalanche?"

He studied me for a long moment. He had always

watched me this way, as if I were an equation that didn't quite tally.

"I want you to know my name," he said. "The name I was given, not the title I took for myself. Will you have it, Alina?"

I could feel the weight of Nikolai's ring in my palm back at the Spinning Wheel. I didn't have to stand here in the Darkling's arms. I could vanish from his grip, slide back into consciousness and the safety of a stone room hidden in a mountaintop. But I didn't want to go. Despite everything, I wanted this whispered confidence.

"Yes," I breathed.

After a long moment, he said, "Aleksander."

A little laugh escaped me. He arched a brow, a smile tugging at his lips. "What?"

"It's just so . . . common." Such an ordinary name, held by kings and peasants alike. I'd known two Aleksanders at Keramzin alone, three in the First Army. One of them had died on the Fold.

His smile deepened and he cocked his head to the side. It almost hurt to see him this way. "Will you say it?" he asked.

I hesitated, feeling danger crowd in on me.

"Aleksander," I whispered.

His grin faded, and his gray eyes seemed to flicker.

"Again," he said.

"Aleksander."

He leaned in. I felt his breath against my neck, then the press of his mouth against my skin just above the collar, almost a sigh.

"Don't," I said. I drew back, but he held me tighter. His hand went to the nape of my neck, long fingers twining in my hair, easing my head back. I closed my eyes.

"Let me," he murmured against my throat. His heel hooked around my leg, bringing me closer. I felt the heat of his tongue, the flex of hard muscle beneath bare skin as he guided my hands around his waist. "It isn't real," he said. "Let me."

I felt that rush of hunger, the steady, longing beat of desire that neither of us wanted, but that gripped us anyway. We were alone in the world, unique. We were bound together and always would be.

And it didn't matter.

I couldn't forget what he'd done, and I wouldn't forgive what he was: a murderer. A monster. A man who had tortured my friends and slaughtered the people I'd tried to protect.

I shoved away from him. "It's real enough."

His eyes narrowed. "I grow weary of this game, Alina."

I was surprised at the anger that surged to life in me. "Weary? You've toyed with me at every turn. You haven't tired of the game. You're just sorry I'm not so easily played."

"Clever Alina," he bit out. "The apt pupil. I'm glad you came tonight. I want to share my news." He yanked his bloody shirt on over his head. "I'm going to enter the Fold."

"Go ahead," I said. "The volcra deserve another piece of you."

"They will not have it."

"You hope to find their appetites changed? Or is this just more madness?"

"I am not mad. Ask David what secrets he left for me to discover at the palace."

I stilled.

"Another clever one," said the Darkling. "I'll be taking him back too, when this is all over. Such an able mind."

"You're bluffing," I said.

The Darkling smiled, though this time the turn of his lips was cold. He shoved off the table and stalked towards me.

"I will enter the Fold, Alina, and I will show West Ravka what I can do, even without the Sun Summoner. And when I have crushed Lantsov's only ally, I will hunt you like an animal. You will find no sanctuary. You will have no peace." He loomed over me, his grey eyes glinting. "Fly back home to your *otkazat'sya*," he snarled. "Hold him tight. The rules of this game are about to change."

The Darkling raised his hand, and the Cut tore through me. I shattered, and gusted back into my body with an icy jolt.

I clutched at my torso, heart hammering in my chest, still feeling the slice of shadow through it, but I was whole and unmarked. I stumbled out of bed, trying to find the lantern, then gave up and fumbled around until I found my coat and boots.

Tamar was standing guard outside my room.

"Where is David lodged?" I asked.

"Just down the corridor with Adrik and Harshaw."

"Are Mal and Tolya sleeping?"

She nodded.

"Wake them up."

She slipped into the guards' room, and Mal and Tolya were outside with us seconds later, awake instantly in the way of soldiers, and already pulling on their boots. Mal had his pistol.

"You won't need that," I said. "At least, I don't think you will."

I considered sending someone to get Nikolai, but I wanted to know what we were dealing with first.

We strode down the hall, and when we got to David's room, Tamar rapped once at the door before pushing in.

Apparently, Adrik and Harshaw had been evicted for the night. A very bleary Genya and David blinked up at us from beneath the covers of a single narrow cot.

I pointed at David. "Get dressed," I said. "You have two minutes."

"What's—" Genya began.

"Just do it."

We slipped back out the door to wait.

Mal gave a little cough. "Can't say I'm surprised."

Tamar snorted. "After his little speech in the war room, even I considered pouncing on him."

Moments later, the door cracked open and a disheveled, barefoot David ushered us in. Genya was seated cross-legged on the cot, her red curls going every which way.

"What is it?" said David. "What's wrong?"

"I've received information that the Darkling intends to use the Fold against West Ravka."

"Did Nikolai—" Tamar began.

I held up a hand. "I need to know if it's possible."

David shook his head. "He can't without you. He needs to enter the Unsea to expand it."

"He claims he can. He claims you left secrets at the Little Palace."

"Wait a minute," said Genya. "Where is this information coming from?"

"Sources," I said curtly. "David, what did he mean?" I didn't want to believe David would betray us, at least not deliberately.

David frowned. "When we fled Os Alta, I left my old notebooks behind, but they're hardly dangerous."

"What was in them?" asked Tamar.

"All kinds of things," he said, his nimble fingers pleating and unpleating the fabric of his trousers. "The designs for the mirrored dishes, a lens to filter different waves of the spectrum, nothing he could use to enter the Fold. And . . ." He paled slightly.

"What else?"

"It was just an idea—"

"*What else?*"

"There was a plan for a glass skiff that Nikolai and I came up with."

I frowned and glanced at Mal, then at the others. They all looked as puzzled as I did. "Why would he want a glass skiff?"

"The frame is made to hold *lumiya*."

I made an impatient gesture. "What's *lumiya*?"

"A variation on liquid fire."

Saints. "Oh, David. You didn't." Liquid fire was one of Morozova's creations. It was sticky, flammable, and created a blaze that was almost impossible to extinguish. It was so dangerous that Morozova had destroyed the formula only hours after he'd created it.

"No!" David held his hands up defensively. "No, no. This is better, safer. The reaction only creates light, not heat. I came up with it when we were trying to find ways to improve the flash bombs for fighting the *nichevo'ya*. It wasn't applicable, but I liked the idea so I kept it for . . . for later." He shrugged helplessly.

"It burns without heat?"

"It's just a source of artificial sunlight."

"Enough to keep the volcra at bay?"

"Yes, but it's useless to the Darkling. It has a limited burn life, and you need sunlight to activate it."

"How much?"

"Very little, that was the point. It was just another way of magnifying your power, like the dishes. But there isn't *any* light in the Fold, so—"

I held out my hands and shadows spilled over the walls.

Genya cried out, and David shrank back against the bed. Tolya and Tamar reached for their weapons.

I dropped my arms, and the shadows returned to their ordinary forms. Everyone gaped at me.

"You have his power?" whispered Genya.

"No. Just a scrap of it." Mal thought I'd taken it from the Darkling. Maybe the Darkling had taken something from me too.

"That's how you made the shadows jump when we were in the Kettle," said Tolya.

I nodded.

Tamar jabbed a finger at Mal. "You lied to us."

"I kept her secrets," Mal said. "You would have done the same."

She crossed her arms. Tolya laid a big hand on her shoulder. They all looked upset, but not as scared as they might have.

"You see what this means," I said. "If the Darkling has even a remnant of my power—"

"Would it be enough to hold off the volcra?" asked Genya.

"No," I said. "I don't think so." I'd needed an amplifier before I was able to command enough light to safely enter the Fold. Of course, there was no guarantee that the

Darkling hadn't taken more of my power when we'd faced each other in the chapel. And yet, if he'd been able to truly wield light, he would have acted before this.

"It doesn't matter," said David miserably. "He only needs enough sunlight to activate the *lumiya* once he's in the Fold."

"Plenty of light for protection," said Mal. "A well-armed skiff of Grisha and soldiers . . ."

Tamar shook her head. "Even for the Darkling, that seems risky."

Tolya answered her with my own thoughts. "You're forgetting the *nichevo'ya*."

"Shadow soldiers fighting volcra?" Genya said in horror.

"Saints," swore Tamar. "Who do you root for?"

"The problem was always containment," said David. "*Lumiya* eats through everything. The only thing that worked was glass, but that presents its own engineering problems. Nikolai and I never resolved them. It was just . . . just for fun."

If the Darkling hadn't solved those problems already, he would.

You will find no sanctuary. You will have no peace.

I put my head in my hands. "He's going to break West Ravka."

And after that, no country would dare to stand with me or Nikolai.

Chapter 10

Half an hour later, we were sitting at the end of a table in the galley, empty glasses of tea in front of us. Genya had made herself scarce, but David was there, his head bent over a pile of drafting paper as he tried to re-create the plans for the glass skiff and the formula for *lumiya* from memory. For better or worse, I didn't believe he'd aided the Darkling intentionally. David's crime was hunger for knowledge, not power.

The rest of the Spinning Wheel was empty and silent, most of the soldiers and rogue Grisha still asleep. Despite being hauled out of bed in the middle of the night, Nikolai managed to look put together, even with his olive drab coat thrown over his nightshirt and trousers. It hadn't taken long to update him on all I had learned, and I wasn't surprised by the first question out of his mouth.

"How long have you known this?" he said. "Why didn't you tell me sooner?"

"An hour, maybe less. I only waited to confirm the information with David."

"That's impossible—"

"Improbable," I corrected gently. "Nikolai . . ." My gut clenched. I glanced at Mal. I hadn't forgotten the way he'd reacted when I'd finally told him I was seeing visions of the Darkling. And this was far worse, because I'd gone looking for him. "I heard it from the Darkling's lips himself. He told me."

"Beg your pardon?"

"I can visit him, like a kind of vision. I . . . I sought him out."

There was a long beat. "You can spy on him?"

"Not exactly." I tried to explain the way the rooms appeared to me, how he appeared. "I can't hear other people or really even see them if they aren't immediately next to him or in contact with him. It's as if he's the only real, material thing."

Nikolai's fingers were drumming on the tabletop. "We could still try to probe for information," he said, his voice excited, "maybe even feed him false intelligence." I blinked. That quickly, Nikolai was strategising. I should have been used to it by now. "Can you do this with other Grisha? Maybe try to get in their heads?"

"I don't think so. The Darkling and I are . . . connected. We probably always will be."

"I have to warn West Ravka," he said. "They'll need to evacuate the area along the shore of the Fold." Nikolai rubbed a hand over his face. It was the first crack I'd seen in his confidence.

"They won't keep to the alliance, will they?" Mal asked.

"I doubt it. The blockade was a gesture West Ravka was willing to make when they thought they were safe from reprisal."

"If they capitulate," said Tamar, "will the Darkling still march?"

"This isn't just about the blockade," I said. "It's about isolating us, making sure we don't have anywhere to turn. And it's about power. He wants to use the Fold. He always has." I restrained the urge to touch my bare wrist. "It's a compulsion."

"What kind of numbers can you raise?" Mal asked Nikolai.

"All told? We could probably rally a force of roughly five thousand. They're spread throughout cells in the north-west, so the problem is mobilising, but I think it can be done. We also have reason to suspect some of the militias may be loyal to us. There have been massive desertions from the base at Poliznaya and the northern and southern fronts."

"What about the Soldat Sol?" asked Tolya. "They'll fight. I know they would lay down their lives for Alina. They've done it before." I rubbed my arms, thinking of more lives lost, of Ruby's fiercely cheerful face marked by the sunburst tattoo.

Nikolai frowned. "But can we rely on the Apparat?" The priest had been instrumental in the coup that had almost brought down Nikolai's father, and unlike Genya, he hadn't been a vulnerable servant victimised by the King. He'd been a trusted adviser. "What exactly does he want?"

"I think he wants to survive," I said. "I doubt he'll risk a head-on confrontation with the Darkling unless he's sure of the outcome."

"We could use the additional numbers," Nikolai admitted.

A dull ache was forming near my right temple. "I don't like this," I said. "Any of it. You're talking about throwing a lot of bodies at the *nichevo'ya*. The casualties will be unheard of."

"You know I'll be right out there with them," said Nikolai.

"All that means is that I can add your number to the dead."

"If the Darkling uses the Fold to sever us from any possible allies, then Ravka is his. He'll only get stronger, consolidate his forces. I won't just give up."

"You saw what those monsters did at the Little Palace—"

"You said it yourself – he won't stop. He needs to use his power, and the more he uses it, the more he'll crave. This may be our last opportunity to bring him down. Besides, rumour has it Oretsev here is quite the tracker. If he finds the firebird, we may just stand a chance."

"And if he doesn't?"

Nikolai shrugged. "We put on our best clothes and die like heroes."

Dawn was breaking by the time we finished hashing out the specifics of what we intended to do next. The *Kingfisher* had returned, and Nikolai sent it right back out again with a refreshed crew and a warning addressed to West Ravka's merchant council that the Darkling might be planning an attack.

They also carried an invitation to meet with him and the Sun Summoner in neutral Kerch. It was too dangerous for Nikolai and me to risk getting caught in what might soon be enemy territory. The *Pelican* was back in the hangar and would soon depart for Keramzin without us. I wasn't sure if I was sorry or relieved that I wouldn't be able to travel with them to the orphanage, but there just wasn't time for a detour. Mal and his team would leave for the Sikurzoi tomorrow aboard the *Bittern*, and I would meet up with them a week later. We would keep to our plan and hope the Darkling didn't act before then.

There was more to discuss, but Nikolai had letters to write, and I needed to talk to Baghra. The time for lessons was over.

I found her in her darkened lair, the fire already stoked, the room unbearably warm. Misha had just brought in her breakfast tray. I waited as she ate her buckwheat kasha and sipped bitter black tea. When she'd finished, Misha opened the book to begin his reading, but Baghra silenced him quickly.

"Take the tray up," she said. "The little Saint has something on her mind. If we make her wait any longer, she may jump out of her seat and shake me."

Horrible woman. Did nothing escape her?

Misha lifted the tray. Then he hesitated, shifting from one foot to the other. "Do I have to come right back down?"

"Stop wriggling like a grub," Baghra snapped, and Misha froze. She gave a wave. "Go on, you useless thing, but don't be late with my lunch."

He raced out the door, dishes rattling, and kicked it shut behind him.

"This is your fault," Baghra complained. "He can never be still any more."

"He's a little boy. It's not something they're known for." I made a mental note to have someone continue Misha's fencing lessons while we were gone.

Baghra scowled and leaned closer to the fire, pulling her furs close around her. "Well," she said, "we're alone. What is it you want to know? Or would you rather sit there biting your tongue for another hour?"

I wasn't sure how to proceed. "Baghra—"

"Either spit it out or let me take a nap."

"The Darkling may have found a way to enter the Fold without me. He'll be able to use it as a weapon. If there's anything you can tell us, we need information."

"Always the same question."

"When I asked you if Morozova could have left the amplifiers unfinished, you said it wasn't his way. Did you know him?"

"We're finished here, girl," she said, turning back to the fire. "You've wasted your morning."

"You told me once that you hoped for redemption for your son. This may be my last chance to stop him."

"Ah, so you hope to save my son now? How forgiving of you."

I took a deep breath.

"Aleksander," I whispered. She stilled. "His true name is Aleksander. And if he takes this step, he'll be lost forever. We may all be."

"That name . . ." Baghra leaned back in her chair. "Only he could have told you. When?"

I'd never spoken of the visions to Baghra, and I didn't think I wanted to now. Instead, I repeated my question. "Baghra, did you know Morozova?"

She was quiet for a long time, the only sound the crackle of the fire. Finally, she said, "As well as anyone did."

Though I'd suspected as much, the fact was hard to believe. I'd seen Morozova's writings, I wore his amplifiers, but he had never seemed real. He was a Saint with a gilded halo, more legend than man to me.

"There's a bottle of *kvas* on a shelf in the corner," she said, "out of Misha's reach. Bring it and a glass."

It was early for *kvas*, but I wasn't going to argue. I brought down the bottle and poured for her.

She took a long sip and smacked her lips together. "The new King doesn't stint, does he?" She sighed and settled back. "All right, little Saint, since you want to know about Morozova and his precious amplifiers, I'll tell you a story – one I used to tell a little boy with dark hair, a silent boy who rarely laughed, who listened more closely than I realised. A boy who had a name and not a title."

In the firelight, the shadowy pools of her eyes seemed to flicker and shift.

"Morozova was the Bonesmith, one of the greatest Fabrikators who ever lived, and a man who tested the very boundaries of Grisha power, but he was also just a man with a wife. She was *otkazat'sya*, and though she loved him, she did not understand him."

I thought of the way the Darkling talked about *otkazat'sya*, the predictions he'd made about Mal and the way I'd be treated by Ravka's people. Had he learned those lessons from Baghra?

"I should tell you that he loved her too," she continued. "At least, I think he did. But it was never enough to make him stop his work. It couldn't temper the need that drove him. This is the curse of Grisha power. You know the way of it, little Saint.

"They spent over a year hunting the stag in Tsibeya, two years sailing the Bone Road in search of the sea whip. Great successes for the Bonesmith. The first two phases of his grand scheme. But when his wife became pregnant, they settled in a small town, a place where he could continue his experiments and hatch his plans for which creature would become the third amplifier.

"They had little money. When he could be pulled away from his studies, he made his living as a woodworker, and the villagers occasionally came to him with wounds and ailments—"

"He was a Healer?" I asked. "I thought he was a Fabrikator."

"Morozova did not draw those distinctions. Few Grisha did in those days. He believed if the science was small enough, anything was possible. And for him, it often was." *Are we not all things?*

"The townspeople viewed Morozova and his family with a combination of pity and distrust. His wife wore rags, and his child . . . his child was rarely seen. Her mother kept her to the house and the fields around it. You see, this little girl had started to show her power early, and it was like nothing ever known." Baghra took another sip of *kvas*. "She could summon darkness."

The words hung in the heated air, their meaning settling over me. "You?" I breathed. "Then the Darkling—"

"I am Morozova's daughter, and the Darkling is the last of Morozova's line." She emptied her glass. "My mother was terrified of me. She was sure that my power was some kind of abomination, the result of my father's experiments. And she may well have been right. To dabble in *merzost*, well, the results are never quite what one would hope. She hated to hold me, could hardly bear to be in the same room with me. It was only when her second child was born that she came back to herself at all. Another little girl, this one normal like her, powerless and pretty. How my mother doted on her!"

Years had passed, hundreds, maybe a thousand. But I recognised the hurt in her voice, the sting of always feeling underfoot and unwanted.

"My father was readying to leave to hunt the firebird. I was just a little girl, but I begged him to take me along. I tried to make myself useful, but all I did was annoy him, and eventually he banned me from his workshop."

She tapped the table, and I filled her glass once more.

"And then one day, Morozova had to leave his workbench. He was drawn to the pasture behind his home by the sound of my mother's screams. I had been playing dolls and my sister had whined and howled and stamped her little feet until my mother insisted that I give over my favourite toy, a wooden swan carved by our father in one of the rare moments that he'd paid me any attention. It had wings so detailed they felt nearly downy and perfect webbed feet that kept it balanced in water. My sister had it in her hand less than a minute before she snapped its slender neck. Remember, if you can, that I was just a child, a lonely child, with so few treasures of my own." She lifted her glass but did not drink. "I lashed out at my sister. With the Cut. I tore her in two."

I tried not to picture it, but the image rose up sharp in my mind, a muddy field, a dark-haired little girl, her favourite toy in pieces. She'd thrown a tantrum, as children do. But she'd been no ordinary child.

"What happened?" I finally whispered.

"The villagers came running. They held my mother back so that she could not get at me. They couldn't make sense of what she was saying. How could a little girl have done such a thing? The priest was already praying over my sister's body when my father arrived. Without a word, Morozova knelt down beside her and began to work. The townspeople didn't understand what was happening, though they sensed power gathering."

"Did he save her?"

"Yes," said Baghra simply. "He was a great Healer, and he used every bit of his skill to bring her back – weak, wheezing, and scarred, but alive."

I'd read countless versions of Sankt Ilya's martyrdom. The details of the story had been distorted over time: He'd healed his child, not a stranger's. A girl, not a boy. But I suspected one thing that hadn't changed was the ending, and I shivered at the thought of what came next.

"It was too much," Baghra said. "The villagers knew what death looked like – that child should have died. And maybe they were resentful too. How many loved ones had they lost to illness or injury since Morozova had come to their town? How many could he have saved? Maybe it was not just horror or righteousness that drove them, but anger as well. They put him in chains – and my sister, a child who should have had the sense to stay dead. There was no one to defend my father, no one to speak on my sister's behalf. We had lived on the outskirts of their lives and made no friends. They marched him to the river. My sister had to be carried. She had only just learned to walk and couldn't manage it with the chains."

I clenched my fists in my lap. I didn't want to hear the rest.

"As my mother wailed and pleaded, as I cried and fought to get free from some barely known neighbour's arms, they shoved Morozova and his youngest daughter off the bridge, and we watched them disappear beneath the water, dragged under by the weight of their iron chains." Baghra emptied her glass and turned it over on the table. "I never saw my father or my sister again."

We sat in silence as I tried to piece together the implications of what she'd said. I saw no tears on Baghra's cheeks. *Her grief is old*, I reminded myself. And yet I didn't think pain like that ever faded entirely. Grief had its own life, took its own sustenance.

"Baghra," I said, pushing on, ruthless in my own way, "if Morozova died—"

"I never said he died. That was the last I ever saw of him. But he was a Grisha of immense power. He might well have survived the fall."

"In chains?"

"He was the greatest Fabrikator who ever lived. It would take more than *otkazat'sya* steel to hold him."

"And you believe he went on to create the third amplifier?"

"His work was his life," she said, and the bitterness of that neglected child edged her words. "If he'd had breath in his body, he would not have stopped searching for the firebird. Would you?"

"No," I admitted. The firebird had become my own obsession, a thread of compulsion that linked me to Morozova across centuries. Could he have survived? Baghra seemed so certain that he had. And what about her sister? If Morozova had managed to save himself, might he have rescued his child from the grasp of the river and used his skill to revive her once more? The thought shook me. I wanted to clutch it tightly, turn it over in my hands, but there was still more I needed to know. "What did the villagers do to you?"

Her rasping chuckle snaked through the room, lifting the hair on my arms. "If they'd been wise, they would have thrown me in the river too. Instead they drove my mother and me out of town and left us to the mercy of the woods. My mother was useless. She tore at her hair and wept until she made herself sick. Finally, she just lay down and wouldn't get up, no matter how I cried and called her name. I stayed with her as long as I could. I tried to make a fire to keep her warm, but I didn't know how." She shrugged. "I was so hungry. Eventually, I left her and wandered, delirious and filthy, until I came to a farm. They took me in and put together a search party, but I couldn't find the way back to her. For all I know, she starved to death on the forest floor."

I stayed quiet, waiting. That *kvas* was beginning to look very good.

"Ravka was different then. Grisha had no sanctuary. Power like ours ended in fates like my father's. I kept mine hidden. I followed tales of witches and Saints and found the secret enclaves where Grisha studied their science. I learned everything I could. And when the time came, I taught my son."

"But what about his father?"

Baghra gave another harsh laugh. "You want a love story too? There's none to be had. I wanted a child, so I sought out the most powerful Grisha I could find. He was a Heartrender. I don't even remember his name."

For a brief moment, I glimpsed the ferocious girl she had been, fearless and wild, a Grisha of extraordinary ability. Then she sighed and shifted in her chair, and the illusion was gone, replaced by a tired old woman huddling by a fire.

"My son was not . . . He began so well. We moved from place to place, we saw the way our people lived, the way they were mistrusted, the lives they were forced to eke out in secrecy and fear. He vowed that we would some day have a safe place, that Grisha power would be something to be valued and coveted, something our country would treasure. We would be Ravkans, not just Grisha. That dream was the seed of the Second Army. A good dream. If I'd known . . ."

She shook her head. "I gave him his pride. I burdened him with ambition, but the worst thing I did was try to protect him. You must understand, even our own kind shunned us, feared the strangeness of our power."

There are no others like us.

"I never wanted him to feel the way I had as a child," said Baghra. "So I taught him that he had no equal, that he was destined to bow to no man. I wanted him to be hard, to be strong. I taught him the lesson my mother and father taught me: to rely on no one. That love – fragile and fickle and raw – was nothing compared to power. He was a brilliant boy. He learned too well."

Baghra's hand shot out. With surprising accuracy, she seized my wrist. "Put your hunger aside, Alina. Do what Morozova and my son could not and *give this up*."

My cheeks were wet with tears. I hurt for her. I hurt for her son. But even so, I knew what my answer would be.

"I can't."

"*What is infinite?*" she recited.

I knew that text well. "*The universe and the greed of men,*" I quoted back to her.

"You may not be able to survive the sacrifice that *merzost* requires. You've tasted that power once, and it almost killed you."

"I have to try."

Baghra shook her head. "Stupid girl," she said, but her

voice was sad, as if she were chastising another girl, from long ago, lost and unwanted, driven by pain and fear.

"The journals—"

"Years later, I returned to the village of my birth. I wasn't sure what I would find. My father's workshop was long gone, but his journals were there, tucked away in the same hidden niche in the old cellar." She released a disbelieving snort. "They'd built a church over it."

I hesitated, then said, "If Morozova survived, what became of him?"

"He probably took his own life. It's the way most Grisha of great power die."

I sat back, stunned. "Why?"

"Do you think I never contemplated it? That my son didn't? Lovers age. Children die. Kingdoms rise and fall, and we go on. Maybe Morozova is still wandering the earth, older and more bitter than I am. Or maybe he used his power on himself and ended it all. It's simple enough. Like calls to like. Otherwise . . ." She chuckled again, that dry, rattling laugh. "You should warn your prince. If he really thinks a bullet will stop a Grisha with three amplifiers, he is much mistaken."

I shuddered. Would I have the courage to take my own life if it came to that? If I brought the amplifiers together, I might destroy the Fold, but I might well make something worse in its place. And when I faced the Darkling, even if I dared to use *merzost* to create an army of light, would it be enough to end him?

"Baghra," I asked cautiously, "what would it take to kill a Grisha with that kind of power?"

Baghra tapped the bare skin of my wrist, the naked spot where the third amplifier might rest in a matter of days.

"Little Saint," she whispered. "Little martyr. I expect we'll find out."

I spent the rest of the afternoon wording a plea for aid to the Apparat. The missive would be left beneath the altar at the Church of Sankt Lukin in Vernost and, hopefully, would make its way to the White Cathedral through the network of the faithful. We'd used a code that Tolya and Tamar knew from their time with the Soldat Sol, so if the message fell into the Darkling's hands, he wouldn't realise that in just over two weeks' time, Mal and I would be waiting for the Apparat's forces in Caryeva. The racing city was as good as abandoned after the summer, and it was close to the southern border. Either we would have the firebird or we wouldn't, but we'd be able to march whatever forces we had north under the cover of the Fold and meet with Nikolai's troops south of Kribirsk.

I had two very different sets of luggage. One was a simple soldier's pack that would be put aboard the *Bittern*. It was stocked with roughspun trousers, an olive drab coat treated to resist the rain, heavy boots, a small reserve of coin for any bribes or purchases I might need to make in Dva Stolba, a fur hat, and a scarf to cover Morozova's collar. The other set was stowed on the *Kingfisher* – a collection of three matching trunks emblazoned with my golden sunburst and stuffed with silks and furs.

When evening came, I descended to the boiler level to say my goodbyes to Baghra and Misha. After her dire warning, I was hardly surprised that Baghra waved me off with a scowl. But I'd really come to see Misha. I reassured him that I had found someone to continue his lessons while we were gone, and I gave him one of the golden sunburst pins worn by my personal guard. Mal wouldn't be able to wear it in the south, and the delight on Misha's face was worth all of Baghra's sneering.

I took my time wending my way back through the dark passages. It was quiet down here, and I'd barely had a moment to think since Baghra had told me her story. I knew she'd intended it as a cautionary tale, and yet my thoughts kept returning to the little girl who'd been thrown into the river with Ilya Morozova. Baghra thought she'd died. She'd dismissed her sister as *otkazat'sya* – but what if she simply hadn't shown her power yet? She was Morozova's child too. What if her gift was unique, like Baghra's? If she had survived, her father might have taken her with him in pursuit of the firebird. She might have lived near the Sikurzoi, her power passed down from generation to generation, over hundreds of years. It might have finally shown itself in me.

It was presumption, I knew. Terrible arrogance. And yet, if we found the firebird near Dva Stolba, so close to the place of my birth, could it really be coincidence?

I stopped short. If I was related to Morozova, that meant I was related to the Darkling. And that meant I'd almost . . . the thought made my skin crawl. No matter how many years and generations might have passed, I still felt as if I needed a scalding bath.

My thoughts were interrupted by Nikolai striding down the hall towards me.

"There's something you should see," he said.

"Is everything all right?"

"Rather spectacular, actually." He peered at me. "What

did the hag do to you? You look like you ate a particularly slimy bug."

Or possibly exchanged kisses and a bit more than that with my cousin. I shuddered.

Nikolai offered me his arm. "Well, whatever it is, you'll have to cringe about it later. There's a miracle upstairs, and it won't wait."

I looped my arm through his. "Never one to oversell it, are you, Lantsov?"

"It's not overselling if you deliver."

We'd just started up the stairs when Mal came bounding down in the opposite direction. He was beaming, his face alight with excitement. That smile was like a bomb going off in my chest. It belonged to a Mal I'd thought had disappeared beneath the scars of this war.

He caught sight of me and Nikolai, arms entwined. It took the briefest second for his face to shutter. He bowed and stepped aside for us to pass.

"Headed the wrong way," said Nikolai. "You're going to miss it."

"Be up in a minute," Mal replied. His voice sounded so normal, so pleasant, I almost believed I'd imagined that smile.

Still, it took everything in me to keep climbing those stairs, to keep my hand on Nikolai's arm. *Despise your heart*, I told myself. Do what needs to be done.

When we reached the top of the stairs and entered the Spinning Wheel, my jaw dropped. The lanterns had been extinguished so that the room was dark, but all around us, stars were falling. The windows were lit with streaks of light cascading over the mountaintop, like bright fish in a river.

"Meteor shower," said Nikolai as he led me carefully

through the room. People had laid blankets and pillows on the heated floor and were sitting in clusters or lying on their backs, watching the night sky.

All at once, the pain in my chest was so bad it nearly bent me double. Because this was what Mal had been coming to show me. Because that look – that open, eager, happy look – had been for me. Because I would always be the first person he turned to when he saw something lovely, and I would do the same. Whether I was a Saint or a queen or the most powerful Grisha who ever lived, I would always turn to him.

"Beautiful," I managed.

"I told you I had a lot of money."

"So you arrange celestial events now?"

"As a sideline."

We stood in the middle of the room, gazing up at the glass dome.

"I could promise to make you forget him," Nikolai offered.

"I'm not sure that's possible."

"You do realise you're playing havoc with my pride."

"Your confidence seems perfectly intact."

"Think about it," he said, leading me through the crowd to a quiet nook near the western terrace. "I'm used to being the centre of attention wherever I go. I've been told I could charm the shoes off a racehorse midstride, and yet you seem impervious."

I laughed. "You know damn well I like you, Nikolai."

"Such a tepid sentiment."

"I don't hear you making declarations of love."

"Would they help?"

"No."

"Flattery? Flowers? A hundred head of cattle?"

I gave him a shove. "No."

Even now I knew that bringing me up here was less a romantic gesture than it was a display. The mess hall was deserted, and we had this little pocket of the Spinning Wheel to ourselves, but he'd made sure we'd taken the long way through the crowd. He'd wanted us to be seen together: the future King and Queen of Ravka.

Nikolai cleared his throat. "Alina, on the very slim chance that we survive the next few weeks, I'm going to ask you to be my wife."

My mouth went dry. I'd known this was where we were headed, but it was still strange to hear him say those words.

"Even if Mal wants to stay on," Nikolai continued, "I'm going to have him reassigned."

Say goodnight. Tell me to leave, Alina.

"I understand," I said quietly.

"Do you? I know I said that we could have a marriage in name only, but if we . . . if we had a child, I wouldn't want him to have to endure the rumours and the jokes." He clasped his hands behind his back. "One royal bastard is enough."

Children. With Nikolai.

"You don't have to do this, you know," I said. I wasn't sure if I was talking to him or myself. "I could lead the Second Army, and you could have pretty much any girl you want."

"A Shu princess? A Kerch banker's daughter?"

"Or a Ravkan heiress or a Grisha like Zoya."

"Zoya? I make it a policy never to seduce anyone prettier than I am."

I laughed. "I think that was an insult."

"Alina, *this* is the alliance I want: the First and Second Armies brought together. As for the rest, I've always known that whatever marriage I made would be political. It would be about power, not love. But we might get lucky. In time, we might have both."

"Or the third amplifier will turn me into a power-mad dictator and you'll have to kill me."

"Yes, that would make for an awkward honeymoon." He took my hand, circling my bare wrist with his fingers. I tensed, and realised I was waiting for the rush of surety that came with the Darkling's touch, or a jolt like the one I'd felt that night at the Little Palace when Mal and I had argued by the *banya*. Nothing happened. Nikolai's skin was warm, his grip gentle. I'd wondered if I would ever feel something so simple again or if the power in me would just keep jumping and crackling, seeking connection the way lightning seeks high ground.

"Collar," Nikolai said. "Fetters. I won't have to spend much on jewellery."

"I have expensive taste in tiaras."

"But only one head."

"Thus far." I glanced down at my wrist. "I should warn you, based on the conversation I had today with Baghra, if things do go wrong with the amplifiers, getting rid of me may require more than your usual firepower."

"Like what?"

"Possibly another Sun Summoner." *It's simple enough. Like calls to like.*

"I'm sure there's a spare around somewhere."

I couldn't help but smile.

"See?" he said. "If we're not dead in a month, we might be very happy together."

"Stop that," I said, still grinning.

"What?"

"Saying the right thing."

"I'll try to wean myself of the habit." His smile faltered. He reached out and brushed the hair back from my face. I froze. He rested his hand in the space where the collar met the curve of my neck, and when I didn't bolt, he slid his palm up to cup my cheek.

I wasn't sure I wanted this. "You said . . . you said you wouldn't kiss me until—"

"Until you were thinking of me instead of trying to forget him?" He moved closer, the light from the meteor shower playing over his features. He leaned in, giving me time to pull away. I could feel his breath when he said, "I love it when you quote me."

He brushed his lips over mine once, briefly, then again. It was less a kiss than the promise of one.

"When you're ready," he said. Then he tucked my hand in his and we stood together, watching the spill of stars streaking the sky.

We might be happy in time. People fell in love every day. Genya and David. Tamar and Nadia. But were they happy? Would they stay that way? Maybe love was superstition, a prayer we said to keep the truth of loneliness at bay. I tilted my head back. The stars looked as if they were close together, when really they were millions of miles apart. In the end, maybe love just meant longing for something impossibly bright and forever out of reach.

Chapter 11

The next morning, I found Nikolai on the eastern terrace taking weather readings. Mal's team was set to depart within the hour and was only waiting for the all clear. I pulled up my hood. It wasn't quite snowing, but a few flakes had settled on my cheeks and hair.

"How does everything look?" I asked, handing Nikolai a glass of tea.

"Not bad," he replied. "Gusts are mild, and the pressure's holding steady. They may have it rough through the mountains, but it shouldn't be anything the *Bittern* can't handle."

I heard the door open behind me, and Mal and Tamar stepped onto the terrace. They were dressed in peasant clothes, fur hats, and sturdy wool coats.

"Are we a go?" Tamar asked. She was trying to seem calm, but I could hear the barely contained excitement in her voice. Behind her, I saw Nadia with her face pressed against the glass, awaiting the verdict.

Nikolai nodded. "You're a go."

Tamar's grin was blinding. She managed a restrained bow, then turned to Nadia and gave her the signal. Nadia whooped and broke into something between a seizure and a dance.

Nikolai laughed. "If only she'd show a little enthusiasm."

"Be safe," I said as I embraced Tamar.

"Take care of Tolya for me," she replied. Then she whispered, "We left the cobalt lace in your trunk. Wear that tonight."

I rolled my eyes and gave her a shove. I knew I would see them all in a week, but I was surprised at how much I was going to miss them.

There was an awkward pause as I faced Mal. His blue eyes were vibrant in the grey morning light. The scar at my shoulder twinged.

"Safe journey, *moi soverenyi*." He bowed.

I knew what was expected, but I hugged him anyway. For a moment, he just stood there, then his arms closed hard around me. "Safe journey, Alina," he whispered into my hair, and quickly stepped back.

"We'll be on our way as soon as the *Kingfisher* returns. I expect to see you all safe and whole in one week's time," Nikolai said, "and packing some all-powerful bird bones."

Mal bowed. "Saints' speed, *moi tsarevich*."

Nikolai offered his hand and they shook. "Good luck, Oretsev. Find the firebird, and when this is over, I'll see you well rewarded. A farmhouse in Udova. A dacha near the city. Whatever you want."

"I don't need any of that. Just . . ." He dropped Nikolai's hand and looked away. "Deserve her."

He hastened back into the Spinning Wheel with Tamar behind him. Through the glass I saw them talking to Nadia and Harshaw.

"Well," said Nikolai, "at least he's learned to make an exit."

I ignored the ache in my throat and said, "How long will it take us to reach Ketterdam?"

"Two to three days, depending on the weather and our Squallers. We'll go north, then over the True Sea. It's safer than travelling over Ravka."

"What's it like?"

"Ketterdam? It's—"

He never finished his sentence. A shadowed blur cut across my vision, and Nikolai was gone. I stood staring at the place where he'd been, then screamed as I felt claws close over my shoulders and my feet lifted from the floor.

I glimpsed Mal bursting through the door to the terrace, Tamar on his heels. He lunged across the distance and seized me around the waist, yanking me back down. I twisted, arms moving in an arc, sending a blaze of light burning through the *nichevo'ya* that had hold of me. It wavered and exploded into nothing. I fell to the terrace in a heap, toppling with Mal, bleeding from where the monster's talons had pierced my skin.

I was on my feet in seconds, horrified by what I saw. The air was full of darting black shapes, winged monsters that moved unlike any natural creature. Behind me, I heard chaos erupting in the hall, the smash of breaking glass as *nichevo'ya* hurled themselves against the windows.

"Get the others out," I yelled to Tamar. "Get them away from here."

"We can't leave you—"

"I won't lose them too!"

"Go!" Mal bellowed at her. He shouldered his rifle, taking aim at the attacking monsters. I lashed out with the Cut, but they were moving so quickly that I couldn't target them. I craned my neck, searching the sky for Nikolai. My heart was pounding. Where was the Darkling? If his monsters were here, then he must be nearby.

He came from above. His creatures moved around him like a living cloak, their wings beating the air in a rippling black wave, forming and re-forming, bearing him aloft, their bodies slipping apart and together, absorbing the bullets from Mal's gun.

"Saints," Mal swore. "How did he find us?"

The answer came quickly. I saw a red shape suspended between two *nichevo'ya*, their black claws sunk deeply into their captive's body. Sergei's face was chalky, his eyes wide and terrified, his lips moving in a silent prayer.

"Shall I spare him, Alina?" said the Darkling.

"Leave him alone!"

"He betrayed you to the first *oprichnik* he could find. I wonder, will you offer him mercy or justice?"

"I don't want him harmed," I shouted.

My mind was reeling. Had Sergei really betrayed us? He'd been on edge since the battle at the Little Palace – what if he'd been planning this all along? Maybe he'd just been trying to slip away during our fight with the militia, maybe he'd let Genya's name drop deliberately. He'd been so ready to leave the Spinning Wheel.

That was when I realised what Sergei was muttering – not prayers, just one word over and over again: *Safe. Safe. Safe.*

"Give him to me," I said.

"He betrayed me first, Alina. He remained in Os Alta when he should have come to my side. He sat on your council, plotted against me. He told me everything."

Thank the Saints we'd kept the location of the firebird a secret.

"So," said the Darkling, "the decision is mine. And I'm afraid that I choose justice."

In one movement, the *nichevo'ya* ripped Sergei's limbs from his body and severed his head from his neck. I had the briefest glimpse of the shock on his face, his mouth open in a silent scream, then the pieces disappeared beneath the cloud bank.

"All Saints," Mal swore.

I gagged, but I had to shove down my terror. Mal and I turned in a slow circle, back to back. We were surrounded by *nichevo'ya*. Behind me, I could hear the sounds of screams and glass shattering in the Spinning Wheel.

"Here we are again, Alina. Your army against mine. Do you think your soldiers will fare any better this time?"

I ignored him and shouted into the misty greyness. "Nikolai!"

"Ah, the pirate prince. I have regretted many of the things I've had to do in this war," said the Darkling. "This is not one of them."

A shadow soldier swooped down. In horror, I saw it held Nikolai struggling in its arms. Any bit of courage I had evaporated. I couldn't see Nikolai ripped limb from limb.

"Please!" The word tore from me, without dignity or constraint. "Please don't!"

The Darkling raised his hand.

I clapped my fingers over my mouth, my legs already buckling.

But the *nichevo'ya* didn't attack Nikolai. It tossed him onto the terrace. His body hit the stone with a sickening thud and rolled to a stop.

"Alina, don't!" Mal tried to hold me back, but I broke free of him and ran to where Nikolai lay, falling to my knees beside him. He moaned. His coat was torn where the creature's claws had shredded the fabric. He tried to push himself up on his elbows and blood dribbled from his mouth.

"This was unexpected," he said weakly.

"You're okay," I said. "It's okay."

"I appreciate your optimism."

I caught movement from the corner of my eye and saw two blots of shadow slip free of the Darkling's hands. They slithered over the lip of the balcony, undulating like serpents, heading directly towards us. I raised my hands and slashed out with the Cut, obliterating one side of the terrace, but I was too slow. The shadows slithered lightning fast across the stone and darted into Nikolai's mouth.

His eyes widened. His breath hitched in surprise, drawing whatever the Darkling had released into his lungs. We stared at each other in shock.

"What – what was that?" he choked.

"I—"

He coughed, shuddered. Then his fingers flew to his chest, tearing open the remains of his shirt. We both looked down, and I saw shadow spreading beneath his skin in fragile black lines, splintering like veins in marble.

"No," I groaned. "No. *No.*"

The cracks travelled across his stomach, down his arms.

"Alina?" he said helplessly. The darkness fractured beneath his skin, climbing his throat. He threw his head back and screamed, the tendons flexing in his neck as his whole body contorted, his back bowing. He shoved up to his knees, chest heaving. I reached for him as he convulsed.

He released another raw scream, and two black shards burst from his back. They unfurled. Like wings.

His head shot up. He looked at me, face beaded in sweat, gaze panicked and desperate. "Alina—"

Then his eyes – his clever, hazel eyes – went black.

"Nikolai?" I whispered.

His lips curled, revealing teeth of black onyx. They had formed fangs.

He snarled. I stumbled backward. His jaws snapped closed a bare inch from me.

"Hungry?" the Darkling asked. "I wonder which one of your friends you'll eat first."

I raised my hands, reluctant to use my power. I didn't want to hurt him. "Nikolai," I begged. "Don't do this. Stay with me."

His face spasmed in pain. He was in there, fighting himself, battling the appetite that had taken hold of him. His hands flexed – no, his *claws*. He howled, and the noise that came from him was desperate, shrieking, completely inhuman.

His wings beat the air as he rose from the terrace, monstrous, but still beautiful, still somehow Nikolai. He looked down at the dark veins coursing over his torso, at the razor-sharp talons that had pushed from his blackened fingertips. He held out his hands as if pleading with me for an answer.

"Nikolai," I cried.

He turned in the air, wrenching himself away, and raced upward, as if he could somehow outpace the need inside him, his black wings carrying him higher as he cut through the *nichevo'ya*. He looked back once, and even from a distance, I felt his anguish and confusion.

Then he was gone, a black speck in the gray sky, while I remained trembling below.

"Eventually," said the Darkling, "he will feed."

I'd warned Nikolai of the Darkling's vengeance, but even I couldn't have foreseen the elegance of this, the perfect cruelty. Nikolai had made a fool of the Darkling, and now the Darkling had taken my polished, brilliant, noble prince and made him into a monster. Death would have been too kind.

A sound came from me, something guttural, animal, a noise I didn't recognise. I raised my hands and brought the Cut blazing down in two furious arcs. They struck the whirring shapes that surrounded the Darkling and I saw some burst apart into nothing, only to have others take their place. I didn't care. I struck him again and again. If I could knock the top off a mountain, surely my power was good for something in this battle.

"Fight me!" I screamed. "Let's end this now! Here!"

"Fight you, Alina? There is no fight to be had." He gestured to the *nichevo'ya*. "Seize them."

They swarmed down from every direction, a seething black mass. Beside me, Mal opened fire. I could smell gunpowder and hear the clink of empty cartridges as bullets hit the ground. I was focusing every bit of power I had, nearly pinwheeling my arms, cutting through five, ten, fifteen shadow soldiers at a time, but it was no good. There were simply too many of them.

Then suddenly they stopped. The *nichevo'ya* hung in the air, bodies limp, wings moving in silent rhythm.

"Did you do that?" Mal asked.

"I—I don't think so . . ."

Silence descended on the terrace. I could hear the wail of the wind, the sounds of the battle raging behind us.

"*Abomination.*"

We turned. Baghra stood inside the doorway, her hand on Misha's shoulder. The boy was shaking, his eyes so wide I could see more white than iris. Behind them, our soldiers were fighting not just *nichevo'ya* but *oprichniki* and the Darkling's own Grisha in their blue and red *kefta*. He'd had his creatures bring them all to the mountaintop.

"Guide me," Baghra told Misha. What courage it must have taken for him to lead her out onto the terrace, past the *nichevo'ya*, who shifted and bumped up against each other, following her passage like a field of glistening black reeds. Only those closest to the Darkling remained moving, clinging to their master, their wings beating in unison.

The Darkling's face was livid. "I should have known I'd find you cloistered with the enemy. Go back inside," he ordered. "My soldiers will not harm you."

Baghra ignored him. When they reached the end of the terrace, Misha placed her hand on the lip of the remaining wall. She leaned against it, releasing an almost contented sigh, and gave Misha a nudge with her stick. "Go on, boy, run to the scrawny little Saint." He hesitated. Baghra reached out and found his cheek, then patted it none too gently. "Go on," she repeated. "I want to talk to my son."

"Misha," Mal said, and the boy bolted over to us, ducking behind Mal's coat. The *nichevo'ya* showed no interest in him. Their attention focused wholly on Baghra.

"What is it you want?" asked the Darkling. "And do not hope to plead for mercy for these fools."

"Only to meet your monsters," she said. Baghra leaned her stick against the wall and held out her arms. The *nichevo'ya* moved forward, rustling and nudging against each other. One nuzzled its head against her palm, as if it were sniffing her. Was it curiosity I sensed in them? Or hunger? "They know me, these children. Like calls to like."

"Stop this," demanded the Darkling.

Baghra's palms began to fill with darkness. The sight was jarring. I'd only ever seen her summon once before. She had hidden her power away as I had once stifled mine, but she had done it for the sake of her son's secrets. I remembered what she'd said about a Grisha turning his power on himself. She shared the Darkling's blood, his power. Would she act against him now?

"I will not fight you," the Darkling said.

"Then strike me down."

"You know I won't."

She smiled then and gave a little chuckle, as if she were pleased with a precocious student. "It's true. That's why I still have hope." Her head snapped to me. "Girl," she said sharply. Her blind eyes were blank, but in that moment, I could have sworn she saw me clearly. "Do not fail me again."

"She isn't strong enough to fight me either, old woman. Take up your stick, and I will return you to the Little Palace."

A terrible suspicion crept into me. Baghra had given me the strength to fight, but she'd never told me to do it. The only thing she'd ever asked of me was to run.

"Baghra—" I began.

"My hut. My fire. That sounds a pleasant thing," she said. "But I find the dark is the same wherever I am."

"You earned those eyes," he said coldly, though I heard the hurt there too.

"I did," she said with a sigh. "And more." Then, without warning, she slammed her hands together. Thunder boomed over the mountain and darkness billowed from her palms like banners unfurling, twisting and curling around the *nichevo'ya*. They shrieked and jittered, whirling in confusion.

"Know that I loved you," she said to the Darkling. "Know that it was not enough."

In a single movement, she shoved herself up on the wall, and before I could draw breath to scream, she tipped forward and vanished over the ledge, trailing the *nichevo'ya* behind her in tangled skeins of darkness. They tumbled past us in a rush, a shrieking black wave that rolled over the terrace and plummeted down, drawn by the power she exuded.

"No!" the Darkling roared. He dove after her, the wings of his soldiers beating with his fury.

"Alina, now!" Through the haze of my horror, I heard Mal's words, felt him pushing me through the door, and suddenly, Mal had Misha in his arms and we were running through the observatory. *Nichevo'ya* streamed past us, pulled towards the terrace by Baghra's trailing skeins. Others simply hovered in confusion as their master drew further away.

Run, Baghra had told me again and again. And now I did.

The heated floor was slippery with melted snow. The massive windows of the Spinning Wheel had been shattered and flurries gusted through the room. I saw fallen bodies, pockets of fighting.

I couldn't seem to think straight. Sergei. Nikolai. Baghra. *Baghra*. Falling through the mists, the rocks rising up to meet her. Would she cry out? Would she close her blind eyes? *Little Saint. Little martyr.*

Tolya was running towards us. I saw two *oprichniki*

come at him, swords drawn. Without breaking stride, he threw out his fists and the soldiers collapsed, clutching their chests, their mouths dripping blood.

"Where are the others?" Mal shouted as we came level with Tolya and pelted for the staircase.

"In the hangar, but they're outnumbered. We need to get down there."

Some of the Darkling's blue-robed Squallers had tried to blockade the stairs. They hurled crates and furniture at us in mighty gusts of wind. I slashed out with the Cut, smashing the crates to kindling before they could reach us, sending the Squallers scattering.

The worst was waiting in the hangar below. All semblance of order had broken down in the panic to get away from the Darkling's soldiers.

People were swarming over the *Pelican* and the *Ibis*. The *Pelican* already hovered above the hangar floor, borne aloft by Squaller current. Soldiers were pulling on its cables, trying to drag it back down and climb aboard, unwilling to wait for the other barge.

Someone gave the order, and the *Pelican* surged free, ploughing through the crowd as it took flight. It rose into the air, trailing screaming men like strange anchors, and disappeared from view.

Zoya, Nadia, and Harshaw were backed against one of the hulls of the *Bittern*, using fire and wind to try to keep back a crowd of Grisha and *oprichniki*.

Tamar was on the deck, and I was relieved to see Nevsky at her side, along with a few other soldiers from the Twenty-Second. But behind them, Adrik lay in a pool of blood. His arm hung from his body at a bizarre angle. His face was white with shock. Genya knelt over him, tears streaming down her face as David stood above her with a rifle, firing down at the attacking crowd with precarious aim. Stigg was nowhere to be seen. Had he fled on the *Pelican* or simply been left behind in the Spinning Wheel?

"Stigg—" I said.

"There's no time," replied Mal.

We shoved through the mob, and at a shouted order from her brother, Tamar slid into place and seized the *Bittern*'s wheel. We lay down cover as Zoya and the other Squallers scrambled on deck. Mal stumbled as a bullet struck his thigh, but Harshaw had hold of him, dragging him aboard.

"Get us moving!" shouted Nevsky. He signalled to the other soldiers, and they arrayed themselves along the hull's railing, opening fire on the Darkling's men. I took a place beside them, sending bright light up against the crowd, blinding them so they couldn't take aim.

Mal and Tolya took their positions at the lines as Zoya filled the sails. But her power wasn't enough.

"Nadia, we need you!" bellowed Tamar.

Nadia looked up from where she'd knelt beside her brother. Her face was streaked with tears, but she rose to her feet, swaying, and forced a draft up into the sails. The *Bittern* started to slide forward on its runners.

"We're too heavy!" Zoya cried.

Nevsky grabbed my shoulder. "Survive," he said roughly. "Help him." Did he know what had happened to Nikolai?

"I will," I vowed. "The other barge—"

He didn't stop to listen. Nevsky shouted, "For the Twenty-Second!" He vaulted over the side, and the other soldiers followed without hesitation. They threw themselves into the mob.

Tamar called the order, and we shot from the hangar. The *Bittern* plunged sickeningly from the ledge, then the sails snapped into place and we were rising.

I looked back and caught one last glimpse of Nevsky, rifle at his shoulder, before he was swallowed by the crowd.

Chapter 12

We bobbed and faltered, the little craft swinging precariously back and forth beneath the sails as Tamar and the crew tried to get control of the *Bittern*. Snow lashed at our faces in stinging gusts, and when the hull nicked the side of a cliff, the whole deck tilted, sending us all scrambling for purchase.

We had no Tidemakers to keep us cloaked in mist, so we could only hope that Baghra had bought us enough time to get clear of the mountains and the Darkling.

Baghra. My eyes skittered over the deck. Misha had tucked himself against the side of the hull, his arms curled over his head. No one could stop to offer comfort.

I knelt beside Adrik and Genya. A *nichevo'ya* had taken a massive bite from Adrik's shoulder, and Genya was trying to stop the bleeding, but she'd never been trained as a Healer. His lips were pale, his skin ice-cold, and as I watched, his eyes began to roll back in his head.

"Tolya!" I shouted, trying not to sound panicked.

Nadia turned, her eyes wide with terror, and the *Bittern* dipped.

"Keep us steady, Nadia," Tamar demanded over the rush of wind. "Tolya, help him!"

Harshaw came up behind Tolya. He had a deep gash in his forearm, but he gripped the ropes and said, "Ready."

I could see Oncat's shape squirming around in his coat.

Tolya's brow was furrowed. Stigg was meant to be with us. Harshaw hadn't been trained to work the lines.

"Just hold her steady," cautioned Harshaw. He looked to where Mal stood braced on the opposite side of the hull, hands tight to the ropes, muscles straining as we were buffeted by snow and wind.

"Do it!" Mal shouted. He was bleeding from the bullet wound in his thigh.

They made the switch. The *Bittern* tilted, then righted itself as Harshaw let out a grunt.

"Got it," he grated through clenched teeth. It wasn't reassuring.

Tolya leapt down to Adrik's side and began working. Nadia was sobbing, but she held the draft steady.

"Can you save the arm?" I asked quietly.

Tolya shook his head once. He was a Heartrender, a warrior, and a killer – not a Healer. "I can't just seal the skin," he said, "or he'll bleed internally. I need to close the arteries. Can you warm him?"

I cast light over Adrik, and his trembling calmed slightly.

We drove onward, sails taut with the force of Grisha wind. Tamar bent to the wheel, coat billowing behind her. I knew when we'd cleared the mountains because the *Bittern* ceased its shaking. The air cut cold against my cheeks as we picked up speed, but I kept Adrik cocooned in sunlight.

Time seemed to slow. Neither of them wanted to say it, but I could see Nadia and Zoya beginning to tire. Mal and Harshaw couldn't be faring well either.

"We need to set down," I said.

"Where are we?" Harshaw asked. His crest of red hair

lay flat on his head, soaked through with snow. I'd thought of him as unpredictable, maybe a little dangerous, but here he was – bloody, tired, and working the lines for hours without complaint.

Tamar consulted her charts. "Just past the permafrost. If we keep heading south, we'll be above more populated areas soon."

"We could try to find woods for cover," panted Nadia.

"We're too near Chernast," Mal replied.

Harshaw adjusted his grip. "Does it matter? If we fly through the day, we're going to be spotted."

"We could go higher," suggested Genya.

Nadia shook her head. "We can try, but the air's thinner up there and we'll use a lot of power on a vertical move."

"Where are we headed, anyway?" asked Zoya.

Without thinking twice, I said, "To the copper mine at Murin. To the firebird."

There was a brief silence. Then Harshaw said what I knew a lot of them had to be thinking. "We could run. Every time we face those monsters, more of us die. We could take this ship anywhere. Kerch. Novyi Zem."

"Like hell," muttered Mal.

"This is my home," said Zoya. "I won't be chased out of it."

"What about Adrik?" Nadia asked, her voice hoarse.

"He lost a lot of blood," said Tolya. "All I can do is keep his heart steady, try to give him time to recover."

"He needs a real Healer."

"If the Darkling finds us, a Healer won't do him any good," said Zoya.

I ran a hand over my eyes, trying to think. Adrik might be stable. Or he might slip more deeply into a coma and never come out of it. And if we set down somewhere and were spotted, we'd all be in for death or worse. The Darkling must know we wouldn't land in Fjerda, deep in enemy territory. He might think we'd flee to West Ravka. He'd send scouts everywhere he could. Would he stop to grieve for his mother? Dashed on the rocks, would there be enough of her left to bury? I looked over my shoulder, sure that at any minute I'd see *nichevo'ya* swooping down on us. I couldn't think about Nikolai. I wouldn't.

"We go to Murin," I said. "We'll figure out the rest from there. I won't force anyone to stay. Zoya, Nadia, can you get us there?" They'd been flagging before, but I needed to believe they had some reserve of strength to call on.

"I know I can," Zoya replied.

Nadia's earnest chin lifted. "Try to keep up."

"We can still be seen," I said. "We need a Tidemaker."

David glanced up from bandaging the powder burns on his hand. "What if you tried bending the light?"

I frowned. "Bend it how?"

"The only reason anyone can see the ship is because light is bouncing off it. Just eliminate the reflection."

"I'm not sure I follow."

"You don't say," said Genya.

"Like a rock in a stream," David explained. "Just bend the light so it never actually hits the ship. There's nothing to see."

"So we'd be invisible?" Genya asked.

"Theoretically."

She yanked off her boot and plunked it down on the deck. "Try it."

I eyed the boot skeptically. I wasn't sure how to begin. This was a completely different way of using my power.

"Just . . . bend the light?"

"Well," said David, "it might help to remember that you don't have to concern yourself with the refractive index. You just need to redirect and synchronise both components of light simultaneously. I mean, you can't just start with the magnetic, that would be ridic—"

I held up a hand. "Let's stick with the rock in the stream."

I concentrated. I didn't summon or hone the light the way I did with the Cut. Instead, I just tried to give it a nudge.

The toe of the boot grew blurry as the air near it seemed to waver.

I tried to think of the light as water, as wind rushing around the leather, parting then slipping back together as if the boot had never been there. I cupped my fingers. The boot flickered and vanished.

Genya whooped. I shrieked and threw my hands in the air. The boot reappeared. I curled my fingers, and it was gone.

"David, have I ever told you you're a genius?"

"Yes."

"I'm telling you again."

Because the ship was larger and in motion, keeping the curve of light around it was more of a challenge. But I only had to worry about the light reflecting off the bottom of the hull, and after a few tries, I felt comfortable keeping the bend steady.

If anyone happened to be standing in a field, peering straight up, they might see something off, a blur or a flash of light – they wouldn't see a winged ship moving through the afternoon sky. At least that was the hope. It reminded me of something I'd once seen the Darkling do when he'd pulled me through a candlelit ballroom, using his power to render us nearly invisible. Yet another trick he'd mastered long before I had.

Genya dug through the provisions and found a stash of *jurda*, the Zemeni stimulant that soldiers sometimes used on long watches. It made me feel jittery and a little nauseated, but there was no other way to keep us on our feet and focused.

It had to be chewed, and soon we were all spitting the rust-coloured juice over the side.

"If this stains my teeth orange—" said Zoya.

"It will," interrupted Genya, "but I promise to put your teeth back whiter than they were before. I may even fix those weird incisors of yours."

"There is nothing wrong with my teeth."

"Not at all," said Genya soothingly. "You're the prettiest walrus I know. I'm just amazed you haven't sawed through your lower lip."

"Keep your hands off me, Tailor," Zoya grumbled, "or I'll poke your other eye out."

By the time dusk came, Zoya didn't have the energy to bicker. She and Nadia were entirely focused on keeping us aloft.

David was able to take over the wheel for brief periods of time so Tamar could see to the wound on Mal's leg. Harshaw, Tolya, and Mal alternated on the lines to give each other a chance to stretch.

Only Nadia and Zoya had no relief as they toiled beneath a crescent moon, though we tried to find ways to help. Genya stood with her back to Nadia's, bracing her so she could rest her knees and feet a bit. Now that the sun had set, we had no need for cover, so for the better part of an hour, I buttressed Zoya's arms while she summoned.

"This is ridiculous," she growled, her muscles shaking beneath my palms.

"Do you want me to let go?"

"If you do, I'll cover you in *jurda* juice."

I was eager to have something to do. The ship was too quiet, and I could feel the day's nightmares waiting to crowd in on me.

Misha hadn't budged from his spot curled into the hull. He was clutching the wooden practice sword that Mal had found for him. My throat tightened as I realised he'd brought it with him on the terrace when Baghra made him escort her to the *nichevo'ya*. I fished a piece of hardtack out of the provisions and took it to him.

"Hungry?" I asked.

He shook his head.

"Will you try to eat something anyway?"

Another head shake.

I sat beside him, unsure what to say. I remembered sitting like this with Sergei in the tank room, searching for words of comfort and failing. Had he been scheming then, manipulating me? His fear had certainly seemed real.

Misha didn't just remind me of Sergei. He was every child whose parents went to war. He was every boy and girl at Keramzin. He was Baghra begging for her father's attention. He was the Darkling learning loneliness at his mother's knee. This was what Ravka did. It made orphans. It made misery. *No land, no life, just a uniform and a gun.* Nikolai had believed in something better.

I took a shaky breath. I had to find a way to shut down my mind. If I thought of Nikolai, I would fall apart. Or Baghra. Or the broken pieces of Sergei's body. Or Stigg, left behind. Or even the Darkling, the look on his face as his mother had disappeared beneath the clouds. How could he be so cruel and still so human?

The night wore on as a sleeping Ravka passed beneath us. I counted stars. I watched over Adrik. I dozed. I moved among the crew, offering sips of water and tufts of dried *jurda* blossoms. When anyone asked about Nikolai or Baghra, I gave them the facts of the battle in the briefest possible terms.

I willed my mind to silence, tried to make it a blank field, white with snow, unmarred by tracks. Some time around sunrise, I took my place at the railing and began shifting the light to camouflage the ship.

That was when Adrik muttered in his sleep.

Nadia's head whipped round. The *Bittern* bobbed.

"Focus!" snapped Zoya.

But she was smiling. We all were, ready to cling to the barest scrap of hope.

We flew through the rest of the day and long into the next night. It was dawn on the second morning when we finally glimpsed the Sikurzoi. At midday, we spotted the deep, jagged crater that marked the abandoned copper mine where Nikolai had suggested we stash the *Bittern*, a murky turquoise pool at its centre.

The descent was slow and tricky, and as soon as the hulls scraped the crater floor, both Nadia and Zoya crumpled to the deck. They had pushed the limits of their power, and though their skin was flushed and glowing, they were completely exhausted.

Tugging on the ropes, the rest of us managed to get the *Bittern* out of sight beneath a ledge of rock. Anyone who climbed down into the mine would find it easily enough, but it was hard to imagine who would bother. The crater floor was littered with rusty machinery. An unpleasant smell came from the stagnant pool, and David said the water's opaque turquoise colour came from minerals leaching out of the rock. There were no signs of squatters.

While Mal and Harshaw secured the sails, Tolya carried Adrik from the *Bittern*. There was blood seeping from the stump where his arm had been, but he was fairly lucid and even drank a few sips of water.

Misha refused to budge from the hull. I tucked a blanket over his shoulders and left him with a piece of hardtack and a slice of dried apple, hoping he would eat.

We helped Zoya and Nadia off the ship, dragged our bedrolls into a nest beneath the shade of the overhang, and, without another word, fell into a troubled sleep. We posted no watch. If we'd been followed, we had no fight left to give.

When I woke, it was late afternoon. Most of the others were still sleeping soundly. Genya was pinning up Adrik's sleeve.

I found Mal coming down the road that led around the side of the crater, carrying a bag full of grouse.

"I thought we'd stay tonight," he said, "make a fire. We can leave for Dva Stolba in the morning."

"All right," I said, though I was eager to get moving.

He must have sensed it because he said, "Adrik could use the rest. We all could. I'm afraid if we keep pushing, one of them will break."

I nodded. He was right. We were all grieving and

frightened and tired. "I'll bring some kindling down."

He touched my arm. "Alina—"

"I won't be long." I pushed past him. I didn't want to talk. I didn't want words of comfort. I wanted the firebird. I wanted to turn my pain into anger and bring it to the Darkling's door.

I made my way up to the woods that surrounded the mine. This far south, the trees were different, taller and more sparse, their bark red and porous. I was on my way back to the mine, my arms full of the driest branches I could find, when I got the eerie feeling I was being watched. I stopped, the hair rising on the back of my neck.

I peered between the sunlit trunks, waiting. The silence was dense, as if every small creature were holding its breath. Then I heard it – a soft rustling. My head jerked up, following the sound into the trees. My eyes fastened on a flicker of movement, the silent beat of a shadowy wing.

Nikolai was perched in the branches of a tree, his dark gaze fastened on me.

His chest was bare and lined in black as if darkness had shattered beneath his skin. He'd lost his boots somewhere, and his bare feet gripped the bark. His toes had become black talons.

He had dried blood on his hands. And near his mouth.

"Nikolai?" I whispered.

He flinched back.

"Nikolai, wait—"

But he leapt into the air, dark wings shaking the branches as he broke through them to the blue sky beyond.

I wanted to scream, so I did. I tossed my kindling to the ground, pressed my fist to my mouth, and screamed until my throat was raw. I couldn't stop. I'd managed not to weep on the *Bittern* or at the mine, but now I sank to the forest floor, my screams turning to sobs, silent, wracking gasps. They hurt, as if they might crack my ribs open, but emerged soundless from my lips. I kept thinking of Nikolai's torn trousers and had the foolish thought that he'd be mortified to see his clothes in such a state. He'd followed us all the way from the Spinning Wheel. Could he tell the Darkling of our whereabouts? Would he? How much of him was left inside that tortured body?

I felt it then, the vibration along that invisible tether. I pushed away from it. I would not go to the Darkling now. I wouldn't go to him ever again. But still, I knew wherever he was, he was grieving.

Mal found me there, head buried in my arms, coat covered in green needles. He offered me his hand, but I ignored it.

"I'm all right," I said, though nothing could have been less true.

"It's getting dark. You shouldn't be out here alone."

"I'm the Sun Summoner. It gets dark when I say it does."

He crouched down in front of me and waited for me to meet his eyes. "Don't shut them out, Alina. They need to grieve with you."

"I don't have anything to say."

"Then let them talk."

I had no solace or encouragement to offer. I didn't want to share this hurt. I didn't want them to see how frightened I was. But I made myself get up and brush the needles from my coat. I let Mal lead me back to the mine.

By the time we got all the way down to the crater floor, it was full dark and the others had lit lanterns beneath the overhang.

"Took your time, didn't you?" said Zoya. "Did we have to freeze while you two frolicked around in the woods?"

There was no point to hiding my tearstained face so I just said, "Turned out I needed a good cry."

I braced myself for an insult. Instead, all she said was, "Next time invite me. I could use one too."

Mal dropped the kindling I'd gathered into the firepit someone had made, and I plucked Oncat from Harshaw's shoulder. She gave a brief hiss, but I didn't care. Right now, I needed to cuddle something soft and furry.

They'd already cleaned and spitted the game Mal had caught, and soon, despite my sadness and worry, the smell of roasting meat had my mouth watering.

We sat around the fire, eating and passing around a flask of *kvas*, watching the flames play over the hull of the *Bittern* as the branches crackled and popped. We had a lot to talk about – who would go with us into the Sikurzoi and who would remain in the valley, whether or not people even wanted to stay. I rubbed my wrist. It helped to focus on the firebird, to think of that instead of the black sheen of Nikolai's eyes, the dark crust of blood near his lips.

Abruptly, Zoya said, "I should have known Sergei couldn't be trusted. He was always a weakling." Though that seemed unfair, I let it pass.

"Oncat never liked him," Harshaw added.

Genya fed a branch to the fire. "Do you think he was planning it all along?"

"I've been wondering that," I admitted. "I thought he'd be better once we got out of the White Cathedral and the tunnels, but he almost seemed worse, more anxious."

"That could have been anything," said Tamar. "Cave-in, militia attack, Tolya's snoring."

Tolya threw a pebble at her and said, "Nikolai's men should have watched him more closely."

Or I should never have let him go. Maybe my guilt over Marie had clouded my judgement. Maybe sorrow was clouding it now and there were more betrayals to come.

"Did the *nichevo'ya* really just . . . tear him apart?" asked Nadia.

I glanced over at Misha. At some point, he'd climbed down from the *Bittern*. Now he was fast asleep beside Mal, still clutching that wooden sword.

"It was horrible," I said softly.

"What about Nikolai?" Zoya asked. "What did the Darkling do to him?"

"I don't know exactly."

"Can it be undone?"

"I don't know that either." I looked to David.

"Maybe," he offered. "I'd need to study him. It's *merzost*. New territory. I wish I had Morozova's journals."

I almost laughed at that. All the time David had been lugging those journals around, I would have gladly thrown them onto a rubbish heap. But now that there was a good reason to want them, they were out of my reach, left behind at the Spinning Wheel.

Capture Nikolai. Put him in a cage. See if we could pull him from the shadow's grasp. The too-clever fox, finally caught. I blinked and looked away. I didn't want to cry again.

Abruptly, Adrik snarled, "I'm glad Sergei's dead. I'm just sorry I didn't get to wring his neck myself."

"You'd need two hands for that," said Zoya.

There was a brief, terrible silence, then Adrik scowled and said, "Okay, *stab* him."

Zoya grinned and passed him the flask. Nadia just shook her head. Sometimes I forgot they were really soldiers. I didn't doubt that Adrik would mourn the loss of his arm. I wasn't even sure how it might impact his ability to summon. But I remembered him standing in front of me at the Little Palace, demanding the right to stay and fight. He was tougher than I'd ever be.

I thought of Botkin, my old teacher, pushing me to run another mile, to take another punch. I remembered the words he'd spoken to me so long ago: *Steel is earned.* Adrik had that steel, and so did Nadia. She'd proven it again in our flight from the Elbjen. A part of me had wondered what Tamar saw in her. But Nadia had been in some of the worst fighting at the Little Palace. She'd lost her best friend and the life she'd always known. Yet she hadn't fallen apart like Sergei or chosen life underground like Maxim. Through all of it, she'd stayed steady.

When Adrik handed the flask back, Zoya took a deep drink and said, "Do you know what Baghra told me at my first lesson with her?" She lowered her voice to imitate Baghra's throaty rasp. "Pretty face. Too bad you have porridge for brains."

Harshaw snorted. "I set fire to her hut in class."

"Of course you did," said Zoya.

"Accidentally! She refused to ever teach me again. Wouldn't even speak to me. I saw her on the grounds once, and she walked right by. Didn't say a word, just whacked me on the knee with her stick. I still have a lump." He yanked up his trouser leg, and sure enough, there was a knob of bone visible beneath the skin.

"That's nothing," Nadia said, her cheeks pinking as we all turned our attention to her. "I had some kind of block where I couldn't summon for a while. She put me in a room and released a hive of bees in it."

"What?" I squeaked. It wasn't just the bees that had shocked me. I'd struggled to summon for months at the Little Palace, and Baghra had never mentioned that other Grisha got blocks.

"What did you do?" Tamar asked incredulously.

"I managed to summon a current to send them up the chimney, but I got stung so many times, I looked like I had firepox."

"I have never been more glad I'm not Grisha," Mal said with a shake of his head.

Zoya lifted her flask. "Let's hear it for the lone *otkazat'sya*."

"Baghra hated me," David said quietly.

Zoya waved dismissively. "We all felt that way."

"No, she really hated me. She taught me once with the rest of the Fabrikators my age, then she refused to ever meet with me again. I used to just stay in the workshops when everyone else had her classes."

"Why?" Harshaw asked, scratching Oncat under the chin.

David shrugged. "No idea."

"I know why," said Genya. I waited, wondering if she really did. "Animal magnetism," she continued. "One more minute in that hut with you, and she would have torn off all your clothes."

David considered this. "That seems improbable."

"Impossible," Mal and I said at the same time.

"Well, not *impossible*," David said, looking vaguely insulted.

Genya laughed and planted a firm kiss on his mouth.

I picked up a stick and gave the fire a poke, sending a gust shooting upward. I knew why Baghra had refused to teach David. He'd reminded her too much of Morozova, so obsessed with knowledge that he'd been blind to his child's suffering, to his wife's neglect. And sure enough, David had created *lumiya* just "for fun," essentially handing the Darkling the means to enter the Fold. But David wasn't like Morozova. He'd been there for Genya when she'd needed him. He was no warrior, but he'd found a way to fight for her.

I looked around at our strange, battered little group, at Adrik with his missing arm, gazing moon-eyed at Zoya; at Harshaw and Tolya, watching as Mal sketched our route in the dirt. I saw Genya grin, her scars pulling taut as David gestured wildly, trying to explain his idea for a brass arm to Nadia, while Nadia ignored him, running her fingers through the dark waves of Tamar's hair.

None of them were easy or soft or simple. They were like me, nursing hurts and hidden wounds, all broken in different ways. We didn't quite fit together. We had edges so jagged we cut each other sometimes, but as I curled up on my side, the warmth of the fire at my back, I felt a rush of gratitude so sweet it made my throat ache. Fear came with it. Keeping them close was a luxury I would pay for. Now I had more to lose.

Chapter 13

In the end, everyone stayed. Even Zoya, though she kept up a steady stream of complaints all the way to Dva Stolba.

We'd agreed to split into two groups. Tamar, Nadia, and Adrik would travel with David, Genya, and Misha. They'd secure lodgings in one of the settlements at the southeast edge of the valley. Genya would have to keep her face hidden, but she didn't seem to mind. She'd wrapped her shawl around her head and declared, "I shall be a woman of mystery." I reminded her not to be *too* intriguing.

Mal and I would travel into the Sikurzoi with Zoya, Harshaw, and Tolya. Because we were so close to the border, we knew we might be facing an increased military presence, but we hoped we could blend in with the refugees trying to get through the Sikurzoi before the first snows came.

If we weren't back from the mountains in two weeks, Tamar would meet with any forces the Apparat might send to Caryeva. I didn't like the idea of sending her and Nadia alone, but Mal and I couldn't cut our group down any further. Shu raiders were known to pick off Ravkan travellers near the border, and we wanted to be prepared for trouble. Tamar at least knew the Soldat Sol, and I tried to reassure myself that she and Nadia were both experienced fighters.

I also wasn't sure what I'd do with any soldiers who did show up, but the message had been sent, and I had to believe that we'd figure out something. Maybe by then I'd have the firebird and the beginnings of a plan. I couldn't think too far ahead. Every time I did, I felt panic tugging at me. It was like being underground again, no air to breathe, waiting for the world to come down around me.

Our team left at sunrise, leaving the others sleeping in the shade of the overhang. Only Misha was awake, watching us with accusatory eyes as he pelted the side of the *Bittern* with pebbles.

"Come here," Mal said, waving him over. I thought Misha might not budge, but then he shuffled to us, his chin jutting out in a sulk. "Do you have the pin Alina gave you?"

Misha nodded once.

"You know what that means, don't you? You're a soldier. Soldiers don't get to go where they want to. They go where they're needed."

"You just don't want me with you."

"No, we need you here to take care of the others. You know David is hopeless, and Adrik is going to need help too, even if he doesn't want to admit it. You'll have to be careful with that one, help him without letting him know you're helping. Can you manage that?"

Misha shrugged.

"We need you to take care of them the way you took care of Baghra."

"But I didn't take care of her."

"Yes you did. You watched over her, and you made her comfortable, and you let her go when she needed you to. You did what had to be done, even though it hurt you. That's what soldiers do."

Misha looked at him sharply, as if considering this. "I should have stopped her," he said, his voice breaking.

"If you had, none of us would be here. We're grateful that you did the hard thing."

Misha frowned. "David *is* kind of a mess."

"True," Mal agreed. "So can we trust you?"

Misha looked away. His expression was still troubled, but he shrugged again.

"Thank you," Mal said. "You can start by getting water boiling for breakfast."

Misha nodded once, then jogged back through the gravel to get the water on.

Mal glanced at me as he rose and shouldered his pack. "What?"

"Nothing. That was just . . . really well done."

"Same way Ana Kuya got me to stop begging her to keep a lantern lit at night."

"Really?"

"Yes," he said starting the climb. "Told me I had to be brave for you, that if I was scared, you'd be scared."

"Well, she told me I had to eat my parsnips to set a good example for you, but I still refused to do it."

"And you wonder why you were always getting the switch."

"I have principles."

"That means, 'If I can be difficult, I will.'"

"Unfair."

"Hey!" Zoya shouted over the edge of the crater above. "If you're not up here before I count to ten, I'm going back to sleep and you can carry me to Dva Stolba."

"Mal," I sighed. "If I murder her in the Sikurzoi, will you hold me accountable?"

"Yes," he said. Then added, "That means, 'Let's make it look like an accident.'"

Dva Stolba took me by surprise. I'd somehow expected that the little valley would be like a graveyard, a grim wasteland of phantoms and abandoned places. Instead, the settlements were bustling. The landscape was dotted with burned-out hulks and empty fields of ash, but new homes and businesses had sprung up right beside them.

There were taverns and hostelries, a storefront advertising watch repair, and what looked like a shop that lent books by the week. Everything felt oddly impermanent. Broken windows had simply been boarded over. Many of the houses had canvas roofs or holes in the walls that had been covered with wool blankets or woven mats. *Who knows how long we'll be here?* they seemed to say. *Let's make do with what we have.*

Had it always been this way? The settlements were constantly being destroyed and rebuilt, governed by the Shu Han or Ravka, depending on how the borders had been drawn at the end of a particular war. Was this how my parents had lived? It was strange to picture them this way, but I didn't mind the idea. They might have been soldiers or merchants. They might have been happy here. And maybe one of them had been harbouring a power, the latent legacy of Morozova's youngest daughter. There were legends of Sun Summoners before me. Most people thought they were hoaxes or empty stories, wishful thinking born of the misery wrought by the Fold. But there might be more to it than that. Or maybe I was clinging to some dream of a heritage I had no real claim to.

We passed through a market square crowded with people, their wares displayed on makeshift tables: tin pans, hunting knives, furs for the trek over the mountains. We saw jars of goose fat, dried figs sold in bunches, fine saddles, and flimsy-looking guns. Strings of freshly plucked ducks, their skin pink and dimpled, hung above one stall. Mal kept his bow and repeating rifle bundled in his pack. The weapons were too finely made not to draw attention.

Children played in the dirt. A squat man in a sleeveless vest was smoking some kind of meat in a big metal drum. I watched him toss a juniper branch inside it, sending up a fragrant, bluish cloud. Zoya scrunched up her nose. Tolya and Harshaw couldn't dig out their coins fast enough.

This was where Mal's family and mine had met death. Somehow the wild, cheerful atmosphere seemed almost unfair. It certainly didn't match my mood.

I was relieved when Mal said, "I thought it would be more grim."

"Did you see how small the graveyard was?" I asked under my breath. He nodded. In most of Ravka, the cemeteries were bigger than the towns, but when the Shu had burned these settlements, there had been no one left to mourn the dead.

Though we'd been well provisioned from the stocks at the Spinning Wheel, Mal wanted to buy a map made by a local. We needed to know which trails might be blocked by landslides or where the bridges had been washed out.

A woman with white braids peeking from beneath her orange wool hat sat on a low, painted stool, humming to herself and beating a cowbell to catch the attention of passersby. She hadn't bothered with a table, but had laid a rug displaying her stock – canteens, saddlebags, maps, and stacks of metal prayer rings – directly on the ground. A mule stood behind her, its long ears twitching off flies, and occasionally, she would reach back and offer it a pat on the nose.

"Snow's coming soon," she said, squinting up at the sky as we poked through the maps. "Need blankets for the journey?"

"We're set," I said. "Thank you."

"Lot of people headed over the border."

"But not you?"

"Too old to go now. Shu, Fjerdans, Fold . . ." She shrugged. "You sit still, trouble passes you by."

Or it smacks right into you, then comes back for seconds, I thought bleakly.

Mal held up one of the maps. "I'm not seeing the eastern mountains, only the west."

"Better off keeping west," she said. "You trying for the coast?"

"Yes," Mal lied smoothly, "then on to Novyi Zem. But—"

"Stay west. People don't come back from the east."

"*Ju weh*," said Tolya. "*Ey ye bat e'yuan.*"

The woman answered back, and they looked over a map together, conversing in Shu while we waited patiently.

Finally, Tolya handed a different map to Mal. "East," he said.

The woman jabbed her cowbell at Tolya and asked me, "What are you going to feed that one in the hills? Better make sure he doesn't put *you* on a spit."

Tolya frowned, but the woman laughed so hard she nearly fell off her stool.

232

Mal added some prayer rings to the maps and gave over his coins.

"Had a brother who went to Novyi Zem," the woman said, still chuckling as she returned Mal's change. "Probably rich now. It's a good place to start a new life."

Zoya snorted. "Compared to what?"

"It's really not bad," said Tolya.

"Dirt and more dirt."

"There *are* cities," Tolya grumbled as we walked away.

"What did that woman have to say about the eastern mountains?" I asked.

"They're sacred," said Tolya, "and apparently haunted. She claims the Cera Huo is guarded by ghosts."

A shiver ran up my spine. "What's the Cera Huo?"

Tolya's golden eyes glinted. "The Firefalls."

I didn't even notice the ruins until we were almost directly beneath them. They were that nondescript – two worn and weather-beaten spires of rock that flanked the road leading south-east out of the valley. They might have once been an arch. Or an aqueduct. Or two mills, as their name indicated. Or just two pointy bits of rock. What had I expected? Ilya Morozova by the side of the road in a golden halo, holding up a sign that read, "You were right, Alina. This way to the firebird"?

But the angles seemed correct. I'd scrutinised the illustration of Sankt Ilya in Chains so often that the image was branded in my mind. The view of the Sikurzoi beyond the spindles matched up to my memory of the page. Had Morozova drawn it himself? Was he responsible for the map left behind in that illustration or had someone else pieced together his story? I might never know.

This is the place, I told myself. *It has to be.*

"Anything familiar?" I asked Mal.

He shook his head. "I guess I hoped . . ." He shrugged. He didn't have to say more than that. I'd been carrying the same hope lodged in my heart, that once I was on this road, in this valley, more of my past might suddenly become clear. Instead, all I had was my same worn set of memories: a dish of beets, a broad pair of shoulders, the sway of ox tails ahead of me.

We spotted a few refugees – a woman with a baby at her breast riding in a pony cart while her husband walked alongside, a group of people our age who I assumed were First Army deserters. But the road beneath the ruins was not crowded. The most popular places to try to enter the Shu Han were further west, where the mountains were less steep and travel to the coast was easier.

The beauty of the Sikurzoi came on me suddenly. The only mountains I'd known were the icy peaks of the far north and the Petrazoi – jagged, grey, and forbidding. These mountains were gentle, rolling, their soft slopes covered in tall grasses, the valleys between them crossed with slow-moving rivers that flashed blue and then gold in the sun. Even the sky felt welcoming, a prairie of infinite blue, thick white clouds stacked heavy on the horizon, the snowcapped peaks of the southern range visible in the distance.

I knew this was no-man's-land, the dangerous boundary that marked the end of Ravka and the beginning of enemy territory, but it didn't feel that way. There was ample water, space for grazing. If there hadn't been a war, if the lines had somehow been drawn differently, this would have been a peaceful place.

We made no fire and camped in the open that night, our bedrolls spread beneath the stars. I listened to the sigh of the wind in the grasses and thought of Nikolai. Was he out there, tracking us as we tracked the firebird? Would he know us? Or had he lost himself completely? Would a day come when we'd simply be prey to him? I peered into the sky, waiting to see a winged shape blotting out the stars. Sleep did not come easily.

The next day, we left the main road and started to climb in earnest. Mal took us east, towards the Cera Huo, following a trail that seemed to appear and disappear as it wended through the mountains. Storms arrived without warning, dense bursts of rain that turned the earth beneath our boots to sucking mud, then vanished as quickly as they'd arrived.

Tolya worried about flash floods, so we left the trail completely and headed for higher ground, spending the rest of the afternoon on the narrow back of a rocky ridge where we could see storm clouds chasing each other over the low hills and valleys, their dark swells glinting with brief flashes of lightning.

The days dragged on, and I was acutely conscious that every step we took deeper into the Shu Han was a step we would have to retrace back to Ravka. What would we find when we returned? Would the Darkling have already marched on West Ravka? And if we found the firebird, if the three amplifiers were brought together at last, would I be strong enough to face him? Mostly, I thought of Morozova and wondered if he'd once walked these same paths, gazed on these same mountains. Had his need to finish the task he'd begun driven him the way my desperation drove me now, forcing me to put one foot in front of the other, to take another step, ford another river, climb another hill?

That night, the temperature dropped enough that we had to set up tents. Zoya seemed to think I should be the one to put ours together, even if we were both going to sleep in it. I was cursing over the pile of canvas when Mal hushed me.

"Someone's out there," he said.

We were in a wide field of feather grass that stretched between two low hills. I peered into the dusk, unable to make anything out, and lifted my hands questioningly.

Mal gave a shake of his head. "As a last resort," he whispered.

I nodded. I didn't want us in another situation like the one we'd had with the militia.

Mal picked up his rifle and signalled. Tolya drew his sword, and we formed up, back to back, waiting. "Harshaw," I whispered.

I heard Harshaw's flint being struck. He stepped forward and spread his arms. A blazing gout of fire roared to life. It swept around us in a shining ring, illuminating the faces of the men crouched low in the field beyond. There were five, maybe six of them, golden-eyed and dressed in shearling. I saw bows drawn and the glint of light off at least one gun barrel.

"Now," I said.

Zoya and Harshaw moved as one, throwing their arms out in wide arcs, the flames flaring across the grass like a living thing, borne by their combined power.

Men shouted. The fire licked out in hungry tongues. I heard a single shot of gunfire, and the thieves turned and ran. Harshaw and Zoya sent the fire after them, chasing them across the field.

"They might come back," said Tolya. "Bring more men. You get good money for Grisha in Koba." It was a city just south of the border.

For the first time, I thought about what it must have been like for Tolya and Tamar, never able to return to their father's country, strangers in Ravka, strangers here too.

Zoya shivered. "They aren't any better in Fjerda. There are witchhunters who don't eat animals, won't wear leather shoes or kill a spider in their homes, but they'll burn Grisha alive on the pyre."

"Shu doctors might not be so bad," said Harshaw. He was still playing with the flames, sending them shooting up in loops and snaking tendrils. "At least they clean their instruments. On the Wandering Isle, they think Grisha blood is a cure-all – for impotence, wasting plague, you name it. When my brother's power showed itself, they cut his throat and hung him upside down to drain like a pig in a slaughterhouse."

"Saints, Harshaw," Zoya gasped.

"I burned that village and everyone in it to the ground. Then I got on a boat and never looked back."

I thought of the dream the Darkling had once had, that we might be Ravkans and not just Grisha. He'd tried to make a safe place for our kind, maybe the only one in the world. *I understand the desire to remain free.*

Was that why Harshaw kept fighting? Why he'd chosen to stay? He must have shared the Darkling's dream once. Had he given its care over to me?

"We'll keep a watch tonight," Mal said, "and head further east tomorrow."

East to the Cera Huo, where phantoms stood guard. But we were already travelling with ghosts of our own.

There was no evidence of the thieves the next morning, only a field scorched in bizarre patterns.

Mal took us further into the mountains. Early in our journey, we'd seen the curling smoke of someone's cookfire or the shape of a hut on a hillside. Now we were alone, our only company the lizards we saw sunning themselves on rocks and, once, a herd of elk grazing in a distant meadow.

If there were signs of the firebird, they were invisible to me, but I recognised the silence in Mal, the deep intent. I'd seen it in Tsibeya when we were hunting the stag and then again on the waters of the Bone Road.

According to Tolya, the Cera Huo was marked differently on every map, and we certainly had no way of knowing if that was where we'd find the firebird. But it had given Mal a direction and now he moved in that steady, reassuring way of his, as if everything in the wild world was already familiar to him, as if he knew all of its secrets. For the others, it became a kind of game, trying to predict which way he would take us.

"What do you see?" Harshaw asked in frustration when Mal turned us away from an easy trail.

Mal shrugged. "It's more what I don't see." He pointed up to where a flock of geese were tacking south in a sharp wedge. "It's the way the birds move, the way the animals hide in the underbrush."

Harshaw scratched Oncat behind the ear and whispered loudly, "And people say *I'm* crazy."

As the days passed, I felt my patience fraying. We had too much time walking with nothing to do except think, and there was no safe place for my thoughts to wander. The past was full of horrors, and the future left me with that breathless, rising panic. The power inside me had once seemed so miraculous, but each confrontation with the Darkling drove home the limitations of my abilities. *There is no fight to be had.* Despite the death I'd seen and the desperation I felt, I was no closer to understanding or wielding *merzost*. I found myself resenting Mal's calm, the surety he seemed to carry in his steps.

"Do you think it's out there?" I asked one afternoon when we'd taken shelter in a dense cluster of pines to wait out a storm.

"Hard to say. Right now, I could just be tracking a big hawk. I'm going on my gut as much as anything, and that always makes me nervous."

"You don't seem nervous. You seem completely at ease." I could hear the irritation in my voice.

Mal glanced at me. "It helps that no one's threatening to cut you open."

I said nothing. The thought of the Darkling's knife was almost comforting – a simple fear, concrete, manageable.

He squinted out at the rain. "And it's something else, something the Darkling said in the chapel. He thought he needed me to find the firebird. As much as I hate to admit it, that's why I know I can do it now, because he was so sure."

I understood. The Darkling's faith in me had been an intoxicating thing. I wanted that certainty, the knowledge that everything would be dealt with, that someone was in control. Sergei had run to the Darkling looking for that reassurance. *I just want to feel safe again.*

"When the time comes," Mal asked, "can you bring the firebird down?"

Yes. I'd had enough of hesitation. It wasn't just that we'd run out of options, or that so much was riding on the firebird's power. I'd simply grown ruthless enough or selfish enough to take another creature's life. But I missed the girl who had shown the stag mercy, who had been strong enough to turn away from the lure of power, who had believed in something more. Another casualty of this war.

"It still doesn't seem real to me," I said. "And even if it is, it may not be enough. The Darkling has an army. He has allies. We have . . ." A band of misfits? Some tattooed zealots? Even with the power of the amplifiers, it seemed a mismatched battle.

"Thanks," Zoya said sourly.

"She has a point," said Harshaw, propped against a tree. He had Oncat perched on his shoulder and was sending little flames dancing through the air. "I'm not really feeling up for much."

"I didn't mean that," I protested.

"It'll be enough," said Mal. "We'll find the firebird. You'll face the Darkling. We'll fight him, and we'll win."

"And then what?" I felt panic press in on me again. "Even if we beat the Darkling and I destroy the Fold, Ravka will be vulnerable." No Lantsov prince to lead. No Darkling. Just a scrawny orphan from Keramzin with whatever force I might piece together from the Grisha who survived and the remnants of the First Army.

"There's the Apparat," said Tolya. "The priest may not be trustworthy, but your followers are."

"And David thought he might be able to heal Nikolai," Zoya put in.

I turned on her, my anger rising. "Do you think Fjerda will wait for us to find a cure? How about the Shu?"

"Then you'll make a new alliance," said Mal.

"Sell my power to the highest bidder?"

"You negotiate. Set your own terms."

"Hash out a marriage contract, pick a Fjerdan noble or a Shu general? Hope my new husband doesn't murder me in my sleep?"

"Alina—"

"And where will you go?"

"I'll stay by your side as long as you let me."

"Noble Mal. Will you stand guard outside our bedchamber at night?" I knew I was being unfair, but in that moment I didn't care.

His jaw set. "I'll do what I have to do to keep you safe."

"Keep your head down. Do your duty."

"Yes."

"One foot in front of the other. Onward to the firebird. Keep marching like a good soldier."

"That's right, Alina. I'm a soldier." I thought he might finally crack and give me the fight I wanted, that I was itching for. Instead, he stood and shook the water from his coat. "And I'll keep marching because the firebird is all I can give you. No money. No army. No mountaintop stronghold." He shouldered his pack. "This is all I have to offer. The same old trick." He stepped out into the rain. I didn't know if I wanted to run after him to apologise or knock him into the mud.

Zoya lifted one elegant shoulder. "I'd rather have the emerald."

I stared at her, then shook my head and released something between a laugh and a sigh. My anger went out of me, leaving me feeling petty and embarrassed. Mal hadn't deserved that. None of them had.

"Sorry," I mumbled.

"Maybe you're hungry," said Zoya. "I always get mean when I'm hungry."

"Are you hungry all the time?" asked Harshaw.

"You haven't seen me mean. When you do, you'll require a very big hanky."

He snorted. "To dry my tears?"

"To staunch the bleeding."

This time my laugh was real. Somehow a little of Zoya's poison was exactly what I needed. Then, despite all my better judgement, I asked the question I'd wanted to ask for nearly a year. "You and Mal, back in Kribirsk—"

"It happened."

I knew that and I knew there had been plenty of others before her, but it still stung. Zoya glanced at me, her long black lashes sparkling with rain. "But never since," she said grudgingly, "and it hasn't been for lack of trying. If a man can say no to me, that's something."

I rolled my eyes. Zoya poked me in the arm with one long finger. "He hasn't been with anyone, you idiot. Do you know what the girls back at the White Cathedral called him? *Beznako.*"

A lost cause.

"It's funny," Zoya said contemplatively. "I understand why the Darkling and Nikolai want your power. But Mal looks at you like you're . . . well, like you're me."

"No he doesn't," said Tolya. "He watches her the way Harshaw watches fire. Like he'll never have enough of her.

Like he's trying to capture what he can before she's gone."

Zoya and I gaped at him. Then she scowled. "You know, if you turned a bit of that poetry on me, I might consider giving you a chance."

"Who says I want one?"

"I want one!" called Harshaw.

Zoya blew a damp curl from her forehead. "Oncat has a better chance than you."

Harshaw held the little tabby above him. "Why, Oncat," he said. "You rogue."

As we closed in on the area where the Cera Huo was rumoured to be, our pace quickened. Mal grew even quieter, his blue eyes moving constantly over the hills. I owed him an apology, but I never seemed to find the right moment to speak to him.

Almost exactly a week into the journey, we came across what we thought was a dry creek bed that ran between two steep rock walls. We'd been following it for nearly ten minutes when Mal knelt and ran his hand through the grass.

"Harshaw," he said, "can you burn some of this scrub away?"

Harshaw struck his flint and sent a low blanket of blue flame rolling over the creek bed, revealing a pattern of stones too regular to be anything but manmade. "It's a road," he said in surprise.

"Here?" I asked. We'd passed nothing except empty mountains for miles.

We stayed alert, searching for signs of what might have

come before, hoping to see etched symbols, maybe the little altars we'd seen carved into the rock closer to Dva Stolba, eager for some kind of proof that we were on the right path. But the only lesson in the stones seemed to be that cities rose and fell and were forgotten. *You live in a single moment. I live in a thousand.* I might live long enough to see Os Alta turn to dust. Or maybe I'd turn my power back on myself and end it all before then. What would life be like when the people I loved were gone? When there were no mysteries left?

We followed the road to where it just seemed to end, buried in a slump of fallen rock covered in grass and yellow wildflowers. We scrambled over it, and when we reached the top, a sliver of ice crept into my bones.

It was as if the colour had been leached out of the landscape. The field before us was grey grass. A black ridge stretched along the horizon, covered in trees, their bark smooth and glossy as polished slate, their angular branches free of leaves. But the eerie thing was the way they grew, in perfect, regular lines, equidistant, as if they had each been planted with infinite care.

"That looks wrong," said Harshaw.

"They're soldier trees," said Mal. "It's just the way they grow, like they're keeping ranks."

"That's not the only reason," said Tolya. "This is the ashwood. The gateway to the Cera Huo."

Mal took out his map. "I don't see it."

"It's a story. There was a massacre here."

"A battle?" I asked.

"No. A Shu battalion was brought here by their enemies. They were prisoners of war."

"Which enemies?" asked Harshaw.

Tolya shrugged. "Ravkan, Fjerdan, maybe other Shu. This was old days."

"What happened to them?"

"They starved, and when the hunger became too great, they turned on each other. It's said the last man standing planted a tree for each of his fallen brethren. And now they wait for travellers to pass too close to their branches, so they can claim a final meal."

"Lovely," grumbled Zoya. "Remind me to never ask you for a bedtime story."

"It's just a legend," Mal said. "I've seen those trees near Balakirev."

"Growing like that?" Harshaw asked.

"Not . . . exactly."

I eyed the shadows in the grove. The trees did look like a regiment marching towards us. I'd heard similar stories about the woods near Duva, that in the long winters, the trees would snatch up girls to eat. *Superstition*, I told myself. Still, I didn't want to take another step towards that hillside.

"Look!" said Harshaw.

I followed his gaze. There, amid the deep shadows of the trees, something white was moving, a fluttering shape that rose and fell, slipping between the branches.

"There's another," I gasped, pointing to where a whorl of white shimmered, then disappeared into nothing.

"It can't be," said Mal.

Another shape appeared between the trees, then another.

"I do not like this," said Harshaw. "I do not like this *at all*."

"Oh, for Saints' sake," sneered Zoya. "You really are peasants."

She lifted her hands, and a massive gust of wind tore up the mountain. The white shapes seemed to retreat. Then Zoya hooked her arms, and they rushed at us in a moaning white cloud.

"Zoya—"

"Relax," she said.

I threw up my arms to ward off whatever horrible thing Zoya had brought down on us. The cloud exploded. It burst into harmless flakes that drifted to the ground around us.

"Ash?" I reached out to catch some of it on my fingers. It was fine and white, the colour of chalk.

"It's just some kind of weather phenomenon," Zoya said, sending the ashes rising again in lazy spirals. We looked back up the hill. The white clouds continued to move in shifts and gusts, but now that we knew what they were, they seemed slightly less sinister. "You didn't really think they were ghosts, did you?"

I blushed and Tolya cleared his throat. Zoya rolled her eyes and strode towards the hill. "I am surrounded by fools."

"They looked spooky," Mal said to me with a shrug.

"They still do," I muttered.

All the way up the rise, weird little blasts of wind struck us, hot and then cold. No matter what Zoya said, the grove was an eerie place. I steered clear of the trees' grasping branches and tried to ignore the goosebumps puckering my arms. Every time a white whorl rose up near us, I jumped and Oncat hissed from Harshaw's shoulder.

When we finally crested the hill, we saw that the trees marched all the way into the valley, though here their branches were lush with purple leaves, their ranks spreading over the landscape below like the folds of a

Fabrikator's robe. But that wasn't what stopped us in our tracks.

Ahead of us stood a towering cliff. It looked less a part of the mountains than the wall of a giant's stronghold. It was dark and massive, nearly flat at the top, the rock the heavy gray of iron. A tangle of dead trees had been blown against its base. The cliff was split down the middle by a roaring waterfall that fed a pool so clear we could see the rocks at the bottom. The lake stretched almost the length of the valley, surrounded by blooming soldier trees, then seemed to disappear belowground.

We made our way down to the valley floor, stepping around and over little pools and rivulets, the thunder of the falls filling our ears. When we reached the largest pool, we stopped to fill our canteens and rinse our faces in the water.

"Is this it?" Zoya asked. "The Cera Huo?"

Setting Oncat aside, Harshaw dunked his head in the water. "Must be," he said. "What's next?"

"Up, I think," said Mal.

Tolya eyed the slick expanse of the cliff wall. The rock was wet with mist from the falls. "We'll have to go round. There's no way of scaling the face."

"In the morning," Mal replied. "Too dangerous to climb in this terrain at night."

Harshaw tilted his head to one side. "We might want to camp a little further off."

"Why?" asked Zoya. "I'm tired."

"Oncat objects to the landscaping."

"That tabby can sleep at the bottom of the pool for all I care," she snapped.

Harshaw just pointed towards the tangle of dead trees

crowded around the bottom of the cliff. They weren't trees at all. They were piles of bones.

"Saints," Zoya said, backing away. "Are those animal or human?"

Harshaw hitched his thumb over his shoulder. "I saw a very welcoming bunch of boulders back that way."

"Let's go there," said Zoya. "*Now*."

We hurried from the falls, picking our way through the soldier trees and up the valley walls.

"Maybe the ash is volcanic," I said hopefully. My imagination was getting the best of me, and I was suddenly sure that I had the ancient remains of burnt men in my hair.

"Could be," said Harshaw. "There might be volcanic activity near here. Maybe that's why they're called the Firefalls."

"No," said Tolya. "That's why."

I looked back over my shoulder to the valley below. In the light of the setting sun, the falls had gone molten gold. It must have been a trick of the mist or the angle, but it was as if the very water had caught fire. The sun sank lower, setting every pool alight, turning the valley into a crucible.

"Incredible," Harshaw groaned. Mal and I exchanged a glance. We'd be lucky if he didn't try to throw himself in.

Zoya dumped her pack on the ground and slumped down on it. "You can keep your damn scenery. All I want is a warm bed and a glass of wine."

Tolya frowned. "This is a holy place."

"Great," she retorted sourly. "See if you can pray me up a dry pair of socks."

Chapter 14

At dawn the next morning, while the others damped the fire and gnawed at pieces of hardtack, I drew on my coat and walked back a little way to look at the falls. The mist was dense in the valley. From here, the bones at the base of the falls just looked like trees. No ghosts. No fire. It felt like a quiet place, somewhere to rest.

We were packing up the ash-covered tents when we heard it – a cry, high and piercing, echoing through the dawn. We halted, silent, waiting to see if it would sound again.

"Could just be a hawk," warned Tolya.

Mal said nothing. He slung his rifle over his shoulder and plunged into the woods. We had to scurry to keep pace with him.

The climb up the back of the falls took us the better part of the day. It was steep and brutal, and though my feet had toughened and my legs were used to hard travel, I still felt the strain of it. My muscles ached beneath my pack, and despite the chill in the air, sweat beaded on my forehead.

"When we catch this thing," panted Zoya, "I'm going to turn it into a stew."

I could feel the excitement rippling through all of us, the sense that we were close now, and we drove each other to push harder up the mountain. In some places, the rise was nearly vertical. We had to pull ourselves higher by grabbing tight to the roots of scraggly trees or wedging our fingers into the rock. At one point, Tolya brought out iron spikes and hammered them directly into the mountain so we could use them as a makeshift ladder.

Finally, late in the afternoon, we hauled our bodies over a ragged stone lip and found ourselves on the flat top of the cliff wall, a smooth expanse of rock and moss, slick with mist and split by the frothing tide of the river.

Looking north, beyond the abrupt drop of the falls, we could see back the way we'd come – the far ridge of the valley, the grey field that led to the ashwood, the indentation of the old road, and beyond it, storms moving over the grass-covered foothills. And they were just foothills. That was clear now. Because if we turned south, we had our first real view of the mountains, the vast, white-capped Sikurzoi, the source of the snowmelt that fed the Cera Huo.

"They just go on and on," said Harshaw wearily.

We made our way to the side of the rapids. It would be tricky fording them, and I wasn't sure there was a point. We could see across to the other side, where the cliff simply ended. There was nothing there. The plateau was clearly and disappointingly empty.

The wind picked up, whipping through my hair and sending a fine mist stinging against my cheek. I glanced south at the white mountains. Autumn was here and winter was on its way. We'd been gone over a week. What if something had happened to the others back in Dva Stolba?

"Well," said Zoya angrily, "where is it?"

Mal walked to the edge of the falls and looked out at the valley.

"I thought you were supposed to be the best tracker in all of Ravka," she said. "Just where do we go now?"

Mal rubbed a hand over the back of his neck. "Down one mountain, up the next. That's the way it works, Zoya."

"For how long?" she said. "We can't just keep on this way."

"Zoya," Tolya cautioned.

"How do we even know this thing exists?"

"What were you expecting?" asked Tolya. "A nest?"

"Why not? A nest, a feather, a steaming pile of dung. Something. *Anything.*"

Zoya was the one saying it, though I sensed the fatigue and disappointment in the others. Tolya would keep going until he collapsed. I wasn't sure Harshaw and Zoya could take much more.

"It's too wet to make camp here," I said. I pointed towards the woods behind the plateau where the trees were reassuringly ordinary, their leaves lit with red and gold. "Head that way until you find a dry spot. Make a fire. We'll figure out what to do after dinner. Maybe it's time to split up."

"You can't go further into the Shu Han without protection," Tolya objected.

Harshaw said nothing, just nuzzled Oncat and failed to meet my eyes.

"We don't have to decide right now. Just go and make camp."

Carefully, I crossed to the edge of the plateau to join Mal. The drop was dizzying, so I looked into the distance instead. If I squinted, I thought I could just make out the burned field where we'd chased off the thieves, but it might have been imagination.

"I'm sorry," he said at last.

"Don't apologise. For all we know, there is no firebird."

"You don't believe that."

"No, but maybe we weren't meant to find it."

"You don't believe that either." He sighed. "So much for the good soldier."

I winced. "I shouldn't have said that."

"You once put goose droppings in my shoes, Alina. A bad mood I can handle." He glanced at me and said, "We all know the burden you're carrying. You don't have to bear it alone."

I shook my head. "You don't understand. You can't."

"Maybe not. But I saw this with soldiers in my unit. You keep storing up all that anger and grief. Eventually it spills over. Or you drown in it."

He'd been telling me the same thing when we'd first arrived at the mine, when he'd said the others needed to grieve with me. I'd needed it too, even if I hadn't wanted to admit it. I'd needed to not be alone. And he was right. I did feel as if I was drowning, fear closing in over me like an icy sea.

"It's not that easy," I said. "I'm not like them. I'm not like anyone." I hesitated then added, "Except him."

"You're nothing like the Darkling."

"I am, even if you don't want to see it."

Mal raised a brow. "Because he's powerful and dangerous and eternal?" He gave a rueful laugh. "Tell me something. Would the Darkling ever have forgiven Genya? Or Tolya and Tamar? Or Zoya? Or me?"

"It's different for us," I said. "Harder to trust."

"I have news for you, Alina. That's tough for everyone."

"You don't—"

"I know, I know. I don't get it. I just know there's no way to live without pain – no matter how long or short your life is. People let you down. You get hurt and do damage in return. But what the Darkling did to Genya? To Baghra? What he tried to do to you with that collar? That's weakness. That's a man afraid." He peered out at the valley. "I may never be able to understand what it is to live with your power, but I know you're better than that. And they all know it too," he said with a nod back to where the others had gone to make camp. "That's why we're here, fighting beside you. That's why Zoya and Harshaw will whine all night, but tomorrow they'll stay."

"Think so?"

He nodded. "We'll eat, we'll sleep, and then we see what happens next."

I sighed. "Just keep going."

He laid a hand on my shoulder. "You move forward, and when you falter, you get up. And when you can't, you let us carry you. You let me carry you." He dropped his hand. "Don't stay out here too long," he said, then turned and strode back over the plateau.

I won't fail you again.

The night before Mal and I had first entered the Fold, he'd promised that we would survive. *We're going to be fine*, he'd told me. *We always are.* In the year since, we'd been tortured and terrorised, broken and rebuilt. We would probably never feel fine again, but I'd needed that lie then, and I needed it now. It kept us standing, kept us fighting another day. It was what we'd been doing our whole lives.

The sun was just starting to set. I stood at the edge of the falls, listening to the rush of the water. As the sun dipped, the falls caught fire, and I watched the pools in the valley turn gold. I leaned over the drop, glimpsing the pile of bones below. Whatever Mal had been hunting, it was big. I peered into the mist rising off the rocks at the base of the falls. The way it billowed and shifted, it almost looked as though it was alive, as if—

Something came rushing up at me. I stumbled backwards and hit the ground with a jarring thud to my tailbone. A cry cut through the silence.

My eyes searched the sky. A huge winged shape soared above me in a widening arc.

"Mal!" I shouted. My pack was at the edge of the plateau, along with my rifle and bow. I made a dash for them, and the firebird came straight at me.

It was huge, white like the stag and the sea whip, its vast wings tinged with golden flame. They beat the air, the gust driving me backwards. Its call echoed through the valley as it opened its massive beak. It was big enough to take my arm off in one bite, maybe my head. Its talons gleamed, long and sharp.

I raised my hands to use the Cut, but I couldn't keep my footing. I slipped and felt myself tumbling towards the cliff's edge, hip, then head, striking damp rock. *The bones*, I thought. *Oh, Saints, the bones at the bottom of the falls.* This was how it killed.

I clawed at the slick stone, trying to find purchase – and then I was falling.

My scream caught on my lips as my arm was nearly wrenched from its socket. Mal had hold of me just below my elbow. He was on his stomach, hanging over the cliff face, the firebird circling above him in the fading light.

"I've got you!" he shouted, but his grip was slipping up

the damp skin of my forearm.

My feet dangled over nothing, my heart pounding in my chest. "Mal . . ." I said desperately.

He leaned out further. We were both going over.

"I've got you," he repeated, his blue eyes blazing. His fingertips closed around my wrist.

The jolt slammed through us at the same time, the same crackling shock we'd felt that night in the woods near the *banya*. He flinched. This time we had no choice but to hold tight. Our eyes met, and power surged between us, bright and inevitable. I had the sense of a door swinging open, and all I wanted was to step through – this taste of perfect, gleaming elation was nothing compared to what lay on the other side. I forgot where I was, forgot everything but the need to cross that threshold, to claim that power.

And with that hunger came horrible understanding. *No,* I thought desperately. *Not this.*

But it was too late. I knew.

Mal gritted his teeth. I felt his grip go even tighter. My bones rubbed together. The burn of power was almost unendurable, a dull whine that filled my head. My heart beat so hard I thought I might not survive it. I needed to walk through that door.

Then, miraculously, he was pulling me higher, inch by inch. I pawed at the rock with my other hand, searching for the top of the cliff, and finally made contact. Mal took hold of both my arms, and I wriggled onto the safety of the plateau.

As soon as his hand released my wrist, the shuddering rush of power relented. We dragged ourselves away from the edge, muscles trembling, panting for breath.

That echoing call sounded again. The firebird hurtled

towards us. We shoved up to our knees. Mal had no time to draw his bow. He threw himself in front of me, arms spread wide as the firebird shrieked and dove, its talons extended directly towards him.

The impact never came. The firebird drew up short, its claws bare inches from Mal's chest. Its wings beat once, twice, driving us back. Time seemed to slow. I could see us both reflected in its great golden eyes. Its beak was razor sharp, and its feathers seemed to blaze with a light of their own. Even through my fear, I felt awe. The firebird was Ravka. It was right that we should kneel.

It gave another piercing cry, then whirled and flapped its wings, soaring into the gathering dusk.

We sank to the ground, breathing hard.

"Why did it stop?" I gasped.

A long moment passed. Then Mal said, "We're not hunting it any more."

He knew. Just as I did. *He knew.*

"We need to get out of here," he said. "It still might come back."

Dimly, I was aware of the others running towards us over the slippery rock as we got to our feet. They must have heard my screams.

"That was it!" shouted Zoya, pointing at the disappearing shape of the firebird. She lifted her hands to try to bring it back in a downdraft.

"Zoya, stop," said Mal. "Let it go."

"Why? What happened? Why didn't you kill it?"

"It's not the amplifier."

"How can you know that?"

Neither of us answered.

"What is going on?" she shouted.

"It's Mal," I said finally.

"What's Mal?" asked Harshaw.

"Mal is the third amplifier." The words came out in a rasp, but solid, so much more even and strong than I ever would have anticipated.

"What are you talking about?" Zoya's fists were clenched, and there were hectic spots of colour on her cheeks.

"We should find cover," said Tolya.

We limped across the plateau and followed the others a short distance up the next hill to the camp they'd made near a tall poplar.

Mal dropped his rifle and unslung his bow. "I'm going to go catch dinner," he said, and melted into the woods before I could think to form a protest.

I slumped on the ground. Harshaw started the fire, and I sat before it, staring at the flames, barely feeling their warmth. Tolya handed me a flask, then dropped into a crouch, and after waiting for a nod from me, slammed my shoulder back into its socket. The pain wasn't enough to stop the images pouring through my head, the connections my mind wouldn't stop making.

A girl in a field, standing over her slain sister, the black wisps of the Cut rising from her body, a father kneeling beside her.

He was a great Healer. Baghra had got it wrong. It had taken more than the Small Science to save Morozova's other daughter. It had taken *merzost*, resurrection. I'd been wrong too. Baghra's sister hadn't been Grisha. She'd been *otkazat'sya* after all.

"You must have known," said Zoya, sitting down on the other side of the fire. Her gaze was accusatory.

Had I? The jolt that night by the *banya*, I'd assumed it was something in me.

And yet, when I looked back, the pattern seemed clear. The first time I'd used my power had been when Mal lay dying in my arms. We'd searched for the stag for weeks, but we'd found it after our first kiss. When the sea whip had revealed itself, I'd been standing in the circle of his arms, close to him for the first time since we'd been forced aboard the Darkling's ship. The amplifiers wanted to be brought together.

And hadn't our lives been bound from the first? By war. By abandonment. Maybe by something more. It couldn't be chance that we'd been born into neighbouring villages, that we'd survived the war that had taken both of our families, that we'd both ended up at Keramzin.

Was this the truth behind Mal's gift for tracking, that he was somehow tied to everything, to the making at the heart of the world? Not a Grisha, and no ordinary amplifier, but something else entirely?

I am become a blade. A weapon to be used. How right he'd been.

I covered my face with my hands. I wanted to blot out this knowledge, carve it from my skull. Because I hungered for the power that lay beyond that golden door, desired it with a kind of pure and aching fever that made me want to tear at my skin. The price for that power would be Mal's life.

What had Baghra said? *You may not be able to survive the sacrifice that* merzost *requires.*

Mal returned a little while later. He'd brought back two fat rabbits. I heard the sounds of him and Tolya working as they cleaned and spitted the animals, and soon

I smelled cooking meat. I had no appetite.

We sat there, listening to the branches pop and hiss in the heat of the flame, until finally Harshaw spoke. "If someone doesn't talk soon, I'm going to set fire to the woods."

So I took a sip from Zoya's flask, and I talked. The words came more easily than I expected. I told them Baghra's story, the horrible tale of a man obsessed, of the daughter he neglected, of the other daughter who had nearly died because of it.

"No," I corrected myself. "She did die that day. Baghra killed her. And Morozova brought her back."

"No one can—"

"He could. It wasn't healing. It was resurrection, the same process he used to create the other amplifiers. It's all in his journals." The means of keeping oxygen in the blood, the method for preventing decay. The power of the Healer and the Fabrikator pushed to their limits and well beyond, taken to a place they were never meant to go.

"*Merzost*," Tolya whispered. "Power over life and death."

I nodded. Magic. Abomination. The power of creation. That was why the journals were incomplete. In the end, there had been no reason for Morozova to hunt for a creature to make into the third amplifier. The cycle had already been completed. He'd endowed his daughter with the power he'd meant for the firebird. The circle had closed.

Morozova had achieved his grand design, but not the way he had expected. *To dabble in* merzost, *well, the results are never quite what one would hope.* When the Darkling had tampered with the making at the heart of the world, the punishment for his arrogance was the Fold, a place where his power was meaningless. Morozova had created three amplifiers that could never be brought together without his daughter forfeiting her life, without his descendants paying in flesh and blood.

"But the stag and the sea whip . . . they were ancient," said Zoya.

"Morozova chose them deliberately. They were sacred creatures – rare, fierce. His child was just an ordinary *otkazat'sya* girl." Was that why the Darkling and Baghra had discounted her so readily? They'd assumed she'd died that day, but the resurrection must have made her stronger – her fragile, mortal life, a life bound by the rules of this world, had been replaced by something else. But in the moment when Morozova gave his daughter a second life, a life that didn't rightly belong to her, would he have cared if it was abomination that made it possible?

"She survived the plunge into the river," I said. "And Morozova brought her south to the settlements." To live and die in the shadow of the arch that would someday give Dva Stolba its name.

I looked at Mal. "She must have passed her power on to her descendants, built into their bones." A bitter laugh escaped me. "I thought it was me," I said. "I was so desperate to believe there was some great purpose to all this, that I didn't just . . . happen. I thought I was the other branch of Morozova's line. But it was you, Mal. It was always you."

Mal watched me through the flames. He hadn't said a word through the whole conversation, through all of a dinner that only Tolya and Oncat had managed to eat.

He said nothing now. Instead he rose and walked to

me. He held out his hand. I hesitated the briefest moment, almost afraid to touch him, then placed my palm in his and let him pull me to my feet. Silently, he led me to one of the tents.

Behind me, I heard Zoya grumble, "Oh, Saints, now I have to listen to Tolya snore all night?"

"You snore too," said Harshaw. "And it isn't ladylike."

"I do not . . ."

Their voices faded as we bent to enter the dim confines of the tent. Firelight filtered through the canvas walls and sent shadows swaying. Without a word, we lay down in the furs. Mal curled around me, his chest pressed to my back, his arms a tight circle, his breath soft against the crook of my neck. It was the way we'd slept with the insects buzzing around us by the shores of Trivka's Pond, in the belly of a ship bound for Novyi Zem, on a narrow cot in the run-down boardinghouse in Cofton.

His hand slid down my forearm. Gently, he clasped the bare skin of my wrist, letting his fingers touch, testing. When they met, that jolting force moved through both of us, even that brief taste of power nearly unbearable in its force.

My throat constricted – with misery, with confusion, and with shameful, undeniable longing. To want this from him was too much, too cruel. *It's not fair.* Stupid words, childish. Senseless.

"We'll find another way," I whispered.

Mal's fingers separated, but he kept my wrist in a loose hold as he drew me closer. I felt as I always had in his arms – complete, as if I was home. Now I had to question even that. Was what I felt real or some product of a destiny Morozova had set into motion hundreds of years ago?

Mal brushed the hair from my neck. He pressed a single brief kiss to the skin above the collar.

"No, Alina," he said softly. "We won't."

The return journey to Dva Stolba seemed shorter. We kept to the high country, to the narrow spines of the hills, as distance and days faded beneath our feet. We moved more quickly because the terrain was familiar and Mal wasn't seeking signs of the firebird, but I also just felt as if time were contracting. I dreaded the reality that awaited us back in the valley, the decisions we would have to make, the explanations I would have to give.

We travelled in near silence, Harshaw humming occasionally or murmuring to Oncat, the rest of us locked in our own thoughts. After that first night, Mal kept his distance. I hadn't approached him. I wasn't even sure what I wanted to say. His mood had changed – that calm was still there, but now I had the eerie sense that he was drinking in the world, memorising it. He would turn his face up to the sun and let his eyes close, or break a stalk of bur marigold and press it to his nose. He hunted for us every night that we had enough cover for a fire. He pointed out larks' nests and wild geranium, and caught a field mouse for Oncat, who seemed too spoiled to do any hunting of her own.

"For a doomed man," said Zoya, "you're remarkably chipper."

"He isn't doomed," I snapped.

Mal nocked an arrow, drew back, and released. It twanged into what looked like a cloudless and empty sky, and a second later, we heard a distant caw as a shape plummeted to the earth nearly a mile ahead of us. He shouldered his bow. "We all die," he said as he jogged off to retrieve his kill. "Not everyone dies for a reason."

"Are we philosophising?" asked Harshaw. "Or were those song lyrics?"

As Harshaw started humming, I ran to catch up with Mal.

"Don't say that," I said as I came level with him. "Don't talk that way."

"All right."

"And don't think that way either."

He actually grinned.

"Mal, please," I said desperately, not even sure what I was asking for. I grabbed his hand. He turned to me, and I didn't stop to think. I went up on my toes and kissed him. It took him the barest second to react, then he dropped his bow and kissed me back, arms winding tight around me, the hard planes of his body pressed against mine.

"Alina—" he began.

I grabbed the lapels of his coat, tears filling my eyes. "Don't tell me this is all happening for a reason," I said fiercely. "Or that it's going to be okay. Don't tell me you're ready to die."

We stood in the tall grass, wind singing through the reeds. He met my gaze, his blue eyes steady. "It's not going to be okay." He brushed the hair back from my cheeks and cupped my face in his rough hands. "None of this is happening for a reason." He skimmed his lips over mine. "And Saints help me, Alina, I want to live forever."

He kissed me again, and this time, he didn't stop – not until my cheeks were flushed and my heart was racing, not until I could barely remember my own name, let alone anyone else's, not until we heard Harshaw singing, and Tolya grumbling, and Zoya cheerfully promising to murder us all.

That night, I slept in Mal's arms, wrapped in furs beneath the stars. We whispered in the dark, stealing kisses, conscious of the others lying only a few feet away. Some part of me wished that a Shu raiding party would come and put a bullet through both of our hearts, leave us there forever, two bodies that would turn to dust and be forgotten. I thought about just leaving, abandoning the others, abandoning Ravka as we'd once intended, striking out through the mountains and making our way to the coast.

I thought of all these things. But I rose the next morning, and the morning after that. I ate dry biscuits, drank bitter tea. Too soon, the mountains faded, and we began our final descent into Dva Stolba. We'd arrived back sooner than expected, in time to retrieve the *Bittern* and still meet any forces the Apparat might send to Caryeva. When I saw the two stone spindles of the ruins, I wanted to level them, let the Cut do what time and weather had failed to, and turn them to rubble.

It took a little while to locate the boarding house where Tamar and the others had found lodging. It was two storeys high and painted a cheerful blue, its porch hung with prayer bells, its pointed roof covered in Shu inscriptions that glittered with gold pigment.

We found Tamar and Nadia seated at a low table in one of the public rooms, Adrik beside them, his empty coat sleeve neatly pinned, a book perched awkwardly on his knees. They sprang to their feet when they saw us.

Tolya enveloped his sister in an enormous hug, while Zoya gave Nadia and Adrik a grudging embrace. Tamar hugged me close as Oncat sprang from Harshaw's shoulders to forage through the leavings of their meal.

"What happened?" she asked, taking in my troubled expression.

"Later."

Misha came pelting down the stairs and hurled himself at Mal. "You came back!" he shouted.

"Of course we did," said Mal, sweeping him into a hug. "Did you keep to your duties?"

Misha nodded solemnly.

"Good. I expect a full report later."

"Come on," Adrik said eagerly. "Did you find it? David's upstairs with Genya. Should I go get him?"

"Adrik," chastised Nadia, "they're exhausted and probably starving."

"Is there tea?" asked Tolya.

Adrik nodded and went off to order.

"We have news," said Tamar, "and it isn't good."

I didn't think it could possibly be worse than our news, so I waved her on. "Tell me."

"The Darkling attacked West Ravka."

I sat down hard. "When?"

"Almost immediately after you left."

I nodded. It was some comfort knowing there was nothing I could have done. "How bad?"

"He used the Fold to take a big chunk out of the south, but from what we've heard, most of the people had already evacuated."

"Any word of Nikolai's forces?"

"There are rumours of cells cropping up fighting under the Lantsov banner, but without Nikolai to lead them, I'm not sure how long they'll hold out."

"All right." At least now I knew what we were dealing with.

"There's more."

I glanced at Tamar questioningly, and the look on her face sent a chill slithering over my skin.

"The Darkling marched on Keramzin."

Chapter 15

My stomach lurched. "What?"

"There are . . . there are rumours that he put it to the torch."

"Alina—" Mal said.

"The students," I said, panic creeping in on me. "What happened to the students?"

"We don't know," said Tamar.

I pressed my hands to my eyes, trying to think. "Your key," I said, my breath coming in harsh gasps.

"There's no reason to believe—"

"The *key*," I repeated, hearing the quaking edge in my voice.

Tamar handed it to me. "Third on the right," she said softly.

I took the stairs two at a time. Near the top, I slipped and banged my knee hard on one of the steps. I barely felt it. I stumbled down the hall, counting the doors. My hands were shaking so badly, it took me two tries to fit the key in the lock and get it to turn.

The room was painted in reds and blues, just as cheerful as the rest of the place. I saw Tamar's jacket thrown over a chair by the tin basin, the two narrow beds pushed together, the rumpled wool blankets. The window was open, and autumn sunlight flooded through. A cool breeze lifted the curtains.

I slammed the door behind me and walked to the window. I gripped the sill, vaguely registering the rickety houses at the edge of the settlement, the spindles in the distance, the mountains beyond. I felt the pull of the wound in my shoulder, the creep of darkness inside me. I launched myself across the tether, seeking him, the only thought in my mind: *What have you done?*

With my next breath, I was standing before him, the room a blur around me.

"At last," the Darkling said. He turned to me, his beautiful face coming into focus. He was leaning against a scorched mantel. Its outline was sickeningly familiar.

His grey eyes were empty, haunted. Was it Baghra's death that had left him this way or some horrific crime he'd committed here?

"Come," the Darkling said softly. "I want you to see."

I was trembling, but I let him take my hand and place it in the crook of his arm. As he did, the blurriness of the vision cleared and the room came to life around me.

We were in what had been the sitting room at Keramzin. The shabby sofas were stained black with soot. Ana Kuya's treasured samovar lay on its side, a tarnished hulk. Nothing remained of the walls but a charred and jagged skeleton, the ghosts of doorways. The curving metal staircase that had once led to the music room had buckled from the heat, its steps fusing together. The ceiling was gone. I could see straight through the wreck of the second storey. Where the attic should have been, there was only grey sky.

Strange, I thought stupidly. *The sun is shining in Dva Stolba.*

"I've been here for days," he said, leading me through the wreckage, over the piles of debris, through what had once been the entry hall, "waiting for you."

The stone steps that led to the front door were smeared with ash but intact. I saw the long, straight gravel drive, the white pillars of the gate, the road that led to town. It had been nearly two years since I'd seen this view, but it was just as I remembered.

The Darkling placed his hands on my shoulders and turned me slightly.

My legs gave way. I fell to my knees, my hands clasped over my mouth. A sound tore from me, too broken to be called a scream.

The oak I'd once climbed on a dare still stood, untouched by the fire that had taken Keramzin. Now its branches were full of bodies. The three Grisha instructors hung from the same thick limb, their *kefta* fluttering slightly in the wind – purple, red, and blue. Beside them, Botkin's face was nearly black above the rope that had dug into his neck. He was covered in wounds. He'd died fighting before they'd strung him up. Next to him, Ana Kuya swayed in her black dress, her heavy key ring at her waist, the toes of her button boots nearly scraping the ground.

"She was, I think, the closest thing you had to a mother," murmured the Darkling.

The sobs that shook me were like the lashes of a whip. I flinched with each one, bent double, collapsing into myself. The Darkling knelt before me. He took me by the wrists, pulling my hands free from my face, as if he wanted to watch me weep.

"Alina," he said. I kept my eyes on the steps, my tears clouding my vision. I would not look at him. "Alina," he repeated.

"Why?" The word was a wail, a child's cry. "Why would

you do this? *How* can you do this? Don't you feel any of it?"

"I have lived a long life, rich in grief. My tears are long since spent. If I still felt as you do, if I ached as you do, I could not have borne this eternity."

"I hope Botkin killed twenty of your Grisha," I spat at him, "a hundred."

"He was an extraordinary man."

"Where are the students?" I made myself ask, though I wasn't sure I could bear the answer. "What have you done?"

"Where are *you*, Alina? I felt sure you would come to me when I moved against West Ravka. I thought your conscience would demand it. I could only hope that this would draw you out."

"*Where are they?*" I screamed.

"They are safe. For now. They will be on my skiff when I enter the Fold again."

"As hostages," I said dully.

He nodded. "In case you get any thoughts of attack rather than surrender. In five days, I will return to the Unsea, and you will come to me – you and the tracker – or I will drive the Fold all the way to West Ravka's coast, and I will march those children, one by one, to the mercy of the volcra."

"This place . . . these people, they were innocent."

"I have waited hundreds of years for this moment, for your power, for this chance. I have earned it with loss and with struggle. I will have it, Alina. Whatever the cost."

I wanted to claw at him, to tell him I'd see him torn apart by his own monsters. I wanted to tell him I would bring all the power of Morozova's amplifiers down on him, an army of light, born of *merzost*, perfect in its vengeance.

I might be able to do it, too. If Mal gave up his life.

"There will be nothing left," I whispered.

"No," he said gently as he folded me in his arms. He pressed a kiss to the top of my hair. "I will strip away all that you know, all that you love, until you have no shelter but me."

In grief, in horror, I let myself break apart.

I was still on my knees, my hands clutching the windowsill, my forehead pressed against the wooden slats of the boardinghouse wall. Outside, I could hear the faint jingle of prayer bells. Inside, there was no sound but the hitch of my breath, the rasp of my sobs as the whip continued to fall, as I bent my back and wept. That was where they found me.

I didn't hear the door open, or their steps as they approached. I just felt gentle hands take hold of me. Zoya sat me down on the edge of the bed, and Tamar settled beside me. Nadia took a comb to my hair, carefully working through the tangles. Genya washed first my face, then my hands with a cool cloth she'd wetted in the basin. It smelled faintly of mint.

We sat there, saying nothing, all of them clustered around me.

"He has the students," I said flatly. "Twenty-three children. He killed the teachers. And Botkin." And Ana Kuya, a woman they'd never known. The woman who had raised me. "Mal—"

"He told us," said Nadia softly.

I think some part of me expected blame, recrimination. Instead, Genya rested her head on my shoulder. Tamar squeezed my hand.

This wasn't just comfort, I realised. They were leaning on me – as I was leaning on them – for strength.

I have lived a long life, rich in grief.

Had the Darkling had friends like this? People whom he'd loved, who had fought for him, and cared for him, and made him laugh? People who had become little more than sacrifices to a dream that outlived them?

"How long do we have?" Tamar asked.

"Five days."

A knock came at the door. It was Mal. Tamar made room for him beside me.

"Bad?" he asked.

I nodded. I couldn't yet stand to tell him what I'd seen. "I have five days to surrender, or he'll use the Fold again."

"He'll do it anyway," said Mal. "You said so yourself. He'll find a reason."

"I might buy us some time—"

"At what cost? You were willing to give up your life," he said quietly. "Why won't you let me do the same?"

"Because I can't bear it."

His face went hard. He seized my wrist and again I felt that jolt. Light cascaded behind my eyes, as if my whole body were ready to crack open with it. Unspeakable power lay behind that door, and Mal's death would open it.

"You *will* bear it," he said. "Or all of these deaths, all we've given up, will be for nothing."

Genya cleared her throat. "Um. The thing is, you may not have to. David has an idea."

"Actually, it was Genya's idea," David said.

We were crowded around a table beneath an awning, a little way down the street from our boarding house. There were no real restaurants in this part of the settlement, but a kind of makeshift tavern had been set up in a burned-out lot. There were lanterns strung over the rickety tables, a wooden keg of sweet fermented milk, and meat roasting in two metal drums like the one we'd seen that first day at the market. The air was thick with the smell of juniper smoke.

Two men were shooting dice at a table near the keg while another plucked his way through a shapeless tune on a battered guitar. There was no discernible melody, but Misha seemed satisfied. He'd taken up an elaborate dance that apparently required clapping and a great deal of concentration.

"We'll make sure to put Genya's name on the plaque," said Zoya. "Just get on with it."

"Remember how you disguised the *Bittern*?" David asked. "The way you bent the light around the ship instead of letting it bounce off of it?"

"I was thinking," said Genya. "What if you did that with us?"

I frowned. "You mean—"

"It's the exact same principle," said David. "It's a greater challenge because there are more variables than just blue sky, but curving light around a soldier is no different from curving light around an object."

"Wait a minute," said Harshaw. "You mean we'd be invisible?"

"Exactly," said Genya.

Adrik leaned forward. "The Darkling will launch from the drydocks in Kribirsk. We could sneak into his camp.

Get the students out that way." His fist was clenched, his eyes alight. He knew those children better than any of us. Some of them were probably his friends.

Tolya frowned. "There's no way we'd get into camp and free them without being noticed. Some of those kids are younger than Misha."

"Kribirsk will be too complicated," said David. "Lots of people, interrupted sight lines. If Alina had more time to practise—"

"We have five days," I repeated.

"So we attack on the Fold," said Genya. "Alina's light will keep the volcra at bay—"

I shook my head. "We'd still have to fight the Darkling's *nichevo'ya*."

"Not if they can't see us," said Genya.

Nadia grinned. "We'd be hiding in plain sight."

"He'll have *oprichniki* and Grisha too," said Tolya. "They won't be short on ammunition like we will. Even if they can't see their targets, they may just open fire and hope they get lucky."

"So we stay out of range." Tamar moved her plate to the centre of the table. "This is the glass skiff," she said. "We place marksmen around the perimeter and use them to thin the Darkling's ranks. *Then* we get close enough to sneak onto the skiff, and once we get the kids to safety—"

"We blow it to bits," said Harshaw. He was practically salivating at the prospect of the explosion.

"And the Darkling with it," Genya finished.

I gave Tamar's plate a turn, considering what the others were suggesting. Without the third amplifier, my power was no match for the Darkling's in a head-on confrontation. He'd proved that in no uncertain terms. But what if I came at him unseen, using light for cover the way others used darkness? It was sneaky, even cowardly, but the Darkling and I had left honour behind long ago. He'd been in my head, waged war on my heart. I wasn't interested in a fair fight, not if there was a chance I could save Mal's life.

As if he could read my mind, Mal said, "I don't like it. Too many things can go wrong."

"This isn't just your choice," said Nadia. "You've been fighting beside us and bleeding with us for months now. We deserve the chance to try and save your life."

"Even if you're a useless *otkazat'sya*," added Zoya.

"Careful," said Harshaw. "You're talking to the Darkling's . . . wait, what are you? His cousin? His nephew?"

Mal shuddered. "I have no idea."

"Are you going to start wearing black now?"

Mal gave a very firm "*No.*"

"You're one of us," said Genya, "whether you like it or not. Besides, if Alina has to kill you, she may go completely crazy *and* she'll have the three amplifiers. Then it will be up to Misha to stop her with the power of awful dancing."

"She is pretty moody," said Harshaw. He tapped his temple. "Not totally *there*, if you know what I mean."

They were kidding, but they might also have been right. *You were meant to be my balance.* What I felt for Mal was messy and stubborn and might leave me heartbroken in the end, but it was also human.

Nadia reached out and nudged Mal's hand. "At least consider the plan. And if it all goes wrong—"

"Alina gets a new bracelet," finished Zoya.

I scowled. "How about I slice *you* open and see how your bones fit?"

Zoya fluffed her hair. "I bet they're just as gorgeous as the rest of me."

I gave Tamar's plate another turn, trying to imagine what this kind of manoeuvre might require. I wished I had Nikolai's mind for strategy. One thing I was sure of. "It will take more than an explosion to kill the Darkling. He survived the Fold and the destruction of the chapel."

"Then what?" asked Harshaw.

"It has to be me," I said. "If we can separate him from his shadow soldiers, I can use the Cut." The Darkling was powerful, but I doubted even he could bounce back from being torn in half. And though I had no claim to Morozova's name, I was the Sun Summoner. I'd hoped for a grand destiny; I would settle for a clean kill.

Zoya released a brief, giddy laugh. "This actually might work."

"It's worth thinking about," I said to Mal. "The Darkling will expect an attack. He won't expect this."

Mal was silent for a long moment. "All right," he said. "But if it does go wrong . . . we all agree what has to happen."

He looked around the table. One by one they nodded. Tolya's face was stoic. Genya dropped her gaze. Finally, only I remained.

"I want your word, Alina."

I swallowed the lump in my throat. "I'll do it." The words tasted like iron on my tongue.

"Good," he said. He grabbed my hand. "Now, let's show Misha how bad dancing's done."

"Kill you, dance with you. Any other requests?"

"Not at the moment," he said, pulling me close. "But I'm sure I'll think of something."

I tucked my head against Mal's shoulder and breathed in his scent. I knew I shouldn't let myself believe in this possibility. We didn't have an army. We didn't have the resources of a king. We only had this ragged crew. *I will strip away all that you know, all that you love.* If he could, I knew the Darkling would use these people against me, but it had never occurred to him that they might be more than liabilities. Maybe he'd underestimated them, and maybe he'd underestimated me too.

It was stupid. It was dangerous. But Ana Kuya used to tell me that hope was tricky like water. Somehow it always found a way in.

We stayed up late that night, talking through the logistics of the plan. The realities of the Fold complicated everything – where and how we would enter, whether or not it was even possible for me to cloak myself, let alone the others, how to isolate the Darkling and get the students clear. We had no blasting powders, so we'd have to make our own. I also wanted to ensure that the others had some way out of the Fold if anything happened to me.

We left early the next morning and crossed back through Dva Stolba to retrieve the *Bittern* from the quarry. It was strange to see it sitting where we'd left it, tucked safely away like a pigeon in the eaves.

"Saints," said Adrik as we clambered into the hulls. "Is that my blood?"

The stain was nearly as big as he was. We'd all been so tired and beaten after our long escape from the Spinning Wheel that no one had even thought to deal with it.

"You made the mess," said Zoya. "You clean it up."

"Need two hands to swab," Adrik retorted, taking a place at the sails instead.

Adrik seemed to relish Zoya's taunts over Nadia's constant fussing. I'd been relieved to learn that he could still summon, though it would take some time for him to be able to control strong currents with just one arm. *Baghra could teach him.* The thought came at me before I remembered that was no longer possible. I could almost hear her voice in my head: *Should I cut off your other arm? Then you'd have something to whine about. Do it again and do it better.* What would she have made of all of this? What would she have made of Mal? I pushed the thought away. We'd never know, and there was no time for mourning.

Once we were in the air, the Squallers set a gentle pace and I used the time to practice bending the light as I camouflaged the ship from below.

The journey took only a few hours, and we landed in a marshy pasture west of Caryeva. The town was the site of the summer horse sales every year. It wasn't known for anything but its racing track and its breeding stables, and even without the war, this late in the year, it would have been all but deserted.

The missive to the Apparat had proposed that we meet at the racecourse. Tamar and Harshaw would scout the track on foot to make sure we weren't walking into a trap. If anything felt wrong, they'd circle back to meet us, and we'd decide what to do from there. I didn't think the Apparat would turn us over to the Darkling, but there was also the possibility that he'd struck some kind of new bargain with the Shu Han or Fjerda.

We were a day early, and the pasture was the perfect

place to practise cloaking moving targets. Misha insisted on being first.

"I'm smaller," he said. "That will make it easier."

He ran out into the centre of the field.

I raised my hands, gave a twist of my wrists, and Misha disappeared. Harshaw gave an appreciative whistle.

"Can you see me?" Misha shouted. As soon as he started waving, the light around him rippled and his skinny forearms appeared as if suspended in space.

Focus. They vanished.

"Misha," instructed Mal, "run towards us."

He appeared, then disappeared again as I adjusted the light.

"I can see him from the side," Tolya called from across the pasture.

I blew out a breath. I had to think about this more carefully. Disguising the ship had been easier because I'd only been altering the reflection of the light from below. Now I had to think about every angle.

"Better!" said Tolya.

Zoya yelped. "That little brat just kicked me."

"Smart kid," said Mal.

I lifted a brow. "Smarter than some."

He had the good grace to blush.

I spent the rest of the afternoon vanishing one, then two, then five Grisha at a time in the field.

It was a different kind of work, but Baghra's lessons still applied. If I concentrated too hard on projecting my power, variables overwhelmed me. But if I thought about the light being everywhere, if I didn't try to prod it and just let it bend, it got much easier.

I thought of the times I'd seen the Darkling use his

power to blind soldiers in a battle, taking on multiple enemies at once. It was easy for him, natural. *I know things about power that you can barely guess at.*

I practised that night, then started up again the next morning after Tamar and Harshaw set out, but my concentration kept faltering. With more marksmen, our attack on the Darkling's skiff might actually stand a chance. What would be waiting at the racecourse? The priest himself? No one at all? I'd imagined a serf army, protected by three amplifiers, marching beneath the banner of the firebird. That wasn't the war we were waging any more.

"I can see him!" Zoya singsonged at me. And sure enough, Tolya's big shape was flickering in and out as he jogged to my right.

I dropped my hands. "Let's break for a bit," I suggested.

Nadia and Adrik unfurled one of the sails so she could help him learn to manage updraft, and Zoya sprawled lazily on the deck to offer less than helpful critique.

Meanwhile, David and Genya bent their heads over one of his notebooks, trying to figure out where they could extract the components for a batch of *lumiya*. It turned out Genya didn't just have a gift for poisons. Her talents had always lain somewhere between Corporalnik and Materialnik; I wondered what she might have become, what path she might have chosen, if not for the Darkling's influence. Mal and Misha headed to the far side of the field with arms full of pine cones and set them along the fence as targets so Misha could learn to shoot.

That left me and Tolya with nothing to do except worry and wait. He sat down beside me on one of the hulls, legs dangling over.

"Do you want to practise some more?" he asked.

"I probably should."

A long moment passed and then he said, "Can you do it? When the time comes?"

I was eerily reminded of Mal asking me if I could bring down the firebird. "You don't think the plan will work."

"I don't think it matters."

"You don't—"

"If you defeat the Darkling, the Fold will remain."

I kicked my heels against the hull. "I can deal with the Fold," I said. "My power will make crossings possible. We can eliminate the volcra." I didn't like to think about that. As monstrous as they were, the volcra had once been human. I leaned back and studied Tolya's face. "You're not convinced."

"You asked me once why I didn't let you die in the chapel, why I let Mal go to you. Maybe there was a reason you both lived. Maybe this is it."

"It was a supposed Saint who started all of this, Tolya."

"And a Saint will end it."

He slid from the hull to the ground and looked up at me. "I know you don't believe as Tamar and I do," he said, "but no matter how this ends, I'm glad our faith brought us to you."

He headed off across the field to join Mal and Misha.

Whether it was coincidence or providence that had made Tolya and Tamar my friends, I was grateful for them. And if I was honest with myself, I envied their faith. If I could believe I had been blessed by some divine purpose, it might make the hard choices easier.

I didn't know if our plan would work, and if it did, there were still too many unknowns. If we bested the Darkling, what would become of his shadow soldiers? And what about Nikolai? What if killing the Darkling caused his death? Should we be trying to capture the Darkling instead? If we survived, Mal would have to go into hiding. His life would be forfeit if anyone learned what he was.

I heard the sound of hoofbeats. Nadia and I climbed up on the captain's platform to get a better look, and as the party came into view, my heart sank.

"Maybe there are more, back at the racecourse," said Nadia.

"Maybe," I said. But I didn't believe it.

I made a quick count. Twelve soldiers. As they drew closer, I saw they were all young and most bore the sun tattoo on their faces. Ruby was there, with her pretty green eyes and blonde braid, and I saw Vladim among them with two other bearded men I thought I recognised from the Priestguards.

I hopped down from the platform and went to greet them. When the party spotted me, they slipped from their horses and each dropped to one knee, heads bowed.

"Ugh," said Zoya. "This again."

I cast her a warning look, though I'd had the exact same thought. I'd nearly forgotten how much I dreaded the burden of Sainthood. But I took on the mantle, playing my part.

"Rise," I said, and when they did, I gestured Vladim forward. "Is this all of you?"

He nodded.

"And what excuse does the Apparat send?"

He swallowed. "None. The pilgrims say daily prayers for your safety and for the destruction of the Fold. He claims that your last command was for him to watch over your flock."

"And my plea for aid?"

Ruby shook her head. "The only reason we knew that you and Nikolai Lantsov had requested help was because a monk loyal to you retrieved the message from the Church of Sankt Lukin."

"So how do you come to be here?"

Vladim smiled and those absurd dimples appeared in his cheeks again. He exchanged a glance with Ruby.

"We escaped," she said.

I'd known the Apparat wasn't to be trusted, and yet some part of me had hoped he might offer me more than prayers. But I'd told him to tend to my followers, to keep them from harm, and they were certainly safer in the White Cathedral than marching into the Fold. The Apparat would do what he did best: wait. When the dust cleared, either I would have defeated the Darkling or found my martyrdom. Either way, men would still take up arms in my name. The Apparat's empire of the faithful would rise.

I laid my hands on Vladim's and Ruby's shoulders. "Thank you for your loyalty. I hope you won't be sorry for it."

They bowed their heads and murmured, "Sankta Alina."

"Let's move," I said. "You're a big enough group that you may have attracted attention, and those tattoos can't have helped."

"Where are we going?" asked Ruby, pulling up her scarf to hide her tattoo.

"Into the Fold."

I saw the new soldiers shift uneasily. "To fight?" she asked.

"To travel," Mal replied.

No army. No allies. We had only three more days until we were to face the Darkling. We would take our chances, and if we failed, there would be no more options. I would murder the only person I'd ever loved and who had ever loved me. I'd dive back into battle wearing his bones.

Chapter 16

It wouldn't be safe to approach Kribirsk on this side of the Fold, so we'd decided to stage our attack from West Ravka, and that meant dealing with the logistics of a crossing. Because Nadia and Zoya couldn't keep the *Bittern* aloft with too many additional passengers, we agreed that Tolya would escort the Soldat Sol to the eastern shore of the Fold and wait for us there. It would take them a full day on horseback, and that would give the rest of us time to enter West Ravka and locate a suitable base camp. Then we'd loop back to lead the others across the Fold under the protection of my power.

We boarded the *Bittern*, and mere hours later, we were speeding towards the strange black fog of the Shadow Fold. This time, when we entered the darkness, I was prepared for the sense of familiarity that gripped me, that feeling of likeness. It was even stronger now that I'd dabbled in *merzost*, the very power that had created this place. I understood it better too, the need that had driven the Darkling to try to re-create Morozova's experiments, a legacy he felt was his.

The volcra came at us, and I glimpsed the dim shapes of their wings, heard their cries as they tore at the circle of light I summoned. If the Darkling had his way, they'd soon be well fed. I was grateful when we burst into the sky above West Ravka.

The territory west of the Fold had been evacuated. We flew over abandoned villages and houses, all without seeing a soul. In the end, we decided to set up in an apple farm just south-west of what was left of Novokribirsk, less than a mile from the dark reach of the Fold. It was called Tomikyana, the name written across the side of the cannery and the barn full of cider presses. Its orchards were thick with fruit that would never be harvested.

The owner's house was lavish, a perfect little cake of a building, lovingly maintained, and topped with a white cupola. I felt almost guilty as Harshaw broke a window and climbed inside to unlock the doors.

"New money," sniffed Zoya as we made our way through the overdecorated rooms, each shelf and mantel brimming with porcelain figurines and curios.

Genya picked up a ceramic pig. "Vile."

"I like it here," protested Adrik. "It's nice."

Zoya made a retching sound. "Maybe taste will come with age."

"I'm only three years younger than you."

"Then maybe you're just doomed to be tacky."

The furniture had been covered with sheets. Misha pulled one free and ran from room to room trailing it behind him like a cape. Most of the cupboards had been emptied, but Harshaw found a tin of sardines that he opened and shared with Oncat. We'd have to send people out to the neighbouring farms to scout for food.

Once we'd made sure there were no other squatters, we left David, Genya, and Misha to get started procuring materials for the production of *lumiya* and blasting powders. Then the rest of us reboarded the *Bittern* to cross back to Ravka.

We'd planned to reunite with the Soldat Sol at the monument to Sankta Anastasia that stood on a low hill overlooking what had once been Tsemna. Thanks to Anastasia, Tsemna had survived the wasting plague that had claimed half the population of the surrounding villages. But Tsemna hadn't survived the Fold. It had been swallowed up when the Black Heretic's disastrous experiments first created the Unsea.

The monument was an eerie sight, a giant stone woman rising out of the earth, arms spread wide, her benevolent gaze fixed on the nothingness of the Fold. Anastasia was rumoured to have rid countless towns of sickness. Had she worked miracles, or was she simply a talented Healer? Was there any difference?

We'd arrived before the Soldat Sol, so we landed and made camp for the night. The air was still warm enough that we didn't need tents, and we laid our bedrolls next to the foot of the statue near a patchy field studded with red boulders. Mal took Harshaw with him to try to find game for dinner. It was scarce down here, as if the animals were just as wary of the Unsea as we were.

I wrapped a shawl around my shoulders and walked down the hill to the edge of the black shore. *Two days*, I thought as I looked into the seething black mists. I knew better than to think I understood what lay ahead of me. Every time I'd tried to predict my fate, my life had been upended.

I heard a soft scraping sound behind me. I turned and froze. Nikolai was perched atop a high rock. He was cleaner than he had been, but he wore the same ragged trousers. His taloned feet gripped the ridge of the rock, and his shadow wings beat gently at the air, his gaze black and unreadable.

I'd been hoping he would show himself again, but now I wasn't sure what to do. Had he been watching us? What had he seen? How much had he understood?

Carefully, I reached into my pocket, afraid any sudden movement might make him bolt.

I held out my hand, the Lantsov emerald resting on my palm. He frowned, a line appearing between his brows, then folded his wings and leapt soundlessly from the rock. It was hard not to back away. I didn't want to be afraid, but the way he moved was so inhuman. He stalked towards me slowly, eyes focused on the ring. When he was less than a foot away, he cocked his head to one side.

Despite the black eyes and the inky lines that coursed up his neck, he still had an elegant face – his mother's fine cheekbones, the strong jaw that must have come from his ambassador father. His frown deepened. Then he reached out and plucked the emerald up in his claws.

"It's—" The words died on my lips. Nikolai turned my palm over and slid the ring onto my finger.

My breath caught between a laugh and a sob. He knew me. I couldn't stop the tears that welled in my eyes.

He pointed to my hand and made a sweeping gesture. It took me a second to grasp his meaning. He was imitating the way I moved when I summoned.

"You want me to call the light?"

His face stayed blank. I let sunlight pool in my palm. "This?"

The glow seemed to galvanise him. He seized my hand and slapped it against his chest. I tried to draw away, but he held my hand in place. His grip was vice-like, made stronger by whatever monstrous thing the Darkling had placed inside him.

I shook my head. "No."

Again, he slapped my hand against his chest, the movement almost frantic.

"I don't know what my power will do to you," I protested.

The corner of his mouth curled, the faintest suggestion of Nikolai's wry smile. I could almost hear him say, *Really, lovely, what could be worse?* Beneath my hand, his heart beat – steady and human.

I released a long breath. "All right," I said. "I'll try."

I summoned the barest bit of light, letting it flow through my palm. He winced, but held my hand firmly in place. I pushed a little harder, trying to direct the light into him, thinking of the spaces between, letting it seep through his skin.

The black cracks on his torso began to recede. I couldn't quite believe what I was seeing. Could it possibly be this simple?

"It's working," I gasped.

He grimaced, then waved me on, asking for more.

I called the light into him, watching the black veins fade and recoil.

He was panting now, his eyes closed. A low, pained whine rose from his throat. His grip around my wrist was iron.

"Nikolai—"

Then I felt something push back, as if the darkness within him was fighting. It shoved against the light. All at once, the cracks exploded outward, just as dark as before, like the roots of a tree drinking deep of poisoned water.

Nikolai flinched and shoved away from me with a

frustrated snarl. He looked down at his chest, misery carved into his features.

It was no good. Only the Cut worked on the *nichevo'ya*. It might well destroy the thing inside Nikolai, but it would kill him too.

His shoulders slumped, his wings roiling with the same shifting movement as the Fold.

"We'll think of something. David will come up with a solution, or we'll find a Healer. . . ."

He dropped to his haunches, elbows resting on his knees, face buried in his hands. Nikolai had seemed infinitely capable, confident in his belief that every problem had a solution and he would be the one to find it. I couldn't bear seeing him this way, broken and defeated for the first time.

I approached him cautiously and crouched down. He wouldn't meet my eyes. Tentatively, I reached out and touched his arm, ready to draw back if he startled or snapped. His skin was warm, the feel of it unchanged despite the shadows lurking beneath it. I slipped my arms around him, careful of the wings that rustled at his back.

"I'm sorry," I whispered.

He dropped his forehead to my shoulder.

"I'm so sorry, Nikolai."

He released a small, shuddering sigh.

Then he inhaled and tensed. He turned his head. I felt his breath on my neck, the scrape of one of his teeth beneath my jaw.

"Nikolai?"

His arms clamped around me. His claws dug into my back. There was no mistaking the growl that issued from his chest.

I pushed away from him and shot to my feet.

"Stop!" I said harshly.

His hands flexed. His lips had pulled back to reveal his onyx fangs. I knew what I saw in him: appetite.

"Don't," I pleaded. "This isn't you. You can control this."

He took a step towards me. Another rumbling, animal growl rolled through him.

I lifted my hands. "Nikolai," I said warningly. "I will put you down."

I saw the moment that reason returned. His face crumpled in horror at what he'd wanted to do, at what some part of him probably still wanted to do. His body was trembling with the desire to feed.

His black eyes brimmed with flickering shadows. Were they tears? He clenched his fists, threw back his head. The tendons in his neck knotted, and he released an echoing shriek of helplessness and rage. I'd heard it before, when the Darkling summoned the *nichevo'ya*, the rending of the fabric of the world, the cry of something that should not be.

He launched himself into the air and hurtled straight for the Fold.

"Nikolai!" I screamed. But he was already gone, swallowed by the seething blackness, lost to the volcra's domain.

I heard footsteps and turned to see Mal, Harshaw, and Zoya running towards me, Oncat yowling and darting between their legs. Harshaw had his flint out, and Mal was unslinging his rifle.

Zoya's eyes were wide. "Was that a *nichevo'ya*?"

I shook my head. "It was Nikolai."

They stopped dead. "He found us?" said Mal.

"He's been tracking us since we left the Spinning Wheel."

"But the Darkling—"

"If he were the Darkling's creature, we'd already be dead."

"How long have you known he was following us?" asked Zoya angrily.

"I saw him once back at the copper mine. There was nothing to do about it."

"We could have had Mal put an arrow through him," said Harshaw.

I jabbed a finger at him. "I wouldn't abandon you, and I'm not abandoning Nikolai."

"Easy," said Mal, stepping forward. "He's gone now, and there's no point to fighting about it. Harshaw, go and start a fire. Zoya, the grouse we caught need cleaning."

She stared at him and didn't budge. He rolled his eyes.

"All right, they need cleaning by *someone else*. Please go find somebody to order around."

"My pleasure."

Harshaw returned his flint to his sleeve. "They're all crazy, Oncat," he said to the tabby. "Invisible armies, monster princes. Let's go and set fire to something."

I rubbed a hand over my eyes as they walked off. "Are you going to yell at me too?"

"No. I've wanted to shoot Nikolai plenty of times, but that seems a little petty now. Curious about that ring, though."

I'd forgotten about the massive jewel on my hand. I pulled it off and shoved it in my pocket. "Nikolai gave it to me back at the Spinning Wheel. I thought he might recognise it."

"Did he?"

"I think so. Before he tried to eat me."

"Saints."

"He flew into the Fold."

"Do you think he meant to—"

"Kill himself? I don't know. Maybe it's like a holiday home to him now. I don't even know if the volcra would see him as prey." I leaned against the boulder Nikolai had been perched on just minutes before. "He tried to get me to me heal him. It didn't work."

"You don't know what you may be able to do once the amplifiers are brought together."

"You mean after I murder you?"

"Alina—"

"We are not talking about this."

"You can't just pull the covers over your head and pretend this isn't happening."

"Can and will."

"You're being a brat."

"And you're being noble and self-sacrificing, and it makes me want to throttle you."

"Well, that's a start."

"That's not funny."

"How am I supposed to deal with this?" he asked. "I don't *feel* noble or self-sacrificing. I'm just . . ."

"What?"

He threw up his hands. "Hungry."

"You're hungry?"

"Yes," he snapped. "I'm hungry and I'm tired and I'm pretty sure that Tolya's going to eat all the grouse."

I couldn't help it. I burst out laughing. "You're *sulking*."

"I am not."

"You are," I said, trying to restrain my giggles.

He snagged my hand and pulled me in for a kiss. He nipped my ear once, hard.

"Ow!"

"I told you I was hungry."

"You're the second person to try to bite me today."

"Oh, it gets worse. When we get back to camp, I'm requesting the Third Tale of Kregi."

"I'm telling Harshaw you're a dog person."

"I'm telling Zoya you don't like her hair."

We kept it up all the way back to the *Bittern*, shoving and taunting each other, feeling a little bit of the strain of the last weeks ease. But as the sun set and I looked over my shoulder into the Fold, I wondered what human things might remain beyond its shores, and if they could hear our laughter.

The Soldat Sol arrived late that night and got only a few hours of sleep before we set out the next day. They were wary as we entered the Fold, but I'd expected them to be far worse, clutching icons and chanting prayers. When we took our first steps into the darkness and I let the light burst forth in a flood around us, I understood: they didn't need to plead with their Saints. They had me.

The *Bittern* drifted high above us, well within the roof of the bright bubble I'd created. I'd chosen to travel on the sands so that I could practise bending light within the confines of the Fold. To the Soldat Sol, this new display of power was one more miracle, further proof that I was a living Saint. I remembered the Apparat's claim: *There is no greater power than faith, and there will be no greater army than one driven by it.* I prayed that he was right, that I wasn't just another leader taking their loyalty and repaying them with useless, honorable deaths.

It took us the better part of that day and night to cross the Fold and escort all of the Soldat Sol up the western shore. By the time we arrived back at Tomikyana, David and Genya had completely taken over. The kitchen looked like a storm had blown through. Bubbling pots covered the cookstove, and a huge kettle had been brought in from the cider press to serve as a cooling tub. David perched on a stool at the big wooden table where the servants had probably rolled dough only weeks before. Now it was littered with glass and metal, smears of some tarlike substance, and countless little bottles of foul-smelling yellow sludge.

"Is this entirely safe?" I asked him.

"Nothing is entirely safe."

"How reassuring."

He smiled. "I'm glad."

In the dining room, Genya had set up her own work space, where she was helping to construct canisters for the *lumiya* and slings that would carry them. The others could activate them as late as they dared during the attack, and if something happened to me on the Fold, they might still have enough light to get out. All of the farm owner's glassware had been conscripted – goblets, snifters, wine and liqueur glasses, an elaborate collection of vases, and a chafing dish in the shape of a fish.

The tea set had been filled with screws and grommets, and Misha sat cross-legged on a silk-cushioned chair, gleefully deconstructing saddles and organizing the strips and bits of leather into careful piles.

Harshaw was dispatched to steal whatever food he could find from nearby estates, work he seemed disturbingly adept at.

I laboured beside Genya and Misha for most of the day. Out in the gardens, the Squallers practised creating an acoustic blanket. It was a variation on the trick Zoya had performed after the cave-in, and we hoped it would allow us to enter the Fold and take up our positions in darkness without attracting the attention of the volcra. It would be a temporary measure at best, but we just needed it to last long enough to enable the ambush. Periodically, my ears would crackle, and all sound would seem to dampen, then I'd hear Nadia as clearly as if she were standing in the room with me, or Adrik's voice booming in my ear.

The pop of gunfire floated back to us from the orchard where Mal and the twins were choosing the best marksmen from the Soldat Sol. We had to be cautious with our ammunition, so they used their bullets sparingly. Later I heard them in the parlour, sorting through weapons and supplies.

We pieced together a dinner of apples, hard cheese, and stale black bread that Harshaw had found in some abandoned larder. The dining room and kitchen were a wreck, so we built a big fire in the grate of the grand receiving room and set out a makeshift picnic, sprawled on the floor and the watered silk couches, toasting bits of bread skewered on the gnarled branches of apple trees.

"If I survive this," I said, wiggling my toes near the fire, "I'm going to have to find some way to compensate these poor people for the damages."

Zoya snorted. "They'll be forced to redecorate. We're doing them a favour."

"And if we don't survive," observed David, "this whole place will be enveloped in darkness."

Tolya pushed aside a flowered cushion. "Might be for the best."

Harshaw took a swig of cider from the jug Tamar had brought in from the press. "If I live, the first thing I'm doing is coming back here and swimming around in a tank of this stuff."

"Go easy, Harshaw," said Tamar. "We need you awake tomorrow."

He groaned. "Why do battles always have to be so early?" Grudgingly, he gave up the jug to one of the Soldat Sol.

We'd gone over the plan until all of us were sure we knew exactly where to be and when. We'd enter the Fold at dawn. The Squallers would go in first to lay down the acoustic blanket and hide our movements from the volcra. I'd heard Nadia whispering with Tamar about not wanting Adrik with them, but Tamar had argued hard in favour of including him. "He's a warrior," she'd said. "If you make him believe he's less now, he'll never know he can be more." I would be with the Squallers, in case anything went wrong. The marksmen and the other Grisha would follow.

We'd planned the ambush at the centre of the Fold, almost directly between Kribirsk and Novokribirsk. Once we spotted the Darkling's skiff, I would illuminate the Unsea, bending the light to keep us invisible. If that didn't bring him to a halt, our marksmen would. They would thin his ranks, and then it was up to Harshaw and the Squallers to create enough chaos that the twins and I could board the skiff, locate the students, and get them to safety. Once they were clear, I would deal with the Darkling. Hopefully, he would never see me coming.

Genya and David would remain at Tomikyana with Misha. I knew Misha would insist on going with us, so Genya had slipped a sleeping draft into his dinner. He was already yawning, curled up near the grate, and I hoped he would sleep through our departure in the morning.

The night wore on. We knew we needed to sleep, though no one much felt like it. Some people decided to bed down by the fire in the receiving room while others trickled out into the house in pairs. Nobody wanted to be alone tonight. Genya and David had work to do in the kitchens. Tamar and Nadia had disappeared early. I thought Zoya might take her pick of the Soldat Sol, but as I slipped out the door, she was still watching the fire, Oncat purring in her lap.

I made my way down the dark hall to the parlour, where Mal was making a final check of the weapons and gear. It was a strange sight, to see the piles of guns and ammunition stacked on a marble tabletop next to the framed miniatures of the lady of the house and a pretty collection of snuffboxes.

"We've been here before," he said.

"We have?"

"When we came out of the Fold the first time. We stopped in the orchard, not very far from the house. I recognised it earlier when we were out shooting."

I remembered. It seemed like a lifetime ago. The fruit on the trees had been too small and sour to eat.

"How did the Soldat Sol do today?"

"Not bad. Only a few of them have much range. But if we're lucky, that's all we'll need. A lot of them saw action in the First Army, so at least there's a chance they'll keep their heads."

Laughter drifted back to us from the receiving room. Someone – Harshaw, I suspected – had started singing. But in the parlour, it was quiet and I could hear that it had begun to rain.

"Mal," I said. "Do you think . . . do you think it's the amplifiers?"

He frowned, checking the sight on a rifle. "What do you mean?"

"Is that what's between us? My power and yours? Is that why we became friends, why . . ." I trailed off.

He picked up another gun, sighted down the barrel. "Maybe that brought us together, but it didn't make us who we are. It didn't make you the girl who could get me to laugh when I had nothing. It sure as hell didn't make me the idiot who took that for granted. Whatever there is between us, we forged it. It belongs to us." Then he set down the rifle and wiped his hands on a rag.

"Come with me," he said, taking my hand and pulling me behind him.

We moved through the darkened house. I heard voices singing something bawdy down the hall, footsteps overhead as someone ran from one room to the next. I thought Mal might lead me up the stairs to the bedrooms; I guess I hoped he would, but instead he took me through the east wing of the house, past a silent sewing room, a library, all the way to a windowless vestibule lined with trowels, spades, and dried cuttings.

"Um . . . delightful?"

"Wait here." He opened a door I hadn't seen, tucked into the wall.

In the dim light, I saw it led to some kind of long, narrow conservatory. The rain beat a steady rhythm against the vaulted roof and glazed glass walls. Mal moved deeper into the room, lighting lanterns that rested on the edge of a slender reflecting pool. Apple trees lined the walls, their boughs dense with clusters of white flowers. Their petals lay like a smattering of snow on the red tile floor and floated on the surface of the water.

I trailed Mal down the length of the pool. The air inside was balmy, sweet with apple blossoms and loamy with the rich scent of soil. Outside, the wind rose and howled with the storm, but in here it was as if the seasons had been suspended. I had the strangest sense that we could be anywhere, that the rest of the house had simply fallen away, and we were completely alone.

At the far end of the room, a desk was tucked into the corner. A shawl had been thrown over the back of a scrollwork chair. There was a basket of sewing things resting on a rug patterned with apple blossoms. The lady of the house must have come here to do her needlework, to sip her morning tea. In the daytime, she would have had a perfect view of the orchards through the big arched windows. A book was open on the desk. I peered at the pages.

"It's a diary," Mal said. "Statistics on the spring crop, the progress of hybrid trees."

"Her glasses," I said, picking up the gold wire frames. "I wonder if she's missing them."

Mal leaned against the stone rim of the pool. "Do you ever wonder what it might have been like if the Grisha Examiners had discovered your power back at Keramzin?"

"Sometimes."

"Ravka would be different."

"Maybe not. My power was useless before we found the stag. Without you, we might never have located any of Morozova's amplifiers."

"*You'd* be different," he said.

I put the delicate frames aside and flipped through the columns of numbers and tidy handwriting. What kind of person might I have been? Would I have become friends with Genya or simply seen her as a servant? Would I have had Zoya's confidence? Her easy arrogance? What would the Darkling have been to me?

"I can tell you what would have happened," I said.

"Go on."

I closed the diary and turned back to Mal, perching on the edge of the desk. "I would have gone to the Little Palace and been spoiled and pampered. I would have dined off golden plates, and I never would have struggled to use my power. It would have been like breathing, the way it always should have been. And in time, I would have forgotten Keramzin."

"And me."

"Never you."

He raised a brow.

"Possibly you," I admitted. He laughed. "The Darkling would have sought Morozova's amplifiers, fruitlessly, hopelessly, until one day a tracker, a no one, an *otkazat'sya* orphan, travelled into the ice of Tsibeya."

"You're assuming I didn't die on the Fold."

"In my version, you were never sent into the Fold. When you tell the story, you can die tragically."

"In that case, carry on."

"This nobody, this nothing, this pathetic orphan—"

"I get it."

301

"He would be the first to spot the stag after centuries of searching. So of course the Darkling and I would have to travel to Tsibeya in his great black coach."

"In the snow?"

"His great black sleigh," I amended. "And when we arrived at Chernast, your unit would be led into our exalted presence—"

"Are we allowed to walk, or do we wriggle in on our bellies like the lowly worms we are?"

"You walk, but you do it with a lot of deference. I would be seated on a raised dais, and I would wear jewels in my hair and a golden *kefta*."

"Not black?"

I paused. "Maybe black."

"It wouldn't matter," Mal said. "I still wouldn't be able to stop looking at you."

I laughed. "No, you would be making eyes at Zoya."

"Zoya's there?"

"Isn't she always?"

He smiled. "I would have noticed you."

"Of course you would. I'm the Sun Summoner, after all."

"You know what I mean."

I looked down, brushing petals off of the desk. "Did you ever notice me at Keramzin?"

He was silent for a long moment, and when I glanced at him, he was looking up at the glass ceiling. He'd gone red as a beet.

"Mal?"

He cleared his throat, crossed his arms. "As a matter of fact, I did. I had some very . . . distracting thoughts about you."

"You did?" I sputtered.

"And I felt guilty for every one of them. You were supposed to be my best friend, not . . ." He shrugged and turned even redder.

"Idiot."

"That fact is well established and adds nothing to the plot."

"Well," I said, taking another swipe at the petals, "it wouldn't matter if you noticed me, because I would have noticed you."

"A lowly *otkazat'sya*?"

"That's right," I said quietly. I didn't feel like teasing him any more.

"And what would you have seen?"

"A soldier – cocky, scarred, extraordinary. And that would have been our beginning."

He rose and closed the distance between us. "And this still would have been our end." He was right. Even in dreams, we had no future. If we somehow both survived tomorrow, I would have to seek an alliance and a crown. Mal would have to find a way to keep his heritage a secret.

Gently, he took my face in his hands. "I would have been different too, without you. Weaker, reckless." He smiled slightly. "Afraid of the dark." He brushed the tears from my cheeks. I wasn't sure when they'd started. "But no matter who or what I was, I would have been yours."

I kissed him then – with grief and need and years of longing, with the desperate hope that I could keep him here in my arms, with the damning knowledge that I could not. I leaned into him, the press of his chest, the breadth of his shoulders.

"Going to miss this," he said as he kissed my cheeks, my jaw, my eyelids. "The way you taste." He set his lips to the hollow beneath my ear. "The way you smell." His hands slid up my back. "The way you feel." My breath hitched as his hips settled against mine.

Then he drew back, searching my eyes. "I wanted more for you," he said. "A white veil in your hair. Vows we could keep."

"A proper wedding night? Just tell me this isn't goodbye. That's the only vow I need."

"I love you, Alina."

He kissed me again. He hadn't answered, but I didn't care, because his mouth was on mine, and in this moment, I could pretend I wasn't a saviour or a Saint, that I could simply choose him, have a life, be in love. That we wouldn't have one night, we would have thousands. I pulled him down with me, easing his body over mine, feeling the cold floor at my back. He had a soldier's hands, rough and calloused, heating my skin, sending hungry sparks through my body that made me lift my hips to try and bring him closer.

I pulled his shirt over his head, letting my fingers trail over the smooth ridges of his muscled back, feeling the lightly raised lines of the words that marked him. But when he slid the fabric of my blouse from my arms, I stiffened, feeling suddenly, painfully aware of every wrong thing about me. Jutting bones, too-small breasts, skin pale and dry as an onion. Then he cupped my cheek, his thumb tracing my lip.

"You are all I've ever wanted," he said. "You are the whole of my heart."

I saw myself then – sour, silly, difficult, lovely in his

eyes. I drew him to me, felt him shudder as our bodies came together, skin against skin, felt the heat of his lips, his tongue, hands moving until the need between us drew taut and anxious as a bowstring waiting for release.

He clasped his hand to my wrist and my mind filled with light. All I saw was Mal's face, all I felt was his body – above me, around me, an awkward rhythm at first, then slow and steady as the beat of the rain. It was all we needed. It was all we would ever have.

Chapter 17

The next morning, I woke to find that Mal had already risen. He'd left me a pot of hot tea on a tray surrounded by apple blossoms. The rain had stopped, but the walls of the conservatory were covered in mist. I rubbed my sleeve against a pane of glass and looked out into the deep blue of early dawn. A deer was moving between the trees, head bent to the sweet grass.

I dressed slowly, drank my tea, lingered by the reflecting pool where the lanterns had long since gone out. In a few hours' time, this place might be buried in darkness. I wanted to remember every detail. On a whim, I picked up a pen and flipped to the last page of the diary and wrote our names.

Alina Starkov
Malyen Oretsev

I wasn't sure why I did it. I just needed to say we had been there.

I found the others packing up in the main hall. Genya waylaid me by the door with my coat in her hands. The olive wool was freshly pressed.

"You should look your best when you put the Darkling in the ground."

"Thanks," I said with a smile. "I'll try not to bleed all over it."

She kissed both of my cheeks. "Good luck. We'll be waiting when you get back."

I took her hand and placed Nikolai's ring in her palm. "If something goes wrong, if we don't make it – take David and Misha and get to Os Kervo. This should buy you all the help you need."

She swallowed, then hugged me hard.

Outside, the Soldat Sol waited in rigid formation, rifles on their backs, canisters of inactive *lumiya* slung over their shoulders. The tattoos on their faces looked fierce in the dawn light. The Grisha wore roughspun. They might have been ordinary soldiers.

Harshaw had left Oncat curled up with Misha, but now she sat in the parlour window, lazily grooming herself and watching us assemble. Tolya and Tamar had their golden sunbursts pinned to their chests. Mal's was still with Misha. He smiled when he saw me, and tapped the space where the pin would have gone, right over his heart.

The deer had scattered. The orchard was empty as we moved through it, boots leaving deep marks on the soft earth. A half hour later, we were standing at the shores of the Fold.

I joined the other Etherealki: Zoya, Nadia, Adrik, and Harshaw. It felt somehow right that we should be the first to enter and that we would do it together. The Squallers raised their arms, summoning current and dropping the pressure as Zoya had done back in the caves. My ears crackled as they layered the acoustic blanket. If it didn't hold, Harshaw and I were ready to summon light and fire to drive the volcra back. We spread out in a line, and with measured steps, we entered the darkness of the Fold.

The Unsea always felt like the end of everything. It

wasn't only the dark, it was the terrible sense of isolation, as if the world had disappeared, leaving only you, the rattle of your breath, the stuttering beat of your heart.

As we stepped onto the dead grey sands and the darkness thickened around us, it took everything in me not to raise my hands and wrap all of us in safe, protective light. I listened closely, expecting to hear the beating of wings, one of those horrible, inhuman shrieks, but I heard nothing, not even our footsteps on the sand. Whatever the Squallers were doing was working. The silence was deep and impenetrable.

"Hello?" I whispered.

"We hear you." I whirled. I knew Zoya was further down the line, though it sounded as if she was speaking right in my ear.

We moved at a steady pace. I heard a click, then almost ten minutes later, a double click. We'd gone a mile. At one point, I heard the distant flap of wings above us, and I felt fear move through our ranks like a living thing. The volcra might not hear us but they could scent prey from miles away. Were they circling above us even now, sensing that something was wrong, that someone was near? I doubted Zoya's trick would keep us safe for long. The absolute madness of what we were doing struck me in that moment. We had dared what no one else ever had: We'd entered the Fold without light.

We kept moving. Two clicks later, we stopped and took up our positions to wait. As soon as we sighted the Darkling's skiff, we'd have to move quickly.

My thoughts turned to him. Cautiously, I tested the tether that bound us. Hunger quaked through me with palpable force. He was eager, ready to unleash the power of the Fold, ready for a fight. I felt it too. I let it echo back to him, that rush of anticipation, that need: *I am coming for you.*

Mal and Tolya – maybe all of the others – believed that the amplifiers had to be brought together, but they had never felt the thrill of using *merzost*. It was something no other Grisha understood, and in the end, it was what bound the Darkling and me most closely – not our powers, not the strangeness of them, not that we were both aberrations, if not abominations. It was our knowledge of the forbidden, our desire for more.

The minutes ticked by, and my nerves began to jangle. The Squallers could maintain the acoustic blanket for only so long. What if the Darkling waited until night to attack? *Where are you?*

The answer came in a pale violet glow, moving towards us from the east.

Two clicks. We fanned out in the formation we had practised.

Three clicks. That was my signal. I raised my hands and set the Fold ablaze. In the same moment, I bent the light, letting it flow around each of our soldiers like a stream.

What did the Darkling see? Dead sands, the flat sheen of a gray sky, the ruined hulks of skiffs falling to dust. And that was all. We were invisible. We were air.

The skiff slowed. As it drew closer, I saw its black sails marked with the sun in eclipse, the strange, smoked-glass quality of its hull. The violet flame of the *lumiya* shimmered over its sides, vague and flickering in the bright glare of my power.

Squallers stood at the masts in their blue *kefta*. A few Inferni lined the railings, flanked by Heartrenders in red, heavily armed *oprichniki* in gray. It was a spare force. The students must be belowdecks. The Darkling stood at the prow, surrounded by his shadow horde. As always, the first sight of him was practically a physical blow. It was like going to him in a vision: He was simply more real, more vibrant than everything else around him.

It happened so fast, I barely had time to register it. The first shot struck one of the Darkling's *oprichniki*. He toppled over the skiff's railing. Then the shots came in a rapid patter, like raindrops on a rooftop at the start of a storm. Grisha and *oprichniki* slumped and fell against one another as confusion broke out aboard the glass skiff. I saw more bodies fall.

Someone shouted, "Return fire!" and the air erupted with the jarring thunder of gunshots, but we were safely out of range. The *nichevo'ya* beat their wings, turning in wide arcs, searching for targets. Flints were struck, and the Inferni who remained on the skiff sent gouts of flame flaring through the air. Cloaked from sight, Harshaw turned the fire back on them. I heard screams.

Then silence, broken only by moaning and shouted orders from the glass skiff. Our sharpshooters had done their job well. The area around the railing was littered with bodies. The Darkling, unharmed, was pointing to a Heartrender and issuing some kind of command. I couldn't make out his words, but I knew this was when he would use the students.

I looked around me, tracking the shooters, the Grisha, feeling their presence in the light.

A single click. The Squallers sent a wave of sand crashing through the air. More shouts rose from the deck as the Darkling's Squallers tried to respond.

That was our cue. The twins and I bolted for the skiff, approaching from the stern. We didn't have much time.

"Where are they?" Tolya whispered as we boarded. It was strange to hear his voice but not to see him.

"Maybe below," I replied. The skiff was shallow, but there was room enough.

We picked our way across the deck, searching for a hatch, careful not to brush against the Darkling's Grisha and guards.

The remaining *oprichniki* had their guns trained on the empty sands beyond the skiff. We were so close that I could see the sweat on their brows, their wide eyes. They twitched, jumping at every real or imagined sound. "*Maleni*," they whispered. Ghosts. Only the Darkling seemed unfazed. His face was serene as he surveyed the destruction I'd loosed. I was close enough to strike, but he was still protected by his shadow soldiers. I had the uneasy sensation that he was waiting for something.

Suddenly, an *oprichnik* yelled, "Get down!"

The people around us dove to the deck and the air exploded with gunfire.

Two other glass skiffs ploughed into view, loaded with *oprichniki*. As soon as they came into contact with the light, the skiffs ignited with the glowing violet flame of *lumiya*.

"Did you think I would come to meet you unprepared, Alina?" the Darkling called over the chaos. "Did you think I would not sacrifice an entire fleet of skiffs to this cause?"

However many he had sent, only two had made it through. But that would be enough to turn the tide. I heard screams, shouting, our soldiers returning fire. A red stain appeared in the sand and with a lurch I realised that one of our people was bleeding. It could be Vladim. Zoya. Mal. I had to get them out of here. Where were the students? I tried to keep my focus. I couldn't let the light falter. Our forces had canisters of *lumiya*. They could retreat into the Fold, but I knew they wouldn't. Not until I was clear of the Darkling's skiff.

I crept around the masts, searching for some sign of a trapdoor or hatch.

Then a searing pain cut through my shoulder. I fell backward, crying out. I'd been shot.

I sprawled on the deck, feeling my hold on the light falter. Tolya's shape flickered into view beside me. I tried to regain control. He disappeared, but through the railing I could see soldiers and Grisha appearing on the sands. *Oprichniki* leapt from the other skiffs, moving in for the attack, and the *nichevo'ya* surged into the battle.

Panic clamoured through me as I scrambled for focus. I couldn't feel my right arm. I made myself breathe. *Stop huffing like a wild boar.* If Adrik could summon with one arm, then I could too.

Tamar appeared near the prow, vanished, stuttered back into view. A *nichevo'ya* slammed into her. She screamed as it sunk its claws deep into her back.

No. I gathered my fractured concentration and reached for the Cut, though I had only one good arm to wield it. I wasn't sure that I could hit the shadow soldier without wounding Tamar, but I couldn't just watch her die.

Then another shape dove into the fray from above. It took me a long second to understand what I was seeing: Nikolai – fangs bared, wings spread.

With his talons, he seized the *nichevo'ya* that held Tamar and wrenched its head back, forcing it to release her. It skittered and writhed, but Nikolai flew upward and hurled it into the blackness beyond. I heard frenzied shrieks from somewhere in the distance – volcra. The shadow soldier did not reappear.

Nikolai swooped back down, barrelling into another of the Darkling's *nichevo'ya*. I could almost imagine his laugh. *Well, if I'm going to be a monster, I might as well be king of the monsters.*

Then I gasped as my good arm was slammed down to the deck. The Darkling loomed over me, his boot pressing down painfully on my wrist.

"There you are," he said in his cool, cut-glass voice. "Hello, Alina."

The light collapsed. Darkness crowded in, lit only by the eerie flicker of violet flame.

I grunted as the Darkling's boot ground down on the bones of my arm.

"Where are the students?" I gritted out.

"They aren't here."

"What did you do to them?"

"They're safe and sound back in Kribirsk. Probably having their lunch." His *nichevo'ya* circled around us, forming a perfect, protective dome that shifted and writhed—wings, talons, hands. "I knew the threat would be enough. Did you really believe I would endanger Grisha children when we've lost so many?"

"I thought . . ." I'd thought he was capable of anything. *He wanted me to believe*, I realised. When he'd shown me Botkin's and Ana Kuya's corpses. He'd wanted me to believe in his ruthlessness. Then I remembered his words from so long ago: *Make me your villain.*

"I know what you thought, what you've always thought of me. It's so much easier that way, isn't it? To puff yourself up with your own righteousness."

"I didn't invent your crimes." This wasn't over yet. All I needed was to reach the flint in my sleeve. All I needed was a spark. It might not kill either of us, but it would hurt like hell, and it might buy the others time.

"Where is the boy? I have my Summoner. I want my tracker too."

Mal was still just a tracker to him, thank the Saints. My good hand curled into my sleeve, brushed the edge of the flint. "I won't let him be used," I said. "Not as leverage. Not as anything."

"On your back, the faithful dying around you, and yet you remain defiant."

He yanked me to my feet. Two *nichevo'ya* slid into place to restrain me as the flint slipped out of my grasp. The Darkling shoved the fabric of my coat aside, his hands sliding down my body. My heart sank as his fingers closed over the first pack of blasting powder. He pulled it from my pocket, then quickly located the second. He sighed.

"I can feel your intent as you feel mine, Alina. Your hopeless resolve, your martyr's determination. I recognise it now."

The tether. An idea came to me then. It was the smallest chance, but I would take it.

The Darkling tossed the packs of blasting powder to a *nichevo'ya* who arced away with them into the darkness. He watched me with cool grey eyes as we waited, the sounds of the battle muffled by the whirring of the shadow soldiers around us. A moment later, a shattering *boom* sounded from somewhere in the distance.

The Darkling shook his head. "It may well take me

another lifetime to break you, Alina, but I will put my mind to the task."

He turned and I acted. Restrained by the *nichevo'ya*, I couldn't use the Cut, but I wasn't powerless. I twisted my wrists. The violet light of the *lumiya* bent around me. At the same time, I reached across the tether between us.

The Darkling's head jerked up and for a moment, though I still stood invisible in the grip of the *nichevo'ya*, I was staring at him from beside the mast. The vision of the girl before him was whole and unwounded. She raised her arms to deliver the Cut. The Darkling didn't stop to think – he reacted. It was the barest second, the brief space between instinct and understanding, but it was enough. His shadow soldiers released me and sprang forward to protect him. I lunged towards the railing and threw myself over the side of the skiff.

I landed on my wounded arm, and pain slammed through my body. The Darkling's howl of rage sounded behind me. I knew I'd lost control of the light, and that meant I was visible. I made myself keep moving, dragging myself across the sand, away from the violet glow of the *lumiya*. I saw sun soldiers and Grisha fighting by the illuminated skiffs. Harshaw down. Ruby bleeding.

I forced myself to my feet. My head spun. I clutched my wounded arm and lurched into the darkness. I had no sight, no sense of direction. I plunged further into the black, trying to make my mind work, to form some kind of plan. I knew the volcra could come for me at any moment, but I couldn't risk the light. *Think*, I berated myself. I was out of ideas. The blasting powders were gone. I couldn't raise the Cut. My sleeve was wet with blood, and my footsteps slowed. I had to find someone to heal my arm.

I had to regroup. I couldn't just run from the Darkling again the way I'd done that first time on the Fold. I'd been running ever since.

"Alina."

I spun. Mal's voice in the dark. *Let it be a trick of sound*, I thought. But I knew the Squallers' blanket had long since been lifted. How had he found me? Stupid question. Mal would always find me.

I gasped as he grabbed my wounded arm. Despite the pain and the risk, I summoned a weak wash of light, saw his beautiful face streaked with dirt and blood. And the knife in his hand. I recognised the blade. It was Tamar's, Grisha-made. Had she offered it to him for this moment? Had he sought her out to ask for it?

"Mal, don't. This isn't over yet—"

"It is, Alina."

I tried to pull away, but he wrapped his hand hard around my wrist, fingers pinching together, the sharp jolt of power moving through both of us, calling me, demanding that I step through that door. With his other hand, he forced my fingers around the knife's grip. The light wavered.

"No!"

"Don't let it all be for nothing, Alina."

"Please—"

An agonised scream rose over the clamour of the battle. It sounded like Zoya.

"Save them, Alina. Don't let me live knowing I might have stopped this."

"Mal—"

"Save them. This once, let me carry you." His gaze locked on mine. "End this," he said.

His grip tightened. *There is no end to our story.*

I would never know if it was greed or selflessness that moved my hand. With Mal's fingers guiding mine, I shoved the knife up and into his chest.

The momentum jerked me forward, and I stumbled. I pulled back, the knife falling from both of our hands, blood spilling from the wound, but he kept his hold on my wrist.

"Mal," I sobbed.

He coughed and blood burbled from his lips. He swayed forward. I nearly toppled as I clutched him to me, his hold on my wrist so tight I thought the bones might snap. He gasped, a wet rattle. His full weight slumped against me, dragging me down, fingers still clenched, pressed against my skin as if he were taking my pulse.

I knew when he was gone. For a moment, all was silent, a held breath – and then everything exploded into white fire. A roar filled my ears, an avalanche of sound that shook the sands and made the very air vibrate.

I screamed as power flooded through me, as I burned, consumed from the inside. I was a living star. I was combustion. I was a new sun born to shatter air and eat the earth.

I am ruination.

The world trembled, dissolved, crashed in on itself.

And then the power was gone.

My eyes flew open. Thick darkness surrounded me. My ears were ringing.

I was on my knees. My hands found Mal's body, the damp crumple of his blood-soaked shirt.

I threw up my hands, calling the light. Nothing happened. I tried again, reaching for the power and finding only absence. I heard a shriek from above. The volcra were circling. I could see bursts of Inferni flame, the dim shapes of soldiers fighting in the violet glow of the skiffs. Somewhere, Tolya and Tamar were calling my name.

"Mal . . ." My throat was raw. I didn't know my own voice.

I sought the light, as I had once done deep in the belly of the White Cathedral, searching for any faint tendril. But this was different. I could feel the wound inside me, the gap where something whole and right had been. I wasn't broken. I was empty.

My fists bunched in Mal's shirt.

"Help me," I gasped.

What is infinite? The universe and the greed of men.

What lesson was this? What sick joke? When the Darkling had toyed with the power at the heart of creation, the Fold had been his reward, a place where his power was meaningless, an abomination that would keep him and his country in servitude for hundreds of years. Was this my punishment, then? Was Morozova truly mad, or was he just a failure?

"Someone help!" I screamed.

Tolya and Tamar were racing towards me, Zoya trailing behind, their bodies lit by glass canisters of *lumiya*. Tolya was limping. Zoya had a burn along one side of her face. Tamar was practically covered in blood from the wounds the *nichevo'ya* had given her. They all stopped short when they saw Mal.

"Bring him back," I cried.

Tolya and Tamar went to their knees beside him, but I saw the look they exchanged.

"Alina—" said Tamar.

"Please," I sobbed. "Bring him back to me."

Tamar opened Mal's mouth, attempting to force air

into his lungs. Tolya placed one hand on Mal's chest, applying pressure to the wound and trying to restore the beat of his heart.

"We need more light," he said.

A choked laugh escaped me. I held up my hands, pleading with the light and with any Saint who had ever lived. It was no good. The gesture felt false. It was a pantomime. There was nothing there.

"I don't understand," I cried as I pressed my wet cheek to Mal's. His skin was already cooling.

Baghra had warned me: *You may not be able to survive the sacrifice that* merzost *requires.* But what was the point of this sacrifice? Had we lived only to be a lesson in the price of greed? Was that the truth of Morozova's madness, some kind of cruel equation that took all our love and loss and added them up to nothing?

It was too much. The hate and pain and grief overwhelmed me. If I'd had my power back for even a second, I would have burned the world to a cinder.

Then I saw it – a light in the distance, a gleaming blade that pierced the dark.

Before I could make sense of it, another appeared – a bright point that became two broad beams, sweeping high and wild above me.

A torrent of light burst from the darkness just a few feet from me. As my eyes adjusted I saw Vladim, his mouth open in shock and confusion as light poured from his palms.

I turned my head and saw them sparking to life, one by one across the Fold, like stars appearing in a twilight sky, Soldat Sol and *oprichniki*, their weapons forgotten, their faces baffled, awed, terrified, and bathed in light.

The Darkling's words came back to me, spoken on a ship that sailed the icy waters of the Bone Road. *Morozova was a strange man. He was a bit like you, drawn to the ordinary and the weak.*

He'd had an *otkazat'sya* wife.

He'd nearly lost an *otkazat'sya* child.

He'd thought himself alone in the world, alone in his power.

Now I understood. I saw what he had done. This was the gift of the three amplifiers: power multiplied a thousand times, but not in one person. How many new Summoners had just been created? How far had Morozova's power reached?

The arcs and cascades of light blossomed around me, a bright garden growing in this unnatural night. The beams met, and where they crossed, the darkness burned away.

The shrieks of the volcra erupted around me as the Fold began to unravel. It was a miracle.

And I didn't care. The Saints could keep their miracles. The Grisha could keep their long lives and their lessons. Mal was dead.

"How?"

I looked up. The Darkling stood behind us, stunned, taking in the impossible sight of the Fold coming apart around us. "This can't be. Not without the firebird. The third—" He stopped short as his eyes settled on Mal's body, the blood on my hands. "It can't be," he repeated.

Even now, as the world we knew was remade in bursts and flashes of light, he couldn't comprehend what Mal truly was. He wouldn't.

"What power is this?" he demanded. The Darkling stalked towards us, shadows pooling in his palms, his creatures swirling around him.

The twins drew their weapons. Without thinking, I lifted my hands, reaching for the light. Nothing happened.

The Darkling stared. He dropped his arms. The skeins of darkness faded.

"No," he said, bewildered, shaking his head. "No. This isn't— What have you done?"

"Keep working," I ordered the twins.

"Alina—"

"*Bring him back to me*," I repeated. I wasn't making sense. I knew that. They didn't have Morozova's power. But Mal could make rabbits out of rocks. He could find true north standing on his head. He would find his way back to me again.

I lurched to my feet, and the Darkling strode towards me.

His hands went to my throat. "No," he whispered.

Only then did I realise the collar had fallen away. I looked down. It lay in pieces beside Mal's body. My wrist was bare; the fetter had broken too.

"This isn't right," he said, and in his voice I heard desperation, a new and unfamiliar anguish. His fingers skimmed my neck, cupped my face. I felt no surge of surety. No light stirred within me to answer his call. His grey eyes searched mine – confused, nearly frightened. "You were meant to be like me. You were meant . . . You're *nothing* now."

He dropped his hands. I saw the realisation strike him. He was truly alone. And he always would be.

I saw the emptiness enter his eyes, felt the yawning void inside him stretch wider, an infinite wasteland. The calm left him, all that cool certainty. He cried out in his rage.

He spread his arms wide, calling the darkness. The *nichevo'ya* scattered like a flock of birds flushed from a hedge and turned on Soldat Sol and *oprichniki* alike, cutting them down, snuffing out the beams of light that blazed from their bodies. I knew there was no bottom to the Darkling's pain. He would just keep falling and falling.

Mercy. Had I ever really understood it? Had I actually believed I knew what it was to suffer? To forgive? *Mercy,* I thought. *For the stag, for the Darkling, for us all.*

If we'd still been bound by that tether, he might have sensed what I was about to do. My fingers twitched in the sleeve of my coat, curling a scrap of shadow around the blade of my knife – the knife I had plucked from the sands, wet with Mal's blood. This was the only power that was left to me, one that had never really been mine. An echo, a joke, a carnival trick. *It's something you took from him.*

"I don't need to be Grisha," I whispered, "to wield Grisha steel."

With one swift movement, I drove the shadow-wrapped blade deep into the Darkling's heart.

He made a soft sound, little more than an exhalation. He looked down at the hilt protruding from his chest, then back up at me. He frowned, took a step, tottered slightly. He righted himself.

A single laugh burst from his lips, and a fine spray of blood settled over his chin. "Like *this*?"

His legs faltered. He tried to stop his descent, but his arm gave way and he crumpled, rolling to his back. *It's simple enough. Like calls to like.* The Darkling's own power. Morozova's own blood.

"Blue sky," he said. I looked. In the distance I saw it, a pale glimmer, almost completely obscured by the black mist of the Fold. The volcra were swooping away from it, looking for somewhere to hide. "Alina," he breathed.

I knelt beside him. The *nichevo'ya* had left off their attacks. They circled and clattered above us, unsure of what to do. I thought I glimpsed Nikolai among them, arcing towards that patch of blue.

"Alina," the Darkling repeated, his fingers seeking mine. I was surprised to find fresh tears filling my eyes.

He reached up and brushed his knuckles over the wetness on my cheek. The smallest smile touched his bloodstained lips. "Someone to mourn me." He dropped his hand, as if the weight were too much. "No grave," he gasped, his hand tightening on mine, "for them to desecrate."

"All right," I said. The tears came harder. *There will be nothing left.*

He shuddered. His eyelids drooped.

"Once more," he said. "Speak my name once more."

He was ancient, I knew that. But in this moment he was just a boy – brilliant, blessed with too much power, burdened by eternity.

"Aleksander."

His eyes fluttered shut. "Don't let me be alone," he murmured. And then he was gone.

A sound like a great sigh rushed over us, lifting my hair. The *nichevo'ya* blew apart, scattering like ashes in wind, leaving startled soldiers and Grisha staring at the places where they'd been. I heard a wrenching cry and looked up in time to see Nikolai's wings dissolve, darkness spilling from him in black wisps as he plummeted to the grey sand. Zoya ran to him, trying to slow his fall with an updraft.

I knew I should move. I should do something. But I couldn't seem to make my legs work. I slumped between

Mal and the Darkling, the last of Morozova's line. I was bleeding from my bullet wound. I touched the bare skin at my neck. It felt naked.

Dimly, I was aware of the Darkling's Grisha retreating. Some of the *oprichniki* went too, the light still flowing from them in uncontrollable fits and starts. I didn't know where they were going. Maybe back to Kribirsk to warn their compatriots that their master had fallen. Maybe they were just running. I didn't care.

I heard Tolya and Tamar whispering back and forth. I couldn't make out the words, but the resignation in their voices was clear enough.

"Nothing left," I said softly, feeling the emptiness inside me, the emptiness everywhere.

The Soldat Sol were cheering, letting light blaze around them in glorious arcs as they burned the Fold away. Some of them had climbed up on the Darkling's glass skiffs. Others had formed a line, bringing the beams of light together, sending a cascade of sunlight speeding through the thinning scraps of darkness, unravelling the Fold in a rippling wave.

They were crying, laughing, joyous in their triumph, so loud that I almost didn't hear it – a soft rasp, fragile, impossible. I tried to keep it out, but hope came at me hard, a longing so acute I knew its end would break me.

Tamar sobbed. Tolya swore. And there it was again: the thready, miraculous sound of Mal drawing breath.

Chapter 18

They took us out of the Fold in one of the Darkling's skiffs. Zoya appropriated the battered glass vessel with effortless command, then kept the curious Soldat Sol distracted as Tolya and Tamar loaded us onto the deck, hidden beneath heavy coats and folded *kefta*. The Darkling's body was wrapped in the blue robes of one of his fallen Inferni. I'd made him a promise, and I intended to keep it.

The Squallers – Zoya, Nadia, and Adrik, all of them alive and as whole as they'd been when the battle began – filled the black sails and carried us over the dead sands as fast as their power would allow.

I lay next to Mal. He was still in terrible pain, drifting in and out of consciousness. Tolya continued to work on him, checking his pulse and his breathing.

Somewhere on the skiff, I heard Nikolai talking, his voice husky and damaged by whatever dark thing had used him. I wanted to go to him, see his face, make sure he was all right. He must have broken bones after that fall. But I'd lost a lot of blood, and I found myself slipping away, my weary mind eager for oblivion. As my eyes began to slide shut, I grabbed Tolya's hand.

"I died here. Do you understand?" He frowned. He thought I was delirious, but I needed to make him hear.

"This was my martyrdom, Tolya. I died here today."

"Sankta Alina," he said softly, and pressed a kiss to my knuckles, a courtly gesture, like a gentleman at a dance. I prayed to all the real Saints that he understood.

In the end, my friends did a good job of my death, and an even better job of Nikolai's resurrection.

They got us back to Tomikyana and stashed us in the barn, tucked away with the cider presses in case the Soldat Sol returned. They got Nikolai cleaned up, cut his hair, filled him with sugary tea and stale bread. Genya even found him a First Army uniform. Within hours, he was headed to Kribirsk, flanked by the twins, along with Nadia and Zoya, dressed in blue *kefta* stolen from the dead.

The story they concocted was simple: He'd been the Darkling's prisoner, slated for execution on the Fold, but he'd escaped and, with the Sun Summoner's help, managed to vanquish the Darkling. Few people knew the truth of what had happened. The battle had been a confusion of violence waged in near darkness, and I suspected the Darkling's Grisha and *oprichniki* would be too busy running or begging for royal pardons to dispute this new version of events. It was a good story with a tragic ending – the Sun Summoner had given her life to save Ravka and its new King.

Most of my hours back at Tomikyana were a blur: The smell of apples. The rustle of pigeons in the eaves. The rise and fall of Mal's breath beside me. At some point, Genya came to look in on us, and I thought I must be dreaming. The scars on her face were still there, but most of the black ridges were gone.

"Your shoulder too," she said with a smile. "Scarred, but not nearly so frightening."

"Your eye?" I asked.

"Gone for good. But I've grown rather fond of my patch. I think it lends me a certain rakishness."

I must have dozed off because the next thing I knew, Misha was standing in front of me with flour on his hands.

"What were you baking?" I asked, my words blurry at the edges.

"Ginger cake."

"Not apple?"

"I'm sick of apples. Do you want to stir the icing?"

I remembered nodding, then fell back asleep.

It wasn't until late that night that Zoya and Tamar came to check on us, bringing news from Kribirsk. It seemed that the power of the amplifiers had reached all the way to the drydocks. The explosion had knocked Grisha and dockworkers from their feet, and mayhem had erupted as light started to pour from every *otkazat'sya* within range.

As the Fold began to disintegrate, they'd dared to step past its shores and join in the destruction. Some of them had picked up guns and started hunting volcra, rounding them up in the few remaining scraps of the Fold and putting them to death. It was said some of the monsters had escaped, braving the light to seek deep shadows elsewhere. Now, between the dockworkers, the Soldat Sol, and the *oprichniki* who had not fled, all that remained of the Unsea were a few dark wisps that hung in the air or trailed over the ground like lost creatures separated from the herd.

When rumours of the Darkling's death had reached Kribirsk, the military camp had descended into chaos – and in strode Nikolai Lantsov. He installed himself in the royal quarters, began assembling First Army captains and Grisha commanders, and simply started giving orders. He'd mobilised all the remaining units of the army to secure the borders, sent messages to the coast to rally Sturmhond's fleet, and had apparently managed it all on no sleep and two fractured ribs. No one else would have had the ability, let alone the nerve – certainly not a younger son and rumoured bastard. But Nikolai had been training for this his entire life, and I knew he had a gift for the impossible.

"How is he?" I asked Tamar.

She paused, then said, "Haunted. There's a difference in him, though I'm not sure anyone else would notice."

"Maybe," objected Zoya. "Though I've never seen anything like it. If he gets any more charming, men and women may start lying down in the street for the privilege of being stepped on by the new Ravkan King. However did you resist him?"

"Good question," Mal murmured from beside me.

"Turns out I don't care for emeralds," I said.

Zoya rolled her eyes. "Or royal blood, blinding charisma, tremendous wealth—"

"You can stop now," said Mal.

I leaned my head against his shoulder. "Those are all nice enough, but my real passion is lost causes." Or just one really. *Beznako*. My lost cause, found again.

"I am surrounded by fools," Zoya said, but she was smiling.

Before Tamar and Zoya returned to the main house,

Tamar checked our injuries. Mal was weak, but given what he'd been through, that was to be expected. Tamar had healed the bullet wound in my shoulder, and aside from being a bit shaky and sore, I felt as good as new. At least, that was what I told them. I could feel the ache of absence where my power had been like a phantom limb.

I dozed on the mattress they'd dragged into the barn, and when I woke, Mal was lying on his side, watching me. He was pale, and his blue eyes seemed almost too bright. I reached out and traced the scar that ran along his jaw, the one he'd gotten in Fjerda when he'd first been hunting the stag.

"What did you see?" I asked. "When—"

"When I died?"

I gave him a gentle shove, and he winced.

"I saw Ilya Morozova on the back of a unicorn, playing a balalaika."

"Very funny."

He eased back and carefully tucked his arm under his head. "I didn't see anything. All I remember is pain. The knife felt like it was on fire, like it was carving my heart from my chest. Then nothing. Just darkness."

"You were gone," I said with a shiver. "And then my power—" My voice broke.

He put out his arm, and I laid my head against his shoulder, careful not to disturb the bandages on his chest. "I'm sorry," he said. "There were times . . . there were times I wished your power away. But I never wanted this."

"I'm grateful to be alive," I said. "The Fold is gone. You're safe. It just . . . hurts." I felt petty. Harshaw was dead, and so were half of the Soldat Sol, including Ruby.

Then there were the others: Sergei, Marie, Paja, Fedyor, Botkin. Baghra. So many lost to this war. The list stretched on and on.

"Loss is loss," Mal said. "You have the right to grieve."

I stared up at the barn's wooden beams. Even the shred of darkness I'd commanded had abandoned me. That power had belonged to the Darkling, and it had left this world with him.

"I feel empty."

Mal was quiet for a long moment, then said, "I feel it too." I pushed up on my elbow. His gaze was far away. "I won't know until I try to track, but I feel different. I used to just know things. Even lying here, I could have sensed deer in the field, a bird resting on a branch, maybe a mouse burrowing in the wall. I never thought about it, but now there's this kind of . . . silence."

Loss. I'd wondered how Tolya and Tamar had brought Mal back. I'd been willing to simply call it a miracle. Now I thought I understood. Mal had possessed two lives, but only one was rightfully his. The other was stolen, an inheritance wrought from *merzost*, snatched from the making at the heart of the world. It was the force that had animated Morozova's daughter when her human life had gone, the power that had reverberated through Mal's bones. His blood had been thick with it, and that purloined bit of creation was what had made him such a remarkable tracker. It had bound him to every living thing. *Like calls to like.*

And now it was gone. The life stolen by Morozova and given to his daughter had reached its end. The life Mal had been born with – fragile, mortal, temporary – was his alone. Loss. This was the price the world had demanded for balance. But Morozova couldn't have known that the person to unlock the secrets of his amplifiers wouldn't be some ancient Grisha who had lived a thousand years and grown weary of his power. He couldn't have known that it would all come down to two orphans from Keramzin.

Mal took my hand, curling his fingers in mine, and pressed it to his chest. "Do you think you could be happy?" he asked. "With a used-up tracker?"

I smiled at that. Cocky Mal, charming, brave, and dangerous. Was that doubt in his voice? I kissed him once, gently. "If you can be happy with someone who stuck a knife in your chest."

"I helped. And I told you I can handle a bad mood."

I didn't know what came next or who I was supposed to be. I owned nothing, not even the borrowed clothes on my back. And yet, lying there, I realised I wasn't afraid. After all I'd been through, there was no fear left in me – sadness, gratitude, maybe even hope, but the fear had been eaten up by pain and challenge. The Saint was gone. The Summoner too. I was just a girl again, but this girl didn't owe her strength to fate or chance or a grand destiny. I'd been born with my power; the rest I'd earned.

"Mal, you'll have to be careful. The story of the amplifiers could leak out. People might still think you have power."

He shook his head. "Malyen Oretsev died with you," he said, his words echoing my thoughts closely enough to raise the hair on my arms. "That life is over. Maybe I'll be smarter in the next one."

I snorted. "We'll see. We're going to have to choose new names, you know."

"Misha is already making a list of suggestions."

"Oh, Saints."

"You have nothing to complain about. Apparently I am to be Dmitri Dumkin."

"Suits you."

"I should warn you that I'm keeping a tab of all of your insults so that I can reward you when I'm healed."

"Easy with the threats, Dumkin. Maybe I'll tell the Apparat all about your miraculous recovery, and he'll turn you into a Saint too."

"He can try," said Mal. "I don't intend to waste my days in holy pursuits."

"No?"

"No," he said as he drew me closer. "I have to spend the rest of my life finding ways to deserve a certain white-haired girl. She's very prickly, occasionally puts goose droppings in my shoes or tries to kill me."

"Sounds fatiguing," I managed as his lips met mine.

"She's worth it. And one day maybe she'll let me chase her into a chapel."

I shuddered. "I don't like chapels."

"I did tell Ana Kuya I would marry you."

I laughed. "You remember that?"

"Alina," he said and kissed the scar on my palm, "I remember everything."

It was time to leave Tomikyana behind. We'd had only one night to recover, but news of the destruction of the Fold was spreading fast, and soon the farm's owners might return. And even if I was no longer the Sun Summoner, there were still things I needed to do before I could bury Sankta Alina forever.

Genya brought us clean clothes. Mal limped behind the cider presses to change while she helped me put on a simple blouse and the *sarafan* that went over it. They were peasant clothes, not even military.

She'd once woven gold through my hair at the Little Palace, but now a more radical change was necessary. She used a pot of hematite and a clutch of shiny rooster feathers to temporarily alter its distinctive white colour, then tied a kerchief around my head for good measure.

Mal returned wearing a tunic and trousers and a simple coat. He had on a black wool cap with a narrow brim. Genya wrinkled her nose. "You look like a farmer."

"I've looked worse." He peered at me. "Is your hair red?"

"Temporarily."

"And she's almost pulling it off," Genya added, and sailed from the barn. The effects would fade in a few days without her assistance.

Genya and David would travel separately to meet with Grisha gathering at the military camp in Kribirsk. They'd offered to take Misha with them, but he'd elected to go with me and Mal. He claimed we needed looking after. We made sure that his golden sunburst was safely hidden away and that his pockets were stuffed with cheese for Oncat. Then we headed into the grey sands of what had once been the Fold.

It was easy to blend in with the crowds crossing to and from Ravka. There were families, groups of soldiers, nobles, and peasants. Children climbed over the ruins of sandskiffs. People gathered in spontaneous parties. They kissed and hugged, handed around bottles of *kvas* and fried bread stuffed with raisins. They greeted each other with shouts of "*Yunejhost!*" Unity.

Amid the celebrations, there were pockets of grief. Silence reigned in the crumbling remains of what had been Novokribirsk. Most of the buildings had slumped into dust. There were only dim suggestions of spaces where the streets had been, and everything had been bleached a nearly colourless grey. The round stone fountain that had stood at the centre of the town looked like a crescent moon, eaten away wherever the Fold's dark power had touched it. Old men poked at the odd ruins and muttered to each other. Even beyond the fallen town's edges, mourners laid flowers on the wrecks of skiffs, and built little altars in their hulls.

Everywhere, I saw people wearing the double eagle, carrying banners, and waving Ravkan flags. Girls wore pale blue and gold ribbons in their hair, and I heard whispers of the tortures the brave young prince had endured at the Darkling's hands.

I heard my name too. Pilgrims were already flooding into the Fold to see the miracle that had occurred and to offer up prayers to Sankta Alina. Once again, vendors had begun setting up carts littered with what they claimed were my finger bones, and my face stared back at me from the painted surfaces of wooden icons. It wasn't quite me, though. This was a prettier girl, with round cheeks and serene brown eyes, the antlers of Morozova's collar resting on her slender neck. Alina of the Fold.

No one spared us a second glance. We weren't nobles. We weren't Second Army. We weren't this strange new class of Summoner soldier. We were anonymous. We were tourists.

In Kribirsk, the party was in full swing. The drydocks were ablaze with coloured lanterns. People sang and drank aboard the sandskiffs. They crowded on the steps of the barracks and raided the mess tent for food. I glimpsed the yellow flag of the Documents Tent, and though some part of me ached to return there, to take in the old familiar smells of ink and paper, I couldn't risk the possibility that one of the cartographers would recognise me.

The brothels and taverns in town were doing a booming business. An impromptu dance was being held in the central square, though just down the street a crowd had gathered at the old church to read the names written on its walls and light candles for the dead. I paused to light one for Harshaw, then another, and another. He would have liked the flames.

Tamar had found a room for us at one of the more respectable inns. I left Mal and Misha there with promises to return that night. The news coming out of Os Alta was still a tangle, and we hadn't had word of Misha's mother yet. I knew he must be hopeful, but he hadn't said a word about it, just solemnly vowed to watch over Mal in my absence.

"Read him religious parables," I whispered to Misha. "He *loves* that."

I barely dodged the pillow Mal threw across the room.

I didn't go directly to the royal barracks, but took a route that led me past where the Darkling's silk pavilion had once stood. I'd assumed that he would rebuild it, but the field was empty, and when I reached the Lantsov quarters, I quickly understood why. The Darkling had taken up residence there. He'd hung black banners from the windows and the carving of the double eagle above the doors had been replaced with a sun in eclipse. Now workmen were pulling down the black silks and replacing them with Ravkan blue and gold. An awning had been set up to catch plaster as a soldier took a massive hammer to the stone symbol above the door, shattering it to dust. A cheer went up from the crowd. I couldn't share in their excitement. For all his crimes, the Darkling had loved Ravka, and he'd wanted its love in return.

I found a guard near the entry and asked after Tamar Kir-Bataar. He looked down his nose at me, seeing nothing but a scrawny peasant girl, and for a moment, I heard the Darkling say, *You're* nothing *now*. The girl I'd once been would have believed him. The girl I'd become wasn't in the mood.

"What exactly are you waiting for?" I snapped. The soldier blinked and jumped to attention. A few minutes later, Tamar and Tolya were jogging down the steps to me.

Tolya swept me up in his huge arms.

"Our sister," he explained to the curious guard.

"Our sister?" hissed Tamar as we entered the royal barracks. "She doesn't look anything like us. Remind me never to let you work intelligence."

"I have better things to do than trade in whispers," he said with dignity. "Besides, she *is* our sister."

I swallowed the lump in my throat and said, "Did I come at a bad time?"

Tamar shook her head. "Nikolai ended meetings early so people could attend the . . ." She trailed off.

I nodded.

They led me down a hall decorated with weapons of war and charts of the Fold. Those maps would have to change now. I wondered if anything would ever grow on those deadened sands.

"Will you stay with him?" I asked Tamar. Nikolai had to be desperate for people he could trust around him.

"For a while. Nadia wants to, and there are still some members of the Twenty-Second alive too."

"Nevsky?"

She shook her head.

"Did Stigg make it out of the Spinning Wheel?"

She shook her head again. There were others to ask after, casualty lists I dreaded reading, but that would have to wait.

"I might stay on," said Tolya. "Depends on—"

"Tolya," his sister said sharply.

Tolya flushed and shrugged. "Just depends."

We reached a set of heavy double doors, their handles the heads of two screaming eagles.

Tamar knocked. The room was dark, lit only by the blaze of a fire in the grate. It took me a moment to pick Nikolai out in the gloom. He was seated in front of the fire, his polished boots propped up on a cushioned stool. A plate of food sat beside him, along with a bottle of *kvas*, though I knew he preferred brandy.

"We'll be outside," Tamar said.

At the sound of the door shutting, Nikolai started. He jumped to his feet and bowed. "Forgive me," he said. "I was lost in thought." Then he grinned and added, "Unfamiliar territory."

I leaned back against the door. A lapse. Covered with charm, but a lapse nonetheless. "You don't have to do that."

"But I do." His smile slipped. He gestured to the chairs by the fire. "Join me?"

I crossed the room. The long table was littered with documents and sheaves of letters emblazoned with the royal seal.

A book lay open on the chair. He moved it aside and we sat.

"What are you reading?"

He glanced at the title. "One of Kamenski's military histories. Really, I just wanted to look at the words." He ran his fingers over the cover. His hands were marred with nicks and cuts. Though my scars had faded, the Darkling had marked Nikolai in a different way. Faint black lines still ran along each of his fingers, scars from where claws had shoved their way through his skin. He would have to pass them off as signs of the torture he'd endured as the Darkling's prisoner. In a way, it was true. At least the rest of the markings seemed to have faded. "I couldn't read," he continued. "When I was . . . I would see signs in store windows, writing on crates. I couldn't understand them, but I remembered enough to know that they were more than scratches on a wall."

I settled deeper into the chair. "What else do you remember?"

His hazel eyes were distant. "Too much. I . . . I can still feel that darkness inside me. I keep thinking it will go, but—"

"I know," I said. "It's better now, but it's still there." Like a shadow next to my heart. I didn't know what that might imply about the Darkling's power, and I didn't want to consider it. "Maybe it will fade in time."

He pinched the bridge of his nose between two fingers. "This isn't what people want of a king, what they expect from me."

"Give yourself a chance to heal."

"Everyone is watching. They need reassurance. It won't be long before the Fjerdans or the Shu try to move against me."

"What will you do?"

"My fleet is intact, thank the Saints and Privyet," he said, referring to the officer he'd left in command when he'd given up the mantle of Sturmhond. "They should be able to neutralise Fjerda for a time, and there are supply ships already waiting in the harbour with deliveries of weapons. I've sent word to every operational military outpost. We'll do our best to secure the borders. I leave for Os Alta tomorrow, and I have emissaries en route to try to bring the militias back under the King's flag." He gave a slight laugh. "My flag."

I smiled. "Just think of all the bowing and scraping in your future."

"All hail the Pirate King."

"Privateer."

"Why dance around it? 'Bastard King' is more likely."

"Actually," I said, "they're already calling you *Korol Rezni*." I'd heard it whispered in the streets of Kribirsk: King of Scars.

He looked up sharply. "Do you think they know?"

"I doubt it. You're used to rumours, Nikolai – this might be a good thing."

He raised a brow.

"I know you love to be loved," I said, "but a little fear couldn't hurt, either."

"Did the Darkling teach you that?"

"And you. I seem to remember a certain story about a Fjerdan captain's fingers and a hungry hound."

"Next time warn me when you're paying attention. I'll talk less."

"*Now* you tell me."

A faint smile tugged at his lips. Then he frowned. "I should warn you – the Apparat will be there tonight."

I sat up straighter. "You pardoned the priest?"

"I had to. I need his support."

"Will you offer him a place at court?"

"We're in negotiations," he said bitterly.

I could offer him all the information I had on the Apparat, though I suspected what would help most was the location of the White Cathedral. Unfortunately, Mal was the only one who might have been able to lead us back there, and I wasn't sure that was a possibility any more.

Nikolai gave the bottle of *kvas* an idle turn.

"It's not too late," he said. "You could stay. You could come back with me to the Grand Palace."

"And do what?"

"Teach, help me rebuild the Second Army, rusticate by the lake?"

This was what Tolya had been alluding to. He'd hoped I might return to Os Alta. It hurt to even think about.

I shook my head. "I'm not Grisha, and I'm certainly not a noble. I don't belong at court."

"You could stay with me," he said quietly. He gave the bottle another turn. "I still need a Queen."

I rose from my chair and nudged his booted feet aside, settling on the little stool to look up at him.

"I'm not the Sun Summoner now, Nikolai. I'm not even Alina Starkov. I don't *want* to return to court."

"But you understand this . . . thing." He tapped his chest.

I did. *Merzost*. Darkness. You could hate it and hunger for it at the same time.

"I'd only be a liability. Power is alliance," I reminded him.

"I do love it when you quote me." He sighed. "If only I weren't so damnably wise."

I reached into my pocket and set the Lantsov emerald on Nikolai's knee. Genya had given it back to me when we'd left Tomikyana.

He picked it up, turned it over. Its stone flashed green in the firelight. "A Shu princess then? A buxom Fjerdan? A Kerch magnate's daughter?" He held out the ring. "Keep it."

I stared at him. "How much of that *kvas* have you drunk?"

"None. Keep it. Please."

"Nikolai, I can't."

"I owe you, Alina. Ravka owes you. This and more. Do good works or commission an opera house or just take it out and gaze at it longingly when you think of the handsome prince you might have made your own. For the record, I favour the latter option, preferably paired with copious tears and the recitation of bad poetry."

I laughed.

He took my hand and pressed the ring into it. "Take it and build something new."

I turned the ring over in my hand. "I'll think about it."

He rolled his eyes. "What is your aversion to the word *yes*?"

I felt tears rising and had to blink them away. "Thank you."

He leaned back. "We were friends, weren't we? Not just allies?"

"Don't be an ass, Nikolai. We *are* friends." I gave him a hard tap on the knee. "Now, you and I are going to settle some things about the Second Army. And then we're going to watch me burn."

On our way to the drydocks, I slipped away and found Genya. She and David were cloistered in a Fabrikator tent on the east side of the camp. When I handed her the sealed letter marked with the Ravkan double eagle, she paused, holding it gingerly, as if the heavy paper were dangerous to the touch.

She ran her thumb over the wax seal, fingers quaking slightly. "Is it . . . ?"

"It's a pardon."

She tore it open and then clutched it to her.

David didn't look up from his worktable when he said, "Are we going to jail?"

"Not just yet," she said. She brushed away a tear. "Thank you." Then she frowned as I handed her the second letter. "What is this?"

"A job offer." It had taken some convincing, but in the end Nikolai had seen the sense in my suggestions. I cleared my throat. "Ravka still needs its Grisha, and Grisha still need a safe haven in the world. I want you to lead the Second Army, along with David. And Zoya."

"Zoya? Are you punishing me?"

"She's powerful, and I think she has it in her to be a good leader. Or she'll make your life a nightmare. Possibly both."

"Why us? The Darkling—"

"The Darkling is gone, and so is the Sun Summoner. Now the Grisha can lead themselves, and I want all the orders represented: Etherealki, Materialki, and you – Corporalki."

"I'm not really a Corporalnik, Alina."

"When you had the chance, you chose red. And I hope that those divisions won't matter so much if the Grisha are led by their own. All of you are strong. All of you know what it is to be seduced by power or status or knowledge. Besides, you're all heroes."

"They'll follow Zoya, maybe even David—"

"Hmm?" he asked distractedly.

"Nothing. You're going to have to go to more meetings."

"I hate meetings," he grumbled.

"Alina," she said, "I'm not so sure they'll follow me."

"You *make* them follow you." I touched her shoulder. "Brave and unbreakable."

A slow smile spread over her face. Then she winked. "And marvellous."

I grinned. "So you accept?"

"I accept."

I hugged her tight. She laughed, then tugged at a lock of hair that had slipped free from my kerchief.

"Already fading," she said. "Should we freshen you up?"

"Tomorrow."

"Tomorrow," she agreed.

I embraced her once more, then slipped outside into the last scraps of daylight.

I wended my way back through camp, following the crowd past the drydocks and into the sands of what had been the Unsea. The sun had almost set and dusk was falling, but it was impossible to miss the pyre, a massive mound of birches, their branches tangled like white limbs.

A shiver passed through me as I saw the girl laid to rest atop it. Her hair spread around her head in a white halo. She wore a *kefta* of blue and gold, and Morozova's collar curled around her throat, the stag's antlers a silvery gray against her skin. Whatever wire or Fabrikator craft held the pieces together had been hidden from view.

My eyes roved over her face – my face. Genya had done an extraordinary job. The shape was just right, the tilt of the nose, the angle of the jaw. The tattoo on her cheek was gone. There was almost nothing left of Ruby, the Soldat Sol who would have lived to be a Summoner if she hadn't perished on the Fold. She'd died an ordinary girl.

I'd baulked at the idea of using her body this way, troubled that her family would have nothing to bury. It had been Tolya who convinced me. "She believed, Alina. Even if you don't, let this be her final act of faith."

Beside Ruby, the Darkling lay in his black *kefta*.

Who had tended him? I wondered, feeling an ache rise in my throat. Who had combed his dark hair back so neatly from his forehead? Who had folded his graceful hands on his chest?

Some in the crowd were complaining that the Darkling had no business sharing a pyre with a Saint. But this felt right to me, and the people needed to see an end to it.

The remaining Soldat Sol had gathered around the pyre, their bare backs and chests emblazoned with tattoos. Vladim was there too, head bowed, the raised flesh of his brand outlined by firelight. Around them, people wept. Nikolai stood at the periphery, immaculate in his First Army uniform, the Apparat at his side. I pulled my shawl up.

Nikolai's gaze touched mine briefly from across the circle. He gave the signal. The Apparat raised his hands. The Inferni struck their flints. Flame leapt in bright arcs, circling and diving between the birches like darting birds, licking at the tinder until it smouldered and caught.

The fire grew, flames shimmering, the shaking leaves of a great golden tree. Around me, the moans and weeping of the crowd grew louder.

Sankta, they cried. *Sankta Alina.*

My eyes burned with the smoke. The smell was sickly sweet.

Sankta Alina.

No one knew his name to curse or extol, so I spoke it softly, beneath my breath.

"Aleksander," I whispered. A boy's name, given up. Almost forgotten.

After

A chapel stood on the coast of West Ravka, south of Os Kervo, on the shores of the True Sea. It was a quiet place, where the waves came nearly to the door. The whitewashed walls were laden with shells, and the dome that floated above the altar looked less like the heavens than the deep blue well of the sea.

There was no grand betrothal, no contract or false ransom. The girl and the boy had no families to fuss over them, to parade them through the nearby town or honour them with feasts. The bride wore no *kokochnik*, no dress of gold. Their only witnesses were an orange cat that slunk between the pews and a child, motherless now too, who carried a wooden sword. He had to stand on a chair to hold the driftwood crowns above their heads as the blessings were said. The names they gave were false ones, though the vows they made were true.

There were still wars, and there were still orphans, but the building that rose over the ruin that had been Keramzin was nothing like the one before. It was not a Duke's home, full of things that shouldn't be touched. It was a place for children. The piano in the music room was left uncovered.

The larder door was never locked. A lantern was always lit in the dormitories to keep away the dark.

The staff did not approve.

The students were too boisterous. Too much money was wasted on sugar for tea, on coal in the winter, on books that contained nothing but fairy stories. And why did each child require a new pair of skates?

Young. Rich. Possibly mad. These were the words whispered about the couple who ran the orphanage. But they paid well, and the boy was so charming that it was hard to stay mad at him, even when he refused to take the switch to some hellion who had tracked mud across the entryway floor.

He was said to be a distant relation of the Duke's, and though his table manners were fine enough, he had a soldier's way about him. He taught the students how to hunt and trap, and the new ways of farming so favoured by Ravka's King. The Duke himself had taken up residence at his winter house in Os Alta. The last few years of the war had been hard on him.

The girl was different, small and strange, with white hair that she wore loose down her back like an unmarried woman, seemingly oblivious to the glares and disapproving clucking of the teachers and the staff. She told the students peculiar stories of flying ships and underground castles, of monsters who ate earth, and birds that rose on wings of flame. Often, she went barefoot in the halls, and the smell of fresh paint never seemed to fade, as she was always starting on some new project or other, drawing a map over one of the classroom walls or covering the ceiling of the girls' dormitory with irises.

"Not much of an artist," sniffed one of the teachers.

"Certainly has an imagination, though," the other replied, peering skeptically at the white dragon that curled around the banister of the stairs.

The students learned maths and geography, science and art. Tradesmen were brought in from local towns and villages to offer apprenticeships. The new King hoped to abolish the draft in a few years' time, and if he succeeded, every Ravkan would need some kind of trade. When the children were tested for Grisha powers, they were allowed to choose whether or not to go to the Little Palace, and they were always welcome back at Keramzin. At night, they were told to keep the young King in their prayers – *Korol Rezni* who would keep Ravka strong.

Even if the boy and the girl weren't quite nobility, they certainly had friends in high places. Presents arrived frequently, sometimes marked with the royal seal: a set of atlases for the library, sturdy wool blankets, a new sleigh and a pair of matched white horses to pull it. Once a man arrived with a fleet of toy boats that the children launched on the creek in a miniature regatta. The teachers noted that the stranger was young and handsome, with golden hair and hazel eyes, but most definitely odd. He stayed late to dinner and never once removed his gloves.

Every winter, during the feast of Sankt Nikolai, a troika would make its way up the snowy road and three Grisha would emerge dressed in furs and thick wool *kefta* – red, purple, and blue – their sledge weighted down with presents: figs and apricots soaked in honey, piles of walnut candies, mink-lined gloves, and boots of butter-soft leather.

They stayed up late, long after the children had gone to bed, talking and laughing, telling stories, eating pickled plums and roasting lamb sausages over the fire.

That first winter, when it was time for her friends to leave, the girl ventured out into the snow to say goodbye, and the stunning raven-haired Squaller handed her another gift.

"A blue *kefta*," said the math teacher, shaking her head. "What would she do with that?"

"Maybe she knew a Grisha who died," replied the cook, taking note of the tears that filled the girl's eyes. They did not see the note that read, *You will always be one of us.*

The boy and the girl had both known loss, and their grief did not leave them. Sometimes he would find her standing by a window, fingers playing in the beams of sunlight that streamed through the glass, or sitting on the front steps of the orphanage, staring at the stump of the oak next to the drive. Then he would go to her, draw her close, and lead her to the shores of Trivka's pond, where the insects buzzed and the grass grew high and sweet, where old wounds might be forgotten.

She saw sadness in the boy too. Though the woods still welcomed him, he was separate from them now, the bond born into his bones burned away in the same moment that he'd given up his life for her.

But then the hour would pass, and the teachers would catch them giggling in a dim hallway or kissing by the stairs. Besides, most days were too full for mourning. There were classes to teach, meals to prepare, letters to write. When evening fell, the boy would bring the girl a glass of tea, a slice of lemon cake, an apple blossom floating in a blue cup. He would kiss her neck and whisper new names in her ear: beauty, beloved, cherished, my heart.

They had an ordinary life, full of ordinary things – if love can ever be called that.

Acknowledgements

A few years back, I started a journey into the dark with a girl who didn't yet have a name. I've been lucky to have wonderful people holding me up and cheering me on every step of the way.

TEAM SCIENCE(!)

The funny thing about the trick Alina pulls by bending light is that it's one of the most sound bits of science in these books. In the real world, it's called "invisibility cloak technology" (which makes me happy on a lot of levels). Google it, and prepare to have your mind blown. Peter Bibring suggested it to me, and Tomikyana is named after his daughter Iris Tommiko. Harper Seiko; I promise to get your name into the next book. I also need to shout out Peter's wife, Michelle Chihara, who is my dear friend and a wonderful writer. When the Grisha trilogy sold to Henry Holt, I danced in her kitchen. That is not a euphemism. Many thanks to John Williams for the spark that led to the acoustic blanket.

TEAM WORDY

Noa Wheeler and I have haggled over titles, bonded over books, and colluded over dumplings. Thank you for making the hard work so much fun. Huge thanks also to Jan Yaged, Jean Feiwel, Laura Godwin, Angus Killick, Elizabeth Fithian, Lucy del Priore, April Ward, Rich Deas, Alison Verost, the relentlessly patient Molly Brouillette, and the wonderful Ksenia Winnicki and Caitlin Sweeny who have done so much to promote the trilogy online. I also want to say a special thank-you to Veronica Roth, John Picacio, Michael Scott, Lauren DeStefano and Rick Riordan, who have been very kind to me and these books.

TEAM NEW LEAF

Joanna Volpe, thank you for being a brilliant agent, a wonderful friend, and for scaring the crap out of me in a hotel room in Belfast. Thanks to Kathleen Ortiz for taking the Grisha international and for putting up with my absurd approach to contracts and travel plans; Pouya Shabazian for laughing at my goofy jokes and helping me navigate the wilds of Hollywood; and Danielle Barthel and Jaida Temperley for manning the barricades with grace and good humor.

TEAM AWESOME LADIES

Morgan Fahey has been an amazing reader and has kept me company with late-night chats and email hilarity. Thank you for talking the Leighyore off many a ledge. Sarah Mesle helped me wade through so many plot woes, and I will never forget our New Year's Eve bunker chat – SkyMall! Kayte Ghaffar, aka Empress of Swag, aka Master Fabrikator, aka Smartypants: I don't know what I would have done without you as conspirator and confidante. Many thanks to Cindy Pon, Marie Rutkoski, Robin Wasserman, Amie Kaufman, Jennifer Rush, Sarah Rees Brennan, Cassandra Clare, and Marie Lu for encouragement, gossip, and inspiration. Also, to Emmy Laybourne, Jessica Brody, and Anna Banks – I feel like we've been to summer camp or possibly war together, and I loved every minute of it. Special thanks to Holly Black, who broke me down and built me back up again in the space of a single cab ride. She has powers, people. I'm just saying.

TEAM LOS ANGELES

Love and gratitude to Ray Tejada, Austin Wilkin, and Rachel Tejada of Ocular Curiosity (aka the League of Unplumbable Fun!). David and Erin Peterson are my favorite power couple – thank you for being so generous with your talent and time. Rachael Martin makes a damn fine date ball, and Robyn Bacon is the woman to trust when it comes to JUSTICE. Jimmy Freeman has coddled me with kindness, encouragement, and hospitality. Gretchen McNeil is a marvellous convention roommate, and for such a Marianne, she's awfully full of great advice. Big thanks to Dan Braun, Brandon Harvey, Liz Hamilton, Josh Kamensky, Heather Joy and the wee Phoebe, Aaron Wilson and Laura Recchi, Michael Pessah, the ridiculously badass Christina Strain, Romi Cortier, Tracey Taylor, Lauren Messiah, Mel Caine, Mike DiMartino, and Kurt

Mattila, who got me hooked on comics all over again. Brad Farwell, you don't live in Los Angeles, but you didn't fit into any of the other categories. Jerk.

TEAM BOOK PUSHER

Huge thanks to the librarians, teachers, bloggers, and booksellers who helped these books find their readers. And as always, love to the Brotherhood without Banners who welcomed me into one of the most supportive and generous fandoms around. They also throw the best parties.

TEAM TUMBLR

Some people supported the Grisha Trilogy early and must be paid due tribute: Irene Koh, who changed the way I see my own characters; Kira, aka Eventhepartofyouthatlovedhim, who blogged early and often; the wonderful ladies of the Grisha Army; Emily Pursel, Laura Maldonaden, Elena of Novelsounds, Laura and Kyra, and Madeleine Michaud, who writes the very best asks. There are so many more of you who have made graphics and fanmixes, who have created art and fic, who have chatted with me, and inspired me, and kept me going. Thank you for making this journey so much more magical.

TEAM FAMILY

Christine, Sam, Ryan, Emily – I love you guys. Shem, you are an amazing artist and the best possible person to see New York with. And finally, all the love and thanks to my adorable, wonderful mumsy, who cried at the right scenes and has learned to speak fluent narwhal.